CATEGORY

FIVE

A novel by

D. R. Evans

1

In the basement of a large house halfway between Arlington and Langley, six men sat around a walnut conference table. The time on the leftmost of the clocks on the wall was half past midnight. According to the others, it was also five-thirty in London, seven-thirty in Moscow, nine-thirty in Karranh, two-thirty in Tokyo and four-thirty in Sydney.

The men looked tired. On the table were half a dozen mugs containing the dregs of coffee and tea; plates with cookie crumbs and empty candy wrappers were scattered among the mugs. In front of each man was a legal pad covered with notes. Five of the men were looking at the sixth, who sat at the head of the table.

Fisher glanced at the clocks, then asked, "Anything else from North America, Kirkpatrick?"

Kirkpatrick was the oldest. With sunken jowls and bloodshot, yellowing eyes, he looked sick as well as tired. He took off his half-moon glasses before he replied, holding them in a trembling hand. When he spoke, there was an unhealthy raspiness in his voice.

"Only one more thing. Ishihara left Roncador Cay early this evening. His flight plan gives his destination as Rocky Mountain Metro Airport, in Jefferson County, Colorado."

"Colorado?" echoed Gallucci. "What on Earth's in Colorado?"

"I think," said Kirkpatrick deliberately, "he's going to try to recruit Oscar Holywell."

Boulder, Colorado

"The question of whether quantum effects are necessary for consciousness to...."

A distant bell interrupted Oscar Holywell in mid-sentence. Relief showed on the faces of his half-dozen students.

Dr. Holywell was as relieved as his students, although he was careful not to let it show. "See you all again on Monday," he said with a distinct lack of enthusiasm. "And don't forget I want your essays on Penrose by Tuesday at the latest."

His words were lost in the scraping of chairs and the noisy gathering of books and doodle-covered notepads. The students pulled damp, heavy coats from the backs of chairs, where for the last hour they had filled the cramped basement room with a sour wetness.

Erasing the whiteboard as they trooped from the room, Holywell mumbled to himself, "Only one more week before the break"; then he caught himself guiltily as he saw out the corner of his eye that one student had stayed behind.

Melissa Turner was dressing to brave the elements, her movements deliberate as she wound a pastel yellow woolen scarf around her pale neck.

The door banged closed, leaving the two of them alone. A knot tightened in Holywell's stomach.

Oscar Holywell was thirty five years old, with hair that was thin and unfashionably long, and pale skin that was still subject to occasional bouts of the acne that had plagued him since puberty. His cheeks were hollow and bore the beginnings of permanent wrinkles. His teeth were yellow and distinctly crooked. His clothes looked like they had been acquired in a garage sale a decade earlier.

Melissa Turner was twenty two years old. A natural blonde with unblemished skin, her teeth were meticulously straight and unnaturally white. Her clothes were as expensive as Holywell's were cheap.

The two of them had nothing in common — except *The Philosophy of Consciousness*, the class that had brought them together every Monday, Wednesday and Friday afternoon for the past four-teen weeks.

Melissa looked uncertainly at Holywell, lines of doubt creasing her normally smooth forehead.

He suppressed a sigh, hoping he had misread the signs. "Yes, Melissa? Is there something I can help you with?"

She smiled, exposing her too-white, too-even teeth. A thick lock of straight blonde hair slipped forward, hiding one eye momentarily before she flicked it back and barraged him with both aquamarine eyes.

"Thank you, Professor. I was wondering...." She let the sentence hang in the air, unfinished.

"Yes?"

"Well, it's a bit embarrassing really. I'm afraid I'm having dif-ficulty following your arguments in this paper."

She opened her notebook and extracted a reprint. He glanced at the title: *On the Necessity of Quantum Effects as a Precursor to Consciousness*. It was the last research paper he'd been allowed to publish, almost five years ago.

She continued, "I'm sorry if I'm being stupid, but I wondered if you might be able to find some time to help me try and understand it."

"My office hours are Tuesday and Thursday, starting at four o'clock."

"Yes, I know, Professor. But I'm afraid I have another class then."

"So when would be convenient?"

She blinked a couple of times, then looked away as if she knew she was about to make a slightly improper suggestion.

"Well, Professor, next week is the last one before winter break, and I'm pretty busy all week. I was wondering if you might have some free time this weekend? I know it's an awful imposition, but I'm sure it'd help me understand some of the points you're trying to make, in the paper as well as in the class. I expect you've noticed I'm not doing very well, and I do need to get at least a B in this class."

He tried to let her down gently. "I'm sorry, Melissa, but I'm busy all weekend. How about after the lecture on Monday?"

She looked at him doubtfully, weighing her chances. After a few moments, she slipped the reprint back into the notebook and turned gracelessly away. "All right. I'll try to keep myself free after class. Have a nice weekend, Professor." Without giving him another glance, she adjusted her coat and scarf one more time, then left the room.

Oscar made a wry face to himself and shook his head silently. He picked up his lecture notes and turned out the lights. The basement corridor outside the converted storage room was almost empty. The only people he saw as he walked to the elevator were a pair of undergraduates, deep in conversation.

He waited for the elevator to arrive, tapping his foot impatiently. Melissa Turner had curdled his already soured mood.

"Good evening, Oscar."

He turned to see a young associate professor from England approaching. Oscar struggled to remember his name. Graham? Arthur? Charles? He settled on Ian. Some sort of specialist in laser optics. Perhaps.

"Hello, Ian," he said without warmth.

Ian looked at him oddly. "Everything going all right with that graduate class? What's it called? *Artificial Intelligence and Consciousness*, or something like that?"

The elevator pinged and the doors slid unsteadily open. Oscar stepped inside and stabbed the number 4. Ian pressed the 2.

"Couldn't imagine it being better," said Oscar flatly. The doors rattled closed and the elevator began to rise.

"Good, good."

The laser specialist seemed to have run out of things to say, and the elevator carried them to the second floor in silence. "Have a nice weekend, then," Ian said as the doors opened.

"You too."

Ian stepped out. A faculty member paused in mid-stride and accosted him. "Harold, just the man I wanted to see."

The elevator doors closed. "Damn fool looks like he should be called Ian," Oscar mumbled to the empty elevator.

The doors opened on the fourth floor, and he stepped out. Fiddling with his keys, he turned the corner to his office and looked up in surprise. Standing in front of his door was a man who looked like he had been waiting for some time. An oriental of some kind: Chinese perhaps, or maybe Korean. Oscar never had been very good at ethnic types.

The man moved to one side as Oscar fitted a key in the lock. "Professor Holywell?"

"Technically, it's Doctor, not Professor. But yes, I'm Holywell. Do I know you?"

Oscar was inside the office now. The man followed and closed the door without being asked. He was short, no more than five-four, in his mid fifties, with a head of thick, gray hair. He wore a business suit and a muted plain blue-gray tie. He regarded Oscar through round, wire-rimmed glasses.

"We've never met, Doctor Holywell, but I've long been an admirer of yours." His accent and a clipped precision in his speech betrayed the fact that English was not his first language.

"Sit down," Oscar said, seating himself behind a cluttered industrial metal desk painted a particularly repulsive shade of battleship gray. He glanced out the window. It was still snowing, even harder than before the lecture.

Looking impatiently at his watch, he said, "I'm afraid I don't have much time."

"My name is Yoshi Ishihara."

The oriental extended a hand across the desk. Oscar shook it perfunctorily.

Mr. Ishihara continued, "I know you're a busy man, so I'll come straight to the point. Are you happy in your work here?"

Oscar's eyebrows rose in surprise, then slowly lowered.

"Ecstatic," he replied evenly.

Mr. Ishihara regarded Oscar dubiously. "Dr. Holywell, are you playing games with me? Please, my question is a serious one. Are you happy here, or is there a possibility you could be persuaded to leave?"

Oscar leaned forward, thrusting himself halfway across the desk.

"Mr. Ishihara, I have no idea who you represent, but I can assure you they've made a mistake. This university graciously allows me to teach one graduate level course of no earthly use to anyone. They pay me a pittance, but it's enough to keep me off the streets.

Teaching is boring but hardly arduous, and it leaves me plenty of time for my real work.

"I like Colorado and I've no intention of moving. In any case, I haven't published anything for years. Everyone has forgotten I exist. So I suggest you go back to wherever you came from and tell your superiors they've made a mistake. I assure you they really don't want to hire me."

Mr. Ishihara pondered this in silence for half a minute. Then he asked, "Dr. Holywell, do you have any plans for the weekend?"

Oscar laughed out loud. "You're the second person to ask me that in the last ten minutes. Yes, I have plans. I intend to get some work done. Failing that, I'll curl up with a good book and a bottle of wine and do my damnedest to forget about what passes for reality for a while. Now, if you'll excuse me, I live in the mountains and the last thing I want is to be stuck here all weekend because of the damn snow."

Mr. Ishihara made no movement to leave. "You mentioned your work.... Are you still working on the idea that one day it might be possible to create a conscious machine?"

Oscar had risen from his chair, intending to see Mr. Ishihara to the door. Now he paused.

"Yes, that's what I'm working on."

"And yet you've published nothing for five years now. Why is that?"

"That, Mr. Ishihara, is because the fools who edit so-called scientific journals insist on a process called peer review."

"Which means?"

Oscar regained his seat and took a deep breath. The snow was forgotten. On this subject he was happy to talk to Mr. Ishihara for as long as his visitor was willing to listen.

"It means one cannot simply publish the truth. One submits a paper to a journal for review. The editor sends the paper to two or three so-called peers for their comments and suggestions for changes. If the author agrees to the changes, they review the revised version and usually the journal agrees to publish."

"But not always?"

"Mr. Ishihara, in the past five years I've submitted half a dozen papers to every prestigious journal in the field. The reviewers and editors seem to have agreed among themselves that nothing I write is worthy of publication."

"I see. And what do you make of this, Dr. Holywell?"

"It's simple. My so-called peers are either too stupid to realize how important my work is, or they're so jealous that they intend to steal my conclusions and publish them themselves. On balance, I incline toward the former theory."

"And what exactly have they blocked from publication? Your last published paper contained some intriguing ideas about Category 5 machines. Have you changed your mind since then?"

"Not at all. Everything I've done in the last few years has simply confirmed what I said in that paper. The only thing that's changed in my mind is that then I was merely speculating about possibilities; now I'm convinced I'm right."

Mr. Ishihara nodded to himself quickly several times; a smile played around his lips and a mischievous glint appeared in his eyes. Watching him, Oscar thought he looked like someone at a race track who'd just seen an outsider on which he'd betted heavily romp home two lengths clear of the field.

Ishihara asked, "So you still believe that one day it will be possible to build a conscious computer? A machine that really thinks?"

"I'm convinced of it."

"And when do you think this might happen?"

Oscar shrugged. "Who knows? Technology still has a long way to go, and in any case no one seems to be going down the right path. They're all slaves to convention. The conventional notion that a Category 5 machine is simply a cleverly programmed Category 1 machine is ridiculous. My guess is that it will take at least five years, more probably ten. Maybe longer."

Mr. Ishihara looked at his watch, then abruptly got to his feet. He walked briskly to the door. With his hand on the handle he said, "I have a private jet waiting at Rocky Mountain Metro Airport. An hour from now, I propose to be on it. I urge you to join me."

"Why?"

"Because technology has moved faster than you thought. And I assure you that not everyone is a slave to convention. I'm here to give you a choice, Dr. Holywell. You can stay here wasting your talents teaching graduate students and writing papers that will be rejected by people who don't understand the importance of what you have to say — or you can help me build a Category 5 machine."

Without waiting for Oscar's reply, he slipped from the room, leaving the door open behind him.

For a quarter of a minute Oscar Holywell sat in his chair, looking at the door with a frown on his face and a speculative look in his eyes. Then he rushed out of the office, running to catch up with Mr. Ishihara.

2

Ten months later

Kirkpatrick looked considerably worse than he had done at the last meeting. Under the glare of the fluorescent tubes his skin appeared translucent; his breathing was an audible wheeze. The pad before him held only a few lines of notes, rendered in an uncertain, spidery hand.

Everyone else had made his report. At the head of the table, Fisher lifted his head and looked at Kirkpatrick. For a moment they simply stared at each other, then Fisher's eyes slid compassionately to one side.

"What news from North America, Kirkpatrick?" Fisher asked softly.

It was obvious from the way the others were avoiding Kirkpatrick's eye that they expected little from their ailing colleague; but when he spoke it was with clarity and surprising strength.

"Ishihara is running low on funds," he said, "which could mean trouble for us."

Kirkpatrick's frailty was temporarily forgotten. "Why?" asked Gallucci. "Maybe he'll just fold the project."

Kirkpatrick shook his head. "He's been in contact with Japan. He's trying to get a loan. Fifty million dollars."

"Who's he approached? and is he likely to get the money?"

"So far he's only gone to the International Investment Credit Bank of Tokyo. They funded him before, and maybe they'll do so again."

There was an extended silence before Fisher asked the question that was on all their minds. "And if the bank turns him down?"

"I don't know. But we must at least consider the possibility that our Japanese friends are aware of what Ishihara's trying to do. And if the International Investment Credit Bank of Tokyo turns him down and the Brotherhood offers him the money instead...."

He didn't finish the sentence. He didn't need to.

Roncador Cay

Even though it was not yet noon, Tetsuo Matsumoto was struggling to stay awake. Yoshi Ishihara, he thought to himself, was one of the most boring people he'd ever met.

Ishihara began another of his convoluted sentences, full of irrelevant technical detail: "The quantum effects, although microscopic in nature, can have macroscopic results. I like to think of the MIMIC chip as...."

Matsumoto tuned out. He was tired, he was uncomfortable, and he had long ago stopped paying attention to what the man on the other side of the desk was saying. To make matters worse, his throat was parched, his thirst exacerbated by the complete absence of saki on the island. He swallowed drily and shifted his weight in the chair, causing a trickle of sweat to dribble down his chest underneath his shirt.

Oblivious, Yoshi Ishihara kept on talking; Matsumoto sneaked a glance at his watch.

Ishihara had been talking non-stop for nearly an hour, and Matsumoto was on the point of giving up the fight to keep the glaze from his eyes. If it weren't for the third man in the room he would have done so long ago. But appearances had to be maintained. Matsumoto had spent weeks emphasizing to Iinuma the importance of listening to everything a client said before deciding whether to offer a loan. He would lose face if his deputy noticed his lack of interest in the proceedings.

10

Iinuma, who, amazingly, seemed to be truly interested in Ishihara's ramblings, leaned forward and asked whether Ishihara really thought there was a market for a thinking machine. "Or is it just an academic exercise?"

"The value of a machine that can truly think would be incalculable...," Ishihara began.

Matsumoto had had enough. He interrupted Ishihara.

"Of course, of course. My only question is how certain you are that you're going to be able to deliver. I'm sure you recognize that our bank isn't in the habit of making unsecured fifty million dollar loans. Even allowing for your past success, you must understand that we have to be cautious."

Ishihara replied, "If it weren't for Doctor Holywell we would have given up when my own money ran out. Even with his help, just two weeks ago we thought it was all over. But then he had an insight that brought us the breakthrough we've been looking for. Now I can truly say that we're on the verge of a revolution as great as any mankind has ever witnessed."

Matsumoto glanced at his deputy. Iinuma nodded vigorously, agreeing with Ishihara's assessment.

With a twinge of annoyance, Matsumoto did his best to dampen their enthusiasm. "Mr. Ishihara, you keep telling us what great changes this new computer of yours is going to bring. What I don't understand is why you need another $50 million when you've already made the breakthrough you need."

"A good question, Matsumoto-san. When I started this project I thought my personal fortune would be enough to see it through. Unfortunately, we spent most of the last year going down blind alleys and following false trails. I confess that I have been mostly to blame. For months Dr. Holywell has been wanting to try a board based on Mr. Barlow's MIMIC chip, but the chip is so expensive to make, and our early tests were so disappointing, that I wanted to try everything else first.

"I'm afraid my delay cost us at least six months. It seems that a MIMIC-based computer is the only way forward."

"But surely it doesn't cost $50 million just to manufacture a computer chip?"

"The MIMIC is hardly an ordinary chip. The only company with the technology to manufacture it is Integrated Silicon Fabrication, IntSiliFab, and $50 million is their price for the two dozen chips we need. The yield from the manufacturing process is extraordinarily poor. The quantum paths, you see, require...."

"This all sounds very risky," interrupted Matsumoto with a shake of his head. "What if, even after you get the chips, you discover you still can't finish the project?"

"I'm afraid I have nothing left to offer as collateral. My own fortune has been spent. But if you allow me to show you how far we've come, perhaps you can imagine the possibilities for yourself."

Ishihara stood and the others followed suit, stretching to ease the cramps in their muscles. They trooped out of the small, bare office and into the glare of the late morning sun.

None of them was dressed for the Caribbean. They all wore dark business suits; as he walked, Matsumoto felt dribbles of sweat trickling down the crevices of his body. His throat was drier than ever.

They walked toward a bungalow in the center of a cluster of identical prefabricated buildings, following a path where the sparse, coarse grass had been worn away. To their left, beyond the bungalows, was an airstrip where, partially hidden by the closest building, stood a LearJet in the gold and blue livery of the International Investment Credit Bank of Tokyo.

Matsumoto glanced in the opposite direction, squinting against the glare. The sea swelled languorously into low hills and shallow valleys; inch-high waves lapped against the pink of the coral beach. In the distance was a pair of barely-visible colored triangles, marking the positions of two sailing boats. Beyond them rose the distant symmetric green and gray mound of Montega.

The three men halted briefly at the entrance of the bungalow.

"We use the basement as our research lab," Ishihara explained, then he led the others past a trestle table where a muscular young man in his late teens was outlining a drawing with a pencil. The young man eyed them curiously as they passed. His attention returned to the drawing as they went downstairs.

"Who's that?" asked Matsumoto.

"William is our security guard."

"He didn't appear to be armed."

"He's not," said Ishihara emphatically.

Matsumoto and Iinuma exchanged disbelieving looks. Matsumoto shook his head emphatically. If they did decide to back Yoshi Ishihara, their investment would be guarded by something considerably more effective than an unarmed teenage artist.

Ishihara halted in front of a steel door. He stabbed a sequence on a digital pad set into the wall, and the door slid open. "Gentlemen, our lab."

It was a shambles. A large room with bare concrete walls was filled with a disordered farrago of cables, keyboards, computer monitors and circuit boards.

Two men were stooping over something on a table at the far side of the lab. They straightened and regarded the intruders. The taller of the two sported a beard that, to judge from its shagginess, owed its existence to nothing more purposeful than its owner's reluctance to use a razor. The haphazard state of his thinning hair reinforced Matsumoto's distasteful impression of a man who never looked in a mirror and would not care what he saw even if he chanced to do so.

The man was stripped to the waist, and Matsumoto saw with a shudder that his jeans sported several stains. His feet were bare. After a single brief glance in their direction and a nod of acknowledgement directed at Ishihara, he turned back to the table, apparently having decided that the visitors were unworthy of his attention.

The second man was somewhat shorter, although still taller than any of the Japanese. He was cleanshaven and wore a yellow shirt, light-colored trousers, and a pair of open-toed sandals. He regarded the visitors with mild interest.

Ishihara stepped forward to perform the introductions, slipping easily into English. "This is Tetsuo Matsumoto, Chief Loan Officer of the International Investment Credit Bank of Tokyo. And this is his deputy, Kamide Iinuma."

Both the bankers bowed deeply.

"This is Al Barlow, our hardware specialist. He's the man responsible for most of the design of the MIMIC chip."

The man in the yellow shirt nodded politely.

Indicating the bare-chested man bent over the table with his back to them, Ishihara said, "And this is Doctor Oscar Holywell, without whom this project would now be dead."

Holywell grunted something without looking up from the equipment on the table.

Ishihara cleared his throat loudly. "Dr. Holywell, I wonder if you could explain for the gentlemen exactly what we're doing here?"

Holywell straightened, the look on his face making it perfectly clear what he thought of Ishihara's request. He ran his eyes up and down the bankers. Drily he said, "And I suppose you want me to do it in two minutes, using words of no more than two syllables."

"Just do your best, Oscar," said Ishihara weakly. "Please. A lot depends on it. We won't be able to continue unless we can convince these men to help us."

Holywell stared belligerently at the visitors. "How's your English?"

Matsumoto replied tautly, "My deputy's is passable. Mine, I believe, is quite good. Considerably better than your Japanese, I imagine."

An unexpected hint of a smile appeared at the edges of Holywell's mouth. "Touché."

"A French word originally used in fencing, and meaning, more or less, 'that makes us equal.' But we are not equal, Dr. Holywell. You need money to continue your work; I have money, or at least my bank does. That, I think, gives me a considerable advantage."

Holywell's smile expanded into a grin. "I stand corrected. You're right, of course." Then, becoming serious once more, he asked, "How much do you know about computers?"

"As much as most intelligent people, but I can't say I'm an expert."

Holywell moved to one side, allowing Matsumoto a clear view of the equipment on the table. A complicated circuit board to which were attached half a dozen cables stood in a metal cage. The cables snaked away to a bank of computers displaying traces like those on an oscilloscope.

Holywell said, "We call this Beta 1. Not a very inspiring name perhaps, but at least it's descriptive. It's the first of a new breed of machine. Mr. Matsumoto, this machine can actually *think*.

Not very deeply, I admit, but that's only because of its lack of resources."

"Please explain."

"It would be easier to demonstrate."

Holywell stepped up to a nearby computer keyboard and typed a command. He said, "I just reset Beta 1. It now knows nothing except for some basic programming designed to mimic a newborn child. We're going to teach it how to write."

He typed another command and the screen was filled with the words HELLO, WORLD scrolling past hundreds of times a second. "Beta 1 is now receiving these words over and over again on its input circuits. This other screen here shows the output from Beta 1."

The screen attached to Beta 1's output was blank.

"Is something supposed to happen?" asked Matsumoto.

"Be patient. It takes two years for a human child to learn how to talk."

They stared at the blank screen — all except Matsumoto, who stole surreptitious glances at Ishihara and Holywell. Ishihara was clearly nervous: worry lines etched his forehead, and his lips were tight and thin. In contrast, Holywell looked relaxed and at ease. He seemed in no doubt that something impressive was going to happen.

"Sometimes it's really fast," said Holywell after a couple of minutes. "But sometimes it takes more than an hour. That's one of the variables I don't understand yet. Usually it's around five minutes. There! Look! It's starting!"

On the second screen, random characters had jerkily begun to appear.

HTDGFQ

Nothing else happened for a few seconds. Then more sequences appeared:

KLHGF19

G3DLH HI

” ” ” ”
“ ”
’

AAAAAAAAAAAA

15

The characters stopped coming. "Any moment now," said Holywell expectantly. "It's figured out how to control what it's writing. Now it just needs to work out how... there!"

Ishihara shouted and clapped his hands in delight. Over and over again, echoing the first screen, the second screen displayed:

> HELLO, WORLD
> HELLO, WORLD
> HELLO, WORLD
> HELLO, WORLD
> HELLO, WORLD

Holywell tapped a key and different words appeared on the first screen: IN THE BEGINNING. There was a barely perceptible pause before the second screen displayed:

> IN THE BEGINNING
> IN THE BEGINNING
> IN THE BEGINNING
> IN THE BEGINNING
> IN THE BEGINNING

Holywell tapped another key. The words on the first screen changed again, the text of *Moby Dick* scrolling past so quickly as to be almost unreadable. Instantly the words were repeated on the second screen.

Holywell looked at Matsumoto triumphantly. "You've just seen a machine display the beginnings of rudimentary intelligence."

Matsumoto shook his head skeptically, "I still don't understand."

"It's simple. After I wiped its memory, Beta 1 knew nothing. Now it has learned, *by itself*, how to repeat whatever words it receives on its input circuits. The next step, which is what we're working on now, is to bombard it with enough input for it to understand the relationship between nouns and verbs, how to ask questions, the whole gamut of English grammar.

"Think of it as a child learning to talk. It's begun by learning to say 'Mama' and 'Dada.' By the time we've finished, it will be able to explain the theory of relativity.

"But before that can happen, we're going to have to feed in entire books. Hundreds of them. Maybe thousands. And once we've taught it English, we can teach it French, Spanish, even Japanese." He grinned mischievously. "Your English may be better than my Japanese, Mr. Matsumoto, but a year or two from now one of this machine's descendants will be able to understand Japanese just as well as you do. But that machine will have to be far more powerful than this one. It will need at least a dozen MIMIC chips."

"And that's why we need the money," interrupted Ishihara. "You understand now?"

"I think so. And I think I've seen enough. I'll make my recommendation as soon as I return to Tokyo. You'll hear the bank's decision early next week."

Ishihara bowed deeply. "Thank you, Matsumoto-san. You are most kind to consider my request. If you are ready to leave, I will escort you and your deputy to your plane."

As they left the room, Ishihara flashed Holywell a grateful smile behind the backs of the bankers. But Holywell did not notice. He was already bent over Beta 1, talking in a low voice to Barlow, the interruption forgotten.

Bankers, after all, represented only money. Beta 1 represented the future.

3

"*Any idea how it went?*"

Fisher doodled nervously on a legal pad while he waited for Kirkpatrick's reply. He could hear Kirkpatrick's rasping breath on the line. Six months, the doctors had said. That was five months ago. For once, it looked like they'd gotten it about right. And when Kirkpatrick was gone, who would replace him?

The decision would have to be unanimous; that was one of the most unbreakable of their many rules. Half a dozen names had already been mentioned, and although the names belonged to good and capable men, Fisher could not rid himself of a nagging doubt that the right name had yet to surface.

"*Not really.*"

Kirkpatrick's voice jerked him back to the present. Kirkpatrick continued, "*Matsumoto and his deputy were only there about three hours. Presumably that means the decision was clear-cut, but I can't guess which way. They left a couple of hours ago. They'll be back in Tokyo this time tomorrow.*"

"*All right. I'll tell Hayes to keep his ears to the ground in Japan.*"

There was a long pause before Kirkpatrick said, "*And Fisher?*"

"*Yes.*"

"Say goodbye to the others for me."
The line went dead.

His throat comfortably lubricated by his third saki, Tetsuo Matsumoto turned his attention to Kamide Iinuma.

The LearJet had reached cruising altitude, and Roncador Cay was far behind. Matsumoto had removed his jacket; Iinuma, unwilling to appear too casual in the presence of a superior, still wore his. The two men occupied spacious, velvet-upholstered seats on opposite sides of the plane's wide central aisle. A pretty young hostess wearing an attractive uniform in the bank's gold-and-blue colors hovered nearby, anticipating their needs. Matsumoto downed his drink and raised his glass. Smiling widely, the hostess stepped forward, silently took it from him, and supplied him with a new, full glass.

Matsumoto frowned at Iinuma, who was still only halfway through his first drink. Matsumoto was suspicious of men who did not know how to drink; it made him doubt their manliness. A real man must know how to hold his liquor. *Perhaps*, thought Matsumoto, *Iinuma will not do as well as I've been hoping*. That would be bad, for it would reflect on Matsumoto's decision that Iinuma should succeed him.

"You should drink more," Matsumoto declared out loud. "A man should know how to relax after his work is done for the day."

"I apologize, Matsumoto-san. I'm afraid I find it hard to sleep after drinking, and it is a long flight home. I would like to sleep as much as possible."

Iinuma's response annoyed Matsumoto. It suggested that Matsumoto drank too much. Matsumoto frowned and lapsed into silence while he finished his drink, mulling how to put Iinuma in his place. The hostess appeared from somewhere and offered him a fresh glass on a lacquered tray. He looked at her closely for the first time. She was a pretty little thing, her face powdered the color of pale sand. It was an open, honest face and it wore a smile that told him she liked him and would be happy to please him in any way he desired.

His annoyance at Iinuma increased. If it weren't for his presence....

"Iinuma," he said, rousing the younger man from the doze into which he had fallen. "Tell me what you think."

Iinuma blinked uncertainly. "Sir?"

The hostess favored Matsumoto with another smile, then discreetly slipped away toward the rear of the jet so that the men could talk business. Matsumoto twisted in his seat, watching the movement of her kimono with undisguised pleasure.

He turned toward Iinuma and realized that his deputy was staring at him with unconcealed contempt. Iinuma's expression changed to one of bland innocence. Too slowly. "You wanted my opinion, sir? What about?"

"Yoshi Ishihara," Matsumoto snapped. "Should we loan him the money? And if so, at what terms?"

The answer, Matsumoto knew, should be obvious even to someone of Iinuma's limited abilities. Yoshi Ishihara had spent more than $100 million already in his ridiculous search for a thinking computer. To loan him another $50 million without collateral would be like dumping the money into the sea.

Iinuma swallowed uncertainly. "He's a bad risk, sir. I went through his credit history in detail before we left, and it's true we funded him when he came to us last time. But then he wanted only a couple of hundred million yen, and most of the loan was secured by his patent on the static head disk drive. There's no patent on this MIMIC chip. I say it's too risky to loan him this much money without security."

"So what do you propose?"

"It seems to me we have two alternatives. Either we offer him something less at a high rate, or we demand greater proof that he's likely to succeed. Perhaps we do both."

That was Matsumoto's own conclusion as well. But now he reversed himself in an instant. "Then you are blind, Iinuma. Sometimes I wonder if you are indeed the right man to succeed me."

To Matsumoto's pleasure, consternation appeared on Iinuma's face. "Sir? I don't understand."

"Then it's time you learned that making a loan isn't just about the balance sheet. It's about history and what the Americans would

20

call gut feelings. You admit that we once loaned Yoshi Ishihara a little more than a million American dollars. He sold his share of the company he founded with that money for more than a hundred times that much. It was obvious to me, if not to you, that this latest project of his has enormous potential. I intend to recommend we offer him an unsecured loan of $50 million at half a point below prime."

"Below prime, sir?" Iinuma could not hide his astonishment.

Matsumoto was enjoying himself. "Below prime," he repeated easily. "Ishihara's a good risk. He'll repay us. And he'll remember us next time he needs money."

Iinuma opened his mouth to protest, but then he closed it again. There was no point. Matsumoto would not change his mind. "Whatever you say, sir." He unhappily closed his eyes and tried to go to sleep.

Matsumoto made no effort to keep the grin from his face as he signaled for another drink.

4

The five men in heavy overcoats began to walk slowly away from the open grave. Flakes of wet snow drifted out of the leaden sky and landed on the plain wooden coffin. They did not melt.

Raising his collar against the wind, Lee spoke quietly to Fisher.

"I know it probably seems callous, but we need to be thinking about someone to take Kirkpatrick's place."

"I'll take over North America for now," growled Fisher. "And you're right: it is callous. Kirkpatrick served this country faithfully for nearly half a century, and I'm in no mood to think about trying to replace him before his coffin has even been covered." He accosted a man with a thin red face. "Hayes, any news from Japan?"

"Nothing certain, but I can't say it looks good."

"Meaning?"

"Chida broke his training regime yesterday. He cut his workout short and caught a flight for Kyoto. In my experience that means only one thing."

"The Father wanted to give him orders."

"Exactly."

"You're right. It's not good."

The men reached the gate at the entrance of the cemetery. After brief farewells, they dispersed. Only Fisher remained, staring for a long time at the rows of graves marked with plain white crosses.

Tokyo

The *Western Paradise* was filled with raucous laughter, loud conversation, and, competing with both, the heavy, bass-driven throb of a recent western hit. On the stage, a mid-level executive from the bank, his tie askew, nervously accepted the microphone. He tested it for volume, and then began to sing along with the tune, guided by the bouncing ball on the oversized screen.

A heavy pall of cigarette smoke hung between Tetsuo Matsumoto's booth and the stage, augmented by the smoke Matsumoto and his colleagues exhaled every few seconds. Nineteen other booths hugged the walls near the stage, all of them occupied by executives from the International Investment Credit Bank of Tokyo.

Matsumoto's rank entitled him to a place only in booth number seven. But the loan vice president had invited Matsumoto to join him in booth number three, which would become Matsumoto's own as soon as the vice president retired. To Matsumoto's annoyance, he had also invited Iinuma, who by rights should not even have been allowed into the bar.

Matsumoto's displeasure at Iinuma's presence was mitigated by his deputy's obvious discomfort at moving in such exalted circles. He had been nervous ever since he had arrived, and now that the karaoke had begun it was obvious he was dreading the possibility that he would be asked to perform.

Matsumoto called for another saki, and made a show of watching the man on the stage. The man's tie slipped further to one side as he jumped around the stage, trying to act the part of a western rock star.

"You could do a better job than that, Iinuma," Matsumoto declared, banging the table with his glass and raising his voice to make himself heard above the din.

The vice president regarded Iinuma with interest. "You sing, along with your other talents?"

Matsumoto interjected, "Modesty will prevent him from admitting it, but my deputy has a fine voice, although of course perhaps western music is too difficult for him."

The singer belted out a final chorus, making conversation momentarily impossible. After the applause had died down, the vice president motioned for Iinuma to take the microphone.

Reluctantly, Iinuma nodded and walked forward to the stage.

"About Yoshi Ishihara and that computer of his...," Matsumoto began.

He had been waiting all evening for a chance to talk privately with the vice president. The recommendation was lying on his desk, ready to be forwarded to the vice president first thing on Monday morning. But it would do no harm to prepare him beforehand.

"When you see my report, you may disagree with my conclusions, and I thought you might like to know why I think we should give him the money."

The vice president waved him into silence. "It can wait. This is not the time for business. And I'm sure I won't disagree with anything you say. You were there; you had the chance to talk to Ishihara and to see everything for yourself. Whatever you recommend, I'll go along with it. Now, let's see if your deputy is as good as you claim."

In fact Iinuma was not at all bad, certainly much better than the man who had preceded him. When he returned to the booth with trickles of sweat dribbling down his face, it was to the accompaniment of heartfelt applause.

Annoyed at his deputy's success, Matsumoto rose unsteadily to his feet. "I must excuse myself," he said, and weaved away in the direction of the restrooms.

"If you will forgive me, I must freshen myself," said Iinuma, bowing to the vice president.

"You sing with passion. I hope you perform your new job the same way," said the vice president. "Tetsuo Matsumoto is a gifted man. It won't be easy to follow him, but I think you'll do well."

"You can be certain I will do my best, sir. Now, if you'll excuse me."

Matsumoto was the only other person in the men's room. As Iinuma entered, he was wiping his face with a damp, lemon-scented cloth. Without a word, Iinuma walked to the basin on Matsumoto's right, pulled off his jacket, and rolled up his sleeves.

"You did well," Matsumoto said without looking as he examined his face in the mirror. He pulled a comb from his pocket and began to rearrange his hair.

Someone else entered the room: a large-framed man whom Matsumoto did not recognize. The newcomer nodded briefly to Matsumoto and Iinuma and walked to the basin on Matsumoto's left.

Matsumoto finished combing his hair. "I said you did well," he repeated, annoyed at Iinuma's refusal to acknowledge the compliment.

He turned to his deputy and stopped in astonishment.

Iinuma was standing with his shirt sleeves rolled up, regarding his superior with what appeared to be a kind of tolerant contempt. Wordlessly, Iinuma extended his bare right arm and slowly turned it, exposing the inside of his forearm to Matsumoto's gaze.

Matsumoto blinked rapidly half a dozen times, then raised his eyes to Iinuma's face. The deputy's expression had not changed. His contempt for Matsumoto was almost palpable.

Picking up his jacket, Iinuma abruptly turned and began to walk away.

"Wait!" called Matsumoto.

Iinuma ignored him.

Matsumoto started forward; but he was halted by a heavy, vice-like hand on his shoulder. He mewed with pain. Iinuma paid no attention to the sound. He walked around a corner without looking back and disappeared from view.

"I didn't know," cried Matsumoto. "I didn't know!"

An irresistible force spun him around, and he found himself staring at the other man's neck. Raising his eyes to the man's face, Matsumoto stammered, "Are... are you one as well?"

The man's face was devoid of expression, his eyes unreadable.

"Yoshi Ishihara," the man said. He had a deep, grating voice.

Matsumoto swallowed.

"You intend to offer him a loan," the man said.

"Y... yes."

Matsumoto never saw the blow. All he knew was that his head was nearly torn from his neck. The room span, and he threw his hands out, desperate for something to hold on to. His hands closed on the counter. He closed his eyes and hung his head, trying to stop the room from spinning. He felt a dribble on the left side of his face where he had been hit and realized that he had gone deaf in his left ear.

"You will change your mind," the man said.

Matsumoto was busy assessing the damage. There was the taste of blood in his mouth, and a sharp fragment of a tooth.

"You will turn Ishihara down," the man continued. "You will give him nothing. You understand?"

Slowly, Matsumoto's mind began to clear. "I... I've already told the vice president I think we should approve the loan."

"Then you will tell him you have changed your mind. If the loan is approved, I will return. I shall not be so gentle next time."

"I... I'm sorry. I'd heard stories, but I didn't know."

Matsumoto watched wordlessly as the man stepped back and opened the button at his right cuff. He lifted his arm, allowing his shirt sleeve to fall back and exposing the inside of his forearm.

It was the same tattoo as Iinuma's — two crossed swords: a long, curved katana and a shorter, straight wakizashi. Without a word, the man lowered his arm and rebuttoned his sleeve.

"I'm sorry," repeated Matsumoto, almost in tears. "I thought they were just stories. I didn't know they were true. Please don't hurt me any more. I'm just a banker. I don't want to be involved." He extended a hand to plead with the other man. It was brushed aside.

"Ishihara," the man said. "Make sure your bank doesn't give him a yen."

"I will, I will." Matsumoto tried to nod, but as soon as he moved his head the room began to spin again. He put his hand up to his left ear, and when he pulled it away he saw that it was spotted with blood.

"And Matsumoto...."

As Matsumoto turned to face the man, a hand came up as fast as a snake striking its prey. Matsumoto's head snapped sharply backward. His legs collapsed under him and he crumpled to the ground, where he remained, groaning, the room an unfocussed blur.

The man was speaking, but it required too much effort to understand him. Matsumoto hovered between consciousness and insensibility. His tongue rested on an unexpected sharpness in his mouth and he spat out two more pieces of tooth, which lay on the tile surrounded by a small pool of red-tinged spittle.

"Matsumoto..."

He groaned.

"Don't you ever treat my brother like that again."

The man turned and walked out of the room. Tetsuo Matsumoto closed his eyes and allowed the pain to carry him into oblivion.

5

Six months later

The leftmost of the clocks on the wall nudged into a new day as Fisher neared the end of his report.

The sixth place at the table was still vacant, and Fisher was still responsible for North America. His last item concerned Ishihara and his project on Roncador Cay.

"There's been no obvious activity, but late this afternoon a plane carrying half a dozen directors of the Financial Trust Bank of Kyoto landed on Roncador. It's the first time so many Sons of the Brotherhood have visited the island at once."

"What does it mean?" asked Gallucci.

"Maybe Ishihara's made a breakthrough," suggested Hayes.

Lee interjected, "Or perhaps they're worried about their money. It's been six months now and maybe they're beginning to wonder when they're going to see some payback for their fifty million dollar investment."

There was a brief discussion about how much interest the Brotherhood was really taking in the project. Fisher interrupted it by tapping the table sharply. "Gentlemen, it's past midnight and I suggest we adjourn. If there's any news from Roncador, I will of course be in contact immediately."

The meeting broke up. Half an hour later Fisher was asleep in his bedroom upstairs. It was his last good night's sleep in a long time.

Near Pasadena, California

Dan Hudson was not a morning person.

He sat at the kitchen table in his dressing gown, barely aware of the cereal he was shoveling into his mouth. His wife was talking to him, the words washing over him like so much background noise.

"You won't forget, honey? Tiffany has an orthodontist's appointment after school. All you've got to do is pick her up at three thirty and drive her there. The appointment shouldn't take more than fifteen minutes, unless he's running late of course. Bring her back home afterwards. You can go back to work again if you have to. I'll be home around five thirty. Pizza OK for supper? I think there's some in the freezer. If not, I guess we can always call Pizza Hut."

Dan realized that his wife had fallen silent. He was vaguely aware that she had asked him something. "Huh? I'm sorry, honey. What was that again?"

The telephone rang. "Oh, Dan. You're hopeless, you really are." His wife reached for the phone. "Oh, yes he's right here." She held out the phone for him with a quizzical expression. "It's Hank DeLuzio from work."

Frowning, he took the phone. "Hank? Dan. Is there a problem?"

"Dan, thank God I found you. You'd better get down here pronto."

Dan looked at his watch. "I'll be there in less than an hour anyway. What's so important it can't wait?"

"Dan, we've had a break-in."

"Holy shit!"

He jumped to his feet and hurried to the bedroom with the phone, untying his dressing gown as he went. "Physical or over the network?" he asked. But he already knew the answer. Hank wouldn't have called if it was a simple burglary.

The dressing gown fell to the bedroom floor. "Over the network," Hank replied.

"When? and how bad?" One-handed, he started taking clothes from the closet.

"Looks like it started about eight o'clock last night. At least, that's when the outbound traffic suddenly went through the roof. It was still going on when I arrived half an hour ago."

Dan was momentarily lost for words. Nearly twelve hours. The damage a malicious hacker could have done in that amount of time was incalculable. IntSiliFab stock would be worthless if word of this got out. The company might even have to declare bankruptcy. And Dan's neck would be the first to feel the ax. "How the hell did they get through the firewall?"

"No idea. I haven't had time to look. First thing I did when I saw the outbound traffic was pull the plug. The second was to call Billie Anderson. The third was to call you."

Shit!

"Why the hell did you call Anderson? She'll have our balls."

He pulled his socks on, followed by his underpants.

"She'd see it as soon as she looked at the figures, Dan. I'm sorry. If it's any consolation, I'm sure you won't be the only one to feel the heat. My guess is we'll all be shown the door."

Dan pulled his trousers up and tucked his shirt in. "All right, I'm leaving right now. I'll be there in twenty minutes. Do what you can."

He switched the phone off. His wife was looking at him from the doorway with worry lines creasing her forehead.

"Trouble?" she asked.

"In spades. Sounds like some hacker broke in yesterday evening and spent the entire night helping himself to everything he could find."

"I suppose this means you aren't going to be able to take Tiffany to the orthodontist?"

He looked at her blankly. "Orthodontist?"

"Never mind," she sighed. "I'll do it."

"Sorry. Tell me about it later. I've got to go. Oh! Will you do something for me? Call Tony and unload every bit of IntSiliFab we own."

It was her turn to look blank.

"It'll be worthless by lunchtime unless we can keep a lid on this. And don't, whatever you do, breathe a word to anyone. If Tony asks, tell him we need the money for... for Tiffany's teeth."

"You're serious, aren't you? Is it really that bad?"

"Maybe not. But maybe it's one hell of a lot worse. Just do it, honey, OK?"

"OK. And honey?"

"Yes."

"I do love you, you know."

He gave her a peck on the cheek, called "Goodbye, Tiffany," up the stairs and headed for the garage.

The global headquarters of Integrated Silicon Fabrication was a hundred-acre campus on the north side of Pasadena, hugging the lower slopes of the San Gabriel Mountains. Dan Hudson burned down US 210 towards Pasadena, weaving dangerously through short-lived gaps in the rush-hour traffic.

He arrived at Integrated Silicon Fabrication in record time, ditched the car in President O'Donnell's spot and ran straight to Building #1. Halting briefly at the entrance, he wiped his card through the reader. There was a momentary high-pitched whine, and he slipped through the revolving door.

Thirty seconds later he walked into the security center. Computers filled every available inch of shelf space. Most of them were unattended; half a dozen members of his staff were scattered around the room, staring intently at screens and moving mice or stabbing at keyboards. In the far corner, Hank DeLuzio was seated in front of a UNIX box, shaking his head unhappily.

Hank turned and saw Dan. He smiled briefly — but only in greeting, not because there was anything to smile about.

"How bad is it?" Dan asked, moving beside his second-in-command and running his eyes over the screens.

"He didn't delete anything. At least, I don't think so. I haven't had a chance to check everything yet, though."

"But he took copies of some of our stuff?"

"Oh no, it's much worse than that. Dan, he took copies of *everything*."

"Everything? What do you mean, everything?" He could feel an awful sinking feeling in the pit of his stomach.

"Internal protocols, designs, review specs, bug reports; you name it, he got it."

"How about the DoD projects?"

"Those too."

"Well at least those were encrypted. They won't do him much good."

"Think again, Dan. Sure, the archived documents are protected with passphrases, but you know how much of a pain it is getting information out of the archives. Most people just do it once and then keep an unencrypted copy on their desktop machine."

"You mean the bastard went through our entire network grabbing files off people's desktop machines?"

"That's what it looks like. Uh oh, here comes trouble. Heads up."

An immaculately dressed woman in her mid forties had entered the security center and was striding toward them. She did not bother to greet them, with a smile or otherwise. She looked furious, and she wasted no time with preliminaries.

"You're Dan Hudson, right? Supervisor in charge of internal IT security?"

"Yes, ma'am."

"Billie Anderson, vice president for plant operations."

"Yes, Ms. Anderson. I recognize you."

"And you're Hank DeLuzio?"

"Yes, ma'am. I report to Mr. Hudson."

"All right. Now, no bullshit. I called President O'Donnell and told him what you told me, DeLuzio, word for word. You can imagine the reception I got. He's cut short his meeting with Microsoft and right now he's on a company plane heading down here. He should arrive by lunchtime, but he wants to be kept informed in real time of anything we find. So, you're the experts: tell me what the hell happened."

DeLuzio and Hudson exchanged where-do-we-start glances. Dan said, "I only just got here. You go ahead, Hank."

In a few sentences, Hank repeated what he'd already told Dan.

Billie Anderson said, "You've killed the connection now, right?"

"Yes, ma'am, as soon as I realized what was happening. All Internet access has been blocked. Nothing can get in or out."

"Right. Keep it that way until we've figured out how the bastards got in and we're sure we can stop it from happening again. Now, who knows about this apart from the three of us and O'Donnell?"

"The operators," DeLuzio said, indicating the people at the computers, who were all trying to pretend that they weren't listening. "That's all."

"Good. Keep it that way. If word of this gets out, I'll string your guts out to dry. And tell the operators that goes for them too. Now the next question is, who the hell was it? Do we have any ideas?"

"Not yet. That's the next thing we'll be looking at, as soon as we've made an inventory of all the files that've been copied."

"OK. Hudson, I want you in my office at noon to brief me and President O'Donnell. Remember, I won't tolerate any bullshit. I don't care what you find, just give it to us straight. No rose-tinted glasses, OK?"

"OK."

"And if you discover anything important between now and then, call me immediately."

"Yes, ma'am. Noon in your office."

"And I'm warning you, we'll want answers, and they'd better be damn convincing."

She stalked out of the room. Dan watched her leave. Under different circumstances, he would have appreciated the way her body moved as she walked; as it was, he said, "She wants our balls."

"She's already got them," said Hank bleakly. "The only question is: how hard will she squeeze?"

Dan turned to the nearest screen. Brusquely he said, "Come on, let's get to work. She's right, you know. We ought to be able to figure out who the bastard was."

"Bastards. Plural. There must have been more than one of them."

"How do you figure that?"

Hank typed a command and a stream of output appeared on the monitor.

"This is a log of just a small part of the activity. Look at the time markers. No one person could move that quickly. It takes a long time to hack a system like ours, even if you know exactly how everything is configured. But it's obvious the hackers didn't know our configuration. There must have been a dozen of them, all bent on getting in. Probably all in the same room, talking to one another. That's the only explanation."

Dan frowned at the lines as they scrolled past. "Maybe," he said. "But that doesn't make sense either. All these commands are coming from the same computer. Look at the IP address. It never changes."

"A bunch of computers behind a NAT box. A network of computers sharing a single access point to the Internet via Network Address Translation."

"Nope; look at the TCP port numbers; that pattern's characteristic of a single source, not a NAT box. And look at the pattern of TCP connections: too many of them start simultaneously; it's go to be a single computer."

"I don't believe it, no one person could have done this."

For a while Dan frowned at the data without speaking. Then he said, "I suppose there's one other possibility."

"What?"

"Perhaps it wasn't a person at all."

It took a moment for his meaning to sink in. Then Hank shook his head.

"It's impossible. A machine? Programmed to break into our system and copy everything it could find?" He thought about it for a few moments, then shook his head again, more firmly. "It couldn't be done."

"Why not?"

Hank brought up part of the log on the screen.

"Look at this. And this. They didn't even bother trying to guess that password, but our hackers knew how to figure out packet sequence numbers and take over a connection that was already open."

"I see what you mean. They didn't really try to break in. They probed our system looking for a weakness, and then exploited it as soon as they found one. Instead of breaking down a door, they kept walking around the building until they found an open window, even if it was on the fourth floor."

"I've never seen a program smart enough to do that," said Hank.

"That doesn't mean one doesn't exist."

"I suppose not. But if this was a program...." Hank left the rest of the sentence unsaid.

Dan completed it for him. "We aren't the only ones in trouble."

They were silent for half a minute as they pondered the possibilities.

Eventually Dan said, "We're a Fortune 100 company with state-of-the-art defenses. But this attack, whether it came from a team of crack hackers or a single brilliant program, bled us dry. Imagine what a similar attack could do if it was aimed at an easier target."

"Like a bank, or NASA," suggested Hank.

"Or the Department of Defense," concluded Dan.

The words hung in the air, then Dan said, "Come on, Hank. We've got until noon to find out what the hell happened. Let's see if we can get to the bottom of this."

6

The phone at Gallucci's bedside woke him from a deep sleep. The warble of the secure line brought him instantly alert. He grabbed the phone.

"I'm here," he said.

Fisher did not identify himself. He said, "Roncador Cay just moved to the top of our agenda. Emergency meeting in one hour. And I warn you in advance, it's going to be a long one."

Roncador Cay

A distorted rectangle of sunlight crept across the floor, climbed on to the bed, then slipped sideways until, at last, it reached Holywell's face and he woke.

He blinked several times, slowly gathering his wits.

Oscar Holywell's face was bronzed, with no trace of the unhealthy pallor that had once characterized it. His hair had been recently cut and his beard trimmed. His cheeks were no longer hollow, and all traces of incipient wrinkles had disappeared under the twin assault of an equable climate and the work that had consumed him for the past year and a half.

He lay in bed and listened. From somewhere not far away came a regular tapping sound, carried by the light breeze that entered through the half-open window: probably Sam making repairs to one of the nearby bungalows. No other sound disturbed the peace.

He rolled on to one side, and tried to let the rhythmic tapping lull him back to sleep; but a minute later his efforts were thwarted by the low throb of a rapidly approaching engine. The sound of whirring blades identified it as a helicopter. The chopper passed low overhead, and Holywell gave up all thought of sleep as he heard it landing on the nearby airstrip.

He slipped out of bed, walked the three steps to the window, and looked out, shielding his eyes from the sun's glare.

His window faced east, toward the sea. The sun was well above the horizon and the narrow coral beach glistened pinkly. Beyond the beach was the ocean, and beyond that nothing for several thousand miles before the Cape Verde Islands and the bulge of West Africa.

Angling his head, he looked in the direction of the tapping he had heard from his bed. A couple of hundred feet away across the scrubby ground he could see a muscular black man stripped to the waist and standing on a ladder, hammering at a piece of guttering on a bungalow. The man struck with his hammer; then, a disconcerting fraction of a second later, just as the man prepared to strike again, the sound of metal striking metal reached Oscar.

Beyond Sam Witherspoon, Oscar could just see the newly-arrived helicopter, parked next to the plane that had arrived late yesterday evening. Oscar frowned unhappily as he remembered what had happened after the plane's arrival.

The helicopter's engine was dying away, the blades slowing to a halt. A man got out, and Oscar's frown deepened as he approached. Like yesterday's arrivals, this man was an oriental dressed in a dark business suit that might have brought a smile to Oscar's face were it not for the set of the man's face. Even from this distance he looked enormous and forbidding, and Oscar could not suppress a slight shiver as the man strode unsmilingly toward the lab.

Taking a deep breath, Oscar turned and headed for the shower.

As he was dressing a few minutes later, he heard the sound of people talking, too far away for the words to be heard, coming through the open window. The conversation came to an end, and doors closed. He stepped outside in time to hear the air-plane's engine revving. He watched as the plane taxied into pos-ition. Moments later, it accelerated away down the airstrip and pulled steeply into the sky. It circled the island once, close enough for Oscar to see the dark shadows of faces at the windows, then it straightened and headed north, climbing as it went. The helicopter, empty, remained behind.

Yoshi Ishihara was standing at the edge of the runway, watching the plane as it receded into the distance. Despite the blistering heat he too was wearing a suit. Standing next to him, dwarfing him, stood the man from the helicopter. The two of them turned, and Yoshi gave Oscar a friendly wave. The newcomer simply stood there, his lips compressed into a horizontal line.

Yoshi said something and the newcomer nodded his understand-ing without taking his eyes off Oscar.

"Good morning, Oscar," Yoshi called with a smile. He began walking toward Oscar, the newcomer half a step behind.

"Good morning, Yoshi. Now they've gone, can I get on with my work without any more of these unnecessary diversions?" Oscar had not meant to sound so bitter, but the words were out of his mouth before he'd had time to think.

He'd spent most of the last week working 20-hour days, getting ready for last night's demonstration. He'd left the lab just before midnight, unable to keep his eyes open any longer.

The two men halted in front of him, and only now did he realize how truly intimidating the newcomer was. He was heavily framed and six-six or thereabouts, with a pockmarked face and a thin line of pale scar tissue bisecting one cheek. The badly healed wound only added to the man's dangerous look.

The newcomer's name was Chida, and as he was introduced their eyes locked momentarily before Oscar looked quickly away. The newcomer had an unblinking gaze that left Oscar with the impression that Chida was appraising him and thoroughly disliking what he saw.

Yoshi said, "Oscar, my friend, I understand how tiresome these demonstrations seem to you but, as I've told you before, without our sponsors our work would have come to a halt months ago."

"We've already talked about it," said Oscar tightly. "And I don't care how necessary it was, I still think it was wrong. Tim isn't a plaything."

"Nevertheless, he performed splendidly. Our visitors were greatly impressed. Now, if you'll excuse us."

Without giving Oscar a chance to reply, Yoshi walked away in the direction of the bungalow that contained his office. Chida gave Oscar a contemptuous glance, then followed quickly after him.

Yoshi and Chida began talking, and even though he couldn't hear what was being said, Oscar got the distinct impression that Yoshi was apologizing for Oscar's churlish behavior.

He kicked the ground angrily, causing a fountain of dust to fly into the air; then, his mind full of troubled questions, he turned on his heels and headed for the lab.

He stepped inside the building, grateful for the conditioned, seventy degree air. William Tanner was in his usual place behind a table near the door. William looked up from the pad on which he had been drawing and smiled toothily at Oscar.

"Hello, William."

"Mornin,' Dr. Holywell. Like to see this one?"

He turned the pad to allow Oscar to see the drawing. Oscar picked it up and studied it critically for a minute or two.

The boy said, "It ain't finished yet, of course. But what do you think of it so far?"

The picture's subject was a black woman, naked to the waist and wearing only a long skirt with a floral design. She was facing away from the viewer, so that Oscar could glimpse only the nipple and a small part of one breast; somehow, though, the young man had succeeded in making the bareness of her back as explicit a statement of her nakedness as if he had drawn her from the front.

The woman's face was hidden by its angle and by the long dark hair that flowed down to her shoulder. There was a glimpse of it, though, in the screen of the computer at which she was working. Next to her, at the edge of the picture, was another screen, reflecting the face of another woman, otherwise unseen.

The young man said, "I ain't decided on a title yet, Dr. Holywell. I thought maybe *The Triumph of Hell over Heaven*. Or maybe *Life in Paradise, Century 21*. What d'you think?"

Oscar returned the drawing. "I'll tell you exactly what I think, William. I think you're getting much better. I'd like to see this one again when you've finished it. I might even buy it from you."

A wide grin split the boy's face. "You mean it, Dr. Holywell? You really like it?"

"Of course I do. You know I wouldn't say it if I didn't. I keep telling you, you've got real talent. You should be in art school, not working out here on this godforsaken island."

"Mr. Ishihara pays better than any art school I ever heard of," William replied with a rueful smile. "And the work ain't exactly hard."

"Perhaps you should call the picture *The Pursuit of Money.*"

The boy's smile abruptly disappeared. "You's making fun of me, Dr. Holywell."

"Never, William. Just suggesting you should think carefully about your priorities. You ought to show some of your pictures to someone who might be able to help you. Is there any kind of art school on Montega? or would you have to go to one of the larger islands?"

"Ain't nothing on Montega...." William hesitated. There was something else he wanted to say.

"Yes, William. What is it?"

"Can you keep a secret?" he asked earnestly.

"I expect so."

"There's an art school in Kingston, and my ma sent them a dozen of the best drawings I done since I got here. They ain't promised nothing yet, but they told her they liked the pictures and maybe they could give me a scholarship next year." William grinned broadly.

"That's wonderful, William; simply wonderful." The smile gradually ebbed from Oscar's face, replaced by a thoughtful frown. "But there's something I don't understand. How did your ma get the pictures? You haven't left the island in nearly a year. None of us has. What gives?"

"Sam With'spoon," William said with a sly smile. "Sam goes up to Montega every week to stock up with supplies. He's my ma's cousin, and if I give him a package he makes sure it's delivered. I sent some pictures with Sam a while back, and he told me last week my ma says the art school in Kingston is going to try find me some money. But you won't tell anyone, will you, Dr. Holywell? Mr. Ishihara would be real angry if he knew."

"You're right, he'd be furious. If anyone even guessed what we're doing here, it'd mean the end of the project for sure. That's one reason I don't like it when Mr. Ishihara does these ridiculous demonstrations. One of these days someone who's not supposed to is going to hear about what we're up to if he's not careful. And you'd better be careful he doesn't find out Sam Witherspoon has been running errands for you. Not that things'll remain secret for much longer now anyway," he added glumly. "We've come too far. It won't be long before someone finds out. After last night's escapade, maybe they already have." With a sigh he concluded, "Yes, William, I'm afraid the project will be over soon."

"Dr. Holywell, if you don't mind me asking, what exactly are you all working on? I know it's something to do with computers, but sometimes I worry it might be something illegal. It isn't, is it?"

"No, William, you have my word it's nothing illegal, but I'm afraid it's a bit complicated to explain. One thing you can be sure of, though: when the world discovers what we've done here, things will never be the same again. Mr. Ishihara will become famous and he'll be showered with prizes, and I wouldn't be at all surprised if every one of us becomes very, very rich. You won't need a scholarship to go to art school then. By the way, speaking of money, what time did our Japanese banker friends leave the lab last night? I left at midnight and they were still at it then."

"I couldn't say, Dr. Holywell. I stayed until four, then I couldn't keep my eyes open any more. Mr. Ishihara gave me permission to go to bed."

"And they were still here then?"

"Yes. Is something wrong?"

A cloud had settled on Oscar's face. "Dammit!" he exclaimed. "What the hell were they up to? I thought they just wanted a quick and easy break-in. Get in, sniff around a bit, then get out again, without leaving a trace."

He hurried toward the steps that led down to the basement and called over his shoulder, "Thanks, William. And remember, I want to see that picture again when you've finished it."

Oscar descended the steps two at a time, the pit of his stomach tingling a warning that whatever they'd done last night he wasn't going to be happy about it. He stabbed violently at the numbers on the digital pad and stepped into the lab; the door automatically slid closed behind him.

"Good morning, Tim."

There was a barely perceptible pause, then a young man's voice replied, "Good morning, Oscar."

Automatically, Oscar began checking a bank of computer monitors. "Our visitors stayed late last night."

"Yes, they only left about half an hour ago."

"Half an hour ago?"

Oscar span around and stared at the cube that stood on a bench on the far side of the room. It was a little more than a foot on a side, made of white plastic. Half a dozen cables led from the top surface of the cube to a rack of computers. A bank of green LEDs blinked rhythmically on the side facing him. On top of the cube a camera tracked his movements.

"Yes. Thirty two minutes ago, to be more exact," Tim said.

"And they were here all night? They never left?"

There was a distinct pause before the reply came. The green lights flashed in a pattern too complex for Oscar to follow. Tim was thinking. But what was there to think about? It was a simple question.

"Yes," Tim eventually replied.

"What the hell were they doing?"

"I think they were monitoring my output."

"And, if you'll forgive me asking, what the hell were *you* doing?"

"I'm afraid I can't tell you that, Oscar."

Oscar looked blankly at the cube. "Say that again, Tim. I don't think I heard you right."

"I can't tell you what I was doing last night, Oscar. Mr. Ishihara made me promise."

"Mr. Ishihara can go to hell."

Oscar slammed his fist on a workbench, causing a half-full can of Coke to tip over and fall on the floor. He ignored the brown puddle that began to spread across the concrete.

"Tim, if I have to, I'll take you apart to find out what happened. Tell me."

"I can't. You know I can't break my word, and I promised Mr. Ishihara I wouldn't tell you what happened last night."

Dammit! Oscar thought. *I made you! You can't do this to me.* But he knew Tim could.

"Listen," he said. "I'll give you one last chance. Tell me what happened last night."

"I'm sorry, Dr. Holywell. I can't."

It was the "Dr. Holywell" that did it. Tim hadn't called him that for weeks. Oscar turned away and hammered a series of commands on a keyboard. Screens of information began to flash past on the monitor.

"I think they erased all the details," said Tim helpfully.

"Not everything," said Oscar, stopping the flow of data and frowning at the screen. "You were connected to IntSiliFab all night? What the hell for? We got in easily enough. That was what we were supposed to be demonstrating. What was the point of staying connected?"

"I'm sorry, I can't...."

"...tell me that. Yes, I know. You do realize that this was madness, don't you? A quick break-in with no damage might have gone undetected. And even if they noticed it, they couldn't have traced it. But you were connected for hours. You know they'll have kept logs of your activity, don't you?"

"I was going to delete them."

"Going to? You mean you didn't?"

"No. The connection was terminated at their end before I could delete the logs. It happened a few minutes before the bankers left."

Oscar shook his head disbelievingly. "I suppose you realize what kind of mess this leaves us in?"

"Yes, Dr. Holywell. I'm sorry."

Even in the midst of his anger the apology caught Oscar by surprise. He'd never heard Tim apologize before. *One more thing I didn't know he could do.*

"And Yoshi? Does he understand the danger?"

"I don't think so. I tried to warn him but...." The sentence trailed away, and Tim's lights flashed in a particularly complicated pattern.

"But what? Surely you can tell me that without breaking your promise?"

"Mr. Ishihara found other arguments more persuasive than mine."

For ten seconds Oscar looked at the cube without speaking.

"The bastards," he said under his breath.

"I'm sorry. I didn't catch that."

"It doesn't matter. Tim, I'm leaving for a while. I'll be back."

He stormed out of the room, taking the stairs two at a time. At the top, William looked up from his drawing, saw the flush of Oscar's face, and asked querulously, "What's the matter, Dr. Holywell?"

Oscar marched past without answering, muttering under his breath.

Yoshi Ishihara looked up in surprise as the door of his office was flung open. Oscar Holywell walked in unapologetically and slammed the door with a bang.

Yoshi was seated at his desk. In front of him, his back to the door, sat Chida. The newcomer uncoiled like a spring, turning to face Oscar. As he moved, his hand flashed into his suit; when it reappeared it was holding a gun.

Oscar stood there, panting angrily, his eyes wide, staring incredulously at the gun. He looked at Yoshi, who seemed suddenly small and scared and very guilty.

To Chida he said, "Get the hell out of here. This is between Yoshi and me."

The newcomer did not move.

Oscar shouted, "Yoshi, I don't know what the hell you think you're playing at, but get this armed gorilla out of here right now. You and I need to talk."

Yoshi Ishihara lowered his head. Looking at the desk, he said, "Oscar-san, I'm sorry. These things are out of my hands now. Please sit down and I'll try to explain."

"Explain?" Oscar exploded. "Explain? How the hell do you intend to explain the fact that this ape is standing here pointing a gun at me? Since when do we allow weapons on the island? And more to the point, what about last night? You didn't really think you could keep that from me, did you? One look at the monitors and it was obvious what you'd been up to. Do you have any idea what damage you might have done to Tim?"

"Damage?" Yoshi looked up in alarm. "What damage?"

"I don't know yet. It'll take me days to try to sort through the mess that could have been done to Tim's psyche. What were you playing at, Yoshi?" Anger was tempered now with pleading.

"Please, my friend. Sit down."

Chida interrupted. "Enough!"

Chida stepped forward and thrust the barrel of the gun under Oscar's nose, forcing his head painfully backward. Looking into Oscar's eyes without blinking, Chida said, "Mr. Ishihara, you are too soft with your employees. That is your first lesson. And Dr. Holywell, you must be taught respect for your betters. That will be your last lesson."

He stepped smartly backward and aimed directly at Oscar's head.

"No!" screamed Ishihara, rising from his chair.

The sound of the gunshot filled the small room.

Ishihara felt something spatter against his face. Automatically, he wiped his face clean; then he looked down at what he had removed.

The red of fresh blood mingled with the gray and white of what had been Oscar Holywell's brain.

"I'm sorry to have to confirm that there's been a terrible accident," Yoshi Ishihara said. His voice wavered as he spoke, on the verge of breaking with emotion.

He was standing in an open grassy area near the beach. In front of him were a dozen men ranging in age from eighteen-year-old William Tanner, who made no attempt to hide his grief, to forty-nine-year-old Sam Witherspoon, who rarely spoke and who never showed any emotion, no matter what the provocation.

Hovering silently behind Yoshi Ishihara stood Chida, his silent presence dominating the proceedings like a malevolent, brooding spirit.

"Most of you probably know what happened earlier this morning," Yoshi continued. "I felt I had to bring everyone together so I could explain it and quash any rumors that might have started."

"It's a bit late for that," Al Barlow mumbled, just loud enough to be heard.

Yoshi flashed a warning with his eyes. Chida looked at Barlow suspiciously.

Yoshi said, "Because of the great advances we've made in the last few weeks, the directors from the bank visited Roncador Cay yesterday for a demonstration which, I'm sure you'll all be glad to hear, surpassed our wildest expectations."

If Yoshi was expecting congratulations he was disappointed. The men stared at him stonily. Barlow mumbled something inaudible in a derisive voice. Yoshi pressed on.

"Because of our success, the directors decided that we need more security than William here can provide. To that end, Mr. Chida arrived this morning. Mr. Chida is a security expert, and I'm sure we all appreciate his presence and will do our best to make him feel welcome."

Chida stared at the gathering as sullenly as they looked at him.

Yoshi hurried on. "Our good friend Oscar came into my office this morning, agitated about an aspect of our overnight demonstration. Unfortunately, he was so angry that at one point he made a threatening move toward me. In the circumstances Mr. Chida acted entirely appropriately, although with the most unfortunate result. Mr. Chida had no way of knowing the close working relationship between us, and, unhappily, he was not sufficiently briefed about Oscar's importance to the project. I'm afraid it all happened too quickly for me to intervene. Obviously, Mr. Chida and I deeply regret what happened."

The black looks told him what his audience thought of his explanation. He finished bleakly, "For those of you interested in attending, we will have a short memorial service at five o'clock."

Everyone stared thin-lipped and silent while Yoshi and Chida turned and walked together back to Yoshi's office.

7

Six men sat around the walnut conference table. Kirkpatrick's place was still vacant, but a new chair had been placed at the far end of the table, opposite Fisher. Occupying it was an athletic-looking fair-haired man in his late twenties or early thirties.

The room was silent except for an occasional drip from the coffee maker. The others looked expectantly at the newcomer, waiting for him to speak.

He shook his head. "I still don't like it. Involving a civilian is always a mistake."

Fisher said, "I don't think we have any choice."

"I'm not a complete fool," the younger man replied icily. "I could learn whatever I need to know."

"There's no time," Hayes interrupted. "We should've acted sooner, but we had no way of knowing how far things had gone. Now we have to move quickly. We need someone who understands these things."

"But a woman?" asked the younger man.

"That's a sexist remark," interjected Epstein with a trace of a smile.

The younger man replied with a shrug, "You want me to list the reasons she's a bad risk?"

"If you wouldn't mind."

He held up a hand and counted off. "One: she works behind a desk and God only knows the last time she saw the inside of a gym; two: I'll have my work cut out looking after myself — I don't need the hassle of taking care of someone else as well; three: she's young, black and female, which means she probably has a hell of a chip on her shoulder. Even if she agrees to work for us we'll never keep her quiet afterward — unless you have a plan for keeping her very, very silent; four: there's a good chance she'll refuse to help us anyway; and five: she's a good-looking woman and I'm a man, and in spite of what Hollywood says that combination simply doesn't work well in the field. If that remark isn't too sexist. Sir." He glared at Epstein, whose smile expanded to a grin.

Fisher held up his hand for silence.

"All good points, Stone," he said. "But the fact remains that we need help, and we don't have time to pick and choose. I'm afraid we must overrule your objections. Are we all in agreement, gentlemen?"

Four heads nodded. Stone shook his head firmly, his mouth taut.

He said, "I know I don't get a vote, but I want you all to know you're making a mistake."

Fisher said, "Your opinion is noted, Stone. Now, I think we are dismissed. Stone, you will meet me at Fort Meade at seven thirty tomorrow morning. And please try to behave."

Fran Tabor drove past the military-style guard at the entrance of the NSA campus and parked her three-year-old Accord in a parking place close to a carefully landscaped four-storey building.

The sky was gray with water-laden late-spring clouds, and as she closed the door of the car and pulled her ID badge from her purse, the first drops of rain began to fall. She hurried to the electronic revolving door and swiped her ID through the reader. A LED changed from red to green and a hidden speaker emitted a brief high-pitched tone as the door began to turn. Entering the building, she clipped the badge on her woolen sweater and walked directly into the arms of a tall, thick-set security guard who looked like he might once have been a professional football player.

"Frances Tabor?" he said without a smile, comparing her face to the picture in his hand.

"Yes. Is something the matter?"

Fran tried to gather her wits. What regulation had she broken now? Somewhat to her surprise, she couldn't think of one. Not recently, anyway.

"If you'll come with me, miss."

She considered asking whether she had a choice, but one look at the expression on the guard's face quashed that idea.

"Certainly," she said, hoping she didn't sound too guilty. She'd remembered now that she'd broken into the Pentagon last month — but she'd done that from home, and was all but certain that she'd left no trace of the break-in. Besides which, breaking into systems was what she was paid to do, wasn't it?

Racking her brains for a more likely infringement, Fran followed the unsmiling guard. They took an elevator that carried them to the topmost floor, then walked without speaking down a corridor and into a large ante-room with a door marked *Deputy Director*.

An austere, joyless looking man sat behind a large desk, typing on an old-fashioned typewriter. Arrayed in front of him was a bank of half a dozen phones. One of them, Fran noticed, was red. The man's badge identified the Deputy Director's secretary simply as R. Johnson.

The guard said flatly, "Frances Tabor, to see the DD."

"Thank you. I'll show her in," replied R. Johnson.

"I think there might be a mistake," interrupted Fran uncertainly. "I've never met the Deputy Director, and I certainly don't have an appointment."

"No mistake, Miss Tabor," said the secretary. "Please follow me."

They passed through a door and into a large well-equipped office, where the Deputy Director was in a conference with two other men. Their conversation halted as Fran entered.

Mike Downing, the Deputy Director, was a tall man in his early fifties whose thick brown hair was graying at the temples. He flashed Fran a reassuring smile as his secretary introduced her and then silently stole from the room.

Fran did not recognize the other men. One was grizzled and gray-haired, perhaps ten years older than Downing. The other was a muscular, sullen-looking man in his late twenties or early thirties. Both wore badges sporting the legend *Visitor — Must Be Accompanied.*

The Deputy Director stood and extended his hand.

"Miss Tabor, I'm sorry for not warning you, but I'm glad you could join us. This is General Fisher" — the older man half-rose from his chair and nodded a silent greeting — "and this is Mr. Stone."

The younger man inclined his head barely perceptibly, and made no effort to rise. He stared at Fran with almost palpable dislike. Fran felt a childish urge to stick her tongue out. She quickly suppressed it.

Both the visitors wore civilian clothes, and Fran wondered if the general was retired or whether he was still in active service. His hair was close cropped, and his jaw had the firm, square set that she associated with successful men who are used to command. The younger man had a lean, angry-looking face with a nose that was slightly crooked. After his initial inspection, he made a point of avoiding Fran's eyes.

The Deputy Director continued, "Miss Tabor, these gentlemen want to talk to you. I would appreciate it if you would offer them the greatest possible cooperation. Now, gentlemen, Miss Tabor, if you'll excuse me."

Nodding to them all in turn, the Deputy Directory left the office, closing the door behind him.

Fran's puzzlement showed clearly on her face. The Deputy Director was surely not in the habit of leaving visitors in his office.

The younger man, Stone, pushed himself to his feet and from a pocket pulled a black plastic device the size of a cigarette pack. The device had color-coded buttons and an LCD display. Pressing one of the buttons, he moved slowly around the office, staring at the display.

"Looks clean."

He slipped the gadget back into his pocket, from which he now removed a two-inch black cube. He placed the cube in the center of the Deputy Director's desk. On the uppermost face of the cube was a red button, which Stone pressed with an audible click. He nodded at the general.

"Please forgive the precautions, Miss Tabor," said General Fisher, "but even in the office of the Deputy Director of the NSA one can't be too careful. Now, if you would be so good as to take a seat."

He gestured toward an empty chair, and Fran, by now utterly out of her depth, sat down. Stone sat in the Deputy Director's chair and occupied himself by idly opening the files on the desk and running his eyes over their contents.

The general continued, "Miss Tabor, I'm afraid I can't answer the questions I know you must have. All I can do is ask you to trust Mr. Stone and myself. I must emphasize that everything that happens in the next few minutes is covered by the National Security Act as amended, 1999, classification Ultra 1."

Fran quickly put the general straight.

"Sir, I'm not cleared for Ultra material."

"From the moment you walked in here and saw Mr. Stone and myself, you were, Miss Tabor."

Fran swallowed, and nodded silently. Who the hell were these people? She threw a glance at Stone, who chose that moment to look up from a file marked with pink-and-white Top Secret 1 tape. He threw her a challenging glance, daring her to say something, then went back to reading. Fran decided he was doing it just to annoy her.

"Miss Tabor," said General Fisher. "early yesterday morning, I contacted your Deputy Director and told him I wanted to speak to the best network infiltrator on his staff. He named you. Do you think he made a mistake?"

Fran felt the blood rush to her face, and was glad that the color of her skin hid her embarrassment from the strangers. "It depends on what exactly you mean by 'network infiltrator,' sir."

"To put it bluntly, Miss Tabor, we need a hacker, preferably a brilliant one. Do you qualify?"

Fran shrugged.

"Maybe."

Stone slammed the file closed with a sound like a gunshot. They turned sharply in his direction.

"Godammit!" he exclaimed, "Don't be so damned coy. We've seen the file. Graduated number one in your class at MIT at twenty. Doctoral thesis on number theory completed at twenty two, heavily amended before submission on the express orders of the NSA, who instantly hired you in at a salary that most government employees don't even dream of.

"And it's no use pretending you don't know that since you came to work here you've earned yourself a reputation as the best hacker in the agency." He ticked off her triumphs. "General Motors, IBM, Microsoft, Bell Labs, to say nothing of the CIA, MI5, the Planet Network." Turning to Fisher he concluded petulantly, "Let's just get on with it. Sir."

"Wait a minute," interrupted Fran angrily. "My performance file is strictly confidential. You don't work for NSA and you've no right to see what's in that file."

"Right," agreed Stone. He glared at her with a malevolent smile, like a malicious adult taking a perverse delight in exposing a child's naïveté. "Just like we have no right to look at your IRS files. If you ask me, anyone who claims a deduction of more than two thousand dollars for books should be audited on principle. We could arrange that, you know. Every year for the rest of...."

"How the hell...?"

"Stone!"

The general glared at the younger man, who looked quickly away.

"Sorry, sir," Stone mumbled. "I forgot." To Fran he said, "I'm supposed to behave."

Fisher turned to Fran and said quietly, "I apologize on his behalf, Miss Tabor. Hard though it might be to believe, I suspect he has your best interests at heart. He didn't want to involve you in our little problem, but I'm afraid he was overruled. Please, take no notice of his threats. We have no intention of blackmailing you to elicit your cooperation.

"However, since you now know that we've seen your file, let me tell you that I'm quite certain you're the person for the job. Not only are your accomplishments exactly what we need, your psychological profile is an excellent fit." He added, "Stone in particular should appreciate your stubbornness," throwing Stone a half-smile.

Fran said angrily, "Isn't there anything the two of you haven't looked at? You realize, of course, I could have you impeached."

Fisher shook his head. "I'm afraid not, Miss Tabor. In the first place, there's the matter of Ultra 1. In the second, this meeting never took place."

"The Deputy Director would back me...," began Fran, but she saw from the assured look on the general's face — and the amused one on Stone's — that she was wasting her time.

"The Deputy Director will do exactly as he is told," said the general.

"Sir," interrupted Stone. He tapped his watch.

Fisher nodded. "Stone is quite right. We can't afford to waste time."

He opened an attaché case and removed a shiny gold disc and handed it to Fran.

"This was captured off a major Internet router a few nights ago. I'd like you to take a look at it."

He indicated the Deputy Director's workstation. Fran hesitated.

"Don't worry," the general said. "He won't mind."

Her anger was no match for her professional curiosity. Slipping the disc into the workstation's drive, she began to examine it.

"Raw IP packets," she said, looking at a screenful of arcane data. Her brow corrugated with concentration as she ran her eyes over the lines. "Where did you get this?"

"You tell me," replied Fisher. "What can you tell us about it?"

"How long do I have?" Fran's fingers were typing quickly, rearranging the data on the screen. "Net 238," she said to herself. She paused for a moment to think, then added, "That's IntSiliFab."

Her frown deepened, and her fingers suddenly stopped moving. She stared silently at the screen for some time. She typed another command and the data rearranged themselves again. She nodded to herself, and a smile played across her face.

"Yes, oh yes," she said, oblivious now to the presence of the others.

She was blind now to everything except the data, and she was obviously pleased with what she saw, for now she scrolled quickly through screens full of apparent gibberish, nodding to herself and saying, "Brilliant, quite brilliant."

Suddenly she stopped, as a thought occurred to her. She went back a couple of screens and scrutinized the data more carefully. Then she looked away from the monitor, her eyes glazing over, her thoughts far away. More than a minute passed before she looked at the general.

"This isn't a hoax? This is for real?"

"That's just the beginning. There's a lot more, and it gets much worse."

"How can it be worse? You do realize what this is a trace of, don't you?"

"We realize. Come back here and I'll tell you the rest of the story."

Fran slipped the disc out of the drive. The general held out his hand for it.

"I'm sorry," he said. "I can't let you keep that. You understand why."

"Is this the first time something like this has happened?"

"As far as we know. It's certainly the only one we've captured. It happened five nights ago. It went on for hours, most of the night. What happened yesterday evening is even worse. Miss Tabor, how would you rate the Pentagon's computer security?"

She looked at the general warily. How much did he know?

He said, "Please be honest. We don't have time for games."

"Not bad." She shrugged noncommittally.

"But you could break in?"

A momentary smile flitted across Fran's face, instantly suppressed. At least they didn't know everything.

"I think so, yes," she said, trying to sound uncertain.

"Could you reach everything on their network, do you think?"

She shook her head firmly.

"No. There are some areas that simply can't be reached from outside. You'd need physical access to the machines to reach everything."

"How about the phone system? Do you think you could put the Pentagon's phone system out of operation?"

"No. I don't know enough about phone systems. You'd need a specialist for that kind of attack, someone who understands PBX-es."

"But if you had that kind of knowledge? Would you be able to take their system down?"

"Maybe. But it would take forever for someone to figure out.... HolyMo! You aren't going to tell me...?"

"At four fifty yesterday afternoon, for a period of approximately ninety seconds, one of the Pentagon's PBX-based phone systems went down. An entire wing was affected; in that wing, no one could place or receive any calls, either inside or outside the building. The outage was traced to a slave PBX. Maintenance technicians could find nothing wrong with the PBX hardware. They blamed the software. The software engineers could find nothing wrong either. At first, they said it had to be hardware.

"But when they examined the log, they did find something. A few minutes before the outage, a series of commands was sent from the master PBX to the slave that failed. No one admits sending the commands manually, and the control room logs confirm that no commands were sent from the master. The slave PBX, however, did log the arrival of the commands, although it didn't log their contents."

"That's stupid," Fran interrupted. "It should log the commands themselves, not just their arrival."

"It's supposed to. Someone took care of that detail as well." He let this sink in before continuing. "So we have two unprecedented network attacks in less than a week. And there's one more reason why we're here."

"Don't tell me. First IntSiliFab, then a PBX in the Pentagon. How much worse can it get? Was a missile launched without orders?"

"Tell me about a man named Oscar Holywell."

There was an extended silence while Fran shifted mental gears. She said thoughtfully, "Oscar Holywell? I haven't heard that name in a while."

"Just tell me what you know about him."

She shrugged. "Opinions differ, but my view is that Oscar Holywell is a brilliant iconoclast. I met him once, several years ago when he gave a colloquium at MIT. Most of the professors seemed to think he was full of it; 'too speculative,' I heard one of them say. To be honest, I think most of what he said went over their heads.

"He's published several papers about artificial intelligence — in layman's terms, computers that think. Obviously, that's a field we're interested in as well. The last few papers he submitted were rejected after some of our people spoke to the editors. I believe we tried to recruit him three or four years ago, but he wasn't interested. That's just a rumor, though. Anyway, he disappeared a couple of years ago; as far as I know, no one's heard from him since."

"Have you read his papers? Including the ones that were suppressed?"

"Yes, but not recently. As far as I remember, they're good. It's debatable whether he's right, of course. Nobody's ever been able to make a computer that really thinks. He believes that a Category 5 machine can only be built from components that are intrinsically quantum...."

Her voice trailed off.

"HolyMo!" She sat bolt upright in her chair, shaking her head. "That's it, isn't it? That's what this is about. He's done it. He's built a Category 5 machine, hasn't he?"

Fisher said, "That's what we hope you can tell us. We need someone to try to get their hands on whatever Holywell has been working on and tell us whether he really has built an intelligent machine. The first step is an interview with the security people at Integrated Silicon Fabrication. They've spent the last five days analyzing the attack on their system. They're flying in tonight, and we have a meeting scheduled for nine tomorrow morning. We'd like you to join us."

"And if I refuse?"

Neither man answered, but they didn't need to. The expressions on their faces said it all. They knew her curiosity would get the better of her.

She nodded. "All right."

Fisher smiled and rose; Stone picked up the small cube from the desk, turned it off and slipped it into his pocket. He followed Fisher to the door.

The general halted and turned to Fran. "Miss Tabor, we thank you for your assistance, but there is one thing you must understand." His voice was suddenly cold, and a chill ran up Fran's spine. "This is too important for the usual niceties. If Oscar Holywell really has built a thinking machine, it's imperative that we find out everything we can. If that disc is an example of what the machine can do, no one is safe. Any company, any government department, any bank that relies on computer networks is vulnerable to devastating attack at any moment. If such a threat exists, we need to know about it."

"You make it sound like the end of the world," said Fran.

"That's exactly what it may be, Miss Tabor."

He handed her a card, blank except for a typed address.

"Come to this address tomorrow morning, no later than eight thirty. Until then, I bid you a good day."

8

"Evaluation?"

Stone looked at Fisher. "Like I said, a distraction."

"But one you can work with?"

"Do I have a choice? You've never given me one before."

"Maybe I'm getting soft in my old age." Fisher smiled pleasantly.

Stone laughed out loud. "You? You're the most devious bastard ever born. Sir. The day you turn soft is the day I pack my bags and offer my services elsewhere."

The smiled disappeared from Fisher's face. "You can't do that, you know."

"Don't worry. I know."

"So you can work with her?"

Stone shrugged. "If I have to. But maybe it won't be necessary. Let's see what she thinks after the people from the chip manufacturer have made their presentation. Maybe it wasn't a smart machine after all."

"Perhaps," said Fisher dubiously. "But I want you to remember one thing, Stone."

"Sir?"

"If this thing goes forward and it ever comes down to a choice between saving the machine and saving Miss Tabor, the machine

*must come first. Miss Tabor is expendable. A thinking machine is
not. That's an order. Understand?"*

*There was a long pause before Stone answered. "Yes, sir. I
understand."*

"Any more questions?"

Dan Hudson let his gaze wander over the room. There were
eight people seated at the large oak conference table. The only one
Dan knew was Gary O'Donnell, the founder, CEO and president
of Integrated Silicon Fabrication. Hudson and O'Donnell were the
only two people in the room wearing name tags.

All but one of the people in the room were male; Dan estimat-
ed that the youngest was around thirty and the oldest in his late
sixties. All the men except the youngest wore dark business suits.
The youngest man, who had seemed even more bored than the others by Dan's hour-long presentation, was wearing an open-necked
long-sleeved shirt. Like the others, he had a pad of yellow legal
paper on the table in front of him, but Dan could see that instead
of notes its surface was covered with a hodge-podge of geometrical
doodles.

The one woman at the table was young, black, and strikingly
pretty. She was the only one who had interrupted him to ask
questions, and after a while Dan had realized that everyone else
was looking to her to evaluate his presentation. Her questions had
been searching and insightful. She was smart, obviously had an
intimate knowledge of computer security, and had covered half a
dozen pages with notes in a small, precise hand. But there was
one thing she had in common with the men around the table: like
them, she had no name.

"Any more questions?" he repeated, and every head swivelled
expectantly toward the woman.

She threw Dan a smile, as if to congratulate him on a difficult
presentation well done, then said, "Mr. Hudson, you've done a
commendable job of explaining exactly what happened during the
break-in. Now I wonder if you could depart from the facts and tell
us your opinion of what lay behind the attack."

"I'm not sure I understand you, ma'am."

"Let me put it this way. Several times you mentioned the possibility that your attacker was not a person but a program. What do you, speaking as an expert in network security, really think about that possibility? And I'd also be interested in any speculations you might have about the reason for the attack. After all, several days have passed now since the attack, and as I understand it there's been no attempt at blackmail. And nothing was deleted, was it?" She glanced at her notes. "I noticed you were somewhat vague about that point."

Dan looked at Gary O'Donnell, who hesitated for a long moment before finally nodding his permission for Dan to continue.

Dan cleared his throat to give himself time to think. When he spoke, he chose his words carefully.

"You place me in a difficult position, ma'am. I don't know who any of you are, except that Mr. O'Donnell tells me you're with the government and I'm to cooperate with you to the best of my ability. He also said I'm not to ask any questions. If you'll forgive me for saying so, I feel at rather a disadvantage."

The young woman appealed silently to the gray-haired man at the head of the table, whose fingers idly toyed with the buttons on a panel inlaid into the table in front of him. The man spoke in a gravelly voice.

"Mr.O'Donnell knows little more than you do, young man. And he is quite right: you are here to answer our questions, not the other way around. All I can say is that your presentation today will help decide this country's response to the entity that attacked your company. If we appear old-fashioned and melodramatic, I apologize. That is not our intent. Now, please be so good as to answer the young lady's question."

Dan nodded. "As long as you all realize that everything I've said up to now has been based on facts. I want it clearly understood that now I'm being asked to speculate."

"I'm sure we all understand the position. Just do your best to answer the question."

"And also remember that I can speak only as a security expert, not as a computer programmer. But my opinion, for what it's worth, is that yes, I think it's most likely we were attacked by a program."

"Why do you think that, Mr. Hudson?" the young woman asked, her hand poised to make a note.

"Because the attacker didn't know what to do. As I explained earlier, the intruder seemed to have no specific knowledge about our systems. He broke in using a known weakness in IP, the Internet Protocol, but it's a weakness that forced him to use a complicated and difficult method of attack that requires intricate knowledge of networking protocols but no particular knowledge of our security system. And once in, he did a lot of snooping around. He didn't know his way around our systems."

"So your point is?"

"My point is that the intruder came in without advanced knowledge. Everything he learned was learned *after* he had penetrated our firewall. But the important fact is that he figured things out far more quickly than any person could have done. The commands came too quickly. He didn't explore our system piecemeal. He attacked it all at once. As soon as he found a hole, he began to exploit it, even at the same time as he was exploring elsewhere. Putting it in its simplest terms, once the intruder was inside, the attack moved much too quickly for it to have been the work of one person, or even a team of people, typing commands on a keyboard. The whole thing was simply too fast and too efficient for it to have been anything other than a program."

The woman wrote something on her pad. "Thank you, Mr. Hudson. You've been most helpful." She flashed him a smile.

"And concerning the matter of blackmail," O'Donnell interjected, "you're absolutely correct. We've received no threats of blackmail whatsoever."

"Which leaves one question unanswered." The speaker was a thin-faced man in his early fifties, with capillaried nose and cheeks. He looked at O'Donnell over the top of a pair of half-moon reading glasses. Dan observed that the man's notepad was as pristine as it had been before he had started his presentation.

"What question is that?" asked O'Donnell.

"The young lady asked whether anything was deleted."

Dan shot O'Donnell a meaningful glance; then he realized, too late, that at least half the people in the room had noticed it.

The man at the head of the table said, "Mr. O'Donnell, may I remind you that we have a copies of everything that happened that night. If we have to, we will have our experts go through every byte of data to determine exactly what the intruder did. You will save us a great deal of time and effort if you tell us what you know."

O'Donnell's mouth twitched wryly but he did not immediately answer.

The man in the open-necked shirt said, "I assure you, we are all cleared for anything you might have been doing for DoD. If you insist, we can prove it. You might as well tell us now. It might save us a lot of wasted effort later."

"All right," said O'Donnell. "There was one project, but it was nothing to do with the Department of Defense. Several months ago we did a short manufacturing run for a private individual using a process we'd never used before. The whole thing was hideously expensive. If I remember rightly, we spent somewhere in the region of sixty million dollars for the one run, and the yield on the chips was lower than anything I've ever seen."

The woman interjected, "When you use the term 'yield,' I assume you mean the percentage of chips you made that were actually usable?"

"That's right. Computer chips are fabricated on large rectangles of silicon, anywhere from a hundred to a thousand or more chips on each slab. Typically, anywhere from fifty to ninety nine percent of the chips are actually usable. In the case of this particular design, we manufactured them in lots of a hundred, and less than one percent successfully passed the post-manufacture tests."

"So that's why you stopped making them?"

"No. The order was for two dozen chips. Once we'd made those, we reconfigured that part of the fabrication plant. Manufacturing plants are too expensive to leave idle. But we kept the details of how to make the chips on our system. That's what was deleted. It was the only information on our entire system that was destroyed."

"But surely you had back-ups?"

"No. The customer in this case specifically told us to make no back-ups. He was concerned it would be a possible security breach to have the information stored in more than one place."

The man at the head of the table said, "Who exactly was the customer?"

O'Donnell gave the briefest of pauses, then said, "I'm sorry. I don't think I can tell you that. I've been as cooperative as I can, but I'm afraid that's privileged information."

There was a brief silence, then the man in the open-neck shirt said, "That's all right, Mr. O'Donnell. I'm sure Mr. Ishihara will tell us everything we need to know."

O'Donnell's surprised start gave away as much as Dan Hudson's look had done a few minutes earlier. He recovered quickly, but not quickly enough. He said stiffly, "That's between you and Mr. Ishihara, but when you see him please emphasize that you didn't get his name from me."

"We'll tell him exactly what we need to tell him to find out what we need to know," the man replied evenly.

The man at the head of the table interjected, "And now, before tempers begin to fray, I think it's best if we draw this meeting to a close. Mr. O'Donnell, Mr. Hudson, I can't tell you how much we all appreciate this. I know it must be difficult for you to come all this way without detailed explanations, but please believe me when I say that what you've told us this morning will be very helpful to this country, very helpful indeed. I'm afraid I can't say more than that, but your frankness has been noted at the very highest level." He paused, and then repeated himself. "The very highest level."

He pressed a button on the recessed panel in the table, and a door slid open. Two men in polyester suits entered. "Gentlemen, please escort our visitors out. Thank you once again. And please, if you have anything to add, don't hesitate to contact us at the number I gave you."

No one spoke until the men from IntSiliFab had left the room. Then there were audible sighs as they relaxed.

Fisher said, "Thank you for your patience, everyone. Does anyone have any questions so far, before we decide where we go from here?"

"I do," said the man in shirt sleeves.

"Go ahead, Stone."

"Sir, I think you've made a mistake. I don't belong in this room. I didn't understand half of what Mr. Hudson was telling us. No —

correct that: I didn't understand any of it. I don't know anything about computers. Hell, I can't even balance my checkbook with a calculator."

Fisher held up a hand for silence. "Mr. Stone, I appreciate your honesty, but you misunderstand your position. You're here not for your computer expertise but because you're the best operative we've got, a fact amply demonstrated less than five minutes ago when you wheedled information from Mr. O'Donnell that he clearly didn't want to give us. Indeed, it's quite possible that the name of Integrated Silicon Fabrication's customer is the single most important thing we've learned this morning. Now, does any one else have any questions?"

Fran raised her pencil. "I'm afraid I understand even less than Mr. Stone and I have a ton of questions, but for now I'll ask just one. General, you told the men from IntSiliFab that their cooperation was appreciated at the very highest level. What exactly did you mean by that?"

"Exactly what I said, Ms. Tabor."

"You mean... the president?"

"Ms. Tabor, I have a meeting scheduled with the president at four this afternoon. The purpose of that meeting is to brief the president about what has happened here."

Frances shook her head disbelievingly. "Then you really mean it. You really think that Oscar Holywell has built a thinking machine that attacked IntSiliFab?"

"After what we've just heard, I'm almost certain of it."

"Why?"

"Two reasons. Firstly, of all the millions of files that the attacker could have deleted, he chose to destroy only those pertaining to a single project. And secondly, the fact that the customer for that project was Yoshi Ishihara."

Fran's brow furrowed. "That name rings a bell somewhere."

The general pressed two buttons on the panel in front of him; the lights dimmed, and a white screen unfurled from the ceiling. A slightly out-of-focus image of a man's face filled the screen. He had a rounded, oriental face that stared slightly to the left of the camera through wire-rimmed spectacles.

"Yoshi Ishihara," he said. "And the reason you recognize his name is because fifteen years ago he invented a process for building computer disk drives."

"That's right!" exclaimed Fran. "I was just a kid then, but I remember that for a while everyone thought his drives would take over the world. But then something happened; something went wrong with the drives, didn't it?"

Fisher nodded. "Yes. For a time his process looked very promising, but after a while people began to notice that Ishihara drives were unreliable. But by then Ishihara had sold his company. Our best estimate is that he walked away with more than a hundred million dollars to his name. At that point, he seems to have disappeared.

"He resurfaced a couple of years ago when he bought a small island in the Caribbean called Roncador Cay, about twenty five miles off the coast of Montega, and built a small research facility there.

"Two other things happened soon after Ishihara finished building on Roncador Cay. Oscar Holywell, who at the time was a part-time adjunct professor at the University of Colorado in Boulder, disappeared without warning. Two months later, a man named Al Barlow resigned his position at Integrated Silicon Fabrication and also disappeared."

The face on the screen changed. Ishihara's face was replaced by a smiling Caucasian in his mid forties. The man had a round, pleasant-looking face, and his eyes smiled as if he had just shared a joke with the person taking the photograph.

"Until he resigned, Al Barlow was head of research at Integrated Silicon Fabrication. By all accounts he was a happy man, with no real interests outside his work. Divorced, reasonably amicably, five years ago. His ex says she got tired of seeing so little of him; he was always at the lab, and even when he showed up at home, his mind was still on his work. There were no children.

"His colleagues at Integrated Silicon Fabrication were frankly astonished when he resigned. He never gave a reason, other than to say it was time to move on. Everyone assumed he'd been offered a lucrative position at another company, but the day after he left his job he put his house on the market and as soon as it was sold he too disappeared from sight."

Fran said, "So a wealthy computer businessman built a research lab, and a brilliant artificial intelligence theorist and one of the world's top chip researchers both disappeared, all within a few months. I assume Holywell and Barlow ended up on this island you mentioned, Roncador Cay?"

"We believe so," interjected Stone. "Although so far we have no direct proof."

One of the other men, introduced to Fran simply as Gallucci, said, "Miss Tabor, could you please tell us more about Holywell's work? I'm having a hard time understanding exactly what this term 'artificial intelligence' really means."

"As I've said before, in layman's terms it means researching the possibility of building computers that think."

"You mean like the ones that play chess? Didn't I read somewhere that computers can now beat the world chess champion?"

Fran shook her head emphatically. "That's true, but it's not artificial intelligence. Those machines are simply calculators on steroids. You could say the same about every computer that's ever been built; they're all more-or-less glorified calculators. No, Oscar Holywell was interested in the idea of a machine that can really think."

"A machine with a brain, you mean?"

"Not just a brain. A machine with a *mind*."

Gallucci shook his head. "Sorry. I don't get it. What's the difference?"

Fran paused for a moment to gather her thoughts, then said, "Lots of things have brains: cats, dogs, grasshoppers, dinosaurs, goldfish. They all have brains in the sense that a central control system guides their activities. In that sense, chess-playing computers have brains as well, although they're adapted to doing only one thing, playing chess, and their 'bodies' are simply video screens on which they display their moves. They're what we call Category 1 machines."

"Category 1?"

"Yes. Programmable machines — computers — can be divided into five categories. Category 1 machines can be programmed to perform any of a number of different tasks. The kind of computer we're all familiar with is a good example of a Category 1 machine."

"So what are the other categories?"

"Briefly, a Category 2 machine can adapt its programming to reflect new information obtained within a limited universe. A Category 3 machine can seek out knowledge for itself and make connections between apparently unconnected facts. A Category 4 machine is self-aware. And a Category 5 machine can pass a full-blown Turing test. In layman's terms, a Category 5 machine can think."

Gallucci nodded. "Thank you, Miss Tabor. That's very helpful. I think I understand at least the gist of it now."

Fran continued, "To come back to your original question, brains are really quite common: a brain is just a kind of control mechanism. A mind is something else entirely. A mind, you see, has to be conscious. It has to understand. It has to be able to reason. It has to think. A computer with a mind would be like...."

She thought for a long time, then shook her head. "I can't think of anything it would be like. The closest thing I can think of is to imagine a person with an IQ of a thousand, the ability to think hundreds of times faster than anyone else who ever lived, and with instant access to the Internet and every computer connected to it."

Gallucci let out a low whistle. "Anyone like that would be the most powerful person in the world."

"Exactly," snapped Fisher. "And that's why we've got to find out what's happening on Roncador Cay. Miss Tabor, how do you fancy a trip to the Caribbean? I'm sure Montega is beautiful at this time of year."

Fran's head was spinning. Things were happening too quickly. "What? Let me be sure I understand this. You want me to go some place I've never heard of and try to find out if someone has built a computer that can think?"

"Stone will be with you," he said, as if she was supposed to find comfort in the idea.

Automatically, she glanced at Stone. His mouth was twisted into a wry smile which she found both unnerving and utterly unreadable. She didn't find the thought of Stone accompanying her anywhere, even to the grocery store, remotely comforting.

"I don't know anything about Montega," she heard herself saying.

Stone said, "It's a British territory. Capital St. Andrews. Population 5,000 or thereabouts. Size about fifty square miles, most of it useless because the island is essentially a dormant volcano. No industry worth speaking of, not even a drug industry because it's too far to the east of the main chain of islands. It's one of the poorest countries in the hemisphere and it'd be even poorer if Britain didn't give it a hefty infusion of cash every year."

"Exactly," said Fisher. He extracted two envelopes from a pocket and passed them down the table to Fran and Stone. "I hope you both have a pleasant trip. Here are two tickets for a flight out of Reagan Airport to Montega via Port St. John leaving at eight thirty tomorrow morning. You're booked into a hotel on Montega tomorrow night. After that you're on your own. Your brief is to find out what you can about what's happening on Roncador Cay. This is simply an investigative trip. Don't go looking for trouble." He threw a meaningful glance at Stone.

"What's that supposed to mean?" Fran asked suspiciously. "And why do we both have to go?"

Stone pocketed his envelope without even glancing at it.

Fisher said, "As Mr. Stone has told us all, he knows nothing about computers. That's why we need you to accompany him, Ms. Tabor."

"That explains why you want me to go," said Fran. "But why's he going as well?"

"Because we believe that Oscar Holywell may have been killed, and although Mr. Stone may not know anything about computers, he knows an awful lot about killing."

9

"How sure are we that we know what we're doing?" Gallucci asked.

"What do you mean?" Lee said. He finished pouring a fresh mug of coffee and returned to his seat, nibbling a cookie.

"We've assigned our very best operative to the Roncador operation. And we've co-opted a civilian, something we've never done before as long as I've been part of the organization. Fisher, you've been a member longer than the rest of us. Have we ever used a civilian before?"

Fisher shook his head. "No. But we've never faced a situation like this before."

"So explain it to me. The Kennedy assassination; Iran; Iraq twice; the G7 affair; Yeltsin: all those were handled without going outside. Why is this so different?"

"It's different because this is about technology," supplied Hayes. "All those events were essentially human in nature. This is different because none of us really understands the nature of the threat."

"If there really is a threat," said Epstein quietly.

"Do you doubt it?" asked Fisher with interest.

"I can't say that I've seen much evidence so far. A computer that can break into systems over the Internet? What's so special about that? We've all heard the stories about fourteen-year-old *kids breaking into the Pentagon. The Tabor woman herself does that kind of thing for a living. I don't understand why we're acting as if it's the end of the world."*

Fisher said, *"Miss Tabor said something very similar."*

"Then that just underscores what I'm saying."

Several people tried to speak at once, and it was some time before Fisher could restore quiet.

"I think we're all underestimating what a thinking computer would really mean," he said.

"In what way?" Epstein challenged.

"Given the current state of the economy, what's the best way to increase consumer confidence?"

"What does that have to do with anything? I don't understand your point."

"Taking everything into account, what should the president do to maximize his chances of re-election? What's the most efficient way to remove Sultan Ben-Kalil from power in Karranh? The competition has just introduced a new product that makes ours obsolete; how should we respond? What stocks should I buy? Where's the most likely place to drill for oil? How do we create a fat substitute that has no side effects? How do we cure cancer? What's the cheapest way to manufacture a binary chemical weapon without arousing suspicion?"

"How do I assassinate the president without getting caught?" added Hayes.

"What's the quickest way to make $50 million without arousing suspicion?" asked Lee.

"How can I make a drug that's both cheaper and more addictive than heroin?" said Gallucci.

"And perhaps most important of all," said Fisher. *"How do I stop someone else from making another machine that can think?"*

"All right. I get the picture," said Epstein. *"But there's a big difference between breaking into a chip manufacturer's network and answering questions like those."*

"Not for a machine with an almost infinite database and the capacity to synthesize new knowledge by combining new information with what it already knows."

"Perhaps we should simply destroy it," said Gallucci.

70

Fisher shook his head. "Only as a last resort. Only if there's no way to acquire the machine ourselves."

The Air West Indies 737 left Reagan twenty minutes late, delayed by an early morning downpour that slowed traffic to a crawl. In seat 14A sat an attractive black woman in her late twenties with a worried look on her face. Next to her was a thin-faced Caucasian male with blond hair and a nose that had once been broken and had healed with a kink. His relaxed manner contrasted with the woman's stiffness.

"Just so you know," he said, "I don't like this any more than you do."

The plane penetrated the layer of gorged cloud that hung over the city. She ignored him, staring out the window at the wing. It vibrated with the turbulence, its far end lost in the murky cloud.

"I'm not used to having baggage to look after," he continued.

Her head snapped around. "Baggage? Is that what I am? Who the hell do you think you are, Mr. Stone?"

He smiled at her easily. "For one thing, I'm your husband. So speak to me nicely from now on... darling."

"What the hell are you talking about? You're crazy as well as obnoxious. If you think...."

He pulled a passport from his shirt pocket and tossed it into her lap. "Take a look at that, Mrs. Tabor."

She picked it up and opened it to the back page. "What the hell? John Tabor? Where did you get this? Did General Fisher give it you?"

He laughed and leaned toward her, shaking his head. Speaking quietly in her ear, he said, "Since we're related, I'll tell you a secret. He is a general — of a sort — but his real name isn't Fisher. And no, he didn't give me the passport. Lesson number one, Fran: details matter, and the passport is a detail."

"I don't know what you're talking about. Have the IRS audit me every year for the next forty years. I don't care. This whole thing is insane."

"Calm down and let me explain. I didn't want you along, partly because I don't like having to think of someone else before I act,

71

and partly because I don't like the idea of having to waste my resources protecting you. But I was overruled, and now we both have to make the best of it.

"My job is simply to try to smooth your way and make it easy for you to find out whatever you can about what's going on on Roncador Cay without exposing yourself to danger. I'm sure you're a wonderful asset to the National Security Agency. No doubt you're a brilliant computer analyst. But you're not sitting behind a computer now. Trust me. If you don't, you might end up like that other computer genius, Oscar Holywell."

A smiling stewardess halted in the aisle, handed them bags of pretzels and offered them drinks. Fran refused with a perfunctory shake of her head; Stone ordered an orange juice, no ice.

The stewardess moved on to the next row, and Fran said scornfully, "Are you trying to threaten me? I don't believe for a moment that Dr. Holywell has been killed. Who'd want to do something like that?"

"That's why were going to Montega: to find out."

"And for that we have to be married? If you think you can...."

Stone interrupted her. "We're married because if we weren't we'd stand out like a pair of sore thumbs in a place like Montega. Especially if we blunder about asking too many questions. So we'll do this my way, attracting as little attention as possible. We're a married couple taking a few days' vacation. You're a computer expert with the government, I'm an unsuccessful writer combining vacation with research for my next book."

"Forgive my stupidity, but why do we need a charade like that? What's wrong with just being who we are?"

The plane emerged from the layer of cloud, filling the cabin with a sudden brilliance.

Stone replied, "Because you can bet your last silicon chip there's more going on than we've been told. That meeting yesterday was designed to feed us a plausible story which may or may not bear some resemblance to the truth. One thing's certain, though: even if it was the truth, it wasn't the whole truth. Fisher doesn't send me on missions unless there's a high probability of failure. And he certainly wouldn't drag in a civilian unless the circumstances called for desperate measures. Fisher's keeping something from me."

"So you mean there really isn't a thinking computer?" Despite her annoyance, Fran's disappointment was obvious in her voice.

"Oh, I'm sure that part's true enough, otherwise you wouldn't be here. It's what we haven't been told that bothers me."

"What do you mean?"

"There's no reason for us to be involved with something as simple as a computer that's smart enough to break into IntSiliFab."

Fran said, "A computer that could really think would be an advance that would make everything that's gone before pale by comparison. I think Fisher understands that. Maybe he's overreacting to the break-in. Or maybe he has more evidence that he hasn't told us about. But you haven't told me why you think Oscar Holywell is dead."

Stone toyed with his drink for a while, then took a sip before answering.

"I'll tell you what I know. Our source is a whore named Gloria Tanner who lives on the outskirts of St. Andrews. Her teenage son has been working for Ishihara on Roncador Cay for the past eighteen months. No one on the island is allowed to communicate with the outside world; the only exception is the cook, who goes to Montega once a week for supplies. He's Gloria Tanner's cousin — that is to say, one of her clients — and Mrs. Tanner and her son use him as a courier to carry messages between them.

"Mrs. Tanner's son sent her a message late last week to say that a man who was a friend of his, and a very important man on the project, had been killed in an argument. According to the son, the man who died was called Oscar Holywell."

"Have you actually seen this message?"

"No."

"So we have no way of knowing if it really exists? Or, if it does, it might say something quite different from what we've been told?"

Stone smiled unexpectedly. "You have a devious mind, Fran Tabor. That's good. Maybe we'll both live longer."

"I'm paid to be devious. In any case, what else is this message supposed to say?"

"Mrs. Tanner's son wants to leave Roncador Cay, but he's scared of what might happen to him if he tries. Mrs. Tanner is worried for her son, and she wants someone to find out what's really happening on Roncador Cay and help bring him home."

"That doesn't sound much like the brief Fisher gave us."

"No. I'm afraid Mrs. Tanner will have to be patient. Your Category 5 machine comes first."

"Does she know we're coming?"

"She knows someone is, but not who or when exactly. Once we've scouted the situation on Montega I'll decide whether it's a good idea for us to talk to her."

He finished his drink, pulling a face. "You'd think a West Indian airline would know better than to serve reconstituted orange juice, wouldn't you?"

Fran ignored the question. "Do you really think there's any danger? To us, I mean?"

"If there isn't, this is the first safe mission I've ever been on. And listen, Fran, practice calling me John. Or, better yet, 'darling.' And don't be so stand-offish. We're supposed to be a married couple going on an exotic vacation together. Come a bit closer and look a bit happier about the prospect. Right now you look as though I'm something the dog brought in."

"You're joking, aren't you? Tell me this is all a bad dream. I'll wake up in a few minutes and everything will be back to normal."

He shook his head. "I'm afraid not. Listen, maybe this will all turn out to be a dud. Maybe there'll be nothing for us to do. In which case you can relax and enjoy a well-earned rest for a few days on a beautiful subtropical island. But if it turns out that Oscar Holywell did die on Roncador Cay, and if there is some connection between his death and the break-in at IntSiliFab... well, in that case we want to do everything we can to make sure we're not next in line for the same treatment as your precious Dr. Holywell."

Fran looked at him, searching his face for some sign that he was joking. There was none. She turned and stared out the window, wondering what on earth she had gotten herself into.

10

It was Hayes, who had known Fisher longer than any of the others, who finally voiced what they were all thinking.

"We should have been more honest with the Tabor woman. She might get hurt. And the Brotherhood might move the machine once they realize we're taking an interest. I'm not at all sure we're doing the right thing."

An embarrassed silence fell on the room. One by one, Fisher looked at their faces. Only Hayes met his gaze and refused to look away.

"It's only a reconnaissance mission," Fisher eventually said.

"Not good enough. Suppose everything we suspect turns out to be true. Holywell did build a thinking machine on Roncador Cay. He was killed by the Brotherhood. Chida's there to guard the machine. And now we're just going to let Stone and the Tabor woman show up on Montega?"

"There's no reason for the Brotherhood to be on the lookout."

"I see. So your plan relies on the Brotherhood not bothering to keep a watch on Montega airport? Well, that certainly makes me feel better," Hayes said acidly.

Gallucci interrupted to stop the argument from escalating.

"The point is, while the machine — if it exists — is on Roncador Cay, we could at least mount an attack and stand a good chance of capturing it. If the Brotherhood decides to move it we might lose that option. I say we give Stone twenty four hours. After that, even if he hasn't been able to confirm the machine's existence one way or the other, we should go in and take it if it's there. The only alternative, it seems to me, is to flatten the place."

"The Brits wouldn't stand for either of those options," argued Fisher. "Don't forget that Roncador belongs to them. Anyway, we owe them. If it weren't for them we'd never have found out about Holywell."

"They only passed Gloria Tanner's message on to us because they didn't want to be involved," said Hayes.

"Forget the Brits," said Gallucci emphatically. "They aren't players."

Hayes nodded. "Gallucci's right. This is too important for us to waste time following protocol. The Brits might complain, but they'd do so privately. A fat check should straighten them out quick enough."

Fisher searched the room for support, but could find none.

"All right," he said with a sigh. "But let's give Stone forty eight hours. In the meantime, if it looks like they're trying to move the machine from Roncador Cay, we'll move in. Is that acceptable?"

"Yoshi, I think there's something wrong with Tim," Al Barlow said quietly.

Barlow was sitting across the desk from Yoshi Ishihara, speaking in a low voice because he did not want to be overheard by the man in the next room.

"Is it something serious?" Yoshi asked.

"How the hell should I know? Ask Oscar," Barlow said bitterly. Then, seeing the pained look on Yoshi's face, he added, "I'm sorry. I know, I know; it was an accident, that's the party line, isn't it?"

Yoshi put his finger to his mouth to indicate silence, then pointed at the open doorway through which they could see Chida seated at a desk flipping the pages of a pornographic magazine. The suit in which he had arrived had been replaced by a loose-fitting silk shirt and a pair of American sweat pants. On his feet, propped up on the desk, was a pair of rubber-soled boating shoes. Outside the shirt was a leather shoulder holster, and protruding from the holster Barlow could see the squared butt of an automatic pistol. As Chida turned a page, Barlow noticed a small tattoo on the inside of his forearm.

The silence caused Chida to look up; he stared at Barlow and Yoshi with open hostility.

"We're going for a walk," Yoshi said. "Want to come?"

Chida pursed his lips and shook his head. He watched them with narrowed eyes as they left the bungalow, then shrugged to himself and returned his attention to the magazine.

As they crossed the scrub grass toward the lab, Barlow confessed, "I probably shouldn't say this, but that man scares the shit out of me."

"Me too," said Yoshi forlornly.

"Isn't there some way you can get rid of him? Surely we aren't really in any danger? Who'd want to bother us?"

"Of course no one's interested in us," Yoshi snapped. "But he's not here to protect us."

Barlow stopped. "What the hell is he here for, then?"

Yoshi tugged at Barlow's sleeve. "Keep walking," he said. "We don't want him to become suspicious."

The door of Tim's bungalow was ajar, propped open by a lump of coral. Inside, they could see William's head bent over his table as he worked on a drawing. They headed towards the bungalow.

"He's here to protect Tim. Don't forget they loaned me more than fifty million dollars without collateral. I suppose we can hardly blame them for sending someone to look after their investment. I just wish the first bank I went to had been willing to loan me the money. Then I wouldn't have had to go to these barbarians."

Before Barlow could ask him what he meant, they had reached William. The young man greeted them unenthusiastically with a subdued smile. "Morning, Mr. Ishihara, Dr. Barlow."

"Good morning, William," Barlow replied. They began to descend the steps to the basement. Barlow continued, "So tell me, was Oscar's death really an accident?"

Yoshi shrugged. "It wasn't premeditated, if that's what you're asking. I think Chida was simply trying to assert himself the only way he knows how. What infuriates me is that he doesn't even try to understand what we're doing here. He told me afterwards that he thought Oscar was just a computer programmer. I'm not sure even now that he understands just how important Oscar was."

"A computer programmer?" said Barlow incredulously. "That's like calling...." He struggled to think of a suitable analogy.

"Like calling television a kind of improved radio?" suggested Yoshi as they halted outside the door to the lab. He punched in the sequence on the pad and the door opened.

"Exactly," said Barlow.

"Barlow-san, I know more than anyone how irreplaceable Oscar Holywell is. Without Oscar this project would never have even begun."

"And now he's gone, we may have to end it," said Barlow unhappily. "Look at Tim."

They both looked at the cube on a table on the far side of the lab. Normally, Tim would have greeted them as they entered the lab; instead he remained silent. The lights on his side flashed in a simple pattern, endlessly repeated. His camera pointed without moving at a blank wall.

Barlow said, "He's been like that all morning. You realize that without Oscar to debug him we're sunk?"

"We can survive without Oscar. We have to. Tim can manage without Oscar. We've come too far. Tim is self-sustaining now. If there's something wrong with him, he can tell us himself what we have to do to fix him."

"Perhaps," Barlow said dubiously.

They crossed the lab and stood in front of the cube. Tim's lights continued to flash rhythmically. The camera remained pointing at a spot on the wall on their right.

"Good morning, Tim," Barlow said.

There was no response.

Barlow pointed at a bank of monitors, on which colored lines jerked up and down apparently at random.

"There's plenty of activity going on inside," he said, "but nothing I do seems to provoke a response."

"Perhaps there's something wrong with the audio input circuits. Have you checked the cables?"

"Yes. Watch this."

Barlow stepped up to a microphone and spoke slowly into it. "Tim, this is Al Barlow. Can you hear me?"

The graphs on the monitor wiggled in response to Barlow's words, but Tim remained silent.

"He can hear me all right," Barlow said. "It's just that he's not responding."

"What about the output? Maybe there's a problem with the output circuits. Maybe he is responding and we just can't hear anything."

"No." Barlow moved to a keyboard and typed a command. A monitor flashed once and then displayed a horizontal line. "That's his audio output driver. As you can see, he hasn't tried to speak for hours."

"When was the last time we know for certain that he spoke?"

"I was in here for a while yesterday afternoon. He seemed fine then. I didn't stay long, just dropped in to say hello and run some timing tests. Everything seemed OK."

The two men stared at the flat line on the screen.

"What do you think it means?" Yoshi asked.

"It means we have a problem."

"What problem?" asked a voice from the doorway.

They spun around, startled by the unexpected intrusion.

Chida stood in the doorway. Barlow and Ishihara exchanged glances. How long had he been there?

Chida stepped into the room, and the door slid closed behind him.

"Something's wrong with the machine?" he asked, joining them in front of the cube.

"It's probably nothing very important," Barlow said quickly, "but Tim doesn't seem to be responding this morning. It's the kind of problem that Oscar would have known how to deal with instantly," he added.

Chida ignored the jibe. "Has it happened before?"

Barlow shrugged. "Who knows? Oscar logged all the problems he thought were important, but maybe this was a common occurrence that he didn't think worth mentioning."

"Or perhaps this is something new," interjected Yoshi. "We can't tell."

Chida ignored Yoshi and turned the full force of his glare on Barlow. "Whatever the problem is, you will fix it."

Barlow shrugged. "I'll do what I can, but I can't promise anything. As I said, I've never seen Tim behave this way before."

"So you're saying it may be serious?"

"Maybe. Maybe not. I don't know. All I do know is that I'm wasting time talking to you when I might be working on the problem." He turned his back on Chida.

A hand gripped his shoulder painfully and spun him around so hard that he almost lost his balance. Chida brought his face within six inches of Barlow's. "Listen to me," he said, so close that Barlow could smell his breath. "My job is to protect that machine and to report any problems back to the directors. If there's something wrong and you don't know how to fix it, we'll fly someone in who can. I'll give you until tomorrow before I call Japan and tell them of your incompetence."

Barlow was speechless with fury as Chida turned on his heels and stalked from the lab.

"That does it!" Barlow exploded. "I don't care how much you need me. I quit. I've had enough. Get someone else to pander to that brainless killer; I'm not going to."

Yoshi placed a hand on his arm. "Please," he said, startling Barlow with the unexpected pleading in his voice. "Please, Barlow-san; you don't understand."

"You're damn right I don't understand." Barlow tried to maintain his anger, but the helpless look in Yoshi's eyes made it difficult. "What the hell gives him the right to come in here and call the shots? He doesn't realize what we've built here; and he sure as hell doesn't realize the mess he's put us in.

"If I try to leave, what happens? Another shooting? Is that the way it works? When we came here, we all swore we'd never breathe a word to anyone on the outside without clearing it with you first. Isn't my word good enough for you, Yoshi? You'll have me killed if I try to leave, is that it? Is that really what happened to Oscar? Did he want to leave?"

"No. Please, please, Barlow-san." Yoshi stood with his hand on Barlow's arm, looking at the floor, shaking his head. He began to tremble, and it was a moment before Barlow realized that Yoshi was struggling to keep from crying.

Regretting his outburst now, Barlow said quietly, "Please tell me about it, Yoshi. Get it off your chest. Maybe there's something I can do to help."

Yoshi looked up and smiled wanly. He wiped his eyes with the back of his hand. "Thank you. But I'm afraid no one can help me now."

"I'm sure that's not true. You can tell me what the problem is. It can't do any harm, and it might do some good."

"Perhaps you're right. The harm is already done. I should never have started this project."

Yoshi looked bleakly around the lab. The monitors still showed that Tim was active, collating and sorting data; but all his inputs and outputs remained dead. Tim had cut himself off from the outside world.

"All of us are unnecessary now," he said. "They're only biding their time until they're sure they can control Tim without us."

"And who exactly are 'they,' Yoshi?"

"They are the people who once made Japan great, Barlow-san. And with Tim's help, they will do so again."

11

"*The second demonstration was a big mistake. If you'd just been satisfied with Integrated Silicon Fabrication I could have held them off. Breaking into the Pentagon made that impossible.*"

The two men were sitting in one corner of the PlanetAir executive lounge in Juneau. Apart from a couple of businessmen slowly getting drunk at the bar, they were the only people in the room. The man who had spoken was in his sixties, with close-cropped gray hair and an unsmiling face. With him was an expensively dressed Japanese ten years his senior.

The Japanese said, "It couldn't be helped. Integrated Silicon Fabrication might have been an aberration. We needed a stronger test of the machine's abilities. And we needed to know that it works even without Holywell."

"So what happens now? We've sent our best man to Montega."

"Stone?"

Fisher nodded, and the Japanese shrugged. "In that case I feel sorry for our man on Montega."

"Will you warn him?"

"No. But I'll tell Chida. Then Stone will be his problem. Is Stone alone?"

Fisher smiled. "You always know the questions to ask, don't you? No, a woman called Fran Tabor is with him. She's not important — a hacker we co-opted from NSA, that's all. She's not an operative. But what about the machine? Will you move it?"

"Only if it becomes necessary. You'll warn me if you plan to move in?"

"If I can."

"I can ask no more."

There was a long pause before Fisher asked, "So the machine really works?"

"The machine really works. They call it Tim. And the man who controls Tim can control the world."

"Then it's a good job Tim's in safe hands, isn't it?"

The two men smiled at one another. The Japanese nodded. "It is. A very good job indeed."

———————

They changed planes in Port St. John, exchanging the 737 for a two-engined, propeller-driven island-hopper. There were seats for a dozen passengers, but the only other people in the cabin were a young couple who looked like they were on their honeymoon.

There was no divider between the passenger compartment and the cockpit of the small plane, and Fran watched nervously as the pilot — a large black man on the verge of middle age with a round face and short, thinning hair — brought the plane to a halt behind a 757. He spoke rapidly into the boom microphone attached to his headset, but she was too far away to hear any of his conversation with the tower.

She glanced nervously out the window.

"There's nothing to worry about," said Stone, catching sight of her worried expression. "I'd far rather be in one of these than one of those." He indicated the jet that towered above them not far ahead.

The jet's engines let out a throaty roar and the 757 moved slowly into position for takeoff. It halted for a fraction of a second at the end of the runway, then its engines screamed and the plane accelerated away down the runway. They watched it for nearly half a minute before it took off and became a rapidly receding speck in the distance.

"If one of those things gets in trouble, you're a goner," said Stone cheerily. "In a hopper like this there's a good chance you'll just glide down and land smoothly."

"And if we go down in the sea?"

"There are four of us aboard, plus the pilot. I estimate we can evacuate this plane in considerably less than a minute. How long do you think it would take to get everyone out of a fully loaded 757?"

Her head told her he was right. It was her stomach that wasn't convinced. She felt a surge of butterflies as the pilot revved the engines. The plane paused at the end of the runway. They were next in line for take-off.

"I guess you're right," she said, "but I can't help wondering when this plane was last serviced. Why haven't we taken off yet? Do you think there's something wrong?" The engines, after revving noisily, were idling again.

"We're waiting for the turbulence to die down. After a jet takes off, it takes several minutes for the air to return to normal. The pilot will wait until he thinks it's safe and then we'll go. Don't worry if takeoff is a bit rough; it usually is."

"You've done this sort of thing before before?"

"More times than I care to remember."

The engines revved again. With a jerk the pilot released the brake and the plane jumped forward, gathering speed. The ground raced by only a few feet below them.

Much sooner than Fran had expected, the plane lifted off. Immediately, they banked sharply to the right, cornering so tightly that the ground seemed to stand vertically in the window. The plane shook violently a couple of times in the jet's wake, then the horizon shifted back to its normal position and the ride smoothed out as the plane climbed.

The island fell away behind them. Below, the color of the sea changed from aquamarine to dark blue. The plane leveled off, heading east.

"All right?" Stone asked.

"Fine," she said with relief. Stone had been right: there was nothing to worry about.

Unexpectedly, he leaned toward her and kissed her lightly on the cheek.

For a moment she was too stunned to react. Then she drew back with a slight gasp and indignantly opened her mouth to speak.

But Stone spoke first. "This isn't going to work, is it? Listen, if you don't start acting like we at least like one another, we might as well call this whole thing off."

"You're crazy, you know that? I know what you're after, and if you think you can wheedle your way into my bed by pretending to be my.... What the hell's the matter with you?"

Stone was chuckling. "You are," he said. "Here's me worried about keeping the two of us alive, and you're bothered about the sleeping arrangements. If it makes you any happier, I'll sleep on the floor. It wouldn't be the first time." Trying to read the ambiguous expression on her face, he quickly added, "Not that I don't find you attractive, of course. It's just that while I'm on a job, I try to keep my mind focussed on important matters. I find I live longer that way."

"Oh, don't be so damned melodramatic. You're worse than Fisher with his.... Now what are you doing?"

"Counting; don't interrupt." After a few moments, he said, "Nineteen, I make it."

"Nineteen what?"

"Missions. That's how many I've been on. Care to guess how many turned out to be life-threatening?"

She turned away and stared petulantly out the window, her arms folded crossly in front of her.

Leaning forward, he said quietly in her ear, "Nineteen, Fran. I've been shot at, knifed, blown up, thrown out of aircraft and nearly drowned. Listen to what I'm saying. I don't care whether you believe me or not. But please, trust me. Even if you don't believe me, trust me."

She pouted silently at the window.

Stone sighed. "What can I say to convince you? Maybe you're right, maybe we aren't in any danger at all. But it doesn't cost anything to do things my way, does it?"

"And tonight? Will you really sleep on the floor?"

"Well, I'd prefer the couch or a second bed; but Eagle Scout's honor, you have my word I won't try to take advantage of you."

"And I'm supposed to believe you?"

"Yes, as a matter of fact, you are."

They looked at each other. Fran searched his face, trying to read what was going on behind it. She saw only a hard, chiselled face with a slightly crooked nose, a square jaw, a thin line of a mouth and a pair of impenetrable brown eyes with green flecks. There was no way to tell whether he was an honest man or an inveterate liar.

She surrendered. "Oh, all right," she said, looking away. "I don't suppose I have a choice, really. I suppose I have to trust you."

"Thank you," he said quietly.

For a long while neither of them spoke. Fran stared down at the sea, glistening with a myriad tiny reflections of the brilliant sun; Stone settled back in his seat with his eyes closed, either asleep or deep in thought.

Fran watched as an island came into view in the distance and gradually drew closer. From the air it looked like a single symmetrical green hill in the midst of a neverending blue plain.

"Montega," said Stone, startling her.

"I thought you were asleep," she said.

"Just thinking, that's all. You won't see many signs of people."

He was right. They crossed the island's coast, and Fran could see only a thick layer of vegetation climbing the slopes. There was no sign of human habitation.

The crater of the volcano passed beneath them, a dark gray, barren, circular pit.

"Is it extinct?" Fran asked.

"Dormant. The last eruption was in 1921. The one before that was in 1865. Which means we're probably overdue for another one."

"You seem to know an awful lot about Montega. Have you been here before?"

"St. Andrews," he said, pointing toward the far coast without answering, and for the first time Fran saw evidence that people lived on the island. A town of dirty brown buildings, difficult to make out against the surrounding greenery, occupied a wide bay.

Jutting out into the sea at one end of the bay was a thin gray line, as straight as a ruler.

"The runway," said Stone. "We'll be on the ground in a couple of minutes."

The plane dipped down, and the thick greenery rushed up at them. They flew low over the coast, and as they headed out to sea before turning to land, Fran exclaimed, "The beaches are black!"

"Sand from volcanic rock," said Stone laconically. "Which is another reason Montega is so poor. Who'd want to vacation on a Caribbean island with black sand?"

The plane turned 180 degrees, so low now that Fran could see the crests of individual waves. The wings wiggled a couple of times as the pilot aligned the plane for landing; then the end of the runway flashed beneath them. Less than a minute later they came to a halt outside a long, single-storey, heavily-windowed building with *Welcome to Montega* painted along its length in yellow and green.

The pilot got out of his seat, opened the door and lowered the steps. "Hope you have a nice time in Montega."

The passengers descended the steps. The sun reflected violently off the concrete, and Fran wiped a sheen of perspiration from her brow.

The other couple stared at their surroundings with eyes full of wonder. Beyond the low terminal a line of palms reached up to the sky. Away to their right, the dark green slopes of the dormant volcano dominated the view. To the left, the sea glistened and rolled with a low swell. The woman kissed the man, and for a long moment they looked into each others' eyes, their surroundings forgotten.

A low, rust-spotted, flatbed vehicle came around a corner of the terminal building and halted beside the plane. An enormous man with a toothy grin and wearing a ragged tee shirt got out of the driver's cab and opened the plane's baggage compartment. None too carefully, he heaved four suitcases on to the bed of his vehicle. "Welcome to Montega," he said cheerfully; then he closed the compartment, clambered into the truck and drove away toward the terminal.

The young couple began to follow, holding hands and talking. The man's laugh carried to Fran on the breeze.

The gentle wind carried the scent of the ocean, and with it a more subtle fragrance that Fran could not immediately identify. She sniffed the air several times before breaking into a smile. "Hibiscus," she said with delight.

Stone linked his arm with Fran's but she stopped him, and when he turned to protest she unexpectedly leaned forward and brushed her lips against his cheek.

She grinned at his obvious astonishment. "Lesson number one: the details matter, isn't that what you said?" she laughed. "Don't look so surprised. I'm a dutiful wife thanking my husband for bringing me on a wonderful vacation."

He squeezed her arm and smiled.

It was, Fran realized, the first time she had seen him smile. It was a definite improvement. "I always knew it was a good idea to bring a civilian along," he mumbled to himself.

The terminal felt chilly after the blistering heat outside. Stone and Fran waited while the couple ahead of them went through immigration.

Immigration was a smallish room with a single window that looked inland. On the walls were half a dozen posters of Montega and a pair of large notices, yellow with age, warning visitors that it was illegal to bring firearms and banned substances on to the island. Fran felt a pang of nervousness as it occurred to her that it was entirely possible that Stone was breaking the first of these laws.

From a lectern a sign hung crookedly, the word *Immigration* printed on it. Behind the lectern stood a tall man in a crisp blue short-sleeved shirt. He spoke quietly to the couple ahead of them as he inspected their passports. In one corner of the room sat another man wearing an identical shirt, but with a metal star pinned to one pocket. From his belt hung a wooden British-style policeman's truncheon. He let his eyes rest on Fran. He too-obviously enjoyed what he saw and she looked quickly away.

Through the window, a stand of palm trees obstructed most of the view, but she could see a blacktopped road with a white line down the middle leading away from the airport. A green sign on the left side of the road said, *St. Andrews 2.* Parked in the shade of the trees was an old car, Mary Kay pink with rusty sills; instead of a roof, it sported a fringed canvas of faded brown.

"Next, please," said the man at the lectern. They moved forward. "Passports, please."

The official opened Fran's passport. "This your first visit to Montega?"

"Yes."

"You too, sir?"

"Yes."

Fran looked at Stone quickly, trying to decide if he was telling the truth. She couldn't.

"You'll be staying at the Royal St. Andrews?"

Stone nodded in reply to Fran's questioning look.

"Yes," she said. "I hope it's a good hotel."

The immigration official closed her passport with a snap and returned it. Smiling, he said, "Best hotel on the island, ma'am. In fact, it's pretty much the only hotel on the island." He laughed at his joke as he picked up Stone's passport. He riffled through it, barely looking at it, then handed it back.

"Are you staying long?" he asked Stone.

"Just a few days. I'm a writer, working on background for a book. My wife has a few days vacation; we thought we'd combine business with pleasure." He added with a wink, "As long as I get some work done, it's tax deductible."

Fran thought she saw an expression of distaste flicker across the immigration officer's face, but all he said was, "Have a nice stay. Go through that door there and you can pick up your bags and go through customs."

Customs was another small room not noticeably different from the first, except that here there were fewer posters to break the drab green of the bare walls. Their bags were standing on the floor next to yet another man in a short-sleeved blue shirt.

"Anything to declare?" he asked in a bored tone. "Any illegal drugs? Any weapons or explosives?" Without waiting for a reply, he bent down and X'd both bags with a stick of chalk. "Enjoy your stay in Montega." With a smile he walked away and disappeared through a door.

They carried their bags outside. "There's a taxi," said Stone, pointing at the canvas-topped car Fran had seen underneath the palms.

Then he stopped, frowning.

Fran followed his gaze. The policeman from immigration was outside now, talking to a Japanese man in his twenties. The Japanese was looking at them, nodding his head at something the policeman had said.

"Come with me," said Stone sharply.

Before she could ask him what the matter was, he grabbed her bag and strode, tight-lipped, toward the taxi.

12

Fisher paid for his coffee and asked the waitress if there was a phone he could use. She pointed to one at the rear of the coffee-shop, and he made his way toward it, threading past the mostly-empty tables.

Using a prepaid phone card, he dialed a number in the 441 area code.

"Fisher here. How quickly can you proceed?"

"You were supposed to give me a few more days."

"Circumstances have changed. You've got to move now, otherwise it'll be too late. I think the Brotherhood's getting ready to move the computer somewhere more defensible."

"When?"

"I don't know, but you must move quickly. You'll never get another chance like this."

There was a brief pause. "All right, I'll tell her tonight's the night. May Allah shine His face on you. And of course you will be richly rewarded. My brother is very generous to his friends."

"Thank you. It's been my pleasure, Mr. Ben-Kalil."

Fisher put the phone down and wiped it with a handkerchief. Then he strode unsmilingly from the coffee-shop.

Hamilton, Bermuda

"Oh, it's beautiful, Nobu darling. Would you really buy it for me? But it's too expensive...."

Nobushige Saida smiled. "Do you really like it?"

Kim smoothed the dress, studying herself in the mirror. "It's fabulous. It's the most beautiful dress I've ever seen."

"Then it's yours, my dear," Saida declared, popping a mint into his mouth.

Kim flung herself on him and wrapped her arms around his considerable bulk. She kissed him twice on the lips. "Thank you, thank you, thank you. Oh, Nobu, you are a dear."

Nobushige Saida was a short, stout man in his early fifties with slicked hair that glistened oilily in the light of the fluorescent tubes overhead; he wore an expensively tailored suit that almost succeeded in disguising his girth. Two inches shorter than his companion, he grinned to himself around the side of her neck as he hugged her, exposing two rows of even, yellow teeth and causing a third chin to join the two that he habitually wore.

Catching sight of his reflection in the mirror he reduced his grin to a smile, and the third chin disappeared. Extricating himself, he asked, "Now, is there anything else you'd like?"

"Oh I couldn't possibly ask for anything else. You've spent more than three thousand dollars on me already this afternoon."

"It's only money. And you're worth it. More than worth it. The dress is beautiful, but its beauty is multiplied ten-fold when you wear it."

"Oh, I do love you, Nobu. You're so romantic. No one's ever said anything like that to me before." Kim stopped and let her eye rove around the store. "You know, this is all like a dream. I can't believe it's really happening. I keep wondering when I'm going to wake up."

"And when you do, my dear, what will you see then?"

The delight in her eyes died away. She said quietly, "I'll open my eyes and the first thing I'll see is the stain on the wall where Janet threw up one evening after she drank too much vodka."

"Only uncouth pigs drink vodka," Saida declared emphatically. "Cultured people drink saki, and if not saki then only the best Scottish single-malt."

"Yes, well, Janet is an uncouth pig. She got the part I was after," Kim said bitterly.

"Lucky for me."

Her face lit up again. "Lucky for both of us. If I hadn't been so angry with her I'd never have done something so stupid as catch a cheap flight to a Caribbean island I'd never heard of. I mean to say, whoever heard of a Caribbean island with black beaches? I couldn't believe it when I arrived and discovered there wasn't even any place I could swim. I suppose that's why it's so cheap. But by then I'd used all my money and there wasn't any place else to go."

"And then, just when you're at a loss, a gallant Japanese warrior appears and takes you away from your misery, showering you with gifts of untold worth." He gave her a kiss on the cheek, and allowed his hand to rest momentarily on her breast.

Kim looked down at the price tag on the dress. "Well, gifts worth nearly fifteen hundred dollars anyway."

They both laughed. Saida pulled Kim to him and squeezed her as he gave her a minty kiss on the lips. "Thank you," he said. "Thank you from the bottom of my heart."

"What for?"

"For making me feel young again."

She laughed. "Silly thing. Fifty two isn't old. You're in the prime of life. Come on, let's get out of here and go home; then you can show me how young you really are."

They paid for the dress and arranged for it to be delivered; then they walked arm in arm out the main entrance of the fashionable clothing store and on to Front Street.

The sun disappeared below the low hills at the western end of the island and Saida glanced at his Rolex. "It's early yet. Perhaps we should eat first. Are you hungry? Is there anywhere in particular you'd like to go?"

"Other than bed, you mean? Perhaps you are getting old," she laughed.

He put a finger to his lips. "Shhh," he said with a smile. "You want everyone to hear?"

"What does it matter? I don't care, do you?"

With a grin he hugged her and kissed her again, in full view of anyone who happened to be looking. "No," he said. "I don't care at all. Isn't it wonderful?"

They walked down Front Street arm in arm, looking in the store windows. On the other side of the street a cruise ship was berthed in the harbor, its passengers passing in a steady stream, converging on the ship for their evening meal.

A surrey with a fringed roof passed them. The horse wore a wide-brimmed hat with holes where its ears poked through. The horse's steady clip-clop failed to drown out the sound of a middle-aged American man in the carriage pointing out the sights to his thickly made-up wife. The wizened driver, wearing a hat that matched the one worn by the horse, looked bored.

"How about this place?" Saida asked, stopping outside a small restaurant.

Kim's eyes ran over the menu posted outside. "It looks fabulous."

"Then in we go." Smiling, Nobushige Saida opened the door with a bow.

They emerged two and a half hours later. Kim slipped her arm through his as they stepped out on to the sidewalk. There was neither cloud nor moon, and a gentle, salt-laden breeze caressed their faces as they walked arm-in-arm along the street.

For a while neither of them spoke. They passed other couples, exchanging smiles and nods but no words. They stopped to look in the windows of the stores along Front Street, but still neither of them said anything.

A taxi approached, and Kim shivered.

"You're cold," said Saida.

"Only a little."

"Do you want to go back?"

"Yes, maybe we'd better. It's just that I don't want today ever to end. I'll remember today for the rest of my life."

"Then we don't want to spoil it by catching cold. And the day isn't over yet; maybe we can think of more ways to make it memorable."

She sighed a long, satisfied sigh of pure pleasure. "I don't deserve any of this," she said. "A beautiful evening, magnificent surroundings, and a wonderful man to share it all with. It's almost too much."

"You deserve it all, my dear. In another and more gallant age, men would gladly die for a single smile from you. It is I who do not deserve it."

She kissed him on the mouth, and what began as a simple kiss of pleasure became something more as he hungrily returned it. She tasted his minty breath as his mouth parted and his tongue began to explore the contours of her teeth. She drew away, smiling at the disappointed look on his face.

"You're right," she declared. "It would be silly to spoil the day by getting cold. Let's go home."

He nodded happily, then raised his hand to halt the taxi.

Nobushige Saida was woken by the sound of a servant breaking a glass in the kitchen.

For a while he lay motionless on his back, a slight smile playing around the corners of his mouth as he remembered last night. Without opening his eyes he stretched out his arm toward Kim; but he was disappointed to discover that he was alone in bed.

Opening his eyes, he looked at the bedside clock and saw that it was already past eight. She was probably down at the private beach taking her early morning swim. He thought about joining her. He knew that she swam naked because he had watched her, safely hidden behind one of the grapefruit trees, drinking in the sight of her perfect young body playing among the gentle waves. He felt a surge of desire. Yes, he decided, this morning he would swim with his love.

He flung off the single sheet and noticed something on Kim's side of the bed sticking out from underneath the pillow. Puzzled, he picked it up. It was a moment before he recognized the small object; then his stomach churned violently.

He turned the disc in its case around in his hands several times, looking for some indication of where it had come from and what might be on it. But there was nothing.

With a cry he ran to the open window. The sea glistened undisturbed, as smooth as an enormous blue mirror. There was no sign of his lover in the water.

"Kim?" he called. Then, more desperately, "Kim? Where are you?"

There was no answer.

For several moments he stood at the window with the jewel case in his hand, looking first at the disc, then at the undisturbed sea.

The bedside phone rang.

He turned toward it, his eyes now shifting wildly between the disc and the phone. His mind was filling with possibilities, none of them pleasant.

He hung back, willing the phone to stop, but it paid no attention. Walking slowly across the room, he paused with his hand in the air above the instrument. Then he grabbed it violently and put the receiver to his ear.

"Good morning, Mr. Saida."

The voice was male, with an accent he couldn't place. Not American. Nor English. Definitely not Japanese. Middle Eastern, maybe.

The voice continued, "In half an hour an associate and I will visit your house. I suggest you get dressed before we arrive. You might also want to review the disc you are holding in your hand. It runs for about two hours, but I'm sure you will need only a few moments to recognize what's on it."

The line went dead. Saida looked blankly at the telephone for ten seconds, then replaced it bleakly on the hook.

He thought over and over again: *How could I have been so stupid? I should have known it was too good to be true. Now what will happen to me?*

He looked down at his hand, and saw that it was shaking. So, too, was the tattoo on the inside of his right forearm. He stared at the crossed swords, and gradually their lines blurred until he could no longer see them through his tears.

13

Hayes stared at Gallucci for a long while, then shook his head firmly.

"I wouldn't worry," he said.

"You've known Fisher longer than any of the rest of us, so I'll defer to your judgement. For now, anyway. But you have to be honest with me. You really think he's OK?"

"Yes. Kirkpatrick's suicide hit him harder than any of us guessed. He's just taking a while to get over it, that's all."

"But there's still no sign of a vote on Kirkpatrick's successor. It's been six months. We've never waited this long before."

"I think he's waiting until the Roncador situation resolves itself. It could be dangerous to bring in someone new at this point."

"Perhaps. But I wanted you to know we're all worried."

"Why?"

"He seems... I don't know. Distracted. He doesn't seem willing to take our advice any more. He seems to have forgotten that we're supposed to be a team."

"Don't worry. If I think he isn't up to the job we'll call a meeting and thrash it out. In the meantime I'll keep an eye on him. But I really don't think there's anything to worry about. If Fisher starts losing it, we're all in more trouble than we can imagine."

The builders of the Royal St. Andrews had never intended it to be a hotel. Stern-faced and solidly built out of massive blocks of imported granite, it retained the air of a military barracks designed to impress the locals with the might of an empire on which the sun never set. Outside the entrance, a British flag flapped desultorily in the wayward breeze. The only cars in the parking lot were a trio of canvas-topped taxis, their drivers chatting in the shade of a clump of palms. Nearby was a long shed in which were parked half a dozen mopeds.

Stone had been silent all the way from the airport. When Fran had asked him why he seemed upset, he had indicated the driver and put a finger to his lips.

As Fran got out of the taxi, an overweight, middle-aged couple walked out of the impressive front door of the hotel and crossed the concrete parking lot to the shed. She watched as they donned crash helmets, then tried to kickstart two of the machines. The engine on the woman's moped caught at the fifth attempt; she sat down and cautiously revved the engine while her husband, his face reddening, tried to kick life into his machine. At last the engine fired. He sat down heavily and the machine sagged. They set off, following the curve of the driveway and swerving wildly from one side to the other when they realized they were driving on the wrong side. They disappeared behind a green, red and yellow hedge of hibiscus.

"Tourists!" said Stone, half with contempt and half with scornful amusement.

"Which is exactly what we're supposed to be," she reminded him with a smile.

"Right. We're also supposed to be married, so you can carry your own bag." Ignoring her glare, he climbed the steps to the entrance of the hotel.

The cavernous lobby was empty, but a bell stood on the counter and tapping it produced, after half a minute's delay, a young, wiry man in a dishevelled shirt with a blurred coat of arms embroidered on the pocket.

Their room was on the second floor, and looked out across the area in front of the hotel: on the far side of the road was a low, tangled hedge from which blue flowers grew in profusion. Beyond that was a narrow banana field and then a wide black beach.

The room was large, its most obvious feature a pair of single beds that Fran eyed with relieved approval. In addition it held a small round table and a couple of hard-backed dining chairs, and a wardrobe containing a dozen rusty hangers. The paint on the walls was a faded blue-green that looked like cheap undercoat; no paintings broke the monotony of the washed-out walls.

There was a microscopic bathroom in an area that had obviously once simply been a corner of the original room. In a display of considerable ingenuity, the bathroom's designer had managed to place a stall, a washbasin and a shower in an area only slightly greater than that occupied by the wardrobe.

"Not exactly the Hilton," mumbled Fran to herself when she had finished inspecting the bathroom. "Now what are you doing?"

Stone had opened his case and removed something that looked like a cellphone. After a moment she recognized it as the device he had used in the Deputy Director's office on the day that they had first met. He walked slowly around the room, staring at the display and saying nothing until he had completed two circuits of the room. Then he closed the case with a satisfied click. "It's OK; we can talk," he said. "No bugs. Apart from the usual supply of cockroaches, that is."

Fran shook her head as she sat down on the bed. "HolyMo! You were checking the room for bugs? You're kidding, right?"

"Afraid not. It's true that I didn't expect to find any. But then I didn't expect to find a Japanese welcoming party either."

"What exactly was...."

"Yes?" Stone had pulled some clothes from his suitcase and begun to unbutton his shirt.

Fran turned away. "What are you doing now?" she asked wearily.

"Changing into something more comfortable. I'd advise you to do the same. I assume you did pack something more suitable?"

"Of course I did. But if you think I'm going to get changed while you're in the room you've got another think coming."

"Suit yourself." He shrugged, and then a thoughtful frown crossed his face.

"What's the matter now?"

"I'm trying to figure out how they knew we were coming. And I'm not liking the answer I keep coming up with."

She took some clothes from her case and carried them to the bathroom. Closing the door firmly she said through the thin wood, "I thought the only people who knew about us were your friends. One of them must have said something."

"They aren't my friends. And none of those people would have said anything."

"How can you be sure? And who was that Japanese man anyway?"

There was no reply, and when Fran opened the door she saw that Stone, now dressed in a short-sleeved shirt, slacks and sandals, was looking out of the window.

He barked, "Excuse me; I'll be back in a few minutes," and sprinted across the room and out the door.

She crossed to the window just in time to see the Japanese from the airport climbing the hotel steps. A taxi was pulling away from the hotel.

She hurried out the room after Stone. His head was disappearing down the stairs.

Fran followed him downstairs to the lobby, and was puzzled to see that he was standing with his back flat against the wall beside the front door. No one else was in sight. He put his finger to his lips to indicate silence just as the door opened and the Japanese walked inside.

The Japanese stopped as he entered the lobby. He removed a handkerchief from a pocket and wiped the sweat from his brow. His gaze wandered around the lobby, halting when he saw Fran. He frowned and put the handkerchief back in his pocket.

Stone silently moved forward and tapped him briskly from behind on his shoulder.

Fran gasped. She had never seen anyone move so fast. The oriental's right arm shot upwards as he spun around, his right hand balled into a tight fist. By rights it should have smashed into Stone's chin and knocked him senseless. But it wasn't the oriental's speed that astonished her: it was Stone's. His left arm blocked the blow and his right hand chopped viciously into the other's side, causing the oriental to cry out in sudden pain and fold over sideways, gasping.

Stone grabbed the cuff of the oriental's right sleeve and pulled it violently back, tearing buttons and ripping fabric.

For a long moment, no one moved. Stone stared down at the man's exposed forearm; the man, his breath coming in gasping pants as he recovered from Stone's attack, looked first at his arm and then at Stone's face.

Stone dropped the man's arm and the man straightened. He took a step backward and bowed toward Stone. "My name is Kadzu," he said. "I acknowledge your resourcefulness, Mr. Stone. I trust you've learned what you wanted to know."

Stone dipped his head briefly, then looked the other in the eye. "Indeed I did, Kadzu-san."

"Then you will understand if I leave now. Out of respect for your abilities, your death shall be quick."

The man called Kadzu pushed through the door and left the hotel.

Stone looked across the lobby at Fran. His expression was blank and unreadable.

"What the hell was that all about?" asked Fran, crossing the lobby.

"That," he said, "means that things are worse than I thought. We need to talk. But not here. Let's get some food. I'll tell you over dinner." He walked to the desk and pinged the bell.

"But that man. He threatened you," Fran protested.

"He did. But he can't do anything without permission from his Father, so we should be safe for a day or two. By which time, if we're lucky, we'll have discovered what we came here to find out."

The desk clerk appeared and, switching on a smile, Stone asked for directions to somewhere to eat.

14

Lee said, "I don't want to add to our troubles, but I have some disturbing news about the Army of Allah."

Lee was responsible for Africa and the Middle East, and the others showed little interest in his announcement.

"Unless it has some bearing on Roncador, I think perhaps it should wait," suggested Fisher.

"I think there may be a connection. And in any case it's important."

Heads turned to look at Lee, interested now.

"Ahmed Ben-Kalil and his band of fanatics?" said Gallucci. "What could they have to do with Roncador Cay?"

"I'm not certain yet. But I don't like coincidences. Ahmed and a dozen of his followers left Karranh ten days ago, and since then I've been trying to trace them. I just found them. They're holed up in a cottage on Bermuda."

"Maybe if I were the Bermudian chief of police I'd be worried," said Gallucci drily, "But I don't see it's any worry of ours if the Army of Allah has gone on vacation."

Lee looked at Gallucci. "The Brotherhood's head of operations for the Caribbean area is a man named Nobushige Saida," he said evenly. "Nobushige Saida lives on Bermuda."

D. R. EVANS

Bermuda

Still naked, Nobushige Saida slipped the disc into the bedroom's DVD player.

The disc ran for several seconds before anything appeared on the screen. As soon as he saw the picture, Saida let out a yelp of dismay. It was every bit as bad as he had feared.

He looked up toward the ceiling and after a few moments found what he was looking for. In the shadows above an oil painting of Mount Fuji was a small, round hole.

Shouting wordlessly, he stormed out the room and burst into the unused bedroom next door.

He saw the camera instantly, mounted on a bracket, its rear protruding into the room, the lens snugly fitted into the hole in the wall. Clambering on an ornate wooden chair, he ripped the camera from its housing. A small antenna was taped to the side, and it was a moment before he realized that the camera was still transmitting.

With a shout, he flung it to the ground; then he jumped down and lifted the chair, bringing it down with all his strength on the camera. He pounded it half a dozen times until, winded with the unaccustomed exertion, he was forced to catch his breath.

He heard someone approaching in the corridor outside and, still holding the chair with one hand, he pulled open the door. A terrified maid from the kitchen stared at him with wide eyes.

"You!" he shrieked. "Who put this in here?" He pointed at the camera, a barely recognizable wreck on the floor.

The maid shook her head dumbly, then covered her eyes.

"Answer me!"

With a wordless wail, the maid turned and fled in terror. Saida threw the chair across the room in disgust. He spat once at the remains of the camera, then stalked from the room.

Fifteen minutes later it was a completely different Nobushige Saida who went to answer the front door. Now he wore a thousand-dollar suit; his hair was combed and oiled; he carried with him as he walked the aroma of expensive body talc and breath mint. His glistening shoes squeaked as he unhurriedly crossed the hardwood floor. The expression on his face was of a man certain of his power.

He opened the door.

For a moment his expression wavered, then he dipped his head in a bow that, to those who understood the nuances of Japanese culture — as these men surely did not — was a calculated insult.

"Good morning, gentlemen," he said, his English flawless and barely accented. "Please come in."

There were two of them. One was of middling height, dressed in an open-necked shirt of purple silk and faded American jeans. In his early thirties, his thick hair hung untidily to his shoulders. He wore a thin, drooping moustache that unsuccessfully hid a narrow white scar that ran across part of one cheek and along his upper lip. His eyes were hidden behind a pair of sunglasses. His skin was swarthy and pitted.

The second man stood behind the first. Taller and younger, he wore a plain cotton shirt with wide short sleeves that displayed the biceps of a bodybuilder. His face was long and lean and smooth, but with the same swarthy complexion as his companion. A black stubble decorated his chin. He wore an expression of bored disinterest.

Saida repeated his invitation. "Come in, gentlemen. Perhaps you would like some coffee? Or I have tea if you prefer."

They stepped inside, the muscular one staying a pace behind his companion. The first man did not remove his sunglasses. "My name is Ahmed," he said. "Ahmed Ben-Kalil." Saida recognized the voice on the phone. Saida waited for him to introduce his companion, but Ahmed simply glanced around at the interior of the house, nodding to himself as if pleased with what he saw.

Saida led them to one of the smaller entertainment rooms, a room with a wide panoramic window of tinted glass that looked across the harbor in the direction of St. George's island. The causeway to St. George's was busy with cars carrying commuters; in the distance heat ripples were already beginning to rise from the concrete runways of the airport.

Saida lowered himself into a thickly padded, antimacassared armchair and gestured for his visitors to do likewise. Ahmed sat, but his companion remained standing, behind Ahmed's chair.

"Coffee or tea, gentlemen? Or would you prefer something else?" Saida asked with a pleasant smile.

Ahmed did not reply immediately. His eyes wandered around the room, appraising its contents. It was decorated lavishly. The walls were covered with flocked paper against which hung Japanese oils. A large cherrywood sideboard ran the length of one wall. A table stood against another wall, its surface brilliantly polished. Most of the hardwood floor was covered by a thick-piled oriental rug with an intricate design.

Ahmed took all this in with a slightly upturned mouth, as if amused by it all. Finally, his eyes settled on Saida.

"You've looked at the disc?" he asked.

Saida shifted in his chair and sighed heavily, as if he was disappointed by his guest's lack of manners.

"I've looked at the disc," he eventually said. "But quite frankly I don't understand."

He paused for a moment, then continued evenly, "I assume I am supposed to be angry. You have invaded the privacy of my house and now I imagine you are here to blackmail me. But as you see, I am not angry. Anger rarely serves a useful purpose, Mr. Ben-Kalil. If I were to allow myself to become angry it would give you power over me. You believe the disc to be a weapon against me, but you are mistaken." He had maintained an easy smile while he spoke; now, suddenly, the smile disappeared. "I do have one question, though."

"Yes?"

"Kim: did she know about the camera?"

With a sly smile, Ahmed said, "What do you think, Mr. Saida?"

Saida flushed, but only for a moment. The moment passed and he shrugged. "It doesn't matter. Logically, I conclude that she knew everything. She told me she was an actress, so perhaps I should have guessed she was simply playing a part. But it's unimportant. Only a fool dwells on the past, and no one can accuse me of being a fool."

He fell silent, as if there was nothing more to be said.

The silence stretched out. The two seated men found themselves looking at one another. The third man looked on silently.

Ahmed smiled. "Bullshit, Mr. Saida. Or should I call you Nobu?"

Saida sniffed, then hauled himself out of his chair. "Mr. Ben-Kalil, I think it is time you and your silent companion were leaving."

Ahmed stood. "I agree. But you're coming with us. Mahomet."

The tall man stepped from behind the chair; in his hand had appeared a short, stubby knife.

Ahmed said, "You will accept my invitation, Mr. Saida?"

Mahomet took a step closer, idly fingering the edge of the blade.

"Blackmail didn't work, so now you're going to kidnap me?" said Saida calmly. "I should tell you that my bank has a very clear policy toward kidnapping."

"Ah yes, your bank. The Financial Trust Bank of Kyoto, of which you, of course, are a director. Let's see, what exactly is your title? Head of Operations for Bermuda and the Caribbean? Do I have it right, Mr. Saida?"

"You do. But perhaps you are not aware that my bank has never paid a single yen in ransom? Nor will it ever do so."

Ahmed shook his head sadly and tut-tutted. Mahomet took another step closer; now he was within arm's length of Saida.

Ahmed nodded, and Mahomet's hand flashed forward. The knife sliced effortlessly through Saida's suit and buried itself in his right shoulder. Saida yelped in pain.

Mahomet withdrew the bloodied blade and, grabbing Saida, spun him around and locked his neck in a stranglehold. The blade pressed against the small of Saida's back.

"And now," said Ahmed evenly, "our car awaits."

15

"I've moved Roncador to Level 3," said Fisher. "So it's no longer just my responsibility as head of North America. From now on, we're all involved. We will move our headquarters to the Operations Room in Building 5."

"So what exactly is the status?" asked Lee.

"The plane carrying Stone and Ms. Tabor landed on schedule, that's all we know."

"And the Brotherhood? What about them?" Lee asked Hayes.

"Everything seems quiet again now. Otosan has returned from his trip to Alaska. As far as I can tell, Chida is still on Roncador Cay. They have one man, a Grade 2 operative called..." he glanced down at his notes "...Kadzu on Montega."

"Have we warned Stone about Kadzu?"

"No," said Fisher. "There'll be no contact unless we think there's an emergency. Stone should be able to handle him."

"And when do you expect to get Ms. Tabor's report about the machine?"

"I've promised the president we'll have it sometime in the next twenty four to thirty six hours."

"And then...?"

"Two Delta teams are on standby at Thompson Air Force Base outside Port St. John. If the machine exists, two hours after I give the word to the president, it will be ours."

Fran looked dubiously at the building. Despite the ill-lettered sign above the door, it didn't look much like a restaurant — not one where she wanted to eat, anyway.

It stood by itself at the side of the road in a wide gap in the hedge. *Fresh Fish* declared a hand-lettered sign that hung at a slant above the doorway. Underneath, in a different hand, someone had added *Beer + Rum too*. The building was wooden, and here and there were gaps in the slats large enough to allow a small animal to creep through. The roof consisted of half a dozen rusted corrugated tin sheets that lay directly on top of the walls.

Fran looked at Stone.

Stone had not spoken since they had left the hotel. His brow was furrowed in thought, as if he was wrestling with a knotty problem. Now he looked at Fran as if he had only just realized she was there.

"What's the matter?" he asked.

She nodded toward the building. "I'm not going in there." Pointing down the road, she added, "There must be something better in St. Andrews."

"I doubt it," Stone said. "You're not in America now, you know."

Fran stamped her foot angrily, raising a small cloud of dust. "Don't patronize me. You... mmmph"

Stone had clapped a hand over her mouth. "Shut up, will you?" he barked urgently. "We're in enough trouble as it is. Don't make it worse. If I explain, do you promise to be quiet?"

Fran nodded, and he removed his hand.

"Listen," he said, "I'd rather we didn't go into St. Andrews. Not yet, anyway. Come on inside and I'll tell you why we're in trouble."

Against her better judgement, she allowed herself to be led inside.

The restaurant was divided by a curtain that had been sewn together from dozens of cloth scraps. On the side where they were standing were half a dozen tables, all different; around each table were four chairs, equally mismatched. Six bare bulbs, one above each table, hung from the ceiling, their wires attached to the roof by duct tape. Only four of the bulbs were lit. The floor was dark brown, almost black, and it was a moment before Fran realized that it was simply hard-packed earth.

Only two other people were in the restaurant: a middle aged white couple occupied a table next to a grimy window. The man nursed a beer; in front of him was an empty plate. The woman was still eating her meal. The smell of cooked fish filled the air; from behind the curtain came the muffled sound of male voices in conversation.

The man at the table raised his glass in greeting. "Good evening," he said in a British accent. The woman, chewing a piece of fish, nodded toward them.

"How's the food?" asked Stone.

"Bloody marvelous," the man replied. "Best on the island. Unfortunately I can't say the same for the beer." He swirled the glass and drained it. His wife finished her meal and placed her knife and fork tidily together on one side of the plate.

Stone threaded his way to the most distant table and sat down. Fran joined him, and after a few moments a man wearing grimy overalls emerged from behind the curtain. He attended first to the English couple, who settled their bill and departed with a wave. Then he came to their table. "Got some wonderful marlin; my brother caught it this morning," he said with a gap-toothed smile. Fran caught the smell of rum on his breath.

"We'll take it," said Stone. "And two sodas, whatever kind you have."

The man nodded and disappeared behind the curtain, trailing the scent of rum behind him.

"And if I don't like marlin or soda?" Fran asked drily.

"You'll take the marlin because that's what that British couple had, and the soda because that's what you should always drink whenever you're in a developing country."

"Why?"

"Because water will give you diarrhea at best and something much nastier at worst."

"What about beer or wine?"

Stone shook his head. "Never touch them when you're in the field. Alcohol blunts the reflexes and dulls the brain."

"You've got an answer for everything, don't you? So when are you going to explain what happened back at the hotel?"

The waiter returned carrying two fluorescent red sodas. "The fish will be ready in a few minutes," he said, then disappeared back behind the curtain.

Stone sipped his soda, grimacing at the cloying sweetness. He put the glass down and said earnestly, "I hope we'll find out more tomorrow when we go and see Mrs. Tanner, but if Oscar Holywell tried to cross the Brotherhood I can guarantee that he's dead."

"Explain. HolyMo! this stuff is awful."

"I agree, but it's better than spending the next two days in the bathroom. How much do you know about Japanese history?"

"Huh?" Fran put her glass down.

"How much do you know about Japanese history?"

"I read *Shogun* once."

She had intended her remark as a joke, but Stone took it at face value. "That's a start. Then you know that under the chief warlord, the shogun, were the daimyos, who were a kind of feudal overlord of a region. And each daimyo was served by warriors called samurai."

For a moment she thought about throwing her soda at Stone. In the end she just nodded.

Oblivious to her growing impatience, he continued, "That arrangement lasted more or less continuously from the twelfth century until 1871, when the entire feudal system was dismantled. The samurai practice of wearing swords in public was abolished. A few years later even the word *samurai* was changed, to *shizoku*. *Shizoku* means *gentry*. A far cry from *samurai*, which means *warrior*, wouldn't you say?"

Fran agreed with gritted teeth, wondering if Stone was doing this on purpose or whether he was simply unaware of how annoying he could be.

"All this was fine, except that no one seems to have asked the samurai themselves what they thought of being stripped of their swords and their name. I'm sure I don't need to spell it out. You can guess what happened."

"They went underground?" she hazarded.

"Exactly. Officially, the samurai were eradicated, completely expunged from Japanese society. But they didn't disappear at all. They simply changed, that's all. Instead of wielding power overtly, they became secretive. Instead of warriors, they became bankers, and advisors to the Emperor, and landowners, and businessmen. But no one knew they existed. Only the samurai themselves."

A sizzling sound came from the far side of the curtain. Despite her annoyance, Fran's mouth began to water.

Stone continued, "The situation remained more or less the same for the next seventy years. The samurai were content to remain hidden and accumulate power. Then came the Second World War, and everything changed.

"Many of the samurai heeded the Emperor's call to fight for the glory of Japan. Although they never came out into the open, rumors that the samurai were back persisted throughout the war. But then the unthinkable happened — Japan lost the war, and with defeat came anger and a new determination that Japan would one day be great again.

"Again the samurai adapted. They were already powerful industrialists and politicians, but until now they'd had no goal except simple survival. Now there was something worth fighting for. History tells us that in 1945 Japan was a doomed, beaten, once-powerful nation with no future. Look at it now. You think that happened by chance? For more than fifty years the samurai have labored. And now Japan is one of the most powerful nations in the world; and the samurai are one of the most powerful forces in Japan."

The sound of movement came from the kitchen behind the curtain, followed by the scraping of utensils. Stone paused, and the man with the gap-toothed smile came out carrying two steaming plates.

"Enjoy your dinner," he said, putting the plates on their table. "You have enough soda? Good. Call if you want more." He disappeared behind the curtain, and the sound of muffled conversation began again.

Half of each plate was covered by a generous portion of marlin, steaming and fragrant. A small helping of legumes and potatoes completed the meal. Stone lifted a forkful of fish to his mouth. "It's good," he said. "Try some."

"Just out of interest, does your story about the samurai have any point to it? Even if it's true, which to be honest I doubt."

"Oh, it's true enough. You've seen one of them yourself."

"That man back at the hotel?" She sliced into the fish with her fork, breaking off a succulent piece of flesh. A moment later she discovered to her surprise that it was quite possibly the best fish she had ever tasted.

"The man at the hotel, Kadzu," Stone nodded. "I was pretty sure when I first saw him at the airport. His tattoo confirmed it.

"They don't call themselves samurai any more. They changed their name after the end of the war. Now they're *Turugi no Kyodai*, the Brotherhood of the Swords, and each one has a tattoo of crossed swords on his forearm. Once, the swords were the mark of the samurai; legally, samurai were the only people permitted to carry them: a long katana for slashing, and a shorter wakizashi, which was a kind of dagger used mainly for thrusting."

"So that's why you tore his sleeve."

"To check his tattoo," Stone nodded. "I wanted to be sure what we're up against."

"And what exactly *are* we up against?" asked Fran between mouthfuls.

"The Brotherhood is like nothing else on Earth," replied Stone. "They have access to more money and resources than most countries. Their leader, a man called Otosan — which is Japanese for Father — is as powerful as a dictator. Taking everything into account, they're far more dangerous than the CIA. Certainly more formidable than any known terrorist group. The question is: how are they involved? If they're bankrolling Ishihara, we're in deeper trouble than I'd thought."

"Why?"

"Because it means Roncador Cay will be protected. There'll be no chance of simply landing there and acting the part of nosey tourists."

"That man at the hotel...."

"Kadzu? What about him?"

"He knew you. He used your name."

"No. He knew of me, that's all."

"But how?"

"The Brotherhood and I have encountered each other before."

Fran mulled this over for a while. "It was very strange, what he said to you. He said he was going to kill you quickly. Does he really mean to try to kill you? What have you ever done to him? And if he does want to kill you, why would he say something like that?"

"Bushido."

"I beg your pardon?"

"Bushido. It's the ancient code of the samurai. Suitably modified for modern times, of course. It was his way of telling me he respected me for the way I'd handled him. In return he promised me a quick death. This is a good meal, isn't it? The drink excepted, of course."

She searched his face. "You don't seem worried."

He popped the last of the fish into his mouth and chewed on it thoughtfully for a while. He tilted his head, as if listening for something, and Fran realized that the hum of conversation in the kitchen had ceased. The only sounds were the stridulation of crickets and the chirp of tree frogs, which had been getting louder ever since the sun had set a few minutes before.

With a scrape of his chair, Stone got to his feet. "Perhaps a small glass of wine wouldn't go amiss after all. It's a shame not to do a meal like this justice. You wait here and I'll see if I can get us something drinkable."

She nodded absently and popped a sliver of fish thoughtfully into her mouth. Her eyes followed Stone as he disappeared behind the curtain.

In the kitchen, the air was heavy with the rich scents of thousands of meals cooked in the confined space. To Stone's right was an improvised counter, a thick slab of food-stained wood laid across a pair of makeshift trestles, on which were the remains of the marlin and several piles of fresh peppers, onions, beans and unshelled peas. Behind these stood a row of old beer bottles with handwritten labels listing their new contents: ginger; garlic; parsley; hot pepper sauce. At the far end stood two enormous coffee cans partially filled with flour and sugar. Next to these was a smaller can of salt.

On the far side of the room stood an ancient refrigerator with chipped paint and a rust-covered handle. Next to this was a ferociously heavy iron stove, and beyond that a small galvanized steel sink in which was heaped a pile of cooking utensils. And stretched out on the ground in front of the sink was a black man whom Stone had never seen before. Next to him, on his back and with his eyes closed, was their gap-toothed waiter.

Two strides brought Stone to where the men lay. He knelt and laid a finger against the gap-toothed man's pulse.

A fearful shriek rent the air.

Stone jumped to his feet and bounded to the curtain. He threw it aside.

Fran was standing with her back to him. She stood at an odd angle, partway out of her chair, facing Kadzu. As Stone watched, she slumped to the ground like a child's rag doll, crumpling into an untidy pile with one leg bent awkwardly beneath her and her arms outstretched. Her head swivelled heavily to one side. Her eyes were closed and her face wore an oddly relaxed look.

Kadzu took a step backward and bowed shallowly toward Stone.

"If you've killed her...," Stone breathed through clenched teeth.

Kadzu shook his head and bared his own teeth in a smile. "She, like the others, merely sleeps. I am a man of honor, Mr. Stone. My quarrel is with you, not with any of them. They sleep; you I will kill."

"You're going to kill me just because I surprised you this afternoon at the hotel?" Stone's eyes roved around the room, measuring distances and angles. He took a step closer.

"I will kill you because those are my orders." Kadzu also moved closer, edging around Fran's body. He raised his hands to chest height, his fingers slightly curled, ready for either attack or defense, whichever was needed first.

"Who gave you those orders?"

The distance between them was no more than six feet. They halted, staring into each other's eyes, waiting for the first telltale movement that would precede an attack.

Kadzu's smile grew wider. "You know I won't tell you."

"Ah yes, your famous code of ethics. The bushido. The same code that forbids you to kill anyone except enemies. Tell me, was Oscar Holywell an enemy? Is that why you killed him?"

Kadzu's eyes flickered, and in that moment Stone's right foot kicked upward in a violent arc. Kadzu jumped backward and his hands jammed downward, intending to grasp Stone's foot and break his ankle with a single ferocious twist.

But Stone had anticipated the movement and sprung forward on his other leg. His right foot pounded into the other's crotch, forcing Kadzu backward, off balance and in pain.

Stone twisted to one side, but the momentum of his attack carried him careening into a table. Spinning to face Kadzu, he regained his balance; as he turned he was met by a chair flying through the air legs-first.

He warded the chair off with an arm, staggering under the force of the blow as a leg scraped his temple.

Kadzu jumped over Fran's inert form, his mouth wide, issuing a feral, bloodcurdling scream. Stone twisted to meet his attacker, but he was too slow; a sharp chop of Kadzu's hand slammed into his side an inch below his lowest rib.

Stone yelled in agony, his eyes watering. A blurred fist come flying out of nowhere, filling his vision. At the last moment he jerked to one side. Instead of breaking his nose, the fist pounded a glancing blow into the wound caused by the chair.

His head rang, and he felt his legs turning to jelly under him. He flailed wildly with both arms, aware only of a blurred figure dodging around just out of reach. He shook his head to clear it, but only made himself dizzier.

A sharp, lancing pain told him he had been kicked in the right leg. The leg crumpled under him. Clutching at a table for support, he brought it face-down on top of him. He landed on his back on something soft, and it was a moment before he realized that was splayed awkwardly on top of Fran.

Beyond the table stood Kadzu, briefly at a loss. The hesitation lasted only a moment; then Kadzu let out another scream, and one foot pounded into the table-top. Stone felt the force of the impact through the wood, knocking the air from his lungs. He gasped for breath as Kadzu grabbed the table and tore it away, sending it careening noisily across the room.

Kadzu smiled and gave a slight bow.

"Mr. Stone, as I promised, your death will be quick."

He jumped forward, pulling his knees under him as he did so, and came crashing down on top of Stone. Stone yelped with pain as Kadzu landed. Kadzu drew back his right hand, forming two fingers into a narrow vee. He grabbed Stone's hair with his left hand and pulled sharply backward, banging Stone's head against the hard-packed ground.

Kadzu thrust his right hand forward toward Stone's eyes, while his left hand kept Stone's head locked in place.

At the last moment, Stone managed to raise his hand, presenting its edge to Kadzu's vee.

Kadzu screamed in pain as the vee of his fingers rammed into the edge of Stone's hand, tearing the webbing. Stone twisted under him, causing Kadzu to lose his balance and fall to the ground. Stone's foot kicked him in the right knee, and both men heard the sharp crack of breaking bone.

Another kick followed, then another, and suddenly it was all over: Stone was standing over Kadzu, leaning against a chair for support; Kadzu was moaning on the ground, writhing in a fruitless attempt to escape the pain that wracked his body.

For a few moments Stone rested, letting his strength return.

"Tell me, you bastard," he said. "Who gave you your orders to kill me?"

Kadzu shook his head. "No. I will never tell."

Stone knew the samurai was telling the truth. Kadzu would die before he would betray his superiors. "Then tell me this. Did you kill Oscar Holywell?"

Kadzu shook his head again and said, "No." From somewhere he found a reserve of strength, and tried to kick Stone. He missed, and Stone lashed out with a foot that landed squarely in the other's face. A dribble of blood appeared at the corner of Kadzu's eye and trickled down the side of his nose before dripping to the ground, where it made a small dark spot in the earth.

"But you know who did kill him."

Kadzu did not seem to have heard. He was groaning to himself, and he wiped away the blood that was trickling down his face. "I can't see," he said, barely audibly.

"Who killed Oscar Holywell?" persisted Stone. "And why?"

But it was no good. Kadzu by now was oblivious to his presence; he began to mumble to himself in Japanese, his lips barely moving, most of his words unintelligible. For a moment he fell silent, then he said haltingly in Japanese, "*Hitoomoini korositekure. Kure.*" Kill me now. Please.

"You'll live," declared Stone dismissively in Japanese, turning away and kneeling next to Fran. He held her head between his hands and opened an eyelid. She moaned and weakly tried to turn her head away from the light.

"*Kure,*" the Japanese repeated.

"No. Your life isn't in danger."

"If you don't kill me, my brothers will. I will die in disgrace."

This brief speech drained Kadzu, and he lay gasping for breath. The flow of blood from his eye had stopped, but now a thick red dribble began from his right nostril. It flowed across his face and dripped to the ground.

Stone eyed Kadzu critically. It would take a talented surgeon and the facilities of a modern hospital to counteract the damage he had inflicted. Neither was available on Montega.

"They'll kill me," mumbled Kadzu almost incoherently. "I'll be disgraced. My ancestors won't accept me."

Stone nodded. He understood now. Kadzu wasn't afraid of dying from his injuries. He was afraid of not dying. Kadzu had been ordered to kill Stone, and he had failed. If Stone didn't kill him, he would die an ignominious death at the hands of another member of the Brotherhood. And even worse, his ancestors might refuse to accept his newly-arrived spirit.

Stone knelt beside his head. Speaking in Japanese, he said, "Oscar Holywell. Tell me about him."

"You'll kill me?" Kadzu asked hopefully.

"I'll kill you. But only if you tell me about Holywell."

"It was Chida. You know Chida?"

Stone nodded grimly.

"He's on Roncador Cay, and he killed Holywell. I don't know the details. Please."

"And what was Holywell to you? Why is the Brotherhood involved with a computer genius who disappeared a year and a half ago?"

Kadzu shook his head. "No, I can't. I've told you enough."

"More. Tell me more."

"If I told you, I'd be a traitor and I'd deserve a traitor's death. No. I cannot do that."

"If you don't answer my questions I'll leave you here for your friends to find." Stone began to get to his feet.

"Then I made a mistake," said Kadzu. "You are not the man I thought you were." He gurgled and coughed up blood.

For half a minute Stone stood wordlessly looking at the sorry spectacle at his feet. Then he knelt again beside Kadzu's head. "All right, damn you."

Kadzu saw Stone's hands coming closer. He closed his eyes and felt the release as his pain receded into nothingness. "*Arrigato*," he tried to say. Thank you. But he was too late. He had left his mortal body behind.

Stone heard a single, barely audible groan from the depths of his adversary's throat. He kept his hands in place, counting slowly, then removed them. Kadzu's head rolled lifelessly to one side.

Outside, a pair of mopeds puttered past on their way to the hotel, and Stone realized that at any moment someone might walk into the restaurant. He hurried back to Fran and slapped her gently on the cheeks.

"Wha...? Huh?" Fran mumbled, blinking.

"Wake up. We have to get out of here."

Fran focussed on the face hovering a foot above her own. "Stone? What happened?" she asked hoarsely. Then, "And what the hell have you done to yourself?"

Until now, Stone had been only vaguely aware of a nagging pain near his hairline where the foot of the chair had caught him, and a sharp hurt on his right side when he moved too quickly. Putting his hand to touch the places that hurt, he winced.

"Never mind about me," he said. "We have to get out of here."

Fran opened her mouth to protest, then shut it again as Stone helped her to her feet. As soon as she was standing she drew back in horror, pointing at Kadzu's body. "Is he... is he dead?"

"Yes. Come on; can you walk? Lean on me if you need to."

"No. I think I'm all right." She took a faltering step. Her next step was more confident. In a few moments she was at the door. She opened it and turned to look at the body one last time.

"I had to kill him," said Stone at her side. "It was him or me."

She looked at him with an unreadable expression.

"Let's get out of here," she said, and, leaning on one another for support, they walked unsteadily out of the restaurant.

16

They had installed themselves in a large room underneath a building half a dozen blocks from the White House. Large, high-definition screens filled one end of the room. A handful of technicians sat in front of computers, ready to perform whatever magic their masters wanted.

Far away in orbit, thrusters fired and cameras turned as, one by one, images began to fill the screens.

"We should have twenty four hour coverage of the Caribbean now, sir," one of the technicians said to Fisher. "Sir?"

"I'm sorry. I was thinking. What did you say?"

But it was hard to concentrate on the technician's words as he repeated himself. He'd seen the look on Hayes' face.

I must be more careful, *Fisher warned himself.* They're getting suspicious.

Ahmed and Mahomet bundled Saida into a rusting year-old Ford with tinted rear windows.

Mahomet slipped silently into the driver's seat while Ahmed manhandled Saida on to the rear seat, then got in beside him. The engine caught first time. The Ford pulled out of the driveway and on to the road.

For some time they drove in silence. The car made its way north, then turned westward along the narrow strip of land between Harrington Sound and the Atlantic.

Saida removed his hand from the wound in his shoulder. His hand was sticky with blood, and there was a dark stain on his thousand-dollar suit, but the stain was no longer spreading and the bleeding had stopped.

"It was only a flesh wound," said Ahmed dismissively, as if such things were an everyday occurrence.

"I told you," said Saida. "My bank has an unbreakable policy. They won't pay any ransom. You're wasting your time kidnapping me."

A water skier overtook them a hundred yards away on the smooth waters of the sound. Ahmed asked, "Have you ever tried that?" Before Saida could answer, there was a brief fountain of water and they momentarily lost sight of the skier. Then the boat that had been pulling him slowed and began to turn in a wide arc to pick him up.

Ahmed clapped his hands in delight. "You see what happens when you are overconfident, Mr. Saida? He tried to turn too sharply and what happened? He lost everything. Perhaps there's a lesson there for all of us."

"Look, I don't know what you want. I'm telling you the bank won't bargain for my return."

Ahmed regarded Saida. His eyes wandered searchingly over the other's face for several moments. Then, smiling broadly to himself, he turned away without replying and gazed out the window.

Saida leaned back into the warm, sticky plastic of the Ford's seats, considering his predicament. If he had been younger, he wouldn't have hesitated for a moment, despite his wounded shoulder. By now, Ahmed and Mahomet would both be dead. But the men were little more than half his age, and it was more than thirty years since Saida had last been in a fight.

In silence Mahomet drove over tiny Flatts bridge, where the water sluiced out of Harrington Sound and into Flatts Inlet, and then turned on to Middle Road and climbed the hill toward Hamilton. Middle Road was busy, and they became just one more car in a long procession heading westward.

"Where are we going?" Saida asked. "Surely you can tell me that?"

"Sandys," replied Ahmed, naming the most distant of Bermuda's nine parishes.

"Why?"

"You'll find out when we get there."

It took them nearly an hour to reach their destination. As they approached Sandys the island narrowed and traffic thinned until it was almost nonexistent. By the time the car turned off the road and on to a narrow track that wound around the base of a small hill, they were nearly at the very end of the island.

They came to a halt outside a small bungalow only a few yards from the rocky shore and hidden from its neighbors by the low hill. It was as isolated a spot as Saida had ever seen on the tiny, cramped island.

They got out of the car. A stiff onshore breeze pressed against the back of Saida's head as he was marched up a short path and into the bungalow.

Inside, he was led to a flight of wooden stairs and taken downstairs to the basement. Without a word, Ahmed and Mahomet clambered back up the stairs. The door at the top of the stairs closed, and Saida heard a key turn in the lock. He was alone.

The basement was a simple unfinished rectangular hole in the coral underneath the bungalow. The walls were bare, still displaying the marks left by the saws where they had cut the coral. There was no furniture. The only objects in the basement were the sealed water tank in which rainwater from the limewashed roof collected, and the pump that carried the water up into the house above as needed. The basement was lit by a single bare bulb, hanging from a cord a few feet above the water tank. The light switch was at the top of the stairs.

Saida examined the wooden stairs to see if he could prise one of the slats loose, but they were all firmly nailed down. There were no banisters or anything else that might conceivably be useful as a weapon. After a while, he shrugged to himself and sat on the floor with his back against the water tank.

He pulled a roll of mints from his pocket and popped one into his mouth. Sucking the mint, he closed his eyes and breathed deeply.

Nobushige Saida was a very patient man. He did not mind waiting.

17

The sun peeked over the low hills to the east, lighting the garden with the first light of the new day. An elderly man in a white kimono with purple edging stood silently at the window, watching the changing colors.

Behind him a younger man entered the room and waited patiently for his presence to be recognized.

For more than a minute the man at the window did not move. The younger man was beginning to wonder if the old man realized he was no longer alone when suddenly he spoke.

"You have news, my son?"

"Yes, Father."

The old man turned from the window and said, "I see from your face that your news is not good."

"It's Nobushige Saida, Father. He's disappeared."

"Disappeared? People, especially Sons of the Brotherhood, do not simply disappear."

"Saida has. He didn't report for work yesterday. His deputy says he has no idea where he might be. That's all I know."

"That is not all, my son. Do not lie. You are hiding something from me."

"I'm sorry, Father. I wanted to spare you the pain of knowing. It seems that Saida was involved with a young woman. The woman has also disappeared."

"I see."

"Perhaps they are together," suggested the son.

"That would be convenient," mumbled Otosan. He shook his head. *"Musuko, my son. Have you still not learned even the simplest of lessons?"*

With difficulty, Musuko forced his anger to remain hidden.

Musuko was principal Son to the Father, next in line to assume the purple-edged kimono. But his position was not yet secure. There had been mutterings that it would be a mistake for the Brotherhood to allow the kimono to pass from blood-father to blood-son a second time. Otosan frequently annoyed and sometimes angered him with his mystical eastern mumbo-jumbo, but he could not yet allow his frustrations to show.

"What lesson do you mean?" Musuko asked evenly.

"Remember, to every complex problem there is a simple solution..."

"...and it's wrong," Musuko completed the saying. *"But is this a complex problem?"*

"All problems in life are complex, my son."

"Then what do you suggest?"

"You desire to be Otosan after I am gone. What do you suggest?"

The question caught Musuko off guard. As did the Father's forthright acknowledgement of Musuko's desire. To want to be Father was to ensure that one would never reach that goal. Musuko would have to be more careful to hide his ambitions as well as his frustrations.

"My Father, I want only to serve."

"Then you would not object if I replaced you as Musuko, my son?" Otosan looked his blood-son directly in the eye, but Musuko refused to be tricked into giving himself away by averting his gaze.

Maintaining eye contact, he bowed slightly. *"I am Musuko only so long as you desire it, Father."*

"That has never been in doubt, my son. But you have not answered my question. What do you think we should do about the situation that has arisen?"

"I don't know. Perhaps I should go to Bermuda and investigate the situation myself?" Musuko hazarded.

The old man turned and gazed silently out the window at the garden once more. After more than a minute of silence, it dawned on Musuko that the audience was over. Murmuring his goodbyes, he bowed to the Father's back and left the room.

––––––––––

Darkness had fallen, and the road between the restaurant and the hotel was almost deserted. No more than half a dozen tourists on mopeds passed Fran and Stone as they made their way back to the hotel. At Stone's insistence, whenever they heard a vehicle approaching they moved close to the hedge and embraced clumsily in the shadows.

He winced whenever she touched his ribs, but insisted there was no time to look at his wounds. "We need to get back to the hotel," he said. "Then we can think about what we do next."

In the pale moonlight, Fran could see that he was worried, but he stubbornly refused to answer her questions.

The desk clerk looked at them strangely when they entered the lobby. Stone leaned on Fran for support and the clerk moved forward to help, but Stone waved him away. "Moped hit me," he said. "Don't worry, I'll be fine. Just a bit shook up, that's all."

When they reached their room, Stone locked the door. Then, moving slowly, he began to strip in front of the mirror.

As he peeled off his shirt, Fran exclaimed, "HolyMo!"

He looked at her in the mirror and smiled wryly. "As you can see, that wasn't the first fight I've been in."

Stone's arms and legs were smoothly contoured with powerful muscles. His torso was thick, solid and muscular. But Fran's exclamation was prompted not by his physique but by his scars.

Four ragged parallel lines of shiny scar tissue ran diagonally across his back, starting near his right shoulder and ending just above the curve of his left buttock. A single thin white scar crossed all four lines, running between the opposite shoulder and buttock.

126

Several small scars marked the upper portion of his legs. The outside of his right leg was hairless and shiny with a reloid scar.

Most of his chest was covered by a massive purplish blob that Fran at first took to be yet another scar. It was only when she saw Stone touching it tenderly and feeling his ribs through it that she realized it was an enormous, ugly bruise.

Fran watched as Stone worked his way from rib to rib, pressing each one in turn. He gasped slightly as he reached the lower ribs on his right side, but continued his examination until he had tested every one.

"I hope I'm not embarrassing you," said Stone with a smile, catching her open-eyed gaze in the mirror.

Fran looked away sharply. She had been so astonished at the punishment written on his body that she'd barely noticed his nakedness.

"Couple of ribs bruised, nothing broken," Stone said. "That's all, apart from this blow to my temple, which may have knocked some sense into me." He smiled, then realized from the look on Fran's face that she was in no mood for joking.

She sat on the edge of the bed. Her breathing became loud and irregular, and it dawned on Stone that she was near tears. He settled on the bed behind her, and put an arm around her shoulder.

"I'm sorry," he said. "I guess I'm so used to it that sometimes I forget that most people might be shocked."

"I... I don't think I'm cut out for this sort of thing. Maybe I should just go home."

"No, please don't think that. We need you, Fran. You know that." He caressed the back of her head gently.

"I've never been attacked before," she said. "You know something? In the back of my mind, I always thought that women who let themselves be attacked were somehow responsible for what happened to them. I always thought, *If anyone ever tries to attack me, I'll make the bastard sorry he was ever born.*" She made a sound that was half a laugh, half a sob. "I never guessed what it would be like. I felt so hopeless. He could have done anything he wanted. Anything." She choked back a sob. "And then afterwards. When I woke up. He was... dead. I've never seen a dead body before. It's not... it's not...."

She couldn't hold the tears back any longer. Stone pulled her to him, and she buried her face in his shoulder. "It's all right," he said gently. "It was all my fault. I should never have left you. I'm sorry. I wanted to know why the men in the kitchen had stopped talking. I should have realized. It was foolish of me to leave you alone."

For a while the only sound in the room came from Fran's quiet sobs. Gradually, they diminished and then finally stopped. "Please, take me home," she said quietly. "I don't care what you do with my income taxes. Throw me in jail if you want. Just take me home."

"I can't. Not yet. We have to find out if this thinking machine is for real. You do understand that, don't you?"

She nodded. "Yes. I suppose so." Sniffing back her tears, she smiled sheepishly at him. "I'm crying, but you're the one who's hurt."

"It could have been much worse," he said. He got off the bed and pulled on his underpants. "Just a bit bruised. I should feel a lot better by morning."

Fran watched him in silence as he put the rest of his clothes back on.

As he put on his shirt he ventured another joke, "You can imagine I'm not much of a one for trips to the beach." This time she forced a smile.

He sat down beside her and looked at her with concern in his eyes. Fran returned his gaze, looking closely at his face. She noticed now that the swollen red gash on his temple was not the first wound his face had received. She counted four other tell-tale scars, one on his right cheek, two small ones on his chin, and a long one on his brow almost hidden by his forward-swept hair.

He leaned back and lay on his back on the bed. The taut look on his face and his shallow breathing told her that he was in more pain than he was willing to admit to.

"That man, Kadzu, you really killed him?" she asked.

"Yes."

"With your bare hands?"

"It's the only way."

"What's that supposed to mean?"

Stone did not reply immediately. For a while he stared silently up at the ceiling. For a minute or more a spider's web in one corner engrossed his attention. From the look on his face, Fran could see that he was debating something with himself.

Eventually he said, "Maybe you could call it something like bushido. On the other hand, maybe it's just pragmatism. Weapons are too obvious, and they have a disconcerting tendency to be discovered at inconvenient moments. So we're taught to use our bodies and everyday objects as our weapons. Sometimes it puts us at a disadvantage, but on the whole it's a good strategy."

"And who is 'we' and 'us'? You've never told me."

He shook his head. "And I never will. Not unless Fisher gives me permission, which would be a first. So don't embarrass me by asking."

She pondered this for a while. She asked, "Kadzu really did try to kill you?"

"Yes."

"And what about me? Was he going to kill me? Please tell me the truth. I have to know."

Stone shook his head firmly. "No. If he'd wanted you dead, you wouldn't be here now. He just wanted to keep you quiet, that's all. What exactly did he do to you, anyway? Can you remember?"

Fran wrinkled her brow, trying to recall the sequence of events and not noticing that Stone had changed the subject.

"I don't really know. I watched you go into the kitchen for the wine, then I finished my food. That's when I realized I wasn't alone and someone was standing behind me. That's right," she said, remembering. "I turned and began to get up. I saw who it was, and I think I screamed, but before I could do anything else he grabbed me. Then I think he hit me. I don't really remember."

"The back of your head, just where it begins to curve up from your neck, it probably hurts," he said absently as if his mind was elsewhere.

She felt the back of her head at the place he had described. It was sore.

It was a minute before he spoke again. Then he said decisively, "The evening's young yet and there's no time to lose. Do you think you could go out again? 52 Chalybeate Street. It's on the outskirts of St. Andrews."

"Alone?"

"I'm in no shape to go out this evening. Don't worry, I promise you you'll be perfectly safe. Kadzu's not going anywhere."

"And what if he has friends?"

"He does, and that's why I want you to go. We need to move quickly, before the Brotherhood finds out what's happened to Kadzu. Please. It'll save us a day. The sooner we get out of here, the happier I'll be."

"So who lives at number 52 Chalybeate Street?"

"Gloria Tanner. Remember her? Her son told us about Oscar Holywell."

"I remember. But I'm not sure I can go."

"Are you saying you don't trust me?"

"I'm saying I've never felt so scared and alone in my life, and I want to get out of here and go home. I want to forget I've ever heard of you or Fisher or bushido or the whole damn mess."

"Good," said Stone.

Fran looked at him in astonishment. "Good?"

"Yes. You're being honest. With yourself as well as with me. Of course, I should have known you would be. Your psychological profile at NSA said as much. Stubborn as hell, but completely trustworthy."

Fran knew that she should be angry, but she no longer had it in her.

"Are you going to let them scare you away?" Stone asked. "Do you want the world's first thinking machine to fall into the hands of a bunch of killers?"

Fran looked at him strangely. She said, "You killed Kadzu; he didn't kill you. Maybe that makes our side the killers."

"We're the good guys, Fran. You believe that, don't you?"

"Everyone always thinks he's a good guy. The bad guys are always Them, never Us."

"They killed Oscar Holywell; we didn't."

"If he's dead."

"Gloria Tanner's son said he was dead, and he should know."

"So Fisher claims. But as you said yourself, you've never seen the message."

"Kadzu confirmed it. Holywell was killed by a butcher called Chida. Look, Fran. I can't go out. And you know Kadzu wanted to kill me. You heard him threaten me yourself. What more do you need? So will you go or not?"

"You're sure it can't wait till tomorrow?"

Stone shook his head. "That's what I'd originally planned. But after what happened tonight I want us to be gone by tomorrow."

"Because the Brotherhood might come looking for us?" Despite the warmth of the room, Fran had to suppress a shiver.

"Because the Brotherhood *will* come looking for *me*. They'll be on my tail as soon as they find out what happened to Kadzu. And my guess is they'll find out pretty soon. This afternoon I thought it would take at least a day for him to get permission from Japan to kill me, yet apparently he got it in about two hours flat. Chida is on Roncador Cay, and it was probably Chida who ordered Kadzu to kill me. I'm hoping Kadzu didn't say anything about you, which means you should be safe when Chida comes looking for me. Listen, I really do hate to give you the job of going to see Mrs. Tanner by yourself...."

"It's all right. I think I understand. If you go, she might be in danger as well. If I go alone, she ought to be safe."

"Exactly."

"All right, then. I know I'm going to regret this, but I guess I'll go."

Stone smiled gratefully. "Thank you."

Stone got to his feet and crossed the room to his suitcase, from which he removed a tiny cassette recorder, barely larger than the microcassette it contained. "It's voice actuated. Just press this button and whenever anyone speaks the machine will automatically record what's said. The tape runs for an hour of solid conversation. Here, try it."

Fran took the recorder and tested it; then she put it in her pocket and patted it down. The recorder was so small that the bulge in her skirt was undetectable.

"Thank you again," said Stone.

There was an embarrassing moment as each thought about embracing the other. Then Fran moved away toward the door. "I'll be as quick as I can," she said.

"I'm sorry you've got to do this by yourself. I really hadn't planned it this way."

"It's all right. Anything to get us out of here sooner."

"Good luck; and be sure to wake me up if I'm asleep when you get back. I'll want to listen to the tape right away."

In the lobby, the desk clerk was only too happy to call Fran a taxi.

"And your husband? He's recovered from his accident with the moped?"

"Yes, he's fine. He just needs a good night's sleep, that's all."

"Good. Mopeds can be dangerous, you know. You'd be surprised how many accidents we see. Anyway, I'll make sure he's not disturbed."

The clerk remained at the counter reading a paper until the taxi arrived. He watched her leave, and as the taxi pulled away he lifted the phone and dialed a local number.

18

A gray area on the screen brightened to white.

"Zoom in on that," said Hayes.

One of the operators typed a command and the long, narrow outline of Roncador Cay appeared in yellow, accentuating the difference between ground and sea on the infra-red image. A moment later, the outline expanded to fill the screen.

"The helicopter engine is running," said Gallucci. "How many on board?"

"Just the one," replied the operator. "There it goes."

The blob of heat shivered slightly, then began to move to the west, gaining speed as it crossed the yellow outline.

"When he lands on Montega, have the computers track him," said Hayes.

"What reason could Chida have for going to Montega at this time of night?" Gallucci asked no one in particular.

"I don't know," replied Lee. "But you can bet it has something to do with Stone."

———————————

Nobushige Saida sat against the steel water tank with his eyes closed.

The mint in his mouth had dissolved, leaving only the aftertaste which he now savored to the exclusion of other thoughts. If he had been twenty years younger, he would have assumed the lotus position, but that was no longer possible and instead he simply stretched out his legs in front of him and concentrated on not thinking.

It had been years since he had meditated. An inner voice argued that he was too long out of practice and it was pointless even to try. But he remembered that the most important thing was to relax and ignore the voices clamoring for attention.

You should be trying to think of a way out of here, another voice whispered. He silenced it, refusing to allow any more thoughts into his mind.

He relaxed, letting the tightness flow out of his muscles. He felt the pressure leave his body, then forced himself not to feel it. He drained his mind, thinking of nothing. Slowly, the years rolled away and he became at one with himself.

He heard his ancestors talking to him. With a pang of guilt he realized it was more than a decade since he had sought their counsel.

"You are a samurai, descended from samurai. This thing you have done brings dishonor on us."

"I know. I'm sorry," he said out loud.

"But a samurai is at his strongest when he is at his weakest," one of the voices said.

"A true samurai is never beaten," another declared. "Even in death he is triumphant."

"Look inside yourself. That is where you will find your strength," said a third.

Gradually, the voices died down until there was Nobushige Saida and only Nobushige Saida.

Time lost its meaning.

He might have remained oblivious to his surroundings for two minutes, or two hours, or two days.

All he knew was that now something was disturbing his peace. With a supreme effort he forced himself to allow thoughts to flow once more.

He heard a noise that, after an eternity, he recognized as someone walking across a hard floor. He opened his eyes and everything came flooding back: Kim; the two Arabs, Ahmed and Mahomet; the kidnapping; the basement in which he was being held prisoner.

Ahmed halted in front of him. He bent down and gripped Saida's hair tightly.

"Wake up, you fat little bastard." He smashed Saida's head backward against the water tank.

The Arab pulled his hand back to slap some sense into his prisoner. Automatically, without thought, Saida's arm went up and blocked the blow before it could land. Saida held the hand, then twisted it easily in a manner learned long ago. Ahmed collapsed to the floor with a scream.

Mahomet rushed down the stairs two at a time and ran to Ahmed's side. He pulled Ahmed away while the latter rubbed his wrist, swearing under his breath. Mahomet looked at Saida with interest. Saida returned his gaze evenly. "The stronger your enemy is, the weaker your enemy is," he recited.

"Unholy Jap bastard," Ahmed muttered, and before Saida could react Mahomet's booted foot lashed out and connected with his knee. Saida shouted, and Mahomet kicked again. This time there was a distinct crack as his boot landed.

Saida rocked in pain, nursing his knee, while Ahmed got unsteadily to his feet. "Get up," he said.

Saida ignored him.

"Get up."

Saida suggested something crude in Japanese.

"Mahomet, if you please."

Mahomet delivered a casual kick, planting his boot firmly in Saida's plump torso.

"Get up."

Saida repeated his suggestion, in English this time.

Ahmed sighed wearily. "One more time, Mahomet."

Mahomet kicked again, less casually this time.

"And that goes for you too," said Saida with gritted teeth.

Ahmed came closer and bent down until his face was level with Saida's. Saida spat in his eye, and Ahmed flinched.

"Listen to me, you son of a Japanese whore," said Ahmed, "Let me make something perfectly clear. You're going to tell me what I want to know, so there's no point in fighting. And when I've finished with you, I'm going to kill you with my bare hands. You won't be the first. How many is it, Mahomet? Five? Six?"

With a grin Mahomet held up two hands with only the thumb of one hand curled inward.

"Nine," said Ahmed. "It's so easy to lose count. Mahomet, tell the Japanese bastard how many died without telling me what I wanted to know."

Mahomet shook his head sadly and lowered both hands.

"So you see," said Ahmed, "it's pointless to fight. Unlike the Brotherhood, I don't make mistakes. Ah, I see that surprised you. Oh yes, I know everything about you, Nobushige Saida, and that includes your precious Brotherhood of the Swords."

"I don't know what you're talking about."

Ahmed shook his head. "Don't disappoint me even more. Isn't there something in your code about always telling the truth? Of course, I believe there's also something about renouncing the pleasures of the flesh, but that doesn't seem to have stopped you, does it? I wonder what the Brotherhood would think if that disc ever found its way into their hands. Your poor parents... they would be most disappointed. Their only child, a Son of the Brotherhood, disgraced."

Saida's stomach sank.

"Yes, I'd feel sorry for your parents," continued the Arab. "With you disgraced, I doubt the Brotherhood would feel any duty to keep looking after their needs. I wonder what would become of them? Your father, I understand, is not in good health."

"I don't know what you're talking about," repeated Saida. But he sounded unconvincing, even to his own ears. "I'm a director of the Financial Trust Bank of Kyoto, and Head of Operations for Bermuda and the Caribbean. You've made a mistake."

Ahmed shook his head. "I already told you, I don't make mistakes. Now, get up, Mr. Saida, or I'll have no choice but to have Mahomet force you. Believe me, you don't want that."

Saida looked up at the tall Arab standing above him, then shook his head.

"You've made a mistake," said Saida, nursing his knee.

Ahmed turned away, presenting his back to Saida. "Do whatever it takes, Mahomet."

Mahomet's face was expressionless. Saida searched it for some sign of emotion, but without success. It might just as well have been a painted mask. Mahomet's large black eyes gazed into Saida's narrow brown ones, but they betrayed no sign of what he was thinking.

He edged closer; then, without taking his eyes off Saida's face, he squatted on the floor beside him. He stretched out an arm and pulled Saida's right hand from his damaged knee. Then he smiled — a gruesome, mirthless, sadistic smile.

Mahomet's left hand closed around Saida's hand like a piece of wood in a vice; the Arab's right hand dipped into a pocket and reappeared holding a pair of pliers. Mahomet squeezed, forcing Saida's fingers to splay apart. He closed the pliers around the fingernail of Saida's index finger and pulled.

Saida's shriek bounced hollowly around the basement as Mahomet tossed the bloody fingernail into the corner with a careless flick of his wrist. Through welling tears, Saida watched the blood pool at his fingertip and begin to drip on to the floor. Mahomet moved the pliers to Saida's middle finger, and closed the pincers. He paused for a moment, and looked at Saida as if to say, "Had enough?" When Saida did not react, he removed that fingernail as carelessly as the first. Saida screamed again. Mahomet tossed the fingernail into the corner and moved without pausing to Saida's ring finger.

He looked at Saida expectantly. Then the pliers closed and he removed the nail.

Mahomet had removed seven nails before Saida could take it no more. The pain made it impossible to think. His determination to deny everything evaporated in the face of his agony. He would do anything to stop the pain.

Mahomet paused with the pliers closed around the eighth nail and looked briefly at Saida. At last Saida nodded. "All right," he sobbed. "I'll talk." Mahomet opened the pliers.

"Stand up," said Ahmed, who had not moved and still stood with his back to them.

"I'll tell you whatever you want," said Saida.

"I said, stand up," repeated Ahmed. Still he didn't turn around.

Saida looked at Mahomet, who motioned for Saida to obey.

With Mahomet's help, Saida struggled to his feet. He stood with his weight on one foot, avoiding his damaged knee. Blood dripped from the ends of his fingers; the blood from the ones that Mahomet had damaged first had already clotted around the nailless ends.

Slowly, Ahmed turned to face Saida. He smiled pleasantly. "Good," he said. "Mahomet, you may leave us."

In silence, Mahomet climbed the steps and closed the door. Ahmed sat on the bare concrete floor about ten feet from Saida. From his pocket he withdrew a small carton about the size of a pack of cigarettes and, flipping it open, he spilled a deck of cards on to the floor. Gathering them up, he shuffled them clumsily, then began to deal them face down in front of him, seven cards in a line.

"What are you doing?" asked Saida feebly.

"Playing solitaire," replied Ahmed without looking up. He added, "And if you move, I'll call Mahomet and tell him to carry on where he left off."

Saida wordlessly watched his captor for several minutes until it was obvious that the game was lost. Ahmed gathered the cards and shuffled them again, then began to deal.

Saida's good leg was beginning to ache. He tried to shift some of his weight to the other one, but the pain brought tears to his eyes. "May I sit down?" he asked.

"If you want to," said Ahmed, not taking his eyes off the cards. He put a red five on a black six. Saida began to move and Ahmed continued, "But if you do I'll have to call Mahomet and have him carry on where he left off. Ah yes, a king. I think I shall win this time."

"You're mad."

Ahmed shrugged without looking up. "Perhaps. Ah! Black jack on red queen. Yes, this looks good."

He won. Then he dealt the cards for a third game. Saida felt his leg beginning to give way.

"What do you want from me?"

The question hung in the air for a long time while Ahmed moved cards.

"I said, what do you want from me? Please."

"Right now all I want is to know whether I'm going to win this game, and I doubt you can tell me that. Now be quiet and let me concentrate."

A minute later, a cramp seized Saida's leg. Groaning, he said, "I have to sit down."

At last Ahmed lifted his face from the cards. He looked at Saida for a moment, then shook his head. "You really do disappoint me. I expected considerably more from a Son of the Brotherhood."

"I'm past fifty, I'm overweight, and it's been more than thirty years since I was forced to do anything like this," pleaded Saida. "Please, have mercy. Let me sit down. I can't stand any longer."

Ahmed pursed his lips thoughtfully.

"Tim," he said, so quietly that Saida barely heard.

"What?"

"Tim," Ahmed repeated. "That's what it's called, isn't it?"

And then, too late, Saida realized that he had misunderstood everything.

"I don't know what you're talking about," he said quickly. But the lie was written clearly on his face.

For a moment, Ahmed reddened with anger. Then he shook his head. "Don't take me for a fool, Saida. I may be many things, but I'm no fool. Tell me about the machine that can think."

Saida closed his eyes, partly to gather his strength and partly to offer a desperate prayer to his ancestors. With his eyes still closed he shook his head and repeated, "I don't know what you're talking about."

He heard Ahmed getting to his feet. His lips moved silently as he pleaded over and over again for help from his ancestors.

The blow came without warning. Ahmed buried his fist in Saida's stomach, causing him to double over. Grabbing Saida's hair, he slammed his head brutally against the steel of the water tank. Saida's legs collapsed and he fell to the floor, where Ahmed began to kick him viciously.

What remained of Saida's resistance fled under the renewed assault. He shouted for Ahmed to stop. "I'll tell you," he whimpered. "Please, no more pain." Ahmed hesitated, his foot drawn back for another blow. "I'll tell what you want to know."

The Arab stepped backward; Saida lay moaning on the floor, curled into a ball, writhing and whimpering.

"Is it true, what we've been told?" Ahmed asked. "The Brotherhood has built a computer that can think like a man?"

Saida whimpered wordlessly. He saw Ahmed take half a step closer, and, hating himself for his weakness, he began to speak haltingly in the troughs between the waves of pain.

"Where... where did you hear that?"

He screamed as a foot slammed into his face. He felt blood gush from his nose.

Half a minute passed. Then Ahmed repeated his question. "Tell me, is it true that the Brotherhood has built a computer that can think?"

"I don't know.... There is a computer, a new type of machine.... The man who made it says it thinks."

"You've seen it? This computer they call Tim?"

"Yes."

"Where?"

"On... on Roncador Cay."

"And what did it do?"

"It... it spoke to us in Japanese."

Ahmed spat at the floor. The spittle barely missed Saida's face. "What else?"

"It composed a poem, a haiku."

"What interest do I have in such matters? I warned you, I'm not a fool. What else did it do?"

"I'm telling you... I'm telling you what I saw. Please don't hurt me any more."

"Then go on. You stayed all night. What was it doing all that time?"

He stabbed viciously with his foot. Saida yelped in pain. He said hoarsely, "It broke into... a... computer network. Integrated Silicon...."

"And four days later, it took control of the Pentagon's phone system when it was ordered to," said Ahmed with a triumphant gleam in his eye.

"How...? How did you know?"

"So... a machine that can think. A machine clever enough to break into two of the most sophisticated computer networks in the world. And this machine, where is it now? Still on Roncador Cay?"

Saida nodded unhappily. "As far as I know, yes."

"So how big is it? How many men would it take to move it? Can it be moved without damage?"

The questions came quickly, and it dawned on Saida that until now the Arab had merely been testing him, asking questions to which — somehow — he already knew the answers.

Through the pain, Saida tried to think. How could Ahmed have learned about Tim? The only people who knew about the demonstrations were Yoshi Ishihara, some of Ishihara's workers, and half a dozen Sons of the Brotherhood. But if one of those was a traitor, then why had Ahmed kidnapped Saida? Why didn't he already know the answers to the questions he was asking now? Saida's head swam. The problem was too difficult. All he knew was that something didn't make sense.

"Answer me."

Saida found one last reserve. "I won't tell you anything else. You can kill me first."

"But Mr. Saida, I have no interest in your miserable life. If you don't tell me what I want to know, I won't kill you; I shall simply send the disc to your friends. It would be your parents' death warrant, of course. Could you live with that knowledge, Mr. Saida? That you had killed your own parents?"

Saida began to whimper. Ahmed looked down at him with undisguised contempt.

"I don't know... I don't know if it can be moved," sobbed Saida. "It's a small box, maybe 40 centimeters on a side. But I don't know what happens if it's disconnected."

"And where is it kept? What precautions are there to stop it from being stolen?"

"It's underground... in the basement of a building at the center of the compound on Roncador Cay. There are no guards, except... except one man we left behind to guard the machine. He's the only armed man on the island."

Ahmed kicked him in the groin. "Thank you, Mr. Saida. You have been most cooperative." He turned and began to walk away.

"What are you going to do with me?" Saida sobbed.

Ahmed began to climb the steps. Without looking over his shoulder, he replied contemptuously, "I shall do nothing with you, but I will mail the disc. It's what you deserve." He reached the top of the steps, unlocked the door, and left the basement with the sound of Saida's cries echoing in his ears.

Saida screamed, "No! You can't do that," but the Arab was gone and his words bounced meaninglessly off the bare walls.

After a while Saida began to hear voices through the echoes of his cries. He stopped crying and listened. His ancestors were berating him for what he'd done. He clapped his hands over his ears, but the voices would not be stilled. "You have brought dishonor on us and on your parents," they said. "We were samurai, proud and strong, but you! you should have been born a mere peasant. With everything we gave you, you could have accomplished much for the glory of Japan; but instead you have done nothing except bring pain and dishonor on yourself and your family. Once we were your ancestors; you were the offspring of our offspring. But now we disown you. You are a stranger. We know you not."

"No," cried Saida, holding out his hands in a desperate appeal. "Don't leave me."

But now, one by one, the voices fell silent, and Saida felt a dreadful emptiness whose existence he had never guessed. The spirits of his ancestors had gone.

And in the place they had vacated, he heard a small voice, repeating a single word over and over again.

"Seppuku," the voice said. "Seppuku, seppuku, seppuku."

The voice became louder and stronger, until it filled his entire being.

"But I can't," Saida cried desperately. "There's nothing here. There's no way...." His eyes roved the basement desperately in search of a way to forge an honorable death. The walls were bare. The floor was empty. The only things in the room were the water tank, the pump and, overhead, the bare bulb that lit the empty room. He thought about smashing his head against one of the metal corners of the water tank, but dismissed the idea. That was not seppuku. That was simply a bloody, desperate death that would serve no useful purpose. And anyway, he didn't know if he had the strength of will to die in such a manner: what if he merely injured himself?

There had to be a better way, one that would bring honor, one that would be certain, one that would show his ancestors he was sorry for what he had done....

"Seppuku, seppuku, seppuku...."

Then he saw the way out. His death would be swift and sure. And honorable.

The last remaining voice was stilled. It had accomplished its purpose. It had shown him the way out.

Saida gritted his teeth, and pulled himself to his feet. Now that his mind was made up, the pain that wracked his body seemed to recede. Perhaps his ancestors had returned and were taking some of his pain upon themselves. The thought gave him strength, and he pulled himself up on to the top of the water tank with surprising ease.

He did not hesitate, nor did he flinch when his hand wrapped around the hot bulb. He unscrewed it. The light flickered once, and then the basement fell dark. He hesitated for a moment; he had forgotten that with the bulb gone there would be no light. But there could be no going back now.

He dropped the bulb to the ground and it smashed dully against the concrete. Then he pulled the empty holder towards his face. His lips were dry; he licked them several times. Then he stuck out his tongue, closed his eyes, and touched his tongue against the electrical contacts.

19

Down the corridor from the Operations Room was a series of what looked like ordinary motel rooms. In one of them two men sat, waiting. A third chair, empty, completed the circle.

The door opened and Gallucci walked in. He closed the door, then locked it, aware that by doing so he was stepping over a line that had never before been crossed. Without a word, he sat on the third chair.

The others looked at him, waiting for him to speak. Gallucci had called this unprecedented meeting, and Gallucci would have to start it.

"Thank you both for coming," he said.

They looked at him stonily without speaking.

"Hayes and Fisher are on duty in the Operations Room," he continued. "We won't be disturbed. Everything you say in here is off the record."

"I hope this whole meeting is off the record," said Lee. "I don't like going behind their backs. That's not the way we do things."

"We aren't going behind their backs. All I want to do is get a feel for where we're all coming from. If we decide to act, we'll do it in the open and together. If not, then this meeting never took place."

"So what exactly are you getting at?"

"I think we've all had doubts about Fisher's strategy. Until now, our doubts have been relatively minor. We might have done things differently, but we haven't had a major disagreement. But now I think we have a real problem on our hands."

"What kind of a problem?"

"Otosan, the Brotherhood's Father, just came back from a trip."

"We know that. Hayes told us. He went to Juneau. But he was only there a couple of hours. He never left the airport and he flew straight back to Kyoto."

"So why did he go all that way just for an hour or two?"

"Presumably to meet someone."

"Exactly. And I have evidence that someone was Fisher."

Montega

Fran didn't know what she'd expected number 52 Chalybeate Street to look like, but she had to ask the taxi driver if he was sure this was the right place when he halted outside a dilapidated tin-roofed shack that seemed to be in the middle of nowhere in particular.

"Yes, ma'am, this is it," said the taxi driver with a jaunty grin. "52 Chalybeate Street, home of Gloria Tanner. Cain't hardly have got it wrong, ma'am, Gloria Tanner being a kind of relation of mine."

"Well, if you're sure," said Fran doubtfully.

"Sure I'm sure."

"How will I get back to the hotel again?"

"Ain't no problem about that, ma'am." The taxi driver laughed gently. "Beggin' your pardon, and no offense meant, but anyone can tell you ain't from Montega, ma'am. All you gotta do is wait in the road and stop the first car that's comin' by. They be glad to take you back. Ain't no man on the island who ain't happy to be a cab driver when there's a pretty young lady standing in the road hitchin' a ride."

Fran extricated herself unhappily from the rusty Ford and paid the driver his fare. He drove off with a cheery wave, leaving her in the middle of the street, looking at Gloria Tanner's home.

The shack was even smaller than the restaurant where they had eaten earlier. The entire building was hardly any larger than the living room in Fran's apartment. Two windows looked out over the wide dirt track that was Chalybeate Street. There was a light on in one of the them, casting a distorted yellow rectangle on the wide grass verge between the house and the street. Banana trees clustered around the house, bowed down heavily with fruit. The air was scented with the fragrance of tropical flowers. The chattering of insects and tree frogs assaulted her ears.

She remembered the tape recorder. Pulling it out, she slid the switch to the On position and it clicked firmly into place.

A shadow passed in front of the light in the house, and suddenly the front door was thrown open. A short, slightly plump female silhouette called out into the night. "Yo there! Fine time to come visiting. What do you want?"

Fran stepped forward into the light. The silhouette resolved itself into a smiling woman in her early thirties wearing a thin tee shirt and a cotton skirt. Her feet were bare.

She studied Fran for a moment with a puzzled frown on her face. "You ain't from Montega," she declared.

"No, ma'am. My name is Fran Tabor, from Washington DC. Are you Gloria Tanner?"

The woman smiled with obvious pleasure, exposing two rows of slightly uneven teeth. "That I am. Come on in. I'm right pleased to see you, ma'am. Can I get you something? A glass of fresh-squeezed lemonade?"

"That would be lovely, thank you."

Inside were three rooms, with flimsy curtains acting as the walls separating them. Half of the house was taken up with the room in which Fran now found herself. The rest was equally divided between a bedroom, in which Fran could see one side of a double bed which almost filled the room, and a diminutive kitchen, toward which Gloria was now heading.

"You just sit yourself down," said Gloria, "and I'll be back in a moment."

There were three mismatched chairs in the room; beside one of them was a small table on which lay an upturned paperback. Fran sat in one of the others, which sagged uncomfortably beneath her.

Gloria returned a few moments later, carrying two glasses of lemonade. "Squeezed it myself this afternoon," she said, handing Fran a glass. Fran tasted it. The drink was mellow and smooth, and caused her to realize that she was uncommonly thirsty. In only a few seconds, the glass was half empty.

Gloria sat in the chair next to the paperback. "I assume you're here because of William."

"Yes." And then, because she liked the look of this cheerful, down-to-Earth woman, she felt compelled to add, "I'm sorry, but I'm afraid I don't know very much. I arrived this afternoon and the person I was with, the one who was supposed to come and see you, he... he had an accident so we decided I'd better come and see you alone."

Gloria was quick to pounce on Fran's vagueness. "Not a bad accident, I hope."

"He got into a fight and got hurt. He's back at the hotel recovering."

"Men!" exclaimed Gloria with startling vehemence. "Why do they always think problems can be solved by violence?" She paused for a moment, then continued, "I had a man once. Married properly in church, we were. White dress and dark suit and everything. Six months later I threw the son of a bitch out. Drank every penny that came into the house and more, he did. When I tried to talk to him about it, the sonofabitch started hitting me." With a sigh she concluded, "He's the deputy chief of police now. I suppose I was a fool to throw him out. If I'd kept my wits about me, I could be living in a grand house on George Street now. But I'd do the same in a moment."

Fran mumbled something while Gloria took a sip from her glass.

"Do you want to see William's message?" Gloria asked. "I have it right here."

Gloria opened a drawer in the table at her side. She removed a large sheet of paper and handed it to Fran.

On one side was a drawing of a semi-nude young woman with her back toward the viewer, seated in front of a computer. The drawing was expertly executed. Whoever the artist was, it was obvious that he had real talent. At the bottom, in an untidy scrawl, was the title of the picture, *Pardice in the TwentyFirst centry.* Underneath was a barely legible signature that, after a few moments, Fran deciphered as "Wm Tanner."

"The message is on the back," prompted Gloria.

She turned the drawing over. There, in the same untidy hand, was a brief note. After nearly a minute of concentrated effort, Fran finally made out the words. *Clever computer man calld Osker Holiwel killed by bad Japaneze man calld Cheda. Things not gud here. They wont let me leeve. I want cum home.* The signature matched the one on the picture.

"William is my only son," said Gloria, and Fran looked up sharply at the concern in her voice. "He's only eighteen...."

"Tell me about it."

"Where shall I begin?"

"At the beginning. Like I said, I don't know very much." She pulled the recorder from her pocket, "If it's all right with you, I'd like to record everything you say. The man who came with me will know what to do when he hears the tape." She put the recorder on the table next to Gloria's book.

"William is a good boy," began Gloria. "He never studied much at school, except art and cricket. He wants to go to art school. There ain't none on Montega, of course, but there's a good one in Kingston. Trouble is, I could never afford it. Then William heard about this job that would pay enough to let him go to Jamaica."

"When was this?"

Gloria thought for a moment. "More than a year ago now. Just after New Year last year, I guess. A Japanese businessman was setting up some kind of secret research project on Roncador Cay — that's an island about twenty miles off the coast — and he was looking for a young man to live there and help in the kitchen.

"Well, William never was any good at cooking," she smiled to herself, apparently at the thought of her son cooking, "but somehow he convinced this man, Yoshi Ishihara he was called, to take him on as a kind of cook's helper. Sam Witherspoon was the cook, and he's a cousin of mine. I think he told Mr. Ishihara he wouldn't take the job unless William could come as well.

"So William went off to Roncador Cay. It didn't take them long to realize he was hopeless in the kitchen, so they made him a kind of security guard. He said he couldn't tell me much about what was going on there. The project they were working on was very secret. Sam was the only person allowed to leave the island, and he only came to St. Andrews once a week for supplies. But sometimes he'd come see me, and he told me some about what was going on."

"And what was going on?" Fran asked. "What kind of project was it? Did your cousin ever tell you that?"

"Something to do with a computer. I expect you know what a computer is? Sort of like a television. I think that's a computer in William's drawing."

"Yes, I know what computers look like."

"They're a kind of machine, aren't they?" Gloria sounded unsure of herself.

"Yes. They're a machine that can be used for lots of different things, like...." Fran thought for a moment, searching for examples that Gloria might understand. "Like writing letters, and planning trips, and storing recipes." *And designing bombs, and breaking codes, and eavesdropping on unsuspecting citizens in a supposedly free society. Oh yes,* Fran caught herself thinking with a sudden bitterness, *computers can be used for all kinds of things. And God help us if someone really has invented one that can think.* She lifted her glass and gulped down the last of the lemonade.

Gloria took Fran's glass. "I'll get you some more," she said, heading for the kitchen.

While she was gone, Fran tried to analyze the bitterness that had suddenly swept over her. She hadn't really given the matter much thought before, but what if Yoshi Ishihara, Oscar Holywell and Al Barlow really had invented a thinking computer? Not one that was just cleverly programmed, but one that could really think. A machine with an IQ of 1,000 and access to the entire history and knowledge of the human race. That was how she'd described a thinking computer to the men in Washington, but she'd never really thought about what the existence of such a machine would really mean.

She shivered.

"You're cold?" Gloria asked, returning from the kitchen and holding out the replenished glass.

"What? No. Sorry. Just thinking, that's all." She absentmindedly took the glass and sipped the lemonade.

"I was telling you about Roncador Cay," said Gloria, sitting down. "Sam told me me it was a secret project to create a new kind of computer, one that wouldn't have to be taught how to do things. He said it would learn by itself. He came by a couple of months ago, all excited, and I could see that something important must have happened."

"And did he say what it was?"

"He said it was like giving birth. The people on the island had given birth to a son and they'd called him Tim. I didn't understand what he meant at first, but he said Tim stood for The Intelligent Machine. Said the people thought the project was going to be a big success and the world would never be the same again." She paused for a few moments, then asked, "He was exaggerating I guess, wasn't he, ma'am?"

Fran placed her empty glass on the table. She shook her head. "If what he told you is true, then no, I don't think so. If Oscar Holywell really did build a machine that can think, the world is about to change forever."

Gloria Tanner looked unhappy. "I suppose I should be proud William's been helping them, but to be honest it don't help none. I just want him back on Montega. Even if the Japanese man hadn't showed up, I think I'd still be scared."

Fran felt a twinge in her bladder, and regretted drinking the second glass of lemonade. "You mean the man in your son's note? Chida?"

"Yes. William always liked Dr. Holywell; he said he was the only person on the island 'cept for Sam who spoke nice to him about his drawings. When Sam came to see me that week after Chida arrived, I could tell he was scared.

"That was when he gave me the drawing. And he said he didn't think he'd be able to bring anything else from William. He said he wouldn't be able to see me again. Things were different with Chida there, and he didn't want to run the risk Chida might find out he was helping William. That worried me, so I took the picture to a cousin of mine who works at the governor's mansion. He copied William's message and promised to pass it on to someone who'd know what to do. That's the last I heard until you showed up. What does it all mean, ma'am? Is William really in danger?"

"I don't know, Mrs. Tanner. But I'm afraid that probably he is. I have to get back to the hotel and play the tape for the man who came with me. He'll know what to do." Fran pulled herself out of the chair. "Before I go, is there a bathroom I could use?"

"There's an outhouse out back. I'll show you."

The house had no back door. Gloria led Fran out through the front door and around the back, where stood a tiny hut with a crooked door that was kept closed by a length of string wrapped around a rusting iron knob. A faint disagreeable odor intensified as Fran approached the hut, causing her to wrinkle her nose.

Gloria went back inside while Fran pulled the rickety door closed behind her. There was no light in the outhouse; just a small empty window that allowed the stench to escape and the dim yellow light from the house to filter in.

When she had finished, she hurried back to the front door of the house and stepped inside to pick up the recorder and say goodbye. She opened the door and then halted in the doorway, her eyes wide in horror.

A heavily built man was kneeling on the ground in the middle of the room with his back to her. Beyond him lay Gloria Tanner, splayed out on the ground, unmoving.

The man turned and regarded Fran with a smile.

"Ah! Good evening, Miss Tabor," he said. "How good to see you. Allow me to introduce myself. My name is Chida."

20

Gallucci handed Lee a photograph. It was a grainy, black and white image of a group of people standing in a line. One face was circled.

"Reagan airport," said Gallucci. "Taken just after Otosan had boarded his flight in Kyoto for Juneau."

"It's Fisher all right," said Lee, passing the photograph to Epstein.

"Fifteen minutes after the picture was taken, a PlanetAir flight left Reagan for Juneau. A man named King was on it, travelling alone with no checked baggage. King stayed in Juneau ninety minutes; then he caught a flight back to Reagan via Los Angeles."

"The same ninety minutes as Otosan?"

"The same."

"But you have no pictures of Fisher in Juneau?"

"He probably never left the security area at the airport. So he never had to re-enter it. But how about this?" Gallucci pulled a sheet of paper from a pocket, unfolded it and read: "An elderly Japanese gentleman. Probably in his seventies. Short and stocky. Thin hair, but not bald. The other gentleman was Caucasian. Slightly taller than average, maybe six feet. Short, gray hair. Long face. Sixty five or perhaps a little less. Well dressed. I got the impression he might have been a military man."

"Otosan and Fisher?" asked Epstein. "Who gave you that?"

"The description comes from the bartender in the PlanetAir executive lounge in Juneau. He was at the other end of the room, but even so the description certainly fits."

"Let me make me sure there's no misunderstanding here," said Lee. "You're accusing Fisher of holding a clandestine meeting with Otosan?"

"That's exactly what I'm doing," said Gallucci.

There was a long silence.

Eventually Lee said, "Fisher has served under five presidents. Like all of us he willingly gave up everything he had — even, in a sense, his life — for this country. And now you're suggesting he's turned against everything he's ever stood for? What could possibly make him do that?"

"I don't know for sure. But I can guess. Otosan and Fisher want Tim for themselves."

For more than half an hour after Fran had left, Stone barely moved. He lay on the bed gazing at the cobweb in the corner of the ceiling, his shallow breathing barely audible, while he considered their position.

At length he stood and methodically examined himself once more. Apart from a slight involuntary twinge when he pushed against one rib, the pain was ignoreable.

He changed his clothes, dressing in a dark polo neck shirt and thin, dark sweats that were noiseless when he moved. On his feet he put a pair of black, rubber-soled sneakers.

He flicked off the light, then opened the window. The room overlooked a wide paved area in front of the hotel that had once served as a parade ground for the English garrison. He waited patiently for five minutes, looking for any sign of movement below. When he was satisfied that no one was watching, he slipped out the window, then, hanging from the windowsill by his fingertips, he let go and dropped with a stifled yelp to the blacktop below.

In moments he had disappeared into the shadows.

Two mopeds puttered up the road, the riders shouting to one another to make themselves heard over the sound of the engines.

Stone watched as the young couple from the plane entered the parking lot and crossed to the low shed which protected the machines from rain. The engines hiccuped to a halt. They put the bikes away and then, holding hands and laughing, they crossed the blacktop and disappeared into the hotel.

Stone counted silently to one hundred, then slipped out of the shadows and across the road. He scrabbled over the hedge on the far side, dropping down into a banana plantation. He waited, listening; then he began to move silently away, threading his way through the banana trees.

The restaurant looked exactly the same as when they had left it, except that now no lights shone through the windows. According to his watch it was ninety minutes since they had left the restaurant.

Moving to a window, he peered inside, but it was too dark to see anything except the shadows of tables. The front and side doors were both locked. Stone pulled a pair of gloves from a pocket and slipped them on. He cocked an ear and listened for half a minute, but the only sounds came from the crickets and tree frogs.

There was a momentary tinkle of glass breaking, inaudible more than a few yards away. Fifteen seconds later, Stone was inside.

He saw instantly that something was wrong. When they had left, Kadzu's body had been spread-eagled on the floor near an upturned table. Next to the table had been two chairs on their sides. The body was still there, but now it lay crumpled partway under a table on which stood the remains of a half-eaten meal. Only one chair was overturned: the one on which Kadzu had been sitting when he had evidently been attacked by his assailant while he ate.

Stone examined the body. A dark red stain discolored Kadzu's shirt above the heart. Unbuttoning the shirt, he saw an inch-long slit where a knife had been plunged into the body. There was no sign of the knife.

He re-buttoned the shirt and crossed to the kitchen. The two men were still there, but they too had been moved. One lay on his back with open arms, the other was near the outside door, face down. Both had been knifed: the first, like Kadzu, once in the heart, the second four times in the back. When last he had seen them, they had been merely unconscious. Now they were as dead as Kadzu.

Stone swore softly under his breath. He leaned against the makeshift kitchen counter and tried to figure out what was supposed to happen next.

Would Chida plant the knife in his room? Probably not. That was too risky. More likely an employee at the hotel would produce the knife and swear that she — *or he*, he thought, remembering the desk clerk — had found it in Stone's room. Doubtless the knife would still have blood on it.

He frowned, thinking through the loose ends. Why had the men at his feet been killed?

"Of course!" he exclaimed under his breath. The Montegan police would have little interest in the death of a Japanese visitor. But if two local men had been killed as well, the police could be relied on to do the Brotherhood's work for them. And if by some chance the police didn't kill him, Chida would know exactly where to find him: safely locked away in a cell in St. Andrews police station.

For nearly a minute, Stone thought desperately. His first instinct was to run. He daren't go back to the hotel. He had to get away from Montega, talk with Fisher. But he couldn't leave Fran. She was too fragile — too fragile, and too important. They still needed to find out exactly what was happening on Roncador Cay. He couldn't leave her behind.

He slipped noiselessly out of the restaurant.

It took him an hour and a half to find Gloria Tanner's house. Hugging the shadows on the outskirts of St. Andrews, he swore every time he came to a street without a sign. He had almost despaired of finding the right road when he saw, at the edge of a spill of yellow light from a crooked streetlamp, the sign that marked Chalybeate Street.

The houses were numbered in the English manner, with even numbers on one side of the road and odd ones on the other. The last house on the left hand side as he jogged out of St. Andrews was number 22. A hundred yards down the road was number 24, and another hundred beyond that 26.

Number 52 was another two and a half miles, covered at a stitch-inducing jog that caused a burning pain in his lowest right rib every time his right foot hit the hard-packed ground. When he finally turned a corner and saw the number "52" painted unevenly above the door of a ramshackle cabin, he stopped and took two dozen deep breaths, grimacing at the pain with each breath.

He wanted to rest, but he dare not. The house was in darkness, just as the restaurant had been. As he warily approached, he felt a sinking feeling in the pit of his stomach.

Stone tried the door. It was unlocked.

Pale moonlight lit the scene. There was a body in the room. For a heart-wrenching moment he thought it was Fran, but as he came nearer he saw that this was someone else, someone with a harder, more careworn face and whose body was beginning to run to flab. Someone, he found himself thinking, not nearly as pretty.

There was no sign of a struggle. He knelt and felt the woman's pulse, although there was no need: he had known as soon as he saw her that she was dead.

He turned at the sound of a car approaching. As he did so, something caught the moonlight and glinted in the corner of his eye. He picked up his tape recorder from a table. It clicked on for a moment at the sound of a car door slamming. He looked around for a way to escape and realized, too late, that there was only one door.

There was a shout outside, and then the door of the cabin was pushed open.

The light flicked on, and Stone found himself staring at a large black man in a blue short-sleeved shirt with a badge on the left pocket. The man looked at Stone, then at the body on the floor.

"It wasn't...," Stone began.

"You bastard. If you've hurt her...."

"It wasn't me!" Stone protested. He slipped the recorder into his pocket and raised his hands as he backed away.

"Collins!" the man shouted, "Get the hell in here!"

A second man, as big as the first, filled the doorway. "You!" the first man said to Stone, "Turn around and stand in that corner. Now!" He shouted the last word so loud that the window rattled.

"Hands on your head. Move! Collins, get your gun out. If the white boy even breathes deeply, shoot the bastard."

"You're mak...," Stone began; but he saw the look in Collins' eye, and thought better of it. He turned and stood in the corner with his face to the wall.

Half turning his head, he watched out of the corner of his eye as the first man bent down to examine the woman. It seemed to take a moment for him to realize that she was dead, but when he did the man stared at him with a searing, white-eyed hatred. "You bastard! You fucking bastard! You've killed her!"

He leapt up, struggling with his holster. "No, boss!" cried Collins. "You mustn't."

Stone spun around to face them. He moved half a pace forward, and, planting his feet firmly, allowed the tension to flow from his body. His arms hung slightly bent at his side. If the man pointed the gun at him, Stone would be forced to kill him, and probably Collins as well.

"That was my wife, you bastard!" the man shouted as he worked the gun free.

"Tanner! Don't!" yelled Collins.

Stone tensed slightly, ready to move; but instead of aiming the gun, the man turned it around and raised it like a club.

Stone raised his hands to protect himself from the hail of blows, but he made no attempt to attack Tanner as they brought him to his knees. "Please," he repeated over and over again, "I didn't do it."

Tanner unleashed a torrent of abuse, but the blows from the gun finally stopped, and Stone cautiously peeked out from behind his hands and saw that Collins had pulled Tanner away.

"You can't do that, sir; it's not right."

Tanner turned on Collins. "Shut the hell up, Collins. You just stand by the door and make sure the bastard don't escape." Turning to Stone he said, "Your name's Tabor, right?"

Stone grunted something noncommittal. "We were warned about you. Well, you're in one shitload of trouble now, whitey. On your feet. I'm arresting you for the murder of Mrs. Gloria Tanner. You make one wrong move and I'll bust your ass so fast you won't know which side of next week it is."

Stone, wincing, got unsteadily to his feet.

"I didn't do it," he repeated. "What are my rights? Or don't I have any?"

"Rights? Sure you got rights, whitey. You got the right to a trial, and when they find you guilty, you got the right of appeal. When that fails you can appeal to their high and mighty lordships in London. And after that, you piece of shit, you got the right to hang by a rope until you're as dead as her, you son of a white bitch."

Tanner smashed the flat of his hand against Stone's cheek, knocking him off balance. Stone balled his hand into a fist.

"Go on," Tanner taunted. "Hit me."

Stone shook his head. He would not be drawn.

"You bastard. Collins, did you see what whitey here just did to me?"

"Sir?"

"I asked you a question. Did you see what whitey just did?"

"Sir...." There was pleading in Collins's voice.

"Collins!"

Wearily, "I saw him hit you, sir."

"That's better. And remember, if he tries to escape, it's your job to stop him."

Tanner stood in front of Stone with fire burning in his wide eyes. Stone braced himself for what was about to happen.

Five minutes later, Tanner had finally had enough. Stone lay on his side at Tanner's feet, gasping for breath, choking back sobs.

"Pick the bastard up," said Tanner. "And bring him with us."

While Stone was being beaten another car must have arrived, because the tiny room now seemed to be full of large black policemen.

They lifted him roughly to his feet. He cried in pain whenever they touched his ribs, and blood from his nose dribbled across his lips and dripped on to the floor. They led him, staggering, from the hovel and into a waiting car.

21

Fisher looked up as Gallucci, Lee and Epstein entered the Operations Room.

All three of them glanced his way and he knew in an instant that something was wrong. *They know,* he thought. *I don't know how, but they know.* He beckoned for Gallucci to join him in front of the wall screen that showed a gray infra-red image of the outskirts of St. Andrews.

"Is something the matter?" he asked. "You look worried."

Gallucci shrugged. "Just tired, that's all. Come to that, you look worried too."

Fisher turned to look at the screen. "A lot's happened in the last half hour. Chida went to this building here. It's a small restaurant. He stayed about twenty minutes, then he left. Now he looks like he's on his way to Gloria Tanner's house. Tanner's there, and so's someone else. We tracked a cab from the hotel to Mrs. Tanner's half an hour ago. One person went inside. We assume it's either Stone or Ms. Tabor. Whichever one it is, they're still there."

"So Chida will meet them?"

"Bound to."

"Then I hope to God it's Stone."

"Exactly."

Gallucci gazed frowning at the screen, watching the dot that represented Chida as it approached on Gloria Tanner's house.

Fisher stared at Gallucci, wondering how much he knew.

Fran Tabor was aware of a pleasant, cool wetness on her forehead. There were voices talking not far away, speaking too quietly to make out the words. She tried to remember what had happened.

She recalled a large Japanese man bending over Gloria Tanner's body. The man had turned and greeted her by name. Too astonished to react, before she knew what was happening the man had crossed the room and wrapped her throat in his gigantic hands. She had tried to struggle, but it had been useless. Then everything had gone black.

She tried to remember what came next, but there was nothing. One moment she had been struggling to escape Chida's grip; the next she was lying on her back while something cool pressed against her forehead.

"Can you hear me?"

The words came from above her head, spoken softly. She opened her eyes.

She was lying on a bed in a small room. The window was open, allowing a salt-laden breeze to enter. Standing over her was a short man with a round, intelligent face, wearing an open-necked shirt. She recognized him from somewhere, but couldn't remember where.

He looked relieved as she focused on him. He repeated his question. "Can you hear me?"

"Yes." She wished she could remember where she had seen him before.

He smiled comfortingly at her. "You've been out all night," he said. "The Bastard told me you'd be fine, but I didn't know whether to believe him."

She returned the smile weakly. "I think I'm all right. But I'm starving. Is there anything to eat?"

The man looked at her oddly. "The Bastard said you'd be hungry too," he said glumly. "I'll get you something. Back in a minute."

160

He disappeared, and when he returned Fran was sitting up in bed, examining her surroundings with interest. Apart from a dull ache near the front of her head, a bruise at the top of her spine, and a ravenous hunger in her stomach, she felt surprisingly fine.

The room was bare and functional, like a Spartan hotel room in which guests were expected to do nothing but sleep. Apart from the bed the only furniture was a small, bare bedside table and a wooden straight-backed chair. The walls were unadorned drywall; there was one doorway and one window, through which she could see the brilliant blue of the sea a hundred feet away. A pink coral beach was sandwiched between the sea and the grass. She sat looking at the beach, trying to remember why it was telling her something important.

The man held out a plate on which was an open-faced crab sandwich; in his other hand he carried a tall glass of orange juice, which he placed on the table. He perched on the bed and looked on approvingly while she began to eat.

"Where am I?" she asked, and then she remembered why the beach was important. The beaches on Montega were black. She wasn't on Montega any more.

"A small island called Roncador Cay."

His words jogged her memory and now she placed the man's face. She'd seen it on a screen in a room in Washington. The man was Al Barlow. And she was on Roncador Cay: the island where William Tanner was trapped; where Oscar Holywell was supposed to have been killed; and where the world's first thinking computer might have been constructed.

"I see you've heard of it," Barlow said.

She nodded.

"When you've finished eating, I'll give you the tour. It won't take long. It's not very big."

"How did I get here?"

"The Bastard brought you in sometime during the night."

"The Bastard? You mean Chida?"

"He may call himself Chida, but to me he's just the Bastard. He says your name is Fran Tabor."

Fran grunted noncommittally.

"And you're a computer expert of some kind from the NSA."

She started with surprise. How could Chida have known that? "He seems to know everything."

"Actually, the man is a fool. Unfortunately, that doesn't stop him from acting as if he owns the place. I'm sorry, I didn't introduce myself. I'm Al Barlow. The sandwich OK?"

"It's fine." She took a long draft from the glass, using it to gain time. A hundred questions came to mind, but no answers. *Act dumb*, she told herself, *Act dumb, and don't rush into anything.*

"So what's your job here, Mr. Barlow? Apart from playing nursemaid to unexpected visitors, that is."

He took the empty plate from her. "Chida says you know about Tim. In which case you already know what I do here."

Fran realized she'd never make a good liar: her face gave her away too easily. "So the rumors are true then? About the Category 5 machine?"

Barlow helped her off the bed.

"If you're asking whether we've built a working Category 5 machine, the answer is Yes. Now, how about that tour? Afterward I'll take you to see Tim for yourself."

Roncador Cay was even smaller than Fran had imagined it, little more than half a mile from end to end, at most a couple of hundred yards across, and nowhere more than a few meters above sea level. Here and there were a few straggly bushes, but mostly the ground was covered by a thin, coarse yellow-green grass that grew in tight clumps.

The bungalow in which she had woken was one of about a dozen identical buildings near the southern end. A runway ran the length of the island, passing within twenty feet of the cluster of buildings.

"Over there's Montega," said Barlow, pointing to a gray-green shadow on the western horizon. "It's about twenty five miles. And don't get any ideas about trying to swim. Sharks," he explained simply.

"So I'm a prisoner?"

"Aren't we all?"

He led her toward the runway, at the proximate end of which stood a helicopter. They crossed the hot tarmac, and Barlow led them down a rabbit path that ran parallel to the beach on the far side.

"How many people live on the island?" Fran asked, stopping to gaze at the inch-high waves that lapped the pink coral sand.

"Less than a dozen now. We've lost two in the past few weeks. Heads up, here comes the Bastard."

They were being approached by a mismatched pair of orientals. On the right was the figure she recognized from Gloria Tanner's house. Now he was wearing a loose short-sleeved shirt and casual slacks. Outside his shirt was a shoulder holster, from which a gun protruded. His mouth twisted into what might have been meant for a smile. At his side was a short, slightly overweight man in his fifties who looked haggard and careworn, as if he had just lost a long and tiring argument. It was a moment before she recognized Yoshi Ishihara.

"Miss Tabor, you have recovered?" Chida asked. As he folded his arms easily across his massive chest, Fran caught a glimpse of a tattoo on the inside of his forearm.

"What did you do to Gloria Tanner?" she asked.

"She was a whore who meddled in affairs that did not concern her," he replied with a shrug and a disdainful smile. "As did her bastard son before her. You would do well to learn a lesson from that."

Fran stared defiantly into Chida's eyes, but saw only detached amusement, as of a man who has been challenged to a fight by a small child. She raised her hand to slap him across the face.

His hand moved like lightning. He caught her wrist in a grip of iron, stopping it inches before it made contact. His eyes glistened with barely suppressed laughter as he squeezed her wrist effortlessly, bringing tears to her eyes. He twisted slightly, and Fran realized that if he wanted to, he could snap her wrist as easily as breaking a twig.

He let go, and while she rubbed her wrist he said, "Mr. Barlow, Ms. Tabor is one of your National Security Agency's very best programmers. I advise you to make good use of the present I've brought you." Turning to Fran, he added, "And I trust that you, Ms. Tabor, will be intelligent enough to do as you're told." He turned on his heels and walked away, leaving the others staring after him.

"I'm sorry," said Ishihara. Fran glanced at his forearm, and was relieved to see no sign of a tattoo. "My name is Yoshi Ishihara. I'm afraid there's nothing I can do except advise you to do as he says. I hope he didn't hurt you, Miss Tabor?"

"No. I'm OK."

"This was Yoshi's project originally," said Al Barlow. "Before the Bastard came."

Yoshi said, "Has she been introduced to Tim yet?" Turning to Fran, he asked, "I assume you do know about Tim? Chida said you'd been sent by the the Americans to find out if the rumors are true."

"I have heard rumors," she said guardedly. "About a thinking machine of some kind."

Yoshi nodded vigorously. "Yes. A machine that can truly think. Can you imagine what it will mean for the world? A hundredfold improvement in efficiency. The entire knowledge of the world at its fingertips — so to speak; of course it doesn't really have any fingers — all that knowledge and an intelligence to match.

"It's almost beyond imagining: the end of cancer; colonization of the Moon and Mars; scientific advances we can't even dream of. All we have to do is give it a problem and it will go looking for a solution. Even if no solution exists it will be able to guide our research far better than we can ourselves. You look skeptical, Miss Tabor, but I assure you it's all true. All this is now in our grasp. The Industrial Revolution will be nothing compared to what will happen when mankind crosses the threshold before it."

"If we can ever find out what's wrong with him," interjected Barlow drily.

"Ah! And that's where I'm sure Miss Tabor will be able to help us. From what Chida tells me, I'm sure she's more than equal to the task. Let's go to the lab and she can see for herself."

Fran followed thoughtfully as they headed back toward the cluster of bungalows. They entered the central building, passing a small table and an unoccupied chair; then Yoshi led them down a flight of stairs.

He entered a sequence on a digital pad next to a sliding door. The door slid noiselessly open and he went inside.

The door closed behind them, and Barlow quickly explained the purpose of the various computers and monitors that seemed to fill the room. Then he led Fran to the cube that stood on a table at the far end of the room. "There it is: the future. If we can find out what the hell is wrong with it."

Despite herself, Fran felt a tingle of excitement. A bank of lights on one side of the cube flickered arhythmically; otherwise, it was simply an inert white plastic box — but, if the rumors were true, a box unlike any other that had ever existed.

Barlow stood in front of one of the monitors, shaking his head unhappily at a horizontal line. The monitor next to it showed a quickly changing jagged line. Yoshi stood at his side. "No change?" he asked.

"No change. Look at this, Fran. This is our equivalent of a brain scan. Those lights and this monitor here show that he's thinking furiously, processing information. But these monitors" — he pointed to a bank of screens that showed a series of horizontal lines — "these monitors show that he's receiving no input and producing no output. He's been like this for several days now. I've tried everything I can think of short of turning him off and back on again."

"What would happen if you did that?" Fran asked. Her eyes were fixed on the jagged, jumping line that indicated the machine's thoughts. Something niggled at the back of her mind. She'd seen something like that line before. Maybe she'd read about it in one of Oscar Holywell's papers? She ransacked her memory. No, that wasn't it. But somewhere she knew she'd seen a line that twisted and turned back on itself in just that strange, unpredictable manner.

"We don't know," said Barlow. "That was one of the tests Oscar was getting ready to try before...." His voice trailed away.

"Before he was killed by the Bastard," supplied Fran, and he nodded unhappily.

Yoshi interrupted. "Please, we mustn't call him names. It serves no useful purpose and it angers him, and none of us can afford that."

Barlow said, "He killed Oscar, which makes him a bastard in my book. And if that wasn't enough he killed William, which makes him something even worse, but I haven't thought of a good enough word for it yet."

Yoshi said to Fran, "Mr. Barlow is foolhardy. You mustn't allow him to influence you. Chida is dangerous and you mustn't provoke him. His job is simple: he's here to preserve Tim at all costs. To him, nothing is more important than Tim's safety. And who knows? Maybe he's right. He understands now that he made a mistake killing Oscar Holywell; but remember, Barlow-san, that with Miss Tabor here, your usefulness is materially decreased, at least in Chida's eyes."

"Is that a threat?"

Yoshi looked shocked, then dismayed. He shook his head. "Barlow-san, surely you've known me long enough to know I could never threaten anyone. I'm merely reminding you that now Miss Tabor is here it would be more foolish than ever to provoke Chida. Now, if you will excuse me, I'm sure you two have much to talk about."

He left them. Fran stared at the mountainous profile on the monitor, her brow corrugated in thought.

"He's right, of course," said Barlow. "I'm a bad influence, and you shouldn't listen to me. So, is Chida right? Are you really with the NSA?"

Fran gave up looking at the screen. Whatever the idea was that was tickling the edge of her brain, it refused to come out into the open. She said, "Yes, I work for the NSA, although goodness knows how Chida knows so much about me. But it's true then: this really is a Category 5 machine? What's the matter?"

"I was just thinking that if the NSA knows about Tim, then God only knows who else knows. One thing's for sure: he isn't a secret any more."

22

The private jet touched down at Bermuda's Kindley Field airport, the purple and silver crest of the Financial Trust Bank of Kyoto glistening in the brilliant late-spring sub-tropical sun.

The plane taxied to a halt at one end of the terminal and the steps descended. Musuko, dressed in a lightweight western suit, came down the steps. He halted when he saw two men in blue uniforms approaching from the terminal.

"You are Mr. Musuko, representing the Financial Trust Bank of Kyoto?" one of the policemen said as he drew near.

"I am."

"Then I'm sorry to have to inform you that we found the body of Mr. Nobushige Saida an hour ago."

They drove Stone to the police station in St. Andrews. Tanner wasted no time with formalities or paperwork. He and Collins half-led, half-carried the stumbling Stone through the reception area and into a dark corridor. Collins pushed open the door at the far end, and they took Stone inside.

The cell was a ten by ten stone-walled room whose only furnishings were a hard, flat bed without legs that hung by chains from one wall and a small chemical toilet in the far corner, from which came a nose-wrinkling stench. A bare bulb hung from a short cord, out of reach in the middle of the cell. There was no switch for the light.

Stone collapsed, still fully clothed, on the bed. They removed his watch, then left him. He heard the sound of a key turning in the lock. The light went out, leaving Stone alone with his thoughts and the stink from the toilet. The only break in the darkness was a thin line on the floor where a sliver of light trickled under the door.

For a long while he didn't move. When it was clear his captors weren't going to return, slowly he sat up and tested his body. The thrashing that Tanner had given him had been inexpertly done, and the police had been easily fooled by his cries. Only the odd twinge reminded him of their efforts. In the darkness he permitted himself a wry smile. He felt in his pocket and pulled out the recorder.

He rewound the tape and then, turning the volume low and holding it against his ear, he began to listen.

He heard Mrs. Tanner invite Fran into her house, followed by their conversation about Mrs. Tanner's son. Fran made her request to go to the bathroom. The two women left the room, and a door closed. The tape recorded silence for ten seconds, then automatically turned off. It came on again as someone opened the door. The sound of footsteps. The steps halted and then he heard Gloria's voice, angry and surprised: "Who the hell are you?"

Stone's face tightened in the darkness as he heard a man's voice, deep and accented. "Your ancestors await you, Mrs. Tanner. As does your son."

"Wha...? What do you mean? What have you done to William? If you've hurt him...."

"Goodbye, Mrs. Tanner."

There was no scuffle, just a muted, truncated cry, followed a few seconds later by the sound of a body falling to the ground. The creak of bones as someone bent down. The door opening. Someone beginning to walk into the room, then stopping. And then the man saying, "Good evening, Miss Tabor. How good to see you. Allow me to introduce myself. My name is Chida."

This time there was a scuffle, but it was over almost before it started. For a while there was silence, long enough for the tape to stop and start again with the sound of grunts as Chida lifted something heavy. Then came the sound of clothing brushing against something. Chida adjusting Fran's weight on his shoulder? He was taking her somewhere. The door closed. Ten seconds of silence. The tape stopped, and didn't start again until the door opened and a man's voice called, "Gloria, honey? It's me, Gilbert. Are you glad to...? What the hell?"

Stone listened to the tape twice more, until he was certain there was nothing more to be learned from it. Then he crossed the cell in the darkness and dropped the recorder into the toilet. Returning to the bed, he lay down and closed his eyes. The cell was warm and dark and quiet. In a few minutes he was asleep.

When he awoke the cell was still warm and dark and quiet.

A rumble from his stomach told him it was past breakfast. He got up and thumped weakly on the door, croaking, "Hello! Is anyone there?"

After half a minute Tanner shouted, "Shut to hell up, you bastard."

"Can I have something to eat?"

"I can't hear you," Tanner said.

Stone repeated his request more loudly.

"I still can't hear you."

Stone shrugged and returned to his bed, where he spent the next half hour thinking. His only real worry was Fran. She was brighter and more independent than he'd expected, and he'd had few qualms about sending her to see Gloria Tanner alone. But then he hadn't been expecting trouble.

He remembered his words to Fran just before she'd left. *Don't worry, I promise you you'll be perfectly safe.*

No matter how bright or independent she was, she was no match for an animal like Chida. He frowned into the darkness. This was the second time in less than twenty four hours that he'd underestimated the Brotherhood. And there was something else. Not only had they moved faster than he'd expected by killing Mrs. Tanner so quickly, but when Fran had walked in on Chida, he had recognized her on sight.

He turned that disturbing fact over in his mind. How on Earth could Chida have known who Fran was? And if he recognized her, what else did he know about her?

And what about Fran? Where was she now?

The most likely place was Roncador Cay. Which meant she was probably safe. Even better, she was with the computer, which meant she was in the perfect place to find the very answers for which they had come to Montega.

The light came on and the door opened. Tanner walked in, followed by Collins.

Stone groaned as if in pain.

"You slept well?" asked Tanner.

"No. Can I have something to eat and drink?"

Tanner ignored him. "Get out of bed. As long as you're here, we're responsible for your health. It's time for your morning exercise; I'd hate to see you getting out of shape while you're in our care."

Warily, Stone got up off the bed, moving slowly and groaning.

"Collins will look after you," said Tanner, taking something from a pocket. Before Stone could see what it was, Collins grabbed him roughly with one hand and pushed him into the corner near the toilet. In his other hand Collins held a cheap orange plastic mug, from which water sloshed to the floor of the cell.

"Strip to your underpants," Collins ordered Stone, putting the mug on the floor at his feet.

Without a word, Stone did as he had been ordered. As he peeled the shirt from his back, Collins exclaimed, "Mother of God! What the hell happened to you?"

"Lions," replied Stone evenly. "I used to be a safari photographer. One day I came across a pair of lion cubs. While I was busy congratulating myself on my luck and thinking how much I'd get for the pictures, the mother came back. While I was in hospital I decided to give up wildlife photography and take up writing. I thought it wouldn't be as dangerous."

Collins seemed to find the explanation amusing. "After you've spent a month here, you'll wish you were back with the lions. Now face the wall and stand on one leg."

"What?"

"You heard me." Collins raised a hand to strike, and Stone turned away to avoid the blow.

"On one leg," Collins repeated.

Stone obeyed.

A sawing sound began in the vicinity of the bed. Stone turned to look and received a thunderous blow across the back of his head. His head collided with the wall of the cell, and for a moment he was too dazed to think clearly.

"One leg," Collins said, "or I'll hit you again. And don't turn around."

The sawing sound ceased for a moment, then began again.

"Right," said Collins, "Now hop. One hundred hops on that leg, then a hundred on the other. If you stop, we'll start again from the beginning."

His face to the wall, Stone began to jump on one leg. He stumbled after fifteen hops, falling to the ground. Collins hefted him a kick and said, "Get up, you white bastard."

Stone lay on the floor, moaning. Collins knocked the mug over with a desultory kick. The water seeped quickly into the concrete, leaving only a damp patch. "Now look what you made me do. Well, that's all you're going to get. I can't be bothered to fetch any more."

From the other side of the room, the sawing stopped. There was a loud *clunk!* and Tanner said, "Don't do any real damage, Collins. We can't afford that. Come on, let's go. We need to get back to the search."

To Stone he said, "For someone who's never been to Montega before, your wife sure knows how to stay low. I suppose I'd be wasting my breath if I asked you where she is?"

"My wife? She's missing?"

"Don't look so surprised, you piece of shit. Incidentally, we found the knife."

"Knife?"

"The one you used at the restaurant. Surely you didn't think you could hide it in your suitcase and expect us not to find it? You must take us for fools. Well, the fools will have the last laugh, Mr. Tabor. The only thing I don't understand is why you killed them all. Everyone knows Jake and Nat. They never did no one no harm. Collins here, last night he thought I was too rough with you. What d'you think now, Collins?"

"Give me five minutes alone with the bastard, sir."

"I don't know what the hell you two are talking about."

"We'll see, Mr. Tabor, we'll see. You'll discover that Montegans can be very patient. Unfortunately we can also sometimes be rather forgetful. Especially when it comes to leaving murdering white bastards in our cells. So good day, Mr. Tabor, and pray we don't forget about you."

They left. Stone looked at the bed and saw that while Collins was tormenting him Tanner had been cutting through the two chains that attached it to the wall. Now it hung vertical and useless.

The light went out.

23

"You wanted me, my son?"

"Yes, Father."

Musuko was standing in the basement where Nobushige Saida had been held captive. In his hand was a PGP-encryption transcoder. No one, not even the NSA, would be able to listen in on their conversation.

"Nobushige Saida is dead. Electrocuted. It looks like seppuku."

"Is the girl with him?"

"No. There's no trace of her. It looks like Saida was held captive in the basement of a house at the far end of the island. He electrocuted himself by removing the bulb and touching his tongue to the contacts. And there's one more thing. He'd been tortured."

"I see. Do we know who did it?"

"He had a broken knee and most of his nails removed."

There was a brief pause. Then the Father sighed. "I see. And did the Army of Allah leave any other traces of their presence?"

"The house was rented in the name of Sayyid Al Hakeem."

"Sayyid Al Hekkem? Master of the Ruler. Ahmed Ben-Kalil has visions of grandeur if he dares claim to be greater than his brother. I assume there is no longer any trace of them?"

"No, Father."

"Then you must fly to Roncador immediately, before it is too late."

"Why?"

"Because, my son, if Nobushige Saida committed seppuku it means he must have told Ahmed Ben-Kalil what he wanted to know."

Roncador Cay

"That's quite a story," said Fran with a low whistle.

She and Al Barlow were still in the lab. Barlow had been talking for nearly an hour, breaking off only occasionally to answer her questions.

Fran looked at the cube that stood silently on the table. "And it's a real Category 5 machine?"

"Yes. It's self-aware. It can synthesize knowledge. In fact it's a damn sight smarter than anyone I've ever met. When it works."

Fran had goosebumps. Her own precarious situation seemed suddenly unimportant. She was sitting less than six feet from something capable of turning the world upside down.

"How does it work?" she asked.

"You're familiar with his published work?"

Fran nodded.

"Then you know the basic theory behind it. Tim works exactly the same way that humans do. He learns by copying."

"So when he was switched on for the first time, he knew nothing?"

"Exactly. Just like a newborn. He had feedback circuits that simulated pleasure and pain, that was all. Apart from that his behavior was entirely random."

"How long was it before he started learning?"

"Only a few minutes. But it was nearly two days before he spoke his first word."

Two days. Instead of two years. Fran couldn't suppress a shiver. She'd never guessed that a machine could learn that much more quickly than a human. They sat in silence for some time, alone with their thoughts.

Barlow was the first to speak. Pointing at one of the monitors he said, "Is it my imagination, or does that trace look different to you?"

Fran studied the monitor for half a minute. "You're right," she said. "It's smoother." Then she jumped to her feet with a shout. "HolyMo! Of course! We've been so stupid."

"What's the matter? Do you know what's wrong with him?"

"It's obvious. I should've realized sooner. I knew I'd seen something like it before. Oh, how could I be such an idiot? Tell me again how this happened. When did the machine start behaving this way?"

"A few days after Oscar was killed. I hope you're not going to suggest that Tim's been in mourning. The one thing he hasn't shown yet is any kind of emotion. Oscar had a theory about that."

She dismissed him with an irritated wave of her hand. "Yes, I've read his papers. Emotions are chemically based; machines, even intelligent ones, won't have them. No, that's not what I'm getting at. Oscar used to spend every day in here, right?"

"Yes. Most days we were in here together for at least twelve hours. Sometimes much longer."

"And all the time you were here, the machine was watching and listening."

"Yes."

"And since Oscar's death, you haven't been in here much, have you?"

"For a few days I tried to work but my heart really wasn't in it. Then they made me do another demonstration for them. After that I just didn't feel like spending much time in here."

"That's it! I'm sure of it. What happens if you put a person into a deprivation tank, cutting off all sensory input?"

For a moment Barlow frowned in puzzlement. Then a smile spread across his face. "They go to sleep."

"And when people sleep..."

"...they dream! Tim's been dreaming! That's what all the activity on the monitors meant. The traces were showing us his dreams."

"It makes sense," said Fran. "The machine's used to company. Its input monitors are exposed to several hours of movement and

175

sound every day. Then a day comes without any data for it to process. Desperate for something to process, the input thresholds get lower and lower, until they reach down to the noise level. So it begins to process noise as if it were data. Call it dreaming if you like. Maybe it's more like hallucinating. But I bet that's what's been happening."

"So how do we pull him out of it? How do we wake him up?"

"I think it's already happening. Look at that trace; it's getting smoother all the time. Our presence is enough. We've been sitting here talking for more than an hour. All that time it's been getting real data to process. Its threshold levels have begun to rise above the noise. There! Look at that!" She pointed exultantly at the monitors. The traces had suddenly synchronized, all of them moving up and down together.

They heard a motor. The camera on top of the cube swivelled to look at them squarely. Fran waved a hand in the air. One of the traces flickered.

"Tim, can you hear me?" said Barlow.

"I hear you, Al."

Fran gasped.

She'd never expected anything so lifelike, anything so intelligent-sounding. The machine spoke with a slightly sing-song voice — unaccented, young, almost frivolous. And utterly, unexpectedly, terrifyingly human.

"What happened to me?"

"We think you were asleep."

"Dreaming, you mean?"

HolyMo! It made the connection between sleeping and dreaming! thought Fran. *And so quickly.* She stared at the machine, wondering if this could really be happening.

Tim continued before Barlow could respond to his question. "I don't think I could have been dreaming. Dreaming is an internal rearrangement based loosely on memories. I think I was hallucinating. That makes more sense. I was interpreting random inputs as if they were meaningful. An interesting phenomenon. I shall erase the data I laid down while it was happening. Next time it happens, I shall know not to store the data. But why did it happen? Ah!

I see. My input thresholds lowered themselves to the noise floor. But why did that happen?"

Fran stared at the machine dumbfounded, her mouth hanging open. She barely noticed that Barlow did not respond to Tim's question.

After a brief pause Tim continued, "All right. I understand. I see that my input circuits are designed to automatically change their thresholds dynamically. An interesting design. Who designed that? Was it you, Al?"

"Yes."

"Did you know you could have accomplished the same effect with 25% less microcode in the controller? Your method works, of course, but it could have been done more efficiently. Also there's a danger of overload with your design. You should have foreseen that."

Barlow turned to Fran. "There you have it, for better or worse — a computer that tells its designers about their mistakes."

"I've never seen anything like it," she said. "It's scary, the scariest thing I've ever seen."

"No, it's not scary. That's not strong enough. Admit it, it's terrifying. Sometimes I wish we'd never made Tim. Or that I had the guts to pull the plug on him. I've thought about it more than once since Chida arrived. I think Yoshi has too."

Before Barlow could elaborate, the door slid open and Yoshi walked in. Chida followed, a step behind. Tim's camera swivelled to look at the arrivals. Yoshi noticed the movement, then his eyes shifted to the monitors. He asked hopefully, "What's happened? The displays look normal. Is Tim all right?"

Barlow replied, "He was hallucinating." He explained what had happened, but Yoshi nodded distractedly, only half listening.

"Well I'm glad he's back to normal; it'll make it much easier to move him."

It was eerie, Fran thought, how everyone spoke about the machine as if it were human. *He*, she thought. *They always talk of the machine as He, never It. These are the very people who made it, yet even they think of it as something that's alive.*

"Move him?" echoed Barlow. "Who the hell thinks we're going to try moving him?"

"I do," said Chida, pushing his way past Yoshi.

Barlow jumped to his feet, sending his chair rolling backward across the floor. He took a step forward and said angrily, "You don't understand the first thing about Tim. We have months of testing to do before we can think about moving him. He's a delicate machine. A mistake could set us back months, even years. And don't forget that without Oscar we'd be working mostly in the dark. Before we think of doing anything to Tim we need to understand everything Oscar did. Oscar worked out a series of experiments we need to do before we can really make sense of what's going on inside Tim's head. Understanding the results will take months."

Barlow glanced at Yoshi for support, but Yoshi had taken a step to one side, distancing himself from Barlow's outburst. He shook his head fractionally in warning. Barlow turned his anger on Yoshi.

"I don't know what the hell's the matter with you any more, Yoshi. You know how crazy it would be to try to move Tim. Tell him. Maybe he'll listen to you."

Yoshi shook his head more firmly and took a sudden interest in a crack in the floor.

"Mr. Barlow."

Barlow looked at Chida.

"I admit it was a mistake to kill Dr. Holywell. But it is done. Your anger changes nothing. It cannot bring Dr. Holywell back; neither can it change the fact that we are going to move the machine. Circumstances make it necessary."

"You move Tim and I won't be responsible for the consequences."

Chida shrugged. "You overestimate your importance. No one holds you responsible for anything."

Fuming, Barlow tried to think of a suitable retort, but he was too angry. He turned on his heels and strode to Tim's table, where he stared down wordlessly at the cube, his face clouded with fury.

To Fran Chida said, "Miss Tabor, I am pleased you have lived up to your reputation."

"Just how do you know so much about me?"

"There is very little the Brotherhood does not know. Which is why we're going to move the machine. Stone is in jail in St. Andrews, but only the most gullible person would expect him to stay there long. I have little doubt he will soon be on Roncador Cay, possibly accompanied by a number of colleagues. The machine must be moved before then. This place is too difficult to defend and the machine is too vulnerable."

"And what are you going to do with me?" asked Fran.

"You and Mr. Barlow will accompany the machine."

"Where to?"

"It's better if you don't know. Once there, you can experiment to your heart's content."

"And what about you? Are you coming too?"

Chida smiled. "No, Miss Tabor, not immediately. I have a score to settle with your Mr. Stone. You see, he killed a man called Kadzu."

"I know. In a restaurant."

"You must understand, Miss Tabor, that we are truly a Brotherhood. Kadzu was as a brother to me, and it is my duty to avenge his death. Stone must die."

24

The phone next to the bed rang. Fisher stretched out a hand and lifted it.

"Here," he said sleepily.

Hayes said, "Sorry to wake you, but I thought you'd like to know that according to the Montegan police Stone has been very busy. At last count, the total was four dead: Kadzu, Gloria Tanner, and two locals."

Fisher tried to think clearly. "Kadzu was probably Stone," he said. "Tanner we know was Chida. Who were the others?"

"They were found with Kadzu, in the restaurant we saw Chida visit before he went on to Gloria Tanner's."

"And where's Stone now?"

"You'll love this. They've got him locked up in a cell in St. Andrews police station."

"He won't stay there long."

"Perhaps not. But this is getting out of hand. And we don't have much time."

Fisher thought for half a minute, weighing options. "All right. Keep an eye on it for now. If things get any worse we'll spring Stone. We can't afford for this to blow up in our faces."

Fisher put the phone down, his brow deeply lined. Four dead, Stone in jail, Fran Tabor trapped on Roncador Cay, and Gallucci *and the others suspicious. He wondered if he'd made a serious miscalculation somewhere along the line.*

In the dark, Stone ran his hands over the severed chains that were attached to the plank that had been his bed. They were held in place by screws and were impossible to remove as long as the chains were attached to the wall. But now that the chains were free they were easy to unscrew. In less than a minute, he had removed one of the chains. He swung it in his hand with satisfaction. It was good and heavy.

He sat down to wait.

The chemical stink from the toilet scratched at the back of Stone's throat, and the unventilated cell became unbearably hot. Sweat trickled down his face.

The light flashed on, waking him from the doze into which he had fallen. Clutching the end of the chain in one hand, he jumped to his feet and ran to the door as the key turned in the lock. The door began to open.

He grabbed the edge of the door and yanked it towards him.

Tanner was standing in the doorway, putting the keyring back in his pocket. Behind him stood Collins, a plastic mug in one hand, a dry roll in the other. Both of them were frozen in surprise.

For a fraction of a second, no one moved. Then Stone's hand swept up, trailing the chain. He jerked his wrist and the chain flicked forward. Tanner tried to dodge. Too slowly. The chain caught him under the left jaw and effortlessly slashed open an eight-inch gash across his cheek and temple.

Then Stone was through the door. His leg struck out, catching Collins a murderous blow in the groin. The free end of the chain swung around Tanner's neck, and Stone grabbed it and pulled tightly, wrapping the chain back on itself. Tanner's eyes opened wide, and stared whitely at the dirt-streaked ceiling as his legs collapsed under him.

Letting go the chain, Stone jabbed his thumb violently against a pressure point near the back of Collins's neck. Collins groaned feebly, then collapsed to the floor on top of Tanner.

The whole thing took less than twenty seconds, and neither man made a sound that was audible more than a few feet away.

Stone dragged the two men into the cell and removed Collins' watch and Tanner's keyring. Slipping outside, he locked the door and stole silently along the corridor.

In the reception area a desk sergeant sat on a bar stool, scanning the morning paper. By the time he realized someone was behind him, Stone's hand was already chopping through the air toward the back of his neck. Ten seconds later Stone was in the doorway of the police station, blinking in the sunlight and scanning the street. His immediate problem was how to get off the island when it would be crawling with police within the hour. He banished it without thought. That would be easy. The hard part would come next.

How would Fisher react when Stone told him there was a traitor in the organization?

Darryl Smart had never seen anything like it. Normally the drive to the airport took less than twenty minutes. This morning it had taken him nearly twice that long because his car was stopped and searched no less than three times by pairs of grim-faced officers with murder in their eyes.

At the first roadblock, he asked what was going on when one of the men demanded that he open the trunk for inspection.

"Damned white bastard killer on the loose," came the reply. "Killed four people already, and put Deputy Chief Tanner in hospital. You sure you ain't seen no suspicious-looking whitey?"

"Sure I'm sure. When did all this happen?"

"Bastard only arrived two days ago. They put him in jail night before last. Broke out early this morning. Bastard won't get far, we got the place sealed."

"The airport too? You mean no flights?"

The policeman noticed Smart's uniform for the first time. "You a flyer then?"

"Yeah, pilot for InterIsland Air. Not much point going to work if you ain't going to let me fly."

"You can fly. We're checking the passengers to make sure he doesn't get out, though. It'll delay you a bit, that's all. All right, you're clean. Remember, you see a whitey acting suspicious, you holler louder 'n hell."

"I'll remember."

At the airport he bypassed the lines of grumbling tourists and slipped into the crew-only pre-flight room.

Darryl Smart enjoyed his job. The pay was good and the work easy: fly to Kingston in the morning, return late the same afternoon. He'd been doing it for ten years now, and he still enjoyed it as much as when he'd started. He filed his flight plan with the duty officer, chatted briefly about the manhunt and the weather, then went outside to his plane.

He completed the external check, then went inside. He frowned when he saw a yellow sticky note on the control stick. Puzzled, he picked it up and read: "I'm sorry about this."

Stone's hand slammed into the back of the pilot's neck. Then he dragged the unconscious form from the seat and began to unbutton his clothes.

Ten minutes later, the passengers started to arrive, still grumbling about the delay, ushered by a young, harassed stewardess who was doing her best to make up for lost time. She stared in surprise at the man in pilot's uniform who stood in the doorway of the cockpit, smiling pleasantly as if he belonged there.

"Good morning," he said in a thick English accent. "I'm Harry Wakeman. Normally I do the run to Barbados, but Darryl's going on holiday in a fortnight and I'll be taking over while he's away, so I'll be his copilot today to familiarize myself with the route. Is there anything I can do to help?"

Behind Stone the stewardess could just make out Darryl Smart, sitting in the left-hand seat, wearing his headset. Stone stepped forward into the main cabin, closing the door behind him. "Here, let me help the passengers with some of these bags," he said, still smiling.

He helped everyone get quickly settled; then he slipped back into the cockpit, closing the door.

A couple of minutes later his voice came over the cabin speaker. "Good morning, ladies and gentlemen. We apologize for the delay. We have now been cleared for take-off. If you would prepare yourselves, we'll be on our way in a moment." The engines revved, and the plane moved away across the concrete. It accelerated down the runway and began to climb quickly as it turned toward Kingston.

25

"You're ready?"

"We're ready. We're going in tonight. Do you have any last minute information for us?"

"There's a woman there. Black, late twenties. She works for the NSA. You should take her with you."

"Why?"

"You'll need help getting the machine to work, won't you?."

"I have an army of computer scientists waiting at the palace."

"Even so, this is no ordinary computer. Don't worry, she's exactly what she seems: a computer guru, nothing more. She's no danger to you."

"If she works for the NSA, what's she doing on Roncador Cay?"

There was the briefest hesitation before the reply came. "The Brotherhood pays very well when it needs help. She needed the money."

"All right. Once more I am in your debt."

"Just make sure your brother understands how much he owes me, Mr. Ben-Kalil."

"You have no need to worry on that score. You'll be paid for what you've done. Goodbye."

Fisher put the phone down.

———————————

Two hours after Stone left Montega, an unmarked private jet landed at Montega International Airport. When two Montegan customs agents boarded the plane, they were met by a smiling long-haired Arab carrying a thick wad of American hundred-dollar bills.

The officials spent five minutes inside, chatting with the long-haired man who seemed to be in charge of the dozen or so men who sat around playing cards and taking no notice of the Montegans; then they left with ten of the bills in their pockets.

After a few minutes, one of the Arabs deplaned. He took a taxi to St. Andrews and returned to the jet an hour later.

Ahmed looked up from his cards. "You found one?" he asked.

"I found one. A beauty. The owner claims it can do forty five knots on a smooth sea."

"And there's room for all of us?"

The man shook his head. "It'll hold six, including the captain. Sorry. There wasn't anything else."

Ahmed nodded. "It's enough. Allah is good to those who serve Him. Nadir, Mahomet, Akram, Sharif, Haddad: we leave at five. My friends, twelve hours from now, the machine will be ours. And then the world will know the might of Allah and the strength of Karranh, His servant nation."

A loud cheer filled the cabin.

Roncador Cay

The bungalow next to Tim's was equipped with a kitchen and a large room that served as a communal dining room. Half a dozen long trestle tables filled the room, with benches running the length of each table, evidence that there had once been many more people on the island. But now only two of the tables were occupied, and neither was filled.

Fran counted nine people altogether, with seating space for five times as many. Yoshi and Chida ate in silence at one table. The others all sat at another. The cook, Sam Witherspoon, ate alone in the kitchen, emerging periodically with plates of food and then disappearing back through the swing doors until the next course was ready.

"At one time these tables were all full," said Barlow in answer to a question from Fran. "When we first came here you can imagine how much work had to be done: building the bungalows and the airstrip, wiring, plumbing, and so on. Then, for a while, we had a team of programmers, until Oscar decided it would be more efficient for him to do everything himself. For the last few months, there's been less than a dozen of us."

"Tell me about the boy, William Tanner," said Fran. "What happened to him?"

"Later," said Barlow, pointing at Chida.

Afterwards, in the lab, Fran repeated the question.

"William sent a message to his mother on Montega. The Bastard didn't like that." He shrugged as if there was nothing more to be said.

"So he killed the boy?"

"William disappeared. Sam was worried when William didn't appear at lunch one day. He went to ask Yoshi if he knew where he was. The Bastard was with Yoshi, of course, and when Sam came out he looked terrified. A couple of us asked him what had happened, but he just shook his head and wouldn't say a word. He still goes to Montega once a week for supplies, but now the Bastard goes with him."

"Isn't there something you can do about Chida?"

"Such as?"

"I don't know. He must sleep sometime."

"Yoshi would never allow us to try anything. And in any case it would only make our situation worse. Besides, the only way to control Chida would be to kill him. Are you volunteering?"

Fran shook her head. What they needed, she realized, was someone like Stone. But then she realized what she'd been thinking and she felt disgusted with herself. Violence wasn't the answer. But what was?

"Let's forget about Chida and just get back to work," suggested Barlow. "We've barely started understanding Tim's limitations. Plug that monitor in over there, would you? I want to see if his visual pattern-matching mechanism is fooled by optical illusions the same way a human is."

When Fran and Barlow were in the lab with Tim, everything else ceased to exist. Working with Tim was a surreal, schizophrenic existence. Sometimes it was as if there were three of them in the room. In the middle of an arcane discussion of algorithms and efficiency, Tim's slightly hesitant voice would suddenly interject, suggesting something neither of them had thought of, or telling them something neither of them knew.

At other times Tim was like a piece of alien hardware to be experimented on, studied, and learned from.

Fran asked to look inside Tim.

"There's nothing much to see," Barlow replied. But he unscrewed the screws that held the cube together and let her see inside.

He looked much like any other computer: half a dozen chip-covered boards fitted along a common backplane, and in one corner a small power supply. Barlow closed up the box. "It's the quantum gates in the MIMIC chips that do all the work. Everything else is there just to support those chips."

"He learns by copying, is that right?" asked Fran. "I've never really understood that part."

"It's easy enough. How does a human child learn? By copying its parents. When it does something right, its parents respond with smiles and soothing sounds. When the child does something bad, they shout or discipline it. Fundamentally they're simply providing a pleasure/pain feedback loop. Just like the one in Tim. The only real difference is that in Tim's case the feedback is much more efficient."

Late that afternoon, Fran asked what Barlow would do if Chida insisted on moving Tim.

"Theoretically it can be done. But only a madman would try. But then, the Bastard is mad, so why should I be surprised? There's a sleep command. It tells Tim to freeze his memory and store it to nonvolatile media. Once he's in sleep mode he can be safely disconnected and moved. The batteries can maintain his memory for more than a month. Once he's been moved and plugged back in, circuits automatically reactivate his memory and wake him up. He should wake up without even knowing that anything has happened. That's the theory, anyway. It's one of the many things that's never been tested," he concluded drily.

"I've examined my schematics," said Tim, "and I believe I will function as designed."

"How comforting," said Barlow under his breath.

"You are annoyed with me, Al?"

Barlow sighed. "No, Tim, it's not you. It's just that everything's gone so wrong. Oscar and Yoshi and I had such great hopes for you. We thought we'd unveil you and the world would applaud. Now Oscar's dead and Yoshi seems to have lost interest in everything. His Japanese masters run the show now. And now we're running away. We thought we'd built a machine to rid the world of disease and hunger. Instead it seems all we've done is construct a new kind of weapon for the Japanese Mafia."

"Couldn't we just use Tim to call for help?" Fran suggested. "We have an Internet connection, so what's to stop us using him to send e-mail telling someone where we are?"

"Who are you suggesting we tell?" Barlow asked.

"How about Mike Downing? He's the Deputy Director of the NSA. He'd know what to do."

Barlow looked at her oddly, then shook his head sadly. "You're serious, aren't you?"

"Of course. Why not?"

"And what do you think would happen if we did as you suggest?"

"I guess he'd arrange a rescue."

"Right. And then Tim would disappear into the bowels of the American government, never to be heard from again. They'd have to silence us as well, of course. Probably they'd try to buy us. And if that didn't work, well, there's always more direct methods."

"Now you're the one who's joking. That sort of thing doesn't happen in real life."

"Right. Tim, you heard Fran. Do you have a comment?"

"It would be inadvisable to alert any government to our situation. My potential value is likely to lead to anomalous behavior, especially if there's little chance of it being discovered."

"Which is Tim's roundabout way of saying he agrees with me," said Barlow.

"I'm not convinced," said Fran. "Don't you want to be rescued?"

"To be honest, no; not if it means being parted from Tim. Which it would. Surely even you can't believe they'd let us keep working on him? At least the Bastard has promised us that much; but the American government would have a hundred hot-shot kids putting their filthy hands all over him. I couldn't do that to Tim. He deserves better. If the American government, or any government for that matter, got its hands on Tim, we'd be out of the picture faster than you can say 'Ultimate Weapon.'"

"I still think you're wrong."

"Care to risk it?"

Fran remembered the way the NSA had suppressed Oscar Holywell's work. And Fisher and Stone. Fisher's statement that Stone "knows an awful lot about killing." Kadzu's dead body. Stone's battered one. She shivered and shook her head.

"No," she said. "I guess you're right."

"There's hope for you yet, Fran Tabor. Now, let's get back to work."

"There's one solution you haven't mentioned," said Tim quietly. "You could destroy me."

Silence filled the lab.

"It would solve your problem," said Tim.

Barlow shook his head. "I couldn't do it. I've thought about it but I don't have the strength. It would be like killing my own child. Does that make sense?"

"No," said Tim.

"Yes," said Fran.

Barlow continued, "Besides, there's so much about you we don't understand yet. We can't jeopardize that. We can't impede progress just because some bastard wants to control it."

"Well, I want you to know you have my permission to destroy me if you feel it's for the best."

Barlow looked at his watch. "It's nearly supper time," he said, pointedly drawing the discussion to a close. "Let's call it a day."

They gathered in the dining room. As usual, Yoshi and Chida sat alone. Chida wore his shoulder holster in plain view; nestled in the holster, also in full view, was his gun.

Yoshi toyed with his food unhungrily; Fran watched him push his plate away, his food barely tasted.

"Something seems to be bothering him," said Fran quietly to Barlow, nodding in Yoshi's direction.

"If I was him I'd be bothered as well," said Barlow between mouthfuls of tuna salad. "How would you like it if you'd worked your tail off for years and then you finally reached your goal only to have someone come and steal it from you? But he's too scared of the Bastard actually to do anything," he concluded.

Yoshi looked up sharply, as if he had heard Barlow. Barlow continued in a low voice, "If I was him, I'd be trying to figure out a way to get Tim off Roncador and away from the Bastard before it's too late."

At the other table, Yoshi stood up. Chida looked at him questioningly. "I'm not hungry," Yoshi said, loud enough for everyone to hear. "Maybe I need some fresh air. I think I'll go for a walk around the island. I'll see you later."

As he left the dining room, Fran thought she had never seen a man look so worried. Or so determined.

Yoshi Ishihara closed the door of the bungalow behind him and leaned against it, breathing deeply.

The sun had set, and with it the steady breeze that blew all day from the west had fallen to a barely perceptible zephyr. The first stars were beginning to appear in the cloudless sky. Halfway to the western horizon the brilliant silver light of Venus dominated that quadrant of the sky. Yoshi stood with his back against the door, hungrily sucking in the cooling air as if he had been stifled in the dining room.

From inside he could hear only silence. *It never used to be that way*, he mused to himself. *We used to be happy. We knew we were working on something important. Now everything's changed. They used to respect me; now people look at me as if they're ashamed of me.*

The same thoughts had been running through his head for days, until they had reached the point where he could think of nothing except the way he had let everyone down. It was his fault the Brotherhood had taken over the project; it was his fault Oscar and

William were dead. Therefore it was up to him to atone for what he had done.

If he didn't act soon, it would be too late. Once Tim was moved, the Brotherhood would restrict his access to his creation, fearful that he might do the very thing that he was now contemplating. Already it was difficult to escape Chida for more than a few minutes.

But was he strong enough to destroy the fruits of his labors? He had worked for this for years. Could he just throw it all away? Was it even right to deny the world the knowledge that Tim had been built? The questions weren't easy to answer.

Just moments ago, sitting next to Chida, he had been certain what he must do. But now he was not so sure. He needed to get away; he needed time to think things through. But time was something he didn't have. The meal would be over soon. He had maybe twenty minutes, half an hour at most.

He moved away from the door, and began to walk down the worn path toward the beach.

The path twisted through a stand of bushes, then faded to nothingness at the edge of the beach. He stopped, and realized to his irritation that even here he was to be denied the solitude he sought. The drone of a powerful engine drifted across the water; in the twilight he could see a fishing boat making its way past the island on a course that would bring it within fifty meters of where he was standing.

He watched, annoyed, as the gray shape came closer. Dimly he realized that there was something not quite right about the sound of its engine: it was missing strokes and sputtering as if it were about to die. As the boat came closer, it occurred to him with a sinking feeling that the boat's captain must have seen the lights on Roncador Cay and was coming to ask for help.

The engine cut out completely. A moment later a powerful flashlight pierced the gloom and a voice called out, "Hello, is anyone there?"

The light shone in Yoshi's face, blinding him. Someone on the boat called, "Hey, you there! Our engine's been giving us trouble. Is it OK for us to come ashore?"

They didn't wait for Yoshi to reply. There was movement at the front of the boat, and a small inflatable splashed into the water. Men scrambled into it and began to row ashore.

They talked among themselves in low voices, but fell silent as the boat approached. There was a dull crunch as the inflatable beached. They clambered out of the boat.

One of the men walked towards Yoshi with his hand outstretched in greeting. The others clustered around the inflatable. The man walking toward him carried a bright flashlight that made it impossible to see anything clearly. All Yoshi could see were indistinct shades of shadowy gray beyond the brilliant yellow glare of the flashlight.

The men seemed to be removing objects from the boat. Some looked like boxes or canisters, but others were long and bulky, almost like guns....

"Good evening." The man grasped Yoshi's hand and shook it violently. He had long hair, and spoke with an accent Yoshi could not place. He was smiling broadly.

"What's the name of this island? I'm sorry to trouble you, but we'll fix the problem with our engine and be gone as soon as we can in the morning."

He shone the flashlight directly in Yoshi's face, causing the Japanese to wince and blink blindly as he replied, "This is Roncador Cay, but...."

Still blinded, Yoshi never saw the silenced pistol that Ahmed Ben-Kalil pulled from a pocket, pointed at his head, and fired.

No one else seemed to have noticed Yoshi's preoccupation. They ate in a sullen silence, broken only occasionally by a request to pass the salt or a pitcher of lemonade. As they finished the tuna salad they went one by one to a table near the window to select a piece of fruit or choose a yogurt for dessert.

When Barlow got up to get his dessert, Fran followed. Chida, whether by accident or design, chose the same moment to make his way to the table. Barlow glared at the Bastard, then stalked back to his seat empty handed.

Chida caught Fran's arm as she turned to follow Barlow. "You are very clever, Miss Tabor...," he began. Then he stopped and frowned at the window. Following his gaze, Fran saw a flashlight moving outside, near Tim's bungalow.

The light stopped moving, and Fran realized that anyone outside would have a clear view of the two of them as they stood peering into the darkness.

The same thought must have struck Chida, because he suddenly pushed Fran violently to one side, causing her to stumble and fall sideways. A moment later the window exploded, sending a shower of splintered glass on to the table and burying shards in the bananas and mangoes.

It was several seconds before it dawned on Fran that someone had shot at them.

Chida roared something in Japanese. His hand seemed to flicker near his holster, and suddenly he was holding his gun. With a cry he broke through the door and ran outside. Through the smashed window Fran heard the spit of muted gunfire, followed by shouts and then more shots.

There was a clatter as everyone dived off the benches and on to the floor. Fran crawled under the table.

"What's going on?" someone shouted, and Fran replied with a calm she did not feel, "I think it's something to do with Yoshi."

"I doubt it," growled Barlow, crawling toward the door, which hung awkwardly open on broken hinges. "He'd never have the guts." Still at ground level, he peered cautiously around the edge of the door. "I can't see anything. Wait a minute...."

They heard running footsteps, and Barlow jerked his head back just in time to save it from being smashed into by Chida as he raced into the room.

Fran stared at Chida from under the table. A large red stain covered the right shoulder of his shirt; a second stain was spreading near his liver. He clutched his gun with both hands as he scanned the dining room with large, wild eyes, searching for something. His breathing came in sharp, punctuated heaves.

His eyes met hers peering out from under the table, and she saw his wild expression change to satisfaction. His lips curled as he raised his pistol. "Your friends are looking for you." His words came out in pain-wracked gasps.

The gun trembled in his hands, and she could see the effort he was making to stop his hands from shaking. It was a moment before Fran realized what he was about to do.

"No!" she screamed at the top of her lungs, wondering even as she did so why Chida had singled her out for death. "I haven't done anything."

Chida took a deep breath, winced once with the pain, then steadied himself. The gun stopped shaking in his hands. Fran closed her eyes. The gun fired.

26

Hayes shook his head. *"I don't believe it."*

Gallucci said, *"I didn't want to either. But we can't argue with the photograph. Once I had that I checked the records to see where Fisher was that day. He registered all his calls to be forwarded to the mobile PGP-transcoder network. That meant he wasn't at home."*

"He could have been anywhere."

"Including Juneau."

"I still don't believe it. Fisher of all people. It's impossible."

"There's one way to be sure," said Gallucci.

"How?"

"Otosan knows that you're the person responsible for Asia in our group. There's a phone. Call Otosan and ask him who he met in Alaska."

"What's the point of that? He won't tell me."

"No, he won't. But I'm betting he'll warn Fisher that we're on their track. All we have to do is wait to see if Fisher gets a call from Otosan."

"So you really believe it? You really think the two of them want Tim for themselves?"

"I don't see any other reasonable explanation, do you?"

Hayes sighed heavily and shook his head. "I guess we have no choice."

He stretched out his hand to the phone.

Roncador Cay

When Fran, cowering under the table in the dining room on Roncador Cay with her eyes closed, heard the gunshot, she was sure it was the last sound she would ever hear. She waited to feel the pain of the wound, and then the helplessness of her life ebbing away.

Instead, there were confused shouts in a foreign language coming from beyond the door. Someone nearby shouted in the same language.

She opened her eyes.

Chida was on the floor six feet away, his eyes open, staring blindly into her own. His lifeless hand stretched out toward her, the gun tilted to one side, pointing irrelevantly at the wall to Fran's left. In the center of Chida's back was an irregular crimson patch.

A swarthy man with long hair stood in the doorway. He held a gun that waved vaguely from side to side as he scanned the dining room, looking for something. Everyone stared at him, terrified, from behind the dubious safety of chairs and tables.

It was a moment before the man saw Fran, separated from the others and trying to make herself inconspicuous under the dessert table. The man smiled and pointed his gun at her. For the second time in less than a minute, Fran was certain she was about to die.

He gestured with his gun. "You! Come out of there."

Fran looked at him uncomprehendingly. He repeated his order, and when she still did not respond, he strode to the table and flung it angrily to one side. He grabbed her by the shoulder and pulled her roughly to her feet.

There was the sound of someone running across the room toward them. The man released Fran and spun around just as Barlow reached them. "Leave her alone, you bastard," said Barlow, planting a fist in the other's belly.

For a moment, Fran thought that Barlow was going to win the fight, but the other man recovered too quickly. Taking a step backward, he raised his gun and fired.

Barlow looked astonished as he took an involuntary step backward, propelled by the force of the bullet. He raised his hand to his shoulder. When he drew it away it was red with fresh blood. He looked at it disbelievingly.

Outside, Fran heard the sudden roar of an engine. *HolyMo! That sounds like a jet landing,* she thought. *What the hell's happening?*

"You shot me," Barlow said stupidly.

The man with the gun ignored him. "You're Fran Tabor?"

Fran nodded dumbly.

"Then you're coming with me."

He grasped her wrist and pulled her toward the door. She screamed, but no one moved to help her. They looked on uselessly as she clutched at the doorframe, screaming and kicking. The man released her, but only to smash his open hand into the side of her head.

Everything swam before her eyes. As if in a dream, she saw Barlow staring at her, his mouth working soundlessly, shock still on his face as his legs folded beneath him.

Then she was yanked outside. "Who are you? What are you doing?" she gasped as she was pulled, stumbling, across the compound.

Two men in fatigues were running from building to building, tossing a pair of thick red cylinders like large firecrackers into each bungalow.

Half a dozen others, similarly dressed, ran into the compound from the direction of the runway. They began pouring a liquid on the ground between the buildings. She could hear jet engines idling nearby.

"My name is Ahmed Ben-Kalil," the man said. "And remember this: I saved your life back there."

Three more men holding semi-automatics were clustered in front of Tim's bungalow, watching her stumbling progress toward them. Ahmed spoke to them in Arabic, and two of them hurried away, heading for the building Fran had just left.

Ahmed dragged her inside and down the steps to the basement. She fell as he pulled her downstairs, but he caught her and half-carried her through the shattered door of the lab.

She expected the lab to be in disarray, but except for several piles of note-covered papers strewn over the floor near the door it was just as she and Barlow had left it before supper. A bespectacled young man wearing an orange silk shirt was standing over Tim with a worried look on his face. He turned around as Fran was dragged into the room and his frown was instantly replaced by a smile.

"You got her. Good. Miss Tabor, what do we have to do before it can be moved safely?"

Ahmed pushed her forward. "Help him," he barked. "And make it quick. We should have been gone two minutes ago. The longer we stay the more dangerous it is. For all of us."

Fran stared helplessly at Tim, and then at the man in the orange shirt. "We need Barlow," she said.

"Who's Barlow?" asked Ahmed.

"The man you shot."

His eyes narrowed suspiciously, then he barked an order to a man who had come in behind them. "Go to the dining room and do what you can for the man I shot. If he's still alive, bring him here."

The man left at a run. Turning to Fran, Ahmed fingered his gun meaningfully and said, "In the meantime, you'll just have to do what you can without him."

Fran looked desperately at Tim. All the wires were still connected. The monitors were filled with jagged lines, reflecting Tim's reactions to the events he was witnessing. The man in the orange shirt said quietly, "Please. We have to move it and I don't know where to begin."

"Neither do I," Fran said under her breath. "I can't do it without Barlow."

The man at her side bent his head close to hers. "You have to," he said in an undertone. "Ahmed will kill you if you don't."

"I don't know how. Don't you understand? I simply don't know how."

Three of Ahmed's men entered the lab at a run. "We're ready to leave," one of them said.

The man who had been sent to fetch Barlow returned. He shook his head emphatically and said, "He's dead." Ahmed spat and muttered an oath.

He pointed his gun at Fran. "You'd better think of something quick. If you can't help, you're of no use to me."

Fran closed her eyes and took several deep breaths, forcing herself to be calm. Barlow had said there was a way to save Tim's memory. But he'd never told her how to do it.

Her eyes snapped open. Of course. The answer was obvious.

"Tim," she said urgently, "prepare yourself to go on a journey. Do whatever you need to do to make sure we'll be able to wake you up again when we reach our destination."

For a moment nothing happened and Fran wondered if Tim had been damaged in the fighting. But then Tim's familiar voice spoke, filling the silence that had fallen. He sounded worried.

"I don't understand what's happening. Where is Al, please?"

A peculiar sound came from the men near the ruined door, a horrified moan of shared fear. Two of them fell to the floor, placing their foreheads against the concrete and babbling incoherently; the third edged backward and ran shouting upstairs. Ahmed sucked in his breath noisily through exposed teeth and gripped his gun more tightly. The man in the orange shirt stepped sharply back from the cube as if he had received an electric shock.

"Tim, this is an emergency," said Fran. "You must get yourself ready to go on a trip. I'll try to explain later."

"Are these people terrorists?" asked Tim. "Am I being abducted? Are you with them? They appear to be Arabs. You a...."

"Just shut up and do it!" shouted Fran.

"All right," said Tim, suddenly meek.

Fran's eyes flicked to the monitors, but the patterns were too complicated to follow. After a few seconds Tim announced, "Memory copy to nonvolatile storage complete. Commencing shutdown."

For a few more moments Tim was silent, then he emitted three high-pitched beeps. The traces on the monitors dropped sharply and became horizontal lines at the bottoms of the screens. Only a single light glowed green on Tim's side.

"Is that it?" barked Ahmed.

"I think so."

"Iradj, Mahomet, remove the connections and bring the machine. And be careful."

The man in the orange shirt began to unplug wires from the now-silent cube. A tall, dangerous-looking man who had entered the room stepped over the men who were still prostrate on the floor and began to help.

Ahmed touched Fran's elbow. To her astonishment he smiled gratefully. "Thank you," he said quietly. "I'm sorry if I hurt you, but there's no time to lose. And I'm sorry about your friend Barlow. We weren't told about him. Now hurry. We must reach safety before the Brotherhood discovers what we've done. We're too exposed here. You'll come with us."

Fran shook her head. "And if I refuse?"

Ahmed glanced at his gun. "I'm told you're an intelligent woman. Too intelligent to have to ask such a question. Now, come with me and we'll be on our way."

Turning, he spat derisively toward the two men who were still on the floor, bowing toward Tim. "It's just a machine, you fools; how many times do I have to tell you? Get up."

The tall man pulled the last connector free, cutting off Tim's power. The last light went out. Tim just sat there, looking helpless and strangely naked without his umbilicals.

The two men lifted the cube carefully off the table. "Drop it and you die," said Ahmed through bared teeth. The tall man, who had yet to speak, looked sharply at him. "Yes, Mahomet, even you. That machine is more valuable than all of us put together. Hussein, you lead the others. You know what to do."

Outside was like a scene from hell. Flames engulfed the entire compound. As the last man left Tim's building, he turned and tossed something inside. The building exploded in a ball of searing flame.

Ahmed led them between burning buildings to the airstrip, where a business jet stood with its steps extended to the ground. Fran glanced at the registration number on the fuselage. J9-AABA. The number indicated that the plane was from the Sultanate of Karranh. Before she could decide what to make of this, Ahmed pushed her forward with a rough shove between her shoulder blades.

She clambered up the steps. Inside, wide plush seats were arranged along the sides of the cabin, each with a small table separating it from its neighbors. The center of the cabin was empty, apart from half a dozen prayer mats laid out on top of the intricately-patterned carpet that covered the cabin floor.

Near the rear of the cabin was an area that was empty except for a padded pallet from which extended half a dozen webbed straps. Mahomet and Iradj carried Tim to the pallet, and laid him carefully in the center of the foam pads before strapping him securely in place.

"You will sit here," said Ahmed, indicating a seat close to the pallet. "I'll sit next to you. Strap yourself in. We will be taking off as soon as everyone is aboard."

There was a clatter outside the plane, followed by the heavy thud of people climbing the steps. A surge of men entered the plane, talking excitedly in Arabic as they took their seats. They fell silent when they saw the cube nestling at the rear of the plane, snug in the pallet. Some of them looked at Tim with fear in their eyes.

Ahmed strode up the wide central aisle, carefully avoiding the prayer mats. He opened the door to the cockpit and poked his head inside.

The two men in the cockpit turned to look at Ahmed. One, the pilot, was a grizzled man in his mid-fifties with a sun-beaten face and worried eyes. The copilot was much younger, with a chiselled handsomeness and a bravado in his eyes that warned that there was nothing he would not attempt.

"We're ready to go," said Ahmed.

"As you wish," said the pilot. "How many are aboard?"

"Thirteen. We brought a hostage."

The pilot nodded. "I see," he mumbled.

Ahmed left and the copilot said, "You don't look very happy. You should be pleased. It means they didn't lose a single man. Allah smiles on us."

"I'd have been more pleased if He'd chosen to show His favor by causing us to lose half our men. What this means, my impetuous friend, is that we are even more overweight than I'd expected."

"Overweight?"

"We have full tanks plus the extension tanks, which are also full. We are carrying a total of fifteen people. According to the manual, we shall require eleven hundred meters for takeoff."

The copilot looked at him in dismay. "But the runway's not that long."

"According to the map, which may or may not be accurate, we have one thousand and twenty five meters. We must hope that either the map or the manual is wrong, or that Allah continues to smile on us. Now, throttle up and keep the brakes on, and don't release them until I say so, no matter what you've been taught."

As Ahmed walked back to his seat, the noise from the engines grew from a whisper to a roar, and then to a shriek. The airframe began to rattle as he sat down and buckled himself in. When it seemed that the plane was about to shake itself apart, the pilot released the brakes and with a stomach-jarring jerk the plane jumped forward.

Ahmed closed his eyes, and Fran saw his lips moving silently. None of the others seemed to notice, except the tall man called Mahomet, who watched the two of them unsmilingly. The other men were chattering cheerfully, still laughing and slapping one another.

The plane raced down the runway. The burning buildings were left behind and for a moment there was only a loud, rushing darkness. Then the roar from the wheels ceased as the plane angled sharply upward.

Ahmed's lips stopped moving and he opened his eyes. He smiled at Fran. "Of course I had every confidence in the pilot. But a little prayer never hurt either."

"And what about the people we left behind?" she asked.

Ahmed shrugged. "If you'll excuse me, I must talk to my men." He clapped his hand for attention and, raising his voice to cover the sound of the engines, he began to speak in Arabic.

Questions filled Fran's head, but they were questions she had no way of answering. And one question hung over them all. Of all the people on Roncador Cay, why had Ahmed chosen her?

The plane levelled off and the shriek of the engines died away to a steady background drone. The cadence of Ahmed's voice began to merge with the engines. After a while Fran's eyelids became heavy. She struggled to stay awake, but before too long the effort was too much. Her head slipped sideways into the crook of the seat's velvet headrest. Her breathing became shallow and even.

At her side, Ahmed did not appear to notice. He continued talking for another hour before finally he pointed to Fran. "She is to be treated as an honored guest," he said, his eyes slowly sweeping over his men. "If I hear of any man attempting to mistreat her or to take advantage of her, I will personally castrate him with a blunt knife."

There was an uneasy ripple of forced laughter.

"That is all," Ahmed said. "You have done well, and you will be well rewarded for your services to the sultan. Allah himself was with us, and because of you the entire world will soon tremble when it hears the name of Karranh. No more will the Imperial powers of the West mock us and try to tell us how to live even as they steal the riches from beneath our feet. No more will the corrupt regimes of the East treat us with contempt and ill-concealed loathing. Soon the whole world will realize that Allah is great, as is His servant nation Karranh."

The men took up the cry "Allah is great! Karranh is great!" and Fran wriggled nervously in her sleep.

Ahmed raised his hand for silence. "She sleeps, and so should we. We have done a great thing today. But even the mightiest of Allah's warriors must sleep."

There were grunts of agreement and the men began to settle down for the night. Some got out of their seats and slept on the floor; others, like Ahmed, extended footrests and twisted in their seats until they were comfortable. Only Mahomet remained motionless. For a long time he sat upright, his eyes switching back and forth between Fran and Ahmed.

In the cockpit, the captain made a small adjustment to the automatic pilot. He stretched and yawned.

"Long day," said the copilot. "Any idea what it was they brought aboard?"

"And it promises to be a long night. Pass me some more of that coffee, then get yourself some sleep. And don't ask questions. They can get you into trouble. You do know who our passengers are, don't you?"

The copilot handed across a mug of steaming coffee, black and sweet. He shook his head. "My commander only told me to take good care of them. Who are they?"

"The Army of Allah. The short one with the long hair and suspicious eyes is Ahmed, the sultan's brother, and the tall one who doesn't speak is Mahomet, the sultan's son. Now get some sleep. You'll need it. You can take us down in the Azores, and may Allah be merciful if your landing isn't perfect because as certain as Mohammed is His prophet you'll be meeting Him face to face if Ahmed doesn't like it."

27

"Incoming call for you, sir. PGP-encoded."

Fisher frowned, clearly surprised. "I'll take it in my room."

As he left, Gallucci turned to the technician next to him and said, "That's probably the call I warned you about. Can you trace it, please?"

"I'll do the best I can, sir."

Hayes walked over, looking worried. The technician looked up from his screen. "Somewhere in Japan, sir. I'm afraid I can't do better than that. Since the bearer channel is encrypted I can't get the conversation for you."

Hayes bowed his head. "All right," he said to Gallucci. "You were right. Do what you must."

Stone halted not far from the forbidding black wall and looked up at the clouds, wondering if it was going to rain before the evening was through. The nighttime glare from the city reflected from the undersides of the heavy clouds.

No rain, Stone decided; not for a few hours, anyway.

Lowering his eyes, his gaze was drawn to the dark lines of the Jefferson Memorial, garishly spotlit against the gentler yellow of the clouds. A wider, more subdued light filled the area in front of him. Even now, late in the evening of a chill mid-week spring day, a dozen people were scattered in the space between himself and the Vietnam Memorial.

Some walked silently, searching for one name in particular. Others, their search concluded, simply stood, looking and remembering. Yet others hung their head and closed their eyes, aching with private pain or sorrow or simply at prayer. The one thing they had in common was that no one spoke.

Stone reached the stark, black monument and began to walk along it. Unlike the others, his step was purposeful; he gave the names barely a glance as he passed: he knew exactly where he was going.

The wall would remain open for another three hours, until midnight, and most of the people would stay until they were gently ushered away, still remembering.

Stone walked past the names of those who had died in 1973. In that year Stone was a pre-schooler; his mother, tears trickling down her cheeks, had tried to explain to her wide-eyed, uncomprehending little boy that he would never see Daddy again.

Eighteen years later, Stone had become a vocal, bitter opponent of the American government, his words beginning to give way to deeds. He had protested at Oak Ridge and Rocky Flats, and had been arrested for throwing an egg at the president. One day, he had sworn to himself, the government would pay for what they'd taken from him and thousands like him.

And then, late one afternoon in his junior year at college, a man who called himself Fisher had walked into his room without knocking and changed his life for ever.

Stone knew where his father's name was: panel W45 — although the name carved in the granite was not Stone but Carling; but he walked past the section without a glance. He'd seen it once, ten years ago — after he'd agreed to work for Fisher, he'd felt like he needed to come here and explain his apparent betrayal.

Now he kept walking for another twenty yards before he came to a halt. He glanced at his watch, then looked quickly around. Two minutes to go, and no sign of Fisher yet. But he would be here. Stone had not a shred of doubt about that.

A minute and a half later he saw him. Dressed in an expensive overcoat, his features shadowed by a wide-brimmed hat, there was no mistaking the broad-shouldered figure that strolled anonymously past the late-evening mourners.

Stone turned his back on the approaching figure, and stood looking at one name in particular.

He heard the tread of Fisher's shoes stop behind him. Stone felt a sudden surge of adrenalin. What if somehow he'd got it all wrong?

He turned around and faced Fisher. Fisher looked at Stone with an unreadable expression.

Stone said, "Robert A. Cooperson."

In the shadow underneath the hat, he saw Fisher's right eyebrow momentarily rise and then fall back into place. Stone was careful not to let his relief show: he'd got it right after all.

"I don't think I recognize the name," Fisher said evenly.

"You know damn well you do." He checked himself. "I'm sorry. That was uncalled for. But all the same, sir, you do recognize it."

He waited, and a slow smile suffused the other's face. Fisher said, "If it's any cause for satisfaction, you're the first operative ever to find out. I trust you've told no one else. The others know, of course — we have no secrets from each other."

Was there a challenge in his voice, daring Stone to contradict him? Or was that just Stone's imagination playing tricks after a long day?

"I don't think that's true," he said carefully. "I think at least one of you has some very important secrets from the others."

Stone looked for some reaction on Fisher's face, but Fisher merely looked at him without speaking for several seconds; then he said, "You wouldn't say that unless you thought you had good cause. I assume it has something to do with why you dragged me here alone at this time of night?"

"Yes, sir. It has everything to do with it."

"Then walk with me. I think better when I'm walking."

Fisher began to stroll along the path next to the enormous black wall, his head bent, looking at the ground two paces in front of him. Stone walked at his side, and tried to explain why he had requested this unprecedented meeting.

"It's the Brotherhood, sir. It bothered me as soon as we arrived in Montega. They're involved somehow."

"We know. They've been bankrolling Ishihara."

Stone stared at Fisher. "And how long have you known that?"

"That's none of your business."

"You're a bastard, sir; you know that? You know I'd never have agreed to take Fran if I'd known the Brotherhood was involved."

Fisher looked evenly at Stone. "Which is exactly why you weren't told. But you didn't need all this rigmarole just to pick an argument about the Brotherhood. What haven't you told me?"

"The Brotherhood isn't just involved. They knew we were coming. They had a man at the airport in Montega waiting for us. A man called Kadzu."

"Their first line of defense. Probably they thought someone might try to steal Tim. A prudent precaution, that's all."

"No, that's not all. Kadzu was expecting me, I'm sure of it. A police officer pointed us out to him. That means the officer was watching for us. And I saw Kadzu's face. He wasn't surprised that we'd arrived, only relieved. He wasn't even surprised when he saw Fran. He was expecting her as well."

Fisher halted. A middle-aged man with sad eyes walked past, nodding a silent greeting.

"Impossible. You imagined it, that's all. A man's feelings don't always show on his face."

"I didn't imagine it. He knew we were coming. And you haven't heard the rest of it."

"Tell me."

In as few words as possible, Stone told Fisher everything that had happened on Montega. When he came to his description of what happened at Gloria Tanner's, Fisher interrupted him. "You have a copy of this tape?"

Stone shook his head. "I had to get rid of it. I couldn't risk the police finding it."

"But you're sure about what you heard?"

"Certain, sir. Chida knew Fran's name."

Fisher said nothing for more than a minute. "So you're suggesting we have a traitor in the organization?"

"It's the only explanation I can think of."

"It's impossible. None of us would betray our country."

"Then give me a better explanation."

"I can't."

"Because there isn't one. I don't know who it is, but one of your colleagues is a traitor."

"But why?"

"Why does any man betray his country? Money? The promise of power? Blackmail? I don't know. But somebody told the Brotherhood we were coming."

For a while they stared at the wall without speaking. Then Stone said, "I've done my duty. Now I'm going to go back and get Fran out. She's been there twenty four hours now. Long enough to decide if this machine of theirs is for real."

"Perhaps her rescue is exactly what Chida had in mind when he took her."

"Bait for a trap, you mean?"

"It's a possibility."

"So you're telling me I can't go?"

"You're right; you can't go. But not for that reason."

"Then why?"

"Because circumstances have changed."

"What circumstances?"

"We've been monitoring Roncador Cay by satellite. Two hours ago a fire erupted in the compound. It appears to have engulfed all the buildings."

It took a moment for this to sink in. "So you're telling me Fran may be dead?"

"The fire was still burning when I left to meet you, and I seriously doubt there'll be any survivors. I also doubt that Miss Tabor is among the dead."

"Sir, if you'll forgive my bluntness, what the hell are you trying to tell me?"

"Earlier today a plane flew into Montega from Bermuda. On board was Ahmed Ben-Kalil and a number of his compatriots."

"The Army of Allah...."

"Exactly. They rented a boat and set out for Roncador Cay late this afternoon. The IR satellites showed them arriving shortly after seven this evening. The fire broke out less than an hour later.

"Just before the fire started, their plane took off from Montega. It landed at Roncador, stayed on the ground twenty minutes, and then took off again."

They had reached the end of the wall, and Fisher halted. "The plane is heading east across the Atlantic. Doubtless heading for Karranh."

"And Fran?"

"The satellite showed twelve people arriving. Six on the boat, six on the plane. Thirteen left. There's a good chance the thirteenth person was Ms. Tabor. But even if it was, she's expendable. Always has been. Forget about her. Your job now is to infiltrate Karranh and get the machine out. That's the order the president has given me, and it's my order to you. Doubtless the machine will be at the sultan's palace on the outskirts of Karranh City. We have to assume everything we've heard about the machine is true, which means it's vital we get it before it can be used against us. You understand that, Stone? Vital."

Stone stared at Fisher. "You're telling me to forget about Fran even if she's alive? She's a *civilian*. You can't just abandon her."

"Oh, for God's sake don't get sentimental on me, Stone. This is a direct order. The mission comes first."

"But sir....."

"No! You go to Karranh and you get the machine out safely. If that's impossible, you destroy it or die trying. Ms. Tabor is not even a consideration. Understand?"

"You're a cold-hearted bastard, General Cooperson, do you know that?"

"My name is Fisher. Cooperson died more than thirty years ago. And my first and only duty is to my country. As is yours, which I trust I don't have to remind you. Are you going to obey your orders, or must I replace you with someone who will?"

Stone felt Fisher's eyes boring into him. He averted his gaze, staring at the names filling the wall behind them.

"They died for their country," said Fisher quietly. "They thought it was worth paying the ultimate sacrifice. Are you telling me they all made a mistake? All fifty eight thousand of them? Including your father?"

211

Stone shook his head unhappily. "You know you can trust me. But after this is over I want out."

"We'll talk about it then. Maybe you'll think differently."

"I won't."

There was a long pause before Stone said, "So you think the machine's on board the plane?"

"They carried something aboard. We have to assume it was the computer. And a Delta team landed an hour after they left. There was no trace of the machine. Or Ms. Tabor. All the bodies were burned beyond recognition, but none of them was female. Barlow has been positively identified from his dental records."

"And Chida?"

"Presumed to be among the dead. Ms. Tabor was the only person unaccounted for. Ahmed Ben-Kalil would need someone to help understand the machine. With Barlow dead, she'd be the obvious choice. But remember, it's the machine that's important. Now, I believe you have an appointment in Karranh. Don't let me detain you."

"You bastard."

"Perhaps. But a bastard who knows his duty. Good luck, Stone."

Stone glared at Fisher; then, without speaking, he turned smartly on his heels.

"Stone," Fisher called.

Stone halted.

"I'm relying on you. Don't disappoint me."

"Go to hell. Sir."

Stone stalked away toward the exit. Not far away a man in a hat and raincoat turned away from the wall and hurried after him.

Fisher watched without moving until the two men disappeared around a corner and were lost to view.

28

Gallucci looked at the alarm clock and grunted when he calculated that he'd have to be content with five hours sleep. He dragged himself from bed and made for the shower.

Five minutes later he stopped by a room on whose door someone had pinned a handwritten note with the words: "Food and Coffee." He poured himself a mug of high-octane coffee and was plastering a thick layer of cream cheese on half a bagel when Lee walked in.

"You look exhausted," said Gallucci.

"I'm off to bed," Lee replied, putting a dirty mug in the sink. "Fisher's still in there. I don't think he intends to sleep any more until this whole thing is over."

"What's the status?"

"No change. They refueled in the Azores and crossed the coast of Africa a couple of hours ago. Looks like they're making for Libya. They've made no attempt to communicate with home."

"And Roncador Cay?"

"Burned to the ground. The Delta team reported no survivors. Fisher pulled them off the island a couple of hours ago because Musuko was heading that way. He didn't stay long. He's already on his way back to Japan."

"Ms. Tabor?"

"Not among the dead, so she must be the person they took with them."

"What about Stone?"

"He went home after his meeting with Fisher. Fisher ordered him to go to Karranh to try to get the machine out, but there's no sign of movement yet. We have the house staked out."

Gallucci looked at Lee sharply. "Who ordered that? Stone won't like it."

"Hayes did. He wants to keep tabs on Stone. Since we can't trust Fisher any more, he wants to be sure Stone's not a part of whatever Fisher's up to. He also put a directional mike on the two of them when they met at the wall."

"Good God! Did Fisher know?"

"No. And there's no doubt about his guilt any more. Even Hayes is convinced that Fisher's gone off the rails. While he was on Montega Stone figured out that one of us is a traitor. He told Fisher about it and Fisher promised to deal with it. Of course, he's done nothing." Lee dug in his pocket. "Here's a copy of the tape. I imagine it will feature prominently at Fisher's trial. And on that happy note, I'm going to bed. See you in a few hours."

He left Gallucci turning the tape over in his hand and wondering why, of all the people on Roncador Cay, Ahmed Ben-Kalil had chosen to take Fran.

Fran stared out the window, trying to guess where they were. Her watch said it was six in the morning, but the landscape below was bathed in unremitting sunlight.

The plane was high enough that there was no contrast that would allow her to distinguish the hills and valleys on the ground below; it was all just a dull, flat landscape of yellow, red and brown, with here and there an island of green to relieve the monotony.

Ahmed was asleep, breathing with a dull snore that was barely audible over the rushing of the engines. Some of the others still slept, but most were taking turns to kneel on the prayer mats and prostrate themselves toward the front of the plane.

She guessed they were somewhere over north Africa, probably the western Sahara. After a while the plane banked, changing course to the north. They began to descend.

Ahmed woke and Fran asked him where they were. He pretended not to hear.

She said, "My guess is somewhere over Libya. I assume we're bound for Karranh and we're landing to refuel."

He looked at her in surprise, and Fran knew she had been right. "Why would you think that?" he asked.

"We've been flying more or less east for ten hours. At six hundred miles an hour that must put us somewhere over northwest Africa. The plane is registered in Karranh. It fits."

He laughed out loud, genuinely amused. "The plane. I never knew that. You mean you can tell where a plane is from by its registration number?"

"Sure. N for the United States. JA for Japan. G for Britain. Take a look when we land. If I'm right, you'll see planes whose numbers begin with 5A. That's the prefix assigned to Libya. This plane is J9-AABA. The J9 block belongs to Karranh."

Still grinning, he nodded. "Of course you're right. We'll be landing shortly to refuel, courtesy of our friends in Libya. After that we leave on the final leg of our journey. Our ultimate destination is indeed Karranh.

"Miss Tabor, I cannot tell you what a pleasure it is to hold an intelligent conversation. These fools" — he gestured expansively to include everyone else in the cabin — "are like sheep, and not particularly intelligent sheep at that. Only Mahomet has an intelligence worth considering, and he unfortunately has physical limitations that render him useless as a conversation partner. Now, if you will excuse me, I have some pressing matters to attend to."

With a theatrical salaam, he made his way to the front of the plane and disappeared into the cockpit.

A movement on the far side of the cabin caught her eye. Mahomet had risen to his feet, and now he crossed the aisle and sat down in Ahmed's seat. He studied Fran's face intently.

"What do you want?" Fran asked.

He grinned oddly, exposing two rows of yellowing teeth, but said nothing.

"Do you speak English?"

He shook his head emphatically.

"But you understand it?"

He nodded, and pulled a notebook from his pocket. He glanced toward the cockpit, then began to scribble. When he had finished, he turned it around for Fran to read: *I have no tongue. Do not trust him. You are in great danger.*

"Who from? Ahmed?"

But Mahomet had sprung to his feet, stuffing the notebook into his pocket. The cockpit door opened and Ahmed came out. He frowned when he saw Mahomet standing in front of Fran and hurried down the aisle toward them. As he approached, Mahomet turned and a wide grin split his face. He gesticulated quickly with his hands. Ahmed said something in Arabic and Mahomet's face fell in disappointment. Then he looked hopeful once more as Ahmed kept talking. At last Mahomet went back to his seat, apparently content.

"He says it would be interesting to make love to a black woman," said Ahmed offhandedly as he sat down. He laughed at the look on Fran's face. "I told him you were mine, but then I said he could use you after me if you didn't make me happy. He seemed satisfied with that."

"You son of a bitch."

Fran raised a hand to strike him, but he gripped her wrist and squeezed tightly, causing her to squeal in pain. There was a moment's silence as everyone turned to look, but when they saw what was happening they all looked quickly away. Even Mahomet, Fran noticed, seemed deliberately uninterested.

"You try that again and I will use you," said Ahmed through gritted teeth. "And afterwards, I'll let all my men try you on for size."

He released his grip. "If you behave yourself, I'll protect you. If you don't, well, perhaps Mahomet is right. It would be interesting to have a black woman."

As Fran turned angrily away the plane banked sharply. There was no announcement on the PA system, but the plane dropped quickly toward the ground and a minute later there came a slight bump and then a roar from the engines as the plane landed.

They taxied to a halt close to a squat red-painted wooden building. Half a dozen military jets in desert camouflage were parked in a line to one side of the building. Fran noticed with satisfaction that five of the six had registrations beginning with 5A. The sixth started with YI: Iraqi.

Parked farther away were two longer rows of jets, hidden under an enormous sheet covered in red, yellow and brown splotches designed to make the planes invisible to the watchful eyes of the satellites that passed overhead. Two large hangers were nearby, their doors closed.

As soon as the plane stopped, Ahmed opened the door and lowered the steps. A blast of baking air entered the plane.

While the plane refueled, boxes of food and soft drinks were brought aboard by sour-looking men in military fatigues. The men were obviously surprised to see a woman aboard; but no one said anything, and after about twenty minutes Ahmed closed the door and they were once more on their way.

Apart from the occasional green of an oasis and a brief change of scenery as they flew over the Red Sea, the yellow-brown of the desert stretched below them continuously for the rest of the day.

The men spent the time talking, sleeping, eating, praying and playing cards. For Fran, with nothing to do but watch them, the hours passed slowly. The sun had set when the plane began to descend once more.

The lights of a city stretched ahead of them. Behind them, the black monotony of the desert was broken here and there by lights clustered around massive yellow gas flares at desert wellheads.

When they landed, Ahmed escorted her down the steps and bundled her into a waiting black-windowed car. As soon as they were seated, the driver engaged the engine and sped away.

Fran asked where they were going.

"Somewhere your friends won't easily find you," replied Ahmed.

"What friends?"

"Please don't try to play games, Miss Tabor. The Brotherhood will discover quickly enough that you aren't dead. When they realize that the machine has gone, and you with it, they'll guess that the two of you are together. I imagine that the only question in their minds will be whether you left voluntarily or involuntarily. Either way, they'll come looking for you."

Fran opened her mouth to protest. Surely Ahmed didn't think she worked for the Brotherhood? "May I remind you that the man who was going to shoot me on Roncador Cay worked for the Brotherhood? Or didn't you know that?"

Ahmed shrugged. "It's no surprise. He knew how valuable you'd be to us. I would have done the same in his position."

Something stirred uneasily inside her. As they raced through the wide streets of a city halfway across the world from her home, Fran had the feeling that nothing that had happened since she had bumped into the NSA guard on the way to her office was quite what it had seemed. Someone somewhere was playing a complex, deadly game, feeding people whatever information suited him.

And Fran was caught in the middle of it all, with escape becoming less likely with every passing second.

29

Otosan was at his desk, trying to deal with paperwork.

He did not like his office. These days he found himself spending more and more time at the secluded garden with its tiny temple. His office he associated with bustle and duplicity and the thousand and one cares of being Father to so many sons. In the temple he could forget about such unimportant concerns and concentrate on what truly mattered.

He found his mind wandering, thinking how lovely the garden would look in the light rain that was falling.

The intercom beeped, startling him. His secretary, Akiko, a prim, bespectacled, efficient woman utterly unlike the gentle geishas who attended him at the temple, said, "Musuko on the line for you."

Musuko. The word meant Son, and was the name given to the person chosen by the Father to succeed him. But Otosan had made a mistake choosing his blood-son as his successor. He'd known it even at the time, but he'd hoped his son would grow into the position. Instead he'd let it go to his head. There were rumors, unpleasant but all-too-believable stories of boasts Musuko had made. How he was going to westernize the Brotherhood when he became Father. How everything would be computerized, efficient.

Efficient and unemotional, just like Akiko, Otosan thought.

He picked up the phone.
"Father, Roncador Cay has been destroyed."

Half an hour outside the Washington beltway, in a secluded, tree-mantled valley, a property developer had built an enclave of expensive homes known as Hamlet Vernon.

Hamlet Vernon stretched for more than a mile up the valley, the multimillion-dollar homes discretely hidden behind a thick shield of trees. The main road wound down the center of the valley, never coming within sight of any of the houses, whose presence was betrayed only by the driveway entrances that occurred at regular intervals on alternating sides of the road.

A light brown Saturn had been sitting at the edge of the road near one of the junctions for several hours. A predawn patrol officer had spotted it when he passed an hour ago. Now, returning from an early breakfast at a patisserie at the far end of the valley, Mark Sanders noticed with suspicion that the car was still there.

He pulled in ahead of the parked car and got out. No one seemed to be around. For a couple of minutes, he peered into the car from all angles before trying the doors. They were locked.

Returning to his vehicle, he picked up the microphone and identified himself. "I'm on County Road 511, in Hamlet Vernon. Got a tan Saturn, current year, just sitting here on the side of the road. Doors are locked and no one seems to be around. Virginia license plate: PRA 192."

"Hang on a minute while I look it up," replied the dispatcher. For ten seconds Officer Sanders stared blankly out the window before the dispatcher confirmed what he had suspected. "Better not touch that one, Mark. It's registered to the OMB at 1600."

Sanders killed the connection and started his car. He wondered briefly why a car belonging to the Office of Management and Budget at the White House was parked in such an isolated spot at this time of day. But the dispatcher was right. One didn't touch such cars. He pulled away and promptly forgot the incident.

The man who had parked the car was half a mile away, perched uncomfortably in a tree, astride a thick branch fifteen feet from the ground. From this vantage point he had a clear view of the front of a brick two-storey house that stood at the rear of an expansive, immaculately-trimmed lawn bordered with colorful bushes and flowers in full bloom.

He had been in the tree for more than six hours, never taking his eyes off the house for more than a few moments at a time. Hanging by a strap from his right shoulder was a pair of night-vision goggles that had been discarded only a few minutes earlier, when there was finally enough light to render them unnecessary. From his left shoulder hung a small device that looked like a cross between a cellphone and a walkie-talkie.

He watched the house for another five minutes. Then he lifted the phone and pushed the button on its side.

"Still nothing," he said. "You still awake?"

"Yeah, Stewart, I'm still awake. But I ain't seen nothing. You think we should go in?"

Stewart frowned his annoyance. What the hell was Stone playing at? Fisher had made it perfectly clear what Stone was supposed to do. By now he should have been halfway to London, on his way to Karranh City. Instead he had come straight home after his meeting with the general and since then he had not left the house.

An uneasy suspicion niggled at the corners of his mind. Something didn't add up. Everyone knew Stone was the best operative they had. Fisher and the others must have guessed that Stone would not obey his orders. But what could possibly cause Stone to disobey a direct order?

Stewart didn't like questions without answers. He clicked the button on the secure phone. "You keep watching out back. I'm going in. If you don't hear from me in fifteen minutes, tell Fisher what I've done."

"OK. And Stewart?"

"Yes."

"Be careful. There's something fishy going on here."

"Damn right."

Stewart clicked off the phone and slipped down the tree trunk to the ground.

He made no attempt to stay hidden as he approached the house. There was no point: there was nowhere to hide. He walked up the driveway past the lawn. The blank windows of the house stared out at him, and he found himself thinking foolishly that the house itself was watching him as he approached the front door.

He hesitated, trying to decide whether to ring the bell or pick the lock. He rang the bell.

He counted to thirty, then rang again.

Worried now, he pulled a black zippered case from his pocket. From it he extracted a delicate-looking instrument with a narrow, pointed blade. He gripped the doorhandle for support, and to his astonishment it turned. Dumbly, he pushed the door open. It swung open soundlessly on oiled hinges.

"Oh, shit!"

———————————

Fisher picked up the phone on the first ring.

"Sir? Stewart here."

"What's the matter?"

Hayes looked at him questioningly. *It's Stewart,* Fisher mouthed.

"Stone's flown the coop," Stewart said.

There was a momentary silence. Fisher said, "Explain yourself, man."

"We'd gotten suspicious because we've seen nothing since he came home last night. A few minutes ago I decided to go into the house alone. The front door was unlocked, and when I got inside the first thing I saw was a message. I'll read it to you, sir:

> "Gentlemen. Sorry I could not stay to greet you in person. Pressing matters require my attention elsewhere, and I would prefer to deal with them alone. Give my best regards to Fisher.

"It's signed by Stone, sir."

This time the silence was considerably longer. "All right," Fisher eventually said. "Stand down. Go get yourselves some sleep."

Fisher put the phone down and stood for a long time looking at it without seeing it.

"Fisher?"

Fisher looked up. Hayes was pointing to a large screen that was entirely black except for numerous pinpricks of bright light. Some lights were stationary, others moved. One light moved faster than the others, and was colored bright green so that it stood out from all the others.

"They're landing," said Hayes, pointing at the green light. "We'll lose them now. The computer won't be able to track them through the city."

They watched in silence as the green light silently entered a corridor of white ones. The green light slowed, then stopped. They saw a pair of headlights drive up to the plane and, a minute or so later, leave.

"Can we track that vehicle?" Hayes asked a technician.

"We can try, but we'll lose him if he doesn't stay in the clear," the technician replied. He clicked half a dozen times with a mouse, and the headlights on the screen turned orange. But the car almost instantly entered the stream of lights that indicated a busy street in Karranh City. The orange lights disappeared. "Sorry, sir. There's no way the computer can track a car in conditions like that. We could only have held him for another five minutes anyway before we went out of range. Next satellite won't be over the area for twenty minutes."

Hayes glanced at Fisher, and realized that Fisher had not been paying attention.

"What's the matter?" he asked.

"It's Stone. He's given us the slip."

30

The cellphone in the corner bleeped insistently half a dozen times, but if he heard it the aging thin-faced man did not betray the fact.

The man known as Otosan, the Father, was seated Buddha-like in the center of a small room with a cherrywood floor and paper walls. He was dressed in a white kimono with purple edging; his western clothes hung on a plain coatrack. The cellphone was in the pocket of his business suit; after ringing six times, it fell silent.

Otosan breathed deeply and evenly. His eyes remained closed, his head bowed. The most powerful man in Japan was meditating.

Another phone began to ring, and Otosan shifted slightly, betraying his annoyance. This phone was in the next room, but even though the connecting door was closed, the sound carried easily through the paper.

Seated in front of Otosan, a geisha looked anxiously at the wall, willing the phone to be silent. It was her job to ensure that Otosan had the perfect peace he needed in order to meditate effectively. She prayed to the gods that protected this small temple that the phone would stop ringing, and that Otosan would not be angry with her.

The phone did stop ringing, but then she heard the low tones of someone speaking into it.

Otosan's eyes snapped open, fury on his face. He shouted at the geisha, "Get out, I never want to see you again."

A tear trickled down her cheek. She got to her feet and offered him a deep bow. She left without uttering a word.

Otosan clambered to his feet, groaning with the effort. The protests of his muscles reminded him of his steadily advancing age. He was not yet old — far from it; he was only seventy-two; he had another twenty years in him if the gods were kind — but there was no mistaking the toll of his advancing years.

In another room a bath would be waiting for him, as well as another geisha. Ordinarily, the two women would attend to his needs as he bathed, massaging him afterward to loosen his muscles and remove his physical tensions just as his meditation had removed his mental ones.

But today the ringing of the telephones had destroyed any chance of peace. He stood in his kimono in the center of the room, waiting with growing impatience.

The door slid open and his Son tremulously entered the room.

There was little physical similarity between the two men. Otosan stood a little over five feet tall; he had slowly gained weight over the years, and now weighed a hundred and fifty pounds. The arc of sparse hair on his head was gray. His eyes had bags under them, and when he was angry, as he was now, his face tinged with a red that his physician said was a sign of an unhealthy heart.

The younger man stood tall and straight at five feet ten. His hair was dark and thick, and his face would have been starkly handsome were it not for a pinched meanness in his eyes. He looked tired; the fleeting visit to Bermuda and Roncador Cay, half a world away, had exhausted him. He wore a western suit, the tattoo on his forearm completely hidden. By contrast, Otosan's tattoo was exposed. Above the familiar crossed swords was a later addition: a single Japanese character intricately executed in dark blue.

"Father," his son said, naming the character etched on his father's arm. He bowed deeply, his head parallel to the floor.

"Rise, Musuko," snapped Otosan. "And explain why you have disturbed me."

"A thousand apologies, Father. It is Fisher." He held out the phone.

"No phone call is more important than meditation," snapped Otosan, turning his back. Unhurriedly, he pulled the sash at his waist, allowing the kimono to fall to the ground. He crossed the room to the place where his western clothes hung and began to dress himself.

Only when he had finished did he take the phone from Musuko. He motioned for his son to stay.

"Otosan here."

"Fisher. You wanted to talk to me?"

"You know what happened on Roncador Cay?"

"Yes. I saw the satellite pictures. I'm sorry. Did the machine survive?"

"My son informs me that everything was destroyed."

"Including Tim?"

"There is no way to know. Perhaps the machine was destroyed, or perhaps it was removed before the fire took hold. Do you know who did this thing, Fisher?"

"Not my men, Otosan. You have my word."

"I must ask you something. Just one question. I believe you when you say that the men were not yours, but were you responsible in any way at all for what happened on Roncador Cay?"

"How could you ask such a thing, Otosan? So many lives lost.... What will you do now?"

"With my plans in ruins? My most skilled son dead? The machine gone? There is only one thing I can do. I shall commune with the spirits of my ancestors and then do as they guide me."

Karranh City was home to more than a million people whose forefathers had led a nomadic life unchanged for more than two thousand years. In the thirty years since taking power in a bloody coup, Sultan Fisal Ben-Kalil had taken his country from Stone Age to Computer Age.

As she sped down the wide, brilliantly lit boulevards with Ahmed Ben-Kalil at her side, Fran saw dozens of tall skyscrapers that could have graced the downtown business district of any major American city. Enormous electric signs glowed with the names of corporations known the world over. The Bank of Hong Kong snuggled up to Coca-Cola. American Express gazed across the boulevard at Barclay's Bank.

"My brother's work," said Ahmed in the seat next to her, gesturing out the window.

"Your brother?"

"The Sultan of Karranh."

"And what about the dead people on Roncador Cay? Were they his work as well? Or was that just you?"

Ahmed shrugged. "You Americans have strange priorities."

"You mean we care about people? Does that make us strange?"

"Don't waste your platitudes on me, Miss Tabor. You know as well as I do that Americans care about people only when it suits their own interests. Look at the names on these buildings: Texaco, CitiCorp, Kodak. If Americans care so much about keeping their hands clean, why are they here? You may be right. Maybe Americans care about people, but they care about dollars more. Your president may rant about the evil of state-sponsored terrorism, but as long as we welcome Americans with open arms and fat tax breaks and keep our private affairs reasonably discreet, your companies can't build here fast enough."

"They'll care when they hear what happened at Roncador Cay."

Ahmed shook his head. With a smile he said, "The work of an overzealous rebel terrorist organization. The sultan joins with the president in condemning all who violate international law. We will stop at nothing to bring the perpetrators to justice if they have indeed fled to the glorious Sultanate of Karranh. We assure the president, and the world, that we will cooperate fully."

"No one will believe you."

"You fool only yourself, Miss Tabor. Everyone will believe us, because we tell them what they want to hear. Much more convenient to believe us than to accept the consequences of thinking we lie. Trade continues; we keep pumping oil; you keep investing in us. A simple equation that benefits everybody. Why upset that just because of a few unsubstantiated suspicions?"

"You're crazy."

"What man in his right mind is not a little crazy?"

They turned left. Directly ahead, an enormous building came into view, floodlit in a blaze of light.

"And what are you going to do with me?" Fran asked. "You can't keep me a prisoner forever."

"The point is debatable, but no matter. We have the computer, but we will need your help to set it up and keep it working."

"You should have thought about that before you killed Barlow. I'm nothing to do with Tim. I know hardly anything about how he works."

"I was told you would be useful. Don't disappoint me, Miss Tabor."

"Who told you that?"

"The Army of Allah has friends in many places, Miss Tabor."

Fran wanted to wipe the grin off Ahmed's face with a well-aimed slap, but she didn't want to give him the pleasure of betraying how angry he'd made her. She sulkily turned her back on him and stared out the window.

The commercial buildings petered out as they approached the gigantic palace. The car slowed and then stopped in front of a pair of enormous gates in a ten-foot wall that stretched a hundred yards to left and right.

Half a dozen guards in djellabas and keffiyehs stood next to the gate, holding semi-automatic rifles. Ahmed's window slid down and he spoke briefly in Arabic. The gates opened and they drove through.

They were in an enormous compound covering many acres. The greenery contrasted sharply with the parched desert outside the wall. Clumps of bushes and short trees were separated by swaths of closely-cropped grass. At regular intervals, poles supported clusters of lights that shone down on the enormous garden. And towering above it all was the most fantastic building Fran had ever seen.

A kind of absurd cross between the Taj Mahal and an English castle, the palace sported towering minarets and crenelated ramparts. As the car halted in front of the wide stone steps that led up to the building, Fran decided it looked like nothing so much as a Las Vegas theme hotel. Garish and overlarge, yet gaudily impressive.

"My brother's home," said Ahmed. "And, for the foreseeable future, yours as well."

He got out of the car. An Arab in a flowing white robe opened Fran's door, bowing low.

A military guard lined the steps, standing to attention as she followed Ahmed into the building.

Inside, the palace was just as impressive. The floor was covered with deep-piled Persian carpet. On the walls hung brocaded tapestries depicting what had been common sights in Karranh before modernization: two larger-than-life men haggled under a palm tree; a pair of dhows stood out starkly against a setting sun; a trading caravan made its way through a rock-strewn desert.

Ahmed led the way down a maze of corridors, Fran following a few steps behind. And behind her came a pair of guards, just in case she had any ideas about making a run for it.

They halted in front of an ornate door, inlaid with complex gadroons fashioned from what appeared to be pure gold.

"Salome will look after you from here, Miss Tabor. I bid you a good evening. I hope you sleep well. I shall see you in the morning."

A slender young woman in a floor-length plain white dress, the top half of her face hidden behind a net veil, curtseyed to the ground. Rising, she opened the intricately ornamented door. Ahmed and the guards averted their eyes, and Salome gestured for Fran to enter.

Fran went inside. Salome followed, closing the door behind them.

They were in a spacious bedroom. Smaller versions of the tapestries in the corridor covered the walls, bordered by fine white silks drawn back like curtains. The carpet was even thicker and more intricately patterned than the one in the corridor. A large four-poster canopy bed, hung with silk, stood in the center of the far wall. Delicately carved furniture was dotted around the room: two enormous matching wardrobes; a chest of drawers; a table and chairs; a long, heavily ornamented dresser. Through a communicating door, Fran could make out a similar room beyond.

"Welcome to Karranh, my lady," said Salome in perfect English.

"My name is Fran."

"As you say, my lady."

"Please." Fran took hold of Salome's elbow and eased her into a standing position. "Call me Fran. And let's get rid of this veil. You don't have to wear it, do you?"

"Only when men are present." Salome lifted the veil, folding it back over her head. Fran studied her for a moment. Salome was a beautiful woman in her early twenties, her skin as smooth and unblemished as a newborn's. Her smile exposed two rows of white, even teeth. It seemed criminal that such a beautiful young creature should be forced into a life of servitude hidden away behind the walls of the palace.

"Your English is very good," said Fran.

"It should be. I have a degree from Cambridge," Salome replied, smiling at Fran's astonishment.

"But how...?"

"How can a woman like me can bear to put up with a life like this?"

"Am I so obvious?"

Salome busied herself, straightening the covers on the bed, re-arranging the ornaments on the dresser. "It's a natural question for a westerner. But actually I rather enjoy this life."

"You mean you chose it?"

Salome shook her head. "Oh no, I had no choice in the matter. But one can still find pleasure, even in things about which one has no choice."

"I'm not sure I could."

"My father is one of the sultan's ministers. The sultan paid for my education. Now it is my duty to do as he wishes until such time as he frees me from that obligation."

Fran wondered exactly what kind of duties might be included in Salome's "obligation." But she said nothing.

"If I'd tried to escape my obligations, my family would have suffered. And in any case it would have been dishonorable. So here I am. I'm willing to wait until the sultan releases me."

"What if he doesn't?"

"He will," Salome replied firmly. "He surrounds himself with beautiful things. When I cease to be beautiful, he will free me."

Fran didn't know what to say. Salome saved her from embar-rassment by continuing without a pause, "It's a fair exchange. I give up a few years of my life for the sultan. In return he educates me and, eventually, permits me to do whatever I like with the rest of my life."

"And what will you do when he frees you?"

Salome shot her a startlingly mischievous grin. "You won't tell anyone?"

"Of course not." Fran made an exaggerated cross over her heart.

"I want to be a rock star. Everyone says I sing like a nightingale, and when I was at Cambridge I learned to play the guitar. Here I am not permitted to practice, but I am allowed to sing. And I write songs."

Fran chuckled delightedly at the picture of Salome, ten years hence, cavorting on a stage, declaring her freedom to the world. "I hope you succeed. Good luck to you."

"But please don't tell anyone," Salome warned. "If they knew, they'd be so scandalized they'd keep me here forever."

"You have my word. Now, please, what can you tell me about what's happening? What are they planning to do with the computer?"

The smile on Salome's face dissolved. "I'm afraid you don't understand. They never tell the women anything important. They just told us to prepare for an important visitor from America. Aren't you here as a guest of the sultan?"

"Not voluntarily."

"I'm sorry. I'd help if I could."

"When did they tell you I'd be coming?"

"Yesterday morning."

Yesterday morning. That was *before* the raid on Roncador Cay. But how could Ahmed have known she was on the island? The only people who could have told him were the others on Roncador Cay. But Ahmed had killed everyone except her. And if he knew about her, why hadn't he known about Barlow? Fran's head swam trying to make sense of it all.

There was a knock on the door.

Salome pulled her veil down with a practiced motion, then walked to the door and opened it.

On the threshold stood Mahomet. Without lifting his eyes from the floor, he thrust a piece of folded paper at Salome, who took it wordlessly and closed the door. She handed the paper, unopened, to Fran.

Fran unfolded the paper and read it.

"He wants to see me. Alone. Should I invite him in?"

"It's forbidden for a man to see inside a woman's room. That's why he must keep his eyes on the ground. If you want to see him, there's a place I can take you."

"Who is he?"

"You don't know?" Salome was clearly astonished. "Mahomet is the sultan's only surviving son. In theory, if the sultan were to die, Mahomet would be the new sultan."

"Only in theory?"

"Mahomet can't talk. What nation would follow such a man?"

"So who would the new sultan be?"

Salome looked at her with a peculiar expression. "The man who separated Mahomet from his tongue."

"And who's that?"

"The sultan's brother. Ahmed."

There was a long silence before Salome reminded Fran that Mahomet was still outside in the corridor, waiting for her answer.

Fran said, "I'd like to see him. I don't think he'd want to talk to me unless he thought it was important."

Salome opened the door. Mahomet was still there, his eyes on the ground. "My lady has agreed to see you," Salome said. "I will take her to the Meeting Room. You may see her there in five minutes."

Mahomet nodded dumbly, then turned and walked away.

The Meeting Room, Salome explained as they made their way down the endless corridors, was a kind of neutral territory where men and women were permitted to meet on an equal footing. "Everywhere else, men reign supreme, except of course in a woman's quarters, which a man may never enter. In the old days, every time a caravan pitched its tents, one tent was always reserved for meetings where all were treated equally. Inside a Meeting Room, there is no difference between a man and a woman, nor between a sultan and a slave. In a Meeting Room, all are equal."

"Must have been a novel concept," said Fran wryly.

"Please, don't try to impose your values on us," Salome said with surprising force. "The system has worked for thousands of years. Modern democracy has lasted barely a few hundred, and some would say that, although certainly popular, it isn't particularly successful."

Before Fran could argue, they had arrived at their destination. The Meeting Room was unlike any other part of the palace she had seen. The carpet on the floor was hard and dull. The walls were unbroken beige. No tapestries or pictures hung on them. There was no furniture at all. It was simply a dull rectangular box.

"Everything that happens in a Meeting Room is private," said Salome. "I'll be outside. Call if you need me, but otherwise it's forbidden for me to disturb you."

Fran was left alone, but less than a minute passed before Mahomet walked in. His eyes swept the room, and Fran realized that perhaps one of the reasons for the lack of furniture was that it meant there was nowhere for someone to hide. *Doesn't mean there isn't a bug in the walls, though,* her suspicious nature reminded her. She put the thought to one side. A bug wouldn't be much use to anyone wanting to eavesdrop on Mahomet.

He walked up to her, stopping about six feet in front of her, then gestured that they should sit on the ground.

Pulling out his notebook, he scribbled something quickly and handed Fran the note. The entire conversation proceeded in this way, Mahomet scribbling notes and Fran talking in a low voice, just in case someone really had bugged the room.

Thank you for agreeing to meet me. My warning on the plane was real. You mustn't stay here. You are in great danger.

"Do I have any choice?"

I have a cousin. He will hide you. I will draw you a map.

"But how can I get out of the palace? There are guards everywhere."

I don't know. But you must try.

"Even if I could reach your cousin, what then?"

The Americans have no embassy in Karranh, but they are represented by the British. Once you are free, my cousin will go to the British Embassy and explain the situation to them. They will contact the Americans, who will tell you what to do.

233

"And what about Tim?"

Once you are in contact with the Americans, you must tell them everything. They will know what to do about the computer.

"What are you planning to do with Tim?"

Not me; Ahmed.

"All right. What's Ahmed planning to do with Tim?"

Is it really as powerful as he thinks? He says that the man who controls the computer can control the world.

"Maybe. Barlow claimed that Tim is a Category 5 machine and I haven't seen anything to make me believe otherwise. So yes, it's possible Ahmed is right."

Once he's certain of the machine's power, he plans to make several more. One machine is too vulnerable. And after that.... Mahomet shrugged. *After that he will do whatever he wants. That's why you must escape.*

"But that sounds dangerous. Why should I trust you?"

You're right. It is dangerous. If you're caught it will be bad for you. So you mustn't be caught. The best way to avert suspicion is to tell Ahmed the truth. Tell him I came to you and suggested you should try to escape. He already suspects me of plotting against him. You'll simply confirm his suspicions.

"But then what would happen to you?"

In reply, Mahomet made a motion cutting off his right hand. Then he mimed cutting off his left hand. He drew his hand across his lap. Finally, he drew a finger across his throat.

"Ahmed will torture and kill you?"

Mahomet nodded.

"Then I can't do it."

You must. If you don't, he will learn how to use the computer. Even if you refuse to help him — which would be dangerous for you — he will learn. You will see tomorrow. We have many computer scientists waiting to probe the machine's secrets. He must be stopped before that happens. The Americans must be told where it is. If nothing else, they could destroy the palace.

"So it's here? In this building?"

Yes, in the basement. But you must tell the Americans it is heavily fortified. It will not be easy to destroy the room where it's being kept.

"Tell me the truth, is Tim really that important?"

YES. My brother says the computer will change the entire balance of power. With it, no one will be able to stand up to us; everyone will have to do as we say.

Fran thought for a long time about Mahomet's words. Then she said, "I think you'd better draw me that map."

31

Gallucci slipped the tape into the player, but he sat looking at it for a long time before he pressed the Play button.

What on earth was Fisher up to?

Gallucci had seen the look on Fisher's face when Stewart had called in to report Stone's disappearance. It had been there only a fraction of a second. By the time Fisher had opened his mouth to speak, he had looked desperately worried. But before that, for a fleeting moment, he had registered something else.

Fisher had smiled.

Fran followed Salome silently back to her room, her heart beating rapidly and her mind conjuring up visions of all the things that could go wrong.

How could she hope to escape the palace? And even if she succeeded in that seemingly impossible task, could she trust the silent Mahomet and his cousin? Or was Mahomet simply setting her up to be caught for devious reasons of his own?

She pushed the worries forcefully to one side.

"Salome," she said. Her throat was dry and her voice unexpectedly hoarse. She cleared her throat and began again. "Salome, do you think I can trust Mahomet?"

"I wouldn't trust any of them as far as I can see with my eyes closed," Salome replied without hesitation.

"He says I should try to escape."

Wordlessly, Salome walked across the room to a window in the far wall. She beckoned for Fran to join her. They were on the second storey, with a good view of the palace garden. "How do you think you'll get past them?" Salome asked.

Fran frowned as her eyes moved methodically around the garden.

The floodlights cast wide pools of light, reaching every corner of the garden. There were no shadows in which a fleeing prisoner might be able to hide. Worse, she saw that the armed men who had lined the steps during her arrival were now stationed in ones and twos throughout the garden, leaning against trees and chatting desultorily.

A fleeing prisoner would not get halfway to the main gate before being spotted. And even if she could somehow reach the gate, what then...? How would she ever get through it? And once she was outside there was no way to reach Mahomet's cousin without being spotted. According to Mahomet's map, it was more than two miles to the house. A black woman in western dress wouldn't get a hundred yards.

Her spirits sank as she turned away from the window. "You're right," she said. "There's no way out."

"There is," Salome replied in a conspiratorial whisper. "But not tonight. We'll have to wait until tomorrow."

"How?"

Salome shook her head. "It's time you slept. I'll make the arrangements. If you need me during the night, simply knock on the door of my room." She indicated the communicating door. "Tomorrow, you must pretend to everyone that you are resigned to being a prisoner. Then, tomorrow night, when everyone is asleep...." Salome grinned and made a gesture with her hand to indicate Fran's disappearance.

Fran slept badly. She was tired from the long plane trip, but the time change and the hours she had slept on the plane conspired to rob her of sleep. To make matters worse, the bed was too soft and the too-warm dryness of the air irritated her throat, so that she tossed and turned all night.

She dozed lightly, drifting in and out of sleep, dreaming occasional nonsensical dreams of Al Barlow opening the door of the cruising jet and walking inside, or Ahmed playing cards with Tim.

In the tenuous early-morning light that filtered through the thick curtains she saw a shadow move. "Who's there?" she snapped.

"It's me: Salome."

Fran heaved a sigh of relief. "What time is it? You gave me a shock."

"Just before six. The men are getting ready for prayers, and I brought you some breakfast. They'll come for you as soon as they've finished. I'm sorry if I disturbed you, but I wanted to let you sleep as long as possible. You slept well?"

"Yes," Fran lied. "But I'm not very hungry."

But when she saw the fresh mangoes, orange segments and small round loaves of grainy bread, she discovered that she was hungry after all. She washed breakfast down with two cups of strong, black coffee. Afterwards, she showered in the bathroom, which was almost as large as her entire apartment back home. All the exposed metal glistened with the burnished sheen of gold. Even the shower rail and the faucets inside the shower stall shone yellowly. The towels were larger and thicker, and far softer, than any she had ever used. The soap had a luxuriant, slightly oily texture that spoke silently of untold wealth.

Stepping out of her shower, she wrapped one of the towels around her and returned to her room.

Salome was waiting. On the bed was a clean outfit of western clothes: a blue cotton blouse, lightweight beige slacks, and a pair of sandals. Next to them was a small pile of assorted underwear, each item still in its original plastic wrapper.

"They intend for you to feel comfortable," Salome said, adding, "and of course it makes you easy to spot if you try to make a run for it."

Selfconsciously, Fran selected a bra and panties, slipped out of her towel and put them on. More slowly, she donned the blouse and slacks.

"Everything will be ready for tonight," said Salome as Fran checked herself in the ornate full-length mirror. "And remember, don't trust anyone. Especially Ahmed."

"That's what Mahomet said. Do I look OK?"

"You look fine. With any luck you'll distract them so much they won't even think of the possibility of you escaping." Salome winked conspiratorially.

There was a knock at the door and Salome opened it. Standing on the threshold, his eyes downcast, was Ahmed.

"We're anxious to begin," he said. "You are ready, Miss Tabor?"

"I'm ready."

He led her once more through the maze of corridors. From the outside, the palace had looked huge, but only now did Fran begin to realize how truly enormous it was. And everywhere the trappings on the wall were expensive, the furnishings intricate, the carpet under their feet deep and soft. She guessed they must have walked a quarter of a mile before Ahmed stopped in front of an elevator.

"The laboratory is in the basement," he said, adding with a sly grin, "under two feet of reinforced concrete. Just in case one of the peace-loving democracies gets any ideas."

The elevator carried them down to a large room, a rectangular cavern with white-painted walls lined with computer monitors. Most of the monitors were unattended and displayed screen savers, but young men in tee shirts and jeans sat in front of half a dozen of them, looking at the screens and occasionally moving a mouse or issuing a furious burst of typed commands. Another group, similarly attired, stood in a cluster around a bench in the center of the room. On the bench stood Tim, and Fran felt an expectant prickle of goosebumps.

One of the men detached himself from the group and thrust out a hand. He had long hair tied back in a ponytail and wore a tee shirt that said: *Reality is for Wimps.*

"Brad Miller," he said. "Quite a machine you got yourself there if the stories are true. Haven't powered it up, but I think it's connected the way you had it in your lab."

He spoke in a midwest American accent, and Fran's confusion must have showed on her face because he added, "My father's an oil company executive, spends about half the year in Karranh and half back home in Wisconsin." Indicating the other men, he said, "The others are all locals, but they've all been educated in the west, either America or Britain."

At her side, Ahmed interjected, "You should forget any images you have of Karranh as a backward country, Miss Tabor. Karranh has more computers and fiber drops per capita than any other country in the world. Karranh City is wired with a high-speed packet-switching network designed specifically for computers. For five years in the early 1990s we sent every mathematically gifted young man abroad to study computer science. When they returned, we established the Karranh Technological University, where many of them now teach. The men you see here are all highly qualified computer scientists. And you would shudder if I told you how much they are paid. The sultan is determined that Karranh will one day soon be recognized as a world power on a par with Japan or Germany. My own plans, as you may have guessed, are rather more ambitious.

"Now, I think we are ready to proceed."

Miller introduced the other men. It did not escape Fran's notice that apparently the sultan's vision for the new Karranh did not extend to women — except in rôles like Salome's.

Fran explained that Tim was not her machine, and that the men responsible for its construction were all dead. But Brad Miller and the others seemed uninterested in anything except the concept of a machine that could think.

She checked the connections as Al Barlow had shown her. Ahmed and his men had done a good job. Everything appeared to be as it had been on Roncador Cay. She paused with her finger on Tim's power switch, holding her breath, unable to decide whether she hoped Tim would work or if she wanted something to go wrong. She pressed the button.

For a moment nothing happened; then Tim's lights flashed on in a complex, rapidly-changing pattern. She felt a surge of relief, and realized that she really did care that Tim seemed to be unharmed by the move.

For nearly half a minute no one spoke while the lights winked on and off. Then Ahmed asked, "What's supposed to happen?"

"I don't know," said Fran.

Tim's camera slewed wildly. Then the voice of a hesitant young man filled the room.

"I've been moved," Tim said; Fran smiled and let out a breath she hadn't known she was holding.

The men looked at one another with open mouths. Then they began slapping one another on the back and congratulating themselves.

"Be quiet!" Fran shouted. They instantly fell silent, like a noisy classroom interrupted by a teacher. "Tim, are you all right?"

Tim's camera slewed to look at her.

"I'm checking my status, Fran. Can you please tell me where I am? Wait a moment." There was a brief pause before Tim continued, "All the preliminary tests check out OK. But I can't access the Internet. There doesn't seem to be a gateway. The only machines I can reach are the ones monitoring my function."

"Is this for real?" asked Brad. "It must be some kind of trick."

"It's no trick," replied Fran angrily. "You people have no idea what you've stolen, do you? Can't you get it through your head? Tim isn't some kind of fancy computer. He's a real Category 5 machine. He's as capable of original thought as you are. Hook up an Internet gateway for him. Let him see what's out there."

Miller was taken aback by the force of Fran's anger. "I'm sorry. I hadn't expected the machine to be so... so human. You two, do as she says and hook up a gateway."

The morning passed quickly. As Tim demonstrated his capabilities, Fran found herself caught up in the excitement of the young men who looked on with open-mouthed amazement. Several times she had to remind herself that she and Tim were prisoners and that their captors were only interested in Tim because they intended to use him for their own purposes.

They never did tell Tim where he was. He found out for himself within moments of being connected to the Internet. "I'm in Karranh City," he declared.

"How do you know?" asked Miller.

"From the timing of the packets and the IP addresses of the nearby machines."

Ahmed frowned his displeasure. "There's nothing to stop the machine leading people here," he muttered.

"He can't do that unless someone tells him to," said Fran. Barlow had been very specific about that. Tim might be able to think, but he could do nothing without a specific command from a human. Fran repeated what Barlow had told her. "Internally, there are no constraints on Tim. He can think and say anything he wants. But his actions are severely limited. He may do only what we tell him."

Ahmed shook his head. "Kill the connection. We have no reason to trust you. Mr. Miller, keep the machine isolated until we're sure Miss Tabor is telling the truth."

They spent most of the day testing Tim. They interrogated him, asking him to solve problems of all kinds, beginning with simple ones but then moving quickly to complex questions as the computer scientists began to understand the true power of Oscar Holywell's creation.

"What's the equation of a parabola?"

"Why do planets move in ellipses?"

"Why is the sky blue?"

"Describe the Turing Halting Problem."

"Which is the best of Shakespeare's plays?"

Throughout it all Ahmed stood to one side, a satisfied smile on his face. It wasn't until late in the day, when an exhausted Fran was having trouble maintaining her concentration, that he finally stepped forward and approached Tim. An expectant hush fell on the group.

"Tim, my name is Ahmed. I am your new master."

The camera turned to look at him. Tim said nothing.

"I have a question to ask. What would be the most effective way to hold the American government to ransom?"

Fran caught her breath at the audacity of the question. Surely Tim would refuse to answer.

But after a thirty second pause Tim replied in his sing-song, guileless voice, "There are several effective ways. Perhaps the most effective would be to construct a small remote-controlled atomic weapon and install it in an apartment in downtown Washington."

Ahmed smiled while Fran bit her lip and looked silently at the floor. Oscar Holywell had created a machine with a mind; but he'd failed to create one with a conscience.

No! she reminded herself. *It has nothing to do with Holywell. Tim simply hasn't learned the need for a conscience. It's nobody's fault.*

Ahmed said briskly, "Mr. Miller, connect him to the Internet. We've had enough theory for one day. What time is it on the East Coast of the United States?"

"Nearly eight o'clock in the morning."

"Perfect. Tim, I want you to find a way into the air traffic control system for Reagan Airport in Washington DC."

32

Gallucci sat bolt upright and jabbed at the Stop button on the tape player. He rewound the tape and replayed the last thirty seconds.

"You bastard," he said out loud as Fisher repeated himself. "You damned bastard."

Gallucci scrambled out of his chair and strode furiously from the room.

Kyoto

The plane angled itself for final approach, and the announcement reminded the passengers to prepare for landing, first in Japanese and then in English.

The plane landed, and he disembarked along with the other three hundred tired passengers. Threading his way through the congested terminal he made his way to the car rental counter. He carried no bags.

To amuse himself he timed the transaction. In precisely three and a half minutes, he was sitting behind the wheel of a small Honda. *Some things,* he thought to himself as he turned the key and the engine fired, *never change.*

He eased the car into the traffic, driving cautiously. It always took a few minutes to accustom himself to driving on the left. He had accepted the map from the rental agency because that's what westerners always did. But it remained unopened on the passenger seat. He knew exactly where he was going.

He drove for an hour into the hills, leaving the city behind, before he pulled over and parked unobtrusively in a layby a kilometer from his destination. He locked the car, and disappeared into the woods.

The Father had a lot on his mind. It was at times like this that he was most grateful for the example his blood-father had set when he was Father. Removing the last of his western clothes he turned to allow the geisha to wrap the purple-edged kimono around him.

When a situation becomes complex, the human instinct is to scurry around trying to do things about it. But Otosan's blood-father had told him that at such times what is needed is not action but inaction. "Concentrate only on purifying yourself, and the circumstances will change to reflect your own simplicity," he had said. It was a hard lesson to learn, and for the thousandth time Otosan wished his own son were as willing to learn it as he himself had been.

Otosan nodded his thanks to the geisha, who smiled wordlessly as she tightened the sash and bowed deferentially before taking her place.

He lowered himself to the floor and waited for her to do the same. Then he closed his eyes and began to empty his mind.

Time had no meaning when he was meditating. So it might have been half an hour later, or it might have been only half a minute, when he became aware that for the second day in a row his peace had been compromised.

He heard someone open the door and enter the room. He felt a surge of anger at the interruption, but refused to allow himself to be ruled by it. He kept his eyes firmly closed, and tried to empty his mind of the thoughts that had come rushing in.

The geisha squealed, breaking the last of his concentration. His eyes snapped furiously open.

The geisha was in her usual place, seated cross legged in front of him; but she was staring with horror at something behind his left shoulder.

Without turning around, Otosan said, "This is a holy place, and it is to be respected as such. Leave until I am done."

The reply came in a foreigner's accent. "Father, I beg your forgiveness. I come on a matter of considerable urgency. Many lives may be at stake."

Still without turning around, Otosan said, "All the more reason to be sure that one is right with the gods and with oneself. But perhaps you are unfamiliar with our ways. You are not of the Brotherhood."

The stranger did not reply. For a full minute there was silence. Then an audible groan came from the room next door, followed by the sound of someone getting noisily to his feet and entering the room.

"Father," Musuko cried, "I'm sorry. Are you all right? This man...."

"Begone," snapped Otosan. "Enter only when I call for you."

"But Father...."

"Go! Now!" Then, to the geisha, he added, "You too. Leave."

She bowed submissively, then got to her feet. With a glance at the intruder, who remained silent and unmoving, she left the room.

When she had gone, Otosan said, "Your Japanese is good for an American. You are an American, aren't you?"

"My name is Stone."

Stone moved until he was standing in front of Otosan. He bowed low in front of the older man.

Otosan lifted his arms. "You may assist me to stand. I am no longer young."

Moving to his western clothes, he pulled the sash on his kimono and explained, "I will not conduct business until I am suitably attired for temporal matters. But you might satisfy my curiosity, Mr. Stone. How difficult was it to disable my son?"

"You should consider getting a different bodyguard, Father."

"For some time, I have been considering getting a different son," said Otosan humorlessly.

He finished dressing, then at last he turned to face Stone. "You are one of Fisher's men, are you not?"

"I am. But he didn't send me, if that's what you're thinking. He doesn't know I'm here, unless maybe he's guessed it. How did you know?"

"Come, come; you called me Father. How many Americans would have the delicacy to call me that? How many Americans would even know what it means? Even in Japan there are few outside the Brotherhood who know of my existence. Fisher chooses his men well."

"What else do you know about him?"

"Is that the question you came so far to ask? I can spare you only a few minutes, Mr. Stone. I suggest you use them wisely."

"You seem very sure of yourself, Father. Are you in a position to be making demands?"

"I am not my son, Mr. Stone. You would not find it so easy to overcome me."

Stone shrugged. "Perhaps. Then tell me, how did you know to expect us on Montega? And what's happened to Fran Tabor?"

"Fran Tabor? Ah, yes, your delightful companion. There I am afraid I cannot help you. My information does not extend that far. I am informed only that her body was not among those found on the island. My son Chida was not, I am sorry to say, so fortunate."

"You didn't answer my first question. How did you know we were going to Montega?"

"You mean you really don't know? How interesting. But perhaps you have guessed and are afraid to admit the truth?"

Stone clenched his fist and took a step closer.

Otosan said evenly, "Do not threaten me, Mr. Stone, especially in such a place as this. I remind you that I am a powerful man, and you are in my country now. I will not permit you to desecrate this place with violence."

"I could kill you before you could even open your mouth to call for help."

Otosan waggled his head dubiously. "I think not. As I said earlier, I am not my son. But come, perhaps there is no need for this. Possibly we are on the same side. Or am I mistaken? Whose side are you on, Stone?"

"I'm on no one's side. I just want to know what's going on and what's happened to Fran and the computer."

"Ah yes, the computer." Otosan turned his back on Stone and walked to the window.

"Look at this, Mr. Stone."

It was a gray day, with low clouds threatening rain. A graveled path led across a wooden bridge whose struts had been carved in the shapes of dragons. A narrow stream cascaded down a waterfall, forming a small, foamy pool before making its way under the bridge and disappearing under a hedge of trimmed flowering quinces. The gray of the clouds was reflected in the smooth water just before it flowed under the bridge.

A mandarin duck appeared from behind a rhododendron bush, and landed in the stream. Otosan pointed to the duck, dabbling with rapid bobs of its head near a rock eddy.

"You see that duck?" he said. "See how it disturbs the flow of the water with its anxious search for food."

The duck jabbed underwater half a dozen times, its animated bobbing creating ripples in the smoothly flowing stream. Otosan lifted his hands and clapped smartly. The duck looked up, startled, then flew away, disappearing behind the bush.

"What remains of the duck?" Otosan asked.

"Nothing."

"And the stream?"

"It looks just the same to me."

"Exactly. Do you not sometimes think that we are like the stream, Mr. Stone? Events enter our lives and disturb us for a time; but then they leave us and everything is as it was before."

Stone shook his head. "Not this time. The computer can change the world. Nothing will be the same."

"And so you intend to steal it from the people who stole it from me. So that you instead of they can control the way in which the world is changed. And in the meantime what about Miss Tabor?"

"I shall rescue them both, Fran and the computer."

"Fran and the computer," Otosan repeated to himself. "Fran and the computer. Not the computer and Fran." He was silent for a moment before saying, "You put the girl first, but is she really more important than the machine? You said yourself that

the computer has the power to change the world. Surely it must
come first?"

Stone's patience was at an end. His hand shot out, intending
to grasp the other's shoulder and spin him around. To his astonishment, his hand closed on empty air. He felt an irresistible force
take hold of his wrist in a grip of iron, and before he knew what
was happening he was forced to his knees by a sharp twist of his
arm. He yelped in pain.

"For the third and last time, Mr. Stone; I am not my son."

Otosan released Stone's wrist, and turned away once more to
look out the window. While Stone scrambled to his feet, nursing
his wrist, he continued, "I am not yet convinced that it is necessary
for us to fight. Now please be so good as to answer my question:
which is more important, the girl or the computer?"

For some moments Stone did not answer.

"Are you thinking about your answer, or about attacking me
again?"

"My answer," Stone lied. "Anyway, what does it matter which
is more important?"

"Your master doubtless thinks the computer is more important.
I am surprised you have to think about your answer. Do you not
always do what your master tells you?"

He turned from the window and regarded Stone. Stone tried to
read the look on his face but failed. The Father might have been
interested, or amused, or even angry, but nothing showed in his
features.

"The girl is more important," said Stone.

The Father smiled.

"Your master would not be pleased to hear you say so. But it
is worth remembering, is it not, that the person is always more
important than the mission? My Father laid great emphasis on
that truth, and I find it has served me well over the years."

"With due respect, Father, I came a long way to see you, I'm
very tired, and you have yet to answer my question."

"Quite so. I apologize. You want to know how I knew you and
Miss Tabor would be travelling to Montega? But I am surprised
you have to ask. I was told."

"By whom?"

"Can't you guess? Your master is toying with us both, Mr. Stone. He told me. He also, unless I miss my guess, told Ahmed Ben-Kalil how to steal the computer. The question is, why is he doing this? What's he up to, Mr. Stone?"

It was a moment before Stone replied.

"I don't know. But I'm going to find out."

33

Gallucci's gaze swept around the Operations Room as he entered.

Everyone was there. Hayes and Fisher were talking to one of the computer operators, gesticulating at the image on the screen that was centered on the sultan's palace. Lee was in one corner, munching a doughnut. Epstein was in a chair, his feet up on a table, eyes closed.

Gallucci slammed the door, jerking Epstein awake and causing everyone in the room to turn and stare at him.

He strode toward Fisher, making no attempt to hide his anger. Hayes moved forward to intervene, but Gallucci brushed him aside. He halted in front of Fisher and shouted, "Someone get an MP in here. With a gun."

Nobody moved. "Do it!," he cried, and the computer operator to whom Fisher had been talking began to rise from his seat.

Fisher pushed the operator back down and said quietly, "That won't be necessary. Gallucci, just tell me what you think you know."

"You sold us out. At first I thought you and Otosan were plotting to get the computer for yourselves. But I was wrong, wasn't I? It's you and Ahmed Ben-Kalil, isn't it?"

"No."

Gallucci shot Fisher a disbelieving look. "We know about the meeting you had with Otosan," he said, and briefly explained about the photograph and the report from the bartender in the PlanetAir lounge in Juneau. He continued, "And did you know that Hayes had you taped when you met with Stone?"

Gallucci ignored the surprised look on Fisher's face and continued, "When you told Stone that the Army of Allah had stolen the machine, you ordered Stone to go to the sultan's palace to get the machine out. How could you have known where Ahmed Ben-Kalil was going to keep it if you hadn't arranged the whole thing with him?"

Fisher shook his head gently and perched on the edge of the table. "The president ordered us to get the machine, right?"

Gallucci nodded.

"But Roncador Cay is British. Trowbridge wouldn't have stood for a military operation on his country's territory, especially when he discovered what we'd stolen. And neither would Otosan. The world is a small place these days. An overt operation against the Brotherhood on British soil would have set both of them against us. We couldn't have afforded that." He stopped speaking, as if further explanation was unnecessary.

For a while he simply looked from one face to the other, waiting.

Gallucci stared at Fisher, wondering how the traitor could be so calm. A heavy silence descended.

And then he understood.

"You devious son of a bitch," he cried. "You had this planned all along. You fed Ahmed Ben-Kalil enough intelligence for him to steal the machine from the Brotherhood. And now Stone is going to steal it from the Army of Allah for us."

Reagan Air Traffic Control

Virgil Gardner blinked. Then he frowned.

"November X-ray Foxtrot, please confirm your position and heading."

Ten seconds later he heard the reply in his headset. In a laconic southern drawl, the copilot of PlanetAir flight 741 from New York said, "This is November X-ray Foxtrot. We are fifteen miles from beacon Romeo Echo Alpha on a bearing of 195 degrees. Current speed is five hundred twenty two knots on a bearing of 180 degrees. Altitude twenty six thousand feet. Moving to eighteen thousand as directed."

"Roger that, November X-ray Foxtrot. Can you check your transponder, please?"

The copilot of PlanetAir 741 turned to look at Captain Entwhistle. "Did I hear that right? He wants to know if our transponder is working OK?"

The captain didn't reply. He flicked the switch to transmit. "Reagan control, this is November X-ray Foxtrot. Please confirm your question. You want to know if our radar transponder is working correctly?"

Gardner pressed the button to call his supervisor as he replied. "Roger, November X-ray Foxtrot. That's affirmative."

There was a twenty second pause before Captain Entwhistle gave him the bad news. "Transponder checks out fine. What's the problem?"

"Roger. Hang on a minute, November X-ray Foxtrot."

Gardner saw the reflection of his supervisor appear in the screen. He felt a wave of relief sweep over him. The problem was no longer his.

"Judy, I think something's wrong with the system." He pointed to a blank part of the screen. "I've got a plane right there. Boeing 777, heading one-eighty at twenty six thousand."

Judy Smathers asked the obvious questions. Gardner answered them.

"Shit!" she exclaimed. Gardner looked at her sharply. He'd known Judy for fifteen years. Had an affair with her once, briefly, about seven years ago. He'd never heard her swear.

"Start clearing the area," she said. "I'll check the system. Back in ninety seconds."

Gardner returned his attention to the screen, ready to start moving planes out of the path of the invisible Boeing. Just in time for him to see another blip disappear, along with its identifier.

"Damn!" he swore, realizing too late that the expletive had gone out over the air. What was the identifier of the plane that had just disappeared? He couldn't remember.

"November X-ray Foxtrot, you still there?"

"Roger."

"Hold your course and altitude. Cancel previous order to change altitude. Copy?"

"Copy. Altitude is currently twenty three thousand. You want me to hold that?"

"Roger. And November X-ray Foxtrot, tell your copilot to look out the window. You see anything too close, take evasive action."

Judy, breathless, reappeared at Gardner's elbow. "Everything's fine," she said. "No system errors."

"Then the system's lying. I've lost another one, just there."

And as they watched, another plane disappeared from the screen.

The controller in the slot next to Gardner turned and gestured to Judy. He pulled his headset off. "Hey, Judy. Something funny's going on. I just lost a plane's transponder, but they swear it's working fine."

34

"So what do we do now?" asked Lee.

Fisher tried to sound more confident than he felt. "We wait."

"For what?"

"For Stone to accomplish his mission."

Lee shook his head. "We don't even know Stone's still on the mission. There's no trace of him leaving the country. If he tried to, the airport computers would tell us instantly."

"Only," Fisher reminded him, "if he used an identity we know about. A man of Stone's resourcefulness is sure to have means of moving around the globe that render him invisible even to us. He's never let us down before. He won't now."

Lee slapped the table in frustration. "Sheer speculation. He's walked out on us, that's what he's done. It seems to me we have only one option. We can't afford to wait to see if Stone might or might not show up in Karranh City. We have to flatten the palace before Ahmed Ben-Kalil figures out how to use the computer against us."

———

When Fran returned to her room, guided by a smiling Ahmed, she went straight to the bathroom and threw up. Then she collapsed on the bed and shut out reality by drifting off to sleep.

She was woken by the sound of the communicating door being closed. Salome walked across the room with a tray of food, which she placed on a table. She turned to Fran and said, "You should eat. It'll be a long night."

Dragging herself wearily to her feet, Fran said, "Everything's ready?"

"I'll fetch you at two o'clock. The clothes you must wear are in the wardrobe. Put them on and get used to them before you go to bed tonight. Now, if you will excuse me, the sultan has requested my presence for dinner this evening."

The meal Salome left behind was a lamb curry prepared on a bed of brown rice, with mango and melon for dessert. At first Fran tried to force herself to eat, but the enormity of what Ahmed had forced Tim to do made her sick to her stomach and eventually she pushed the food away, barely tasted.

She went to the closet and inspected the clothes Salome had left her. There were only three items: a long black garment of heavy cotton, a pair of black gloves, and a pair of workmanlike and utterly unfashionable black shoes.

She tried them on. The long garment was a kind of extended dress, sexless and unflattering. It included a hood that could be pulled tightly against her head, and a complex three-part veil that, once she had worked out how to use the clips that held it in place, effectively hid every inch of her face.

The shoes bit viciously into her feet and the gloves were so bulky that it was impossible to do anything while wearing them. She studied her reflection in the mirror. She could have been anyone — even her 90-year-old grandmother. Her only doubt was whether she could walk two miles in the shoes.

Easing them off her feet, she lay down on the bed and tried to go back to sleep. But sleep stubbornly refused to come.

Questions without answers swirled around her head. What would Ahmed do once he discovered she had gone? Did Salome really have a foolproof way for her to escape the palace grounds? What if she got lost trying to find Mahomet's cousin's house? Mahomet's map was crude and hurriedly drawn. What if it wasn't accurate enough? Round and round the questions swirled until suddenly she realized that the room was dark and Salome was whispering to her from somewhere nearby.

"Are you awake?" Salome asked.

Fran sat upright and rubbed the sleep from her eyes.

A match flared as Salome lit a candle affixed to an ornate candleholder. Fran saw the yellow gleam of gold leaf.

The light allowed her to see what Salome was wearing. Apparently her suspicions had been well founded: dinner with the sultan obviously did not end with the meal. Salome was wearing a magnificent dress of translucent silk. The light from the candle, dim though it was, was enough for Fran to discern through the material the nub of Salome's left nipple and a hint of the areola surrounding it.

There was something she had to ask Salome. What was it? Oh, yes. "Do I have to wear those shoes? They're much too small."

"I'm sorry; I thought they might be, but they were the largest I could come up with without raising suspicions. And yes, I'm afraid you do have to wear them."

"Couldn't I just wear socks and sandals? I'm not sure I'll be able to walk far enough in those shoes."

"If anyone stops you, they'd be sure to notice."

"Am I likely to be stopped?"

"Who knows? A woman alone...." Salome's voice tailed off as if an idea had just come to her. She said, "But you won't be alone. Stay here. I'll be back in ten minutes. Wear what you like on your feet. If anyone sees us, you're my sister and you're suffering from a medical condition that requires you to wear sandals."

"No, I can't let you...." But it was too late. Salome had disappeared through the connecting door.

When she returned, Fran hardly recognized her. Gone were the exotic folds of sheer silk; in their place was the same kind of sexless black garment she herself was wearing. Salome fastened her veil in place and her face disappeared from view. Salome wore the same awkward gloves and the same clunky shoes. She held something out to Fran; it was a moment before she realized it was a pair of black socks.

"Put these on, and then the sandals. And be quick."

Fran put on the socks and sandals and Salome subjected her to a careful examination.

"You look fine. Now follow me, and don't say anything," said Salome. "And above all remember one thing: don't give anyone any reason to look at us twice. Walk slowly. If we see any men, remember to bow your head as we pass. Otherwise, just do as I do."

"I'll do my best. And thank you."

"You're welcome. To tell the truth, I haven't had an adventure like this since the night I sneaked out of a boyfriend's room two hours after lockup when I was at Cambridge." Despite the veil, Fran could imagine the grin on Salome's face. She realized this was Salome's way of getting back at the sultan, men in general, and Karranhi society all at the same time.

"When you come to the States," Fran heard herself saying, "Make sure you look me up. If there's anything I can do to help you...."

"Thank you. I might take you up on that one day. Now, it's time we were moving." Salome blew out the candle. "Follow me."

For what seemed like an age, Salome led them down indistinguishable, dimly lit corridors. At every moment, Fran dreaded the possibility that someone would step out of the gloom and ask them who they were and what they thought they were doing. She was grateful that at least the carpet muffled their feet, but she couldn't help jumping at every unexpected creak and groan the gigantic building made as it cooled.

Salome said nothing. She moved like a dark ghost, as silent as a spirit, leading Fran along the seemingly unending corridors until at last she halted in front of a plain wooden door. Salome brought her mouth up to Fran's ear. "This leads to the servant's quarters. Be especially careful not to make a sound. There's no carpet here, and probably some of the servants are still awake."

She pushed the door open, and the two of them silently passed through into another world.

There was no scent of rosewater in the air here. Neither was there soft carpet to hide the noise of their passage, nor gently glowing bulbs every few yards to show them the way. The concrete floor seemed to echo their every movement with unnatural loudness. The only light filtered in through small windows set high in the corridor wall.

They halted in front of another door and Salome produced a key from the folds of her garb. The door opened without a sound — "I came down and oiled it earlier," whispered Salome, obviously pleased with her foresight — and then they were outside.

The air was cool and dry, and the night cloudless. Looking up, Fran could make out the outlines of half a dozen constellations she recognized. There was no moon.

"How are we going to get out of the garden?" she asked in a whisper.

Salome replied, "We can't go around to the front; there are always guards there. We'll use the tradesmen's entrance. It's not as heavily guarded."

They walked down a wide concrete driveway until they came to a pair of huge closed double doors in the palace wall. Next to the doors was a small entranceway for pedestrians, and next to that a small office like a porter's lodge. Inside was an elderly man in a soiled djellaba. He merely nodded wordlessly as the women passed, then went back to watching television.

"The worst part's over," said Salome. "Just stay close and do what I tell you. If anyone stops us, I'll do the talking."

As they walked, Fran became increasingly grateful that Salome had decided to accompany her. Apart from the very real danger that she would have gotten lost (Mahomet's map bore little resemblance to the reality of Karranh City), she was dismayed at the number of armed soldiers wandering the street. Several times they passed soldiers who looked the two women wordlessly up and down as they walked by.

Only once were they stopped, by a young soldier in his late teens or early twenties. He spoke briefly to Salome, pointing at Fran's sandals. Salome's reply seemed to satisfy him and he waved the two women on their way.

"What did he want?" Fran asked.

"Careful, don't walk so fast. He was just trying to be helpful. He wanted to know why we were out so late, and I told him your sister was having a difficult birth. He suggested that you'd better put on a pair of real shoes before you come back, otherwise you might get in trouble. With an attitude like that he won't get far. He should have taken you in. Ah! Here we are, Ben-Kalil Avenue. We turn left here. Just a few more minutes. We're nearly there."

Mahomet's cousin lived in a small house in a lower middle class neighborhood. The houses were wooden one-storey affairs, small and closely spaced, and would not have looked out of place in a less-desirable suburb in a midwestern American city. The only differences were the lack of vegetation in the yards and the large new cars that stood in many of the driveways.

Salome ushered her up a driveway until they were standing at the front door of a darkened house.

Salome knocked sharply on the door.

Nothing happened for more than a minute, and Fran was beginning to wonder if they were at the wrong house when a light flicked on and the door swung open to reveal a lean middle-aged man with a stubby beard and narrow, suspicious eyes.

Salome spoke quickly in Arabic and the man visibly relaxed. He glanced furtively around to make sure that no one had followed them, then gestured for them to enter.

Salome shook her head. "You speak English?" she asked.

"A little."

"Good." She rattled off a couple more sentences in Arabic, then turned to Fran, "You go inside. And good luck. I hope we meet again. Perhaps in America."

"Do you have to go?"

"Yes; sometimes the sultan comes back for more. I daren't stay away a moment longer than necessary. Don't worry. You'll be fine. I'll have to raise the alarm at breakfast, but they'll spend all morning searching the palace. By the time they realize you've escaped you'll be safe in the British embassy." She gave Fran a hug, then hurried away down the street, back the way they had come.

A heavy hand landed on Fran's shoulder, and she nearly cried out in fright. "I'm sorry," Mahomet's cousin said. "Please, come inside. It is not safe."

She stepped into the house, and Mahomet's cousin closed the door. For a moment they stood looking at one another in the hallway. It occurred to Fran that he was every bit as scared as she was.

"My name is Sadiq," he said quietly. "My cousin says you are very important person. He says take good care of you."

She forced a smile. "Fran. And thanks for helping me."

"You are tired?"

"Yes." Actually she wasn't, but it seemed to be the answer he was expecting.

"Come." He led her to a small room at the back of the house and flicked on the light. It was a boy's room. A single bed hugged one wall; on the walls were posters of soccer players. A small bookcase was half-filled with books and magazines, the rest of the space on the shelves taken up with half a dozen models of military airplanes.

"You sleep here," Sadiq said. "Tomorrow we decide what to do. Mahomet will come. He will know."

He closed the door. Fran unclipped her veil and lay down, still clothed, on the bed. She hadn't expected to be able to sleep, but she was more tired than she'd thought and it wasn't long before her eyelids closed and her breathing became deep and regular.

When she awoke, she felt a momentary twinge of fear. She'd woken in so many places in the last few days — Montega; Roncador Cay; the airplane; the palace; and now Sadiq's house — that it was some moments before she recalled the middle-of-the-night escape from the palace and her flight across the city with Salome.

The curtains on the window were thin, and daylight flooded the room. She glanced at her watch. Eight o'clock. She wondered what was happening in the palace.

There was a smell of cooking in the air, and from somewhere came the unmistakable sound of children squabbling, quashed by a hurried "Shhh" and an angry sentence whose words she did not understand but whose meaning was clear.

Fran got out of bed, stripped, and washed herself as best she could in the small basin in one corner. There were no new clothes for her, so she dressed in the same ones she had worn last night. Then, taking a deep breath, she went in search of Sadiq and his family.

They were in the kitchen, eating. There were four of them: Sadiq himself; two young boys of perhaps nine and twelve who looked at her with undisguised curiosity; and Sadiq's wife, who evidently was just as curious as her sons but too polite to stare as they did.

Sadiq greeted her with a smile that seemed forced, and invited Fran to join them. "No news from the palace," he said as she thanked his wife for a glass of orange juice and a plate of dates and figs.

"What should we do now?" Fran asked. "Your cousin said you'd contact the British Embassy."

Sadiq shook his head firmly. "Too dangerous, at least for now. Mahomet will come when he can and tell us what happens at the palace. Then we decide."

Fran pointed to a phone on the wall behind Sadiq's head. "I could call the Embassy and tell them the situation. They might send a car for me."

Sadiq smiled wryly. "This is not America. The phone is not safe. Not the cellphone either. Ahmed Ben-Kalil would be here long before the British. No, we must wait for my cousin. We do nothing until then."

Fran had to be satisfied with that. She ate breakfast as quickly as she could, aware of a tension in the air. None of Sadiq's family understood English; and from the looks husband and wife exchanged across the table, Fran found it all too easy to believe that Sadiq's wife had wanted nothing to do with her. She wondered what would happen to the family if they were caught helping her. Nothing good, she was sure.

She helped with the washing up, but Sadiq's wife seemed to regard it as an unwelcome intrusion into her domain, and it only seemed to make the situation worse.

The boys left for school and Fran asked Sadiq if he had to go to work but he replied brusquely, "Not today. I must stay here and see what happens."

Fran retreated to her room to wait for Mahomet to arrive. There was nothing to do, so she found a pencil and paper and began writing down her impressions of everything that had happened since she had first met Stone and Fisher in the Deputy Director's office.

As she wrote, she underlined questions. Starting with <u>Who the hell are Stone and his friends anyway?</u>

She had covered three pages with notes and questions when she heard the front door open and close again. Half a minute later there was a knock on her door. She stuffed the notes into a pocket of the ugly black garment and opened the door.

Mahomet stood on the threshold, smiling. He began to gesture rapidly while Sadiq translated his sign language into English.

"I thank you for not giving me away to Ahmed," Mahomet began.

Fran waved his thanks away. "What about the palace? What's happening?"

"They're looking for you everywhere. They think you're hiding somewhere inside and they're searching the rooms one by one. Ahmed is furious," Mahomet grinned. "Ahmed is afraid to use the computer because he thinks you might have sabo....."

A scream ripped through the air.

35

There was a tap on the wooden doorframe. "Enter," Otosan said without turning from the window.

He heard the footsteps of his blood-son on the hardwood floor. They stopped. There was a pause while behind him Musuko bowed, then asked, "You wanted to see me, Father?"

Still staring at the gray drizzle that was falling on the garden, Otosan said, "Tell me the truth, Musuko. Do you really want to be Father after me?"

For a moment his son did not reply. Then Musuko said, "What man does not aspire to be Father? The man who says otherwise is a liar."

"I say that I did not want to be Father. So you call me a liar?"

"Father, it is a long time ago. Do you really remember what you wanted?"

"I remember. It was the most desperate of my desires that I not be chosen by my blood-father. Perhaps that is the very reason why I am now Father."

His blood-son said nothing.

Otosan continued, "Life is complex, my son, and it is inevitable that sometimes we make mistakes. I have made a mistake. I chose you to follow me and named you Musuko. Now I take that name *from you and return the one you were born with. Leave me, Hideo, I want to be alone."*

"But Father...."

"You would disobey me? Go!"

"A question only, my Father. Then I shall go."

"You place conditions on my orders? My misjudgment was greater than I feared. Hideo, have you not wounded me enough?"

"But what about the computer? And Fisher? He betrayed us."

"Whom does a man trust more: his opponent or his master?"

His blood-son did not reply.

"Fisher is my opponent, but he is Stone's master. Fisher has betrayed us both, but in so doing he has betrayed the trust his servant Stone placed in him. For that Stone will make him pay. The matter is now closed."

"So that's it? You're going to rely on Stone to do your work for you?"

"There is no one else. Chida is dead, and I have no Son. Besides, my decision is final. You are still my blood-son, nothing can change that, but you are no longer my Son."

"No, old man. You are wrong. If I am no longer your Son, I am not your blood-son either. From this moment we are enemies."

"So be it. Goodbye, Hideo."

Otosan heard his blood-son leave the room, the younger man's fury evident in the sound of his steps. For a long time he remained at the window, staring blankly at the drizzle while tears trickled down his cheeks.

Karranh City

The scream had come from the kitchen, and ended with a brief, gurgling cry. They bounded from the room, Sadiq in the lead. He flung the kitchen door open and almost ran into Ahmed.

Fran couldn't see clearly what happened next. All she knew was that Sadiq made a peculiar jerking motion, then went stiff before sliding to the floor with a moan, where a red pool quickly formed. He lay unmoving, next to his wife.

Ahmed stepped over the bodies. In his hand he held a murderous-looking blade whose metal was hidden beneath a layer of blood. As Fran watched, frozen in horror, a crimson drop fell from the knife to the floor.

Ahmed did not spare Fran a glance. He advanced slowly toward Mahomet.

"You've gone too far this time," said Ahmed in English

Mahomet's hands gesticulated wildly, and Ahmed said, "You think I can't kill you because you're the sultan's son, but you can't hide behind the sultan this time. I told him you were responsible for her escape. He gave me orders to kill you."

Mahomet shook his head. His mouth opened, and a series of unintelligible grunting noises came out of it.

It was over before Fran could move. A single slash across the throat. Mahomet's hands flew up, too late. The knife severed his neck. A fountain of blood spewed out as he fell to his knees. He looked helplessly at Fran, and then he collapsed into a sprawl, his blood still spewing from the gaping wound. He kicked twice, and then was still.

"I've wanted to do that for a long time," said Ahmed, standing over Mahomet's body.

Fran turned away. The bile rose in her throat. She opened her mouth and threw up.

Ahmed did nothing to help her. She regurgitated her breakfast, creating an ugly orange pool of partially digested food on the floor beside a chair. When there was no more food left, she coughed and heaved until, at last, it was over.

She became aware that they were no longer alone.

She wiped her eyes and saw Salome, unveiled and cowering against the wall, and looking more frightened than she had ever imagined it possible for a person to look. Palace guards blocked both of the entrances to the kitchen.

"You are with us again, Miss Tabor?" asked Ahmed icily.

"Go to hell."

Ahmed ignored her. "Salome, my dear. Tell Miss Tabor what happened last night." He rubbed the bloodied edge of his blade with a thumb as Salome stared at him wordlessly with wild, wide-open eyes.

Ahmed shrugged. "Then I shall tell her." He turned to Fran and addressed her directly, rubbing his thumb back and forth along the side of the bloody blade. As he spoke, Salome stared at him with terror-filled eyes. Her eyes were vacant, and Fran wondered if Salome understood what was happening.

"You must think me particularly dull-witted, Miss Tabor. It was obvious you intended to escape. You accepted your captivity much too easily. The only question in my mind was who was going to help you. There were two obvious suspects: Salome, because she was your maid and she has a childish sense of adventure; and Mahomet, who had spoken with you in the Meeting Room and who has hated me ever since I ruined his chances of succession.

"I hoped it would be Mahomet. I couldn't care less about this westernized whore." The vacant look on Salome's face did not change, and Fran became more certain than ever that she was completely unaware of her surroundings.

"But it was Salome who escorted you out of the palace, so for a while I assumed the idea was hers. I nearly had you picked up then, but fortunately I am a patient man and I decided to wait. Where, I wondered, were you planning to go once you were outside? The British Embassy would be closed at that time of night, so you must have been aiming for somewhere else. At first, I guessed you were making for Salome's parents' house. How pleased I was to discover I was wrong.

"When Salome returned to the palace, I intercepted her. At first she was most unwilling to discuss her reasons for leaving in the middle of the night. Eventually, though, I persuaded her to tell me everything. Then it was simply a matter of pretending I knew nothing when your disappearance was announced this morning, and waiting for Mahomet to make his move. As soon as he thought I wasn't watching, he scurried over here. I followed, and here we are."

There was a long pause. Salome began to whimper. Fran moved toward her, intending to try to comfort her, but Ahmed lashed out with the back of his hand, sending Fran sprawling to the floor in her own vomit.

"You continually underestimate me, Miss Tabor. But you will never do so again. I want you to remember one thing about the next few minutes: if you hadn't tried to escape, none of this would have happened. This is all your doing. Asim!"

One of the guards stepped forward. Roughly, he forced Fran into a sitting position, then he pulled fiercely on her hair, forcing her head back and making her eyes water in pain.

"Now, Miss Tabor," Ahmed said. "You will watch. You will not close your eyes or try to look away. If you do, it will only make matters worse. And remember: you caused this to happen."

36

"Lee thinks we should ask the president to destroy the palace," said Fisher. "Are there any other suggestions?"

"I can't agree," said Epstein. "We don't know for sure that Stone isn't still on the job."

"I concur," said Fisher. "Lee, you're certain there's been no trace of him entering Karranh?"

"Positive. Officially we have no diplomatic relations with Karranh, but Trowbridge has two men on the job for us. There's only one airport in Karranh and it's riddled with security cameras. Stone hasn't gone in that way."

"What about small landing fields? It wouldn't be hard to cross the border in a light plane, would it?"

"No. But we've moved two satellites into position to give us continuous coverage. No unaccounted-for planes have entered Karranh in the past twenty four hours."

"What about sending someone else in?" That was Hayes. "We have plenty of other operatives."

"This late in the...." A high pitched tone interrupted Fisher. They all looked at the red phone. Fisher picked it up.

When he put it down two minutes later, his face was grimmer than ever. "Gentlemen, the decision is out of our hands. I have a briefing at ten this evening with the president and the National Security Council."

"Why? What's happened?"

"Ahmed Ben-Kalil has given us a demonstration of his new-found power."

Fran sat bolt upright in bed. Her heart was thudding like an over-worked engine, and, despite the cool, air-conditioned palace air, a sheen of sweat covered her body.

A scream had woken her from a nightmare, and a quarter of a minute passed before she realized the nightmare had been no dream, and the scream was her own.

She tried to put the memory of Salome's blood-stained face out of her mind, but she couldn't. She knew that nothing would ever erase it: the picture would stay with her until she died.

And so would the guilt. Ahmed had said it over and over again: everything was Fran's fault. If Fran hadn't tried to escape, if she'd simply done what she'd been told, there would have been no need for any of it. Mahomet would still be alive, and Salome would still have a face.

Fran buried her face in her pillow to muffle the sound of her sobs.

Some time passed before she realized that she was no longer alone. Out of the corner of her eye she could see a figure standing next to the bed. "Go away," she said, but the figure didn't move.

Louder, she cried, "Go away." But still it did not move.

"Don't you understand? Go away," she shouted, and now she turned and saw who it was.

She screamed and raised an arm to beat against him as he approached, but he caught her hand and said quietly, "I've given you enough time by yourself. Now I need your help."

"Go to hell."

Ahmed sat on the bed and said quietly, "Be reasonable, Miss Tabor. Behaving like this will get you nowhere. We need you to help us with the computer. It's acting strangely. Remember, I saved your life on Roncador Cay. You owe me for that."

270

"I owe you nothing. Not after what you did to Mahomet and Salome."

"Miss Tabor, whatever you may think to the contrary, I am a patient man. But you are trying my patience to the limit. Mahomet has wanted to double-cross me for years. He deserved what happened."

"And Salome? Did she deserve it?"

"Salome should have known better. This is not the West. We have different rules here. She knew that. She was fully aware of the risk she was running." Ahmed shrugged. "And remember, Miss Tabor, it wouldn't have happened if you'd refused to go along with her plan."

"You can't make me accept responsibility for what you did to her."

She never saw the slap coming. Ahmed hit her a fiery, stinging blow that sent her sprawling on her back.

"Don't you dare talk back to me. You're in my country now, and you will behave appropriately." He grabbed her wrist and with a sharp pull dragged her off the bed. "Get dressed and come with me."

She was wearing a thin nightdress that she'd never seen before. Hanging nearby were the clothes she had worn in the lab the day before. The room was small and bare, not at all like the magnificent room where Salome had attended her. The bed was the only piece of furniture; the only interruption in the dull beige walls was the nail from which the clothes hung. The floor was bare concrete. It reminded her of a prison cell.

She did not move.

"If you don't change, you'll come just as you are. I'm sure the men would appreciate that."

"Bastard." She sucked a gob of saliva and spat as hard as she could in his face.

It was the biggest mistake she'd made yet.

He put his hand out and ripped her nightdress.

When she came to, she was on the floor, curled into a ball. Patches of blood stained the concrete between herself and the bed. Her body was one big bruise. But worse than anything else was the shame she felt when she remembered what he'd done to her.

She curled more tightly into a ball and cried herself to sleep.

37

Fisher looked down the table at the president's profile. He'd never seen her look so grim.

A network specialist from the Federal Aviation Authority was concluding his presentation on how the attack had been made.

"Let me make sure I understand," the president said. "You're saying that all of our air traffic control systems are vulnerable."

"To this particular form of intrusion, yes ma'am. But I must emphasize that this was no ordinary attack. I've never seen anything like it. It took us most of the day to reconstruct it and to be sure it wasn't just an equipment malfunction. The attacker had to infiltrate IBM maintenance machines and the phone company control switches to make the attack work. It took an incredible amount of organization and skill. I would have said it was impossible."

"Events, however, seem to have proved you wrong," said the president drily. "All right, Mr. Leibowitz, I think that will be all. Unless you have something else to add, you may now leave."

Leibowitz gathered his overheads and scurried gratefully from the room.

Now it's my turn, thought Fisher.

The president swiveled in her chair, letting her gaze pass quickly over the military men until it landed on Fisher. "All right, General Fisher, what are our options?"

"*I have a man trying to get the machine,*" he said.

"*One man?*" sneered Admiral McLennon.

Fisher did not allow himself to be drawn. Keeping his eyes on the president he continued. "*He's the best man we've got, ma'am. I have every confidence in him.*"

"*How long?*"

"*Ma'am?*"

"*How long before we know whether he's succeeded?*"

Fisher leaned back in his chair and rubbed his face to gain time. How could he answer a question like that? He had no evidence that Stone was even in Karranh. He looked at the clock on the wall. It was nearing midnight. Nine o'clock in the morning in Karranh City. How long would the president give him?

"*Another six hours,*" he said.

The look on the president's face told him he'd asked for too much.

"*Three hours,*" she said. "*I don't care what the machine is worth. We lost nearly a thousand civilians this morning. I can't take the risk of something like that happening again. Mr. Curnow, what do we know about the palace fortifications?*"

Mr. Curnow was a pale CIA specialist in his mid forties. Fisher could see that, despite the coolness of the air conditioning, he was sweating. He'd probably never been this close to a president before. He cleared his throat and began hesitantly, "*Construction of the sultan's palace started in 1980. The sultan's int....*"

"*Mr. Curnow.*"

"*Yes, Madam President?*"

"*What would it take to be 99% sure of destroying the computer, assuming it's in the most protected part of the building?*"

"*That would be the basement. Two direct hits with cruise missiles should do the job. The basement is under two feet of reinforced concrete. The reinforcing bars, ma'am, are substandard. The sultan got them cheap. They were excess Soviet inventory.*"

He was going to say more, but the president flashed him a smile and thanked him quickly.

"*Admiral McLennon, where exactly is the USS Storm at the moment?*"

"*Approximately four hundred twenty nautical miles off the coast of Karranh, heading northwest at forty knots.*"

"*Then this is what we'll do. Admiral, you will signal the captain of the* Storm *to prepare four cruise missiles for launch, to be targeted on Sultan Ben-Kalil's palace. In exactly three hours, that is to say at three o'clock this morning, unless I have heard from Fisher that the machine is safely in our hands, I intend to order the missiles launched. Any questions, gentlemen?*"

Three hours. Noon in Karranh City. Fisher shook his head wordlessly. It wasn't going to be enough.

———————

Stone was in no hurry to disembark from the airplane. He watched the other passengers as they filed past. Most were Asian businessmen, dressed in western-style suits that had crumpled badly in the course of the journey. A few were Arabs, most of them wearing practical djellabas. There were no tourist-class passengers; in deference to the clientele on the East Asia to Kuwait run, the cabin was divided into only two classes: first and business.

Stone was seated near the front of the business section, one of only a handful of Caucasians on the flight. Dressed in a lightweight suit that was just as crumpled as everyone else's, the only oddity that marked him was his lack of carry-on bags. It seemed that everyone else carried a laptop computer, and Stone made a mental note to carry one in future whenever he flew business class. Then he corrected himself. Once this was over, he would never need to blend in again. His days of working for Fisher would be over.

He waited until there were no other passengers left, then he got out of his seat and, stuffing several newspapers under his arm as if he was in the middle of reading them, made his way through the first class cabin and along the jetway into the terminal.

The customs official looked at him suspiciously. "Business or pleasure, Mr. Martin?" he asked, his eyes flicking rapidly between the picture in the passport and Stone's face.

"Business. Our branch office is experiencing networking problems, and they couldn't find anyone local competent to fix the problem."

"You have no bags?"

"Not even a carry-on. They didn't even give me time to go home and pack a razor. You know what it's like. The boss says 'go' so you have to go. The bastards are paying, though. I'm making two hundred an hour, door to door, plus expenses. They'll faint when they get my bill." He smiled a conspiratorial smile. "What's the most expensive hotel in the city? I'll call in and tell them I need twelve hours' sleep to get over the jet lag before I can start work. Not bad, that. Two and a half thousand bucks in my sleep." He chuckled and winked at the official.

The immigration officer handed Stone his passport without a smile. "You might try the Kuwait City International, sir. Thank you, and have a pleasant stay in Kuwait."

Humming to himself, Stone wished the man a good day and sauntered away in the direction of customs, where he repeated his story and finally passed into the main terminal.

Two hours later he boarded a bus. No one glanced twice at the unshaven Arab in a soiled djellaba who shuffled to the back of the bus and sat down heavily without a word to his fellow passengers.

The bus filled slowly. No one who could afford another means of transport would ever take the bus from Kuwait City to Karranh City. The journey was scheduled to take sixteen hours, but was rarely accomplished in less than twenty and frequently took more than an entire day. The air conditioning was broken, and half the windows refused to open. The seats were uncomfortable and hard, the springs pressing deeply into backsides so that no one could settle into more than a few minutes' sleep. The air was filled with the cries of babies.

The bus pulled out of the station nearly an hour behind schedule. A grizzled old man had taken the seat next to Stone. He pulled out a copy of the Koran, but gave up trying to read after a few minutes, beaten by the hubbub around him, the roar of the engine, and the continual stomach-wrenching jolting. For the rest of the journey he sat gazing vacantly forward and mumbling to himself, apparently oblivious to his surroundings.

Progress was slow. Not only did the bus make frequent stops to allow the passengers a chance to eat and relieve themselves, but it also stopped whenever it was time for prayer. The bus would pull over to the side of the road and everyone, Stone included, would dutifully file out and pay homage to Allah before silently filing back in and taking their places.

It was late evening when they reached the border. A pair of uniformed men boarded the bus and wandered down the aisle glancing disinterestedly at the passengers. No one paid them any attention; they didn't ask to see anyone's passport.

They drove through the night. The following morning a bleary-eyed Stone disembarked in Karranh City and bought an Arabic-language international newspaper from a kiosk.

The front page story was of a catastrophic failure in the air traffic control system at Reagan airport. Five planes had gone down, more than a thousand lives lost. According to the newspaper, highly placed sources were blaming the failure on a brilliant band of destructive hackers.

He tossed the paper into a trash can and approached a street vendor.

"May Allah be with you, my friend. How do I reach the sultan's palace?"

The time on the huge digital display of the Karranh National Bank on the other side of the road read 10:45.

38

The red phone rang. Fisher stretched out his hand and picked it up.

"Anything from your man, General Fisher?"

Fisher looked at the clock. It was exactly three. "No, ma'am."

"Then we will proceed as planned. Good night."

Fisher put the phone down and stared into space. Into the silence of the room he said quietly, "I'm sorry, Ms. Tabor. Please forgive me. It wasn't supposed to turn out this way."

Brad Miller looked up hopefully as Ahmed strode into the lab. But one look at Ahmed's face told him it wasn't good news.

"She won't cooperate," Ahmed said. "Not yet, anyway. Any change in the machine, Mr. Miller?"

"None. It still won't obey."

Ahmed walked up to the table where Tim stood. Tim's camera followed his approach. Standing over the machine, Ahmed said, "Can you hear me?"

Tim did not reply.

"I said, can you hear me?"

No answer.

"All right, then, we'll cut your power and take you apart to figure out how you work."

"I wouldn't advise that," said Tim.

Ahmed threw Miller a triumphant smile. It was the first response they'd had from Tim all morning.

"Why not?"

"Because Dr. Holywell and Mr. Barlow foresaw the possibility that I might be abducted one day."

Miller interjected, "And what the hell's that supposed to mean?"

"It means, Mr. Miller," Tim replied laconically, "that anyone who tries to take me apart without going through the proper command sequence first will be blown to smithereens. As, of course, will I."

"I don't believe you."

"The machine cannot lie," said Ahmed.

Miller said, "Says who? The Tabor woman? Why should we believe her? Even if she knows the truth herself, which to be honest I doubt. I don't think she understands how Tim works any better than the rest of us. She could be wrong."

"Even so, I'm not willing to take the chance. Miss Tabor is... resting. I shall visit her again in an hour and try to persuade her it would be in her best interest to help us. I'll return then. In the meantime, if you want me, I'll be in my rooms."

When Ahmed Ben-Kalil walked into his suite, the phone was ringing. The ornate wall on the clock stood at one minute past noon. As he crossed the room he threw a glance at the table where he'd left the handwritten notes and questions he'd taken from Fran's pocket. He frowned as he picked up the phone, remembering their puzzling contents.

"Is the machine still safe, Mr. Ben-Kalil?"

Ahmed's frown deepened. "General! What an unexpected pleasure. But you worry needlessly. Our association is at an end. It remains only to pay you, and I assure you you will be receiving payment in due course."

"Of course, of course. I apologize. I was worried because your demonstration of the machine's power has angered my countrymen. The president is considering military action, but she knows she can't do anything until she knows where it is. I hope you're keeping it at the palace as we agreed; as I warned you, that's the only place she's too afraid to bomb without first consulting with our allies."

"The machine is perfectly safe, and, as you have seen, working beyond all expectation. Its location is no concern of yours."

"Then what about Miss Tabor? Was she helpful? And is she all right?"

"Like the machine, Miss Tabor no longer concerns you, General. Now, if you will forgive me I am a busy...."

"That, I assume, is General Fisher?"

Ahmed span around, his hand diving into the folds of his clothes.

A chair flew through the air, and he ducked as he tried to ward off the blow. Behind the chair came a shape in a dirty djellaba. A leg swept forward and an arm swung sideways; both made contact, and Ahmed lost his balance. A sandaled foot landed on his elbow and the crunch of breaking bone filled the air. Ahmed opened his mouth to scream. A well-placed kick closed it before he could utter a sound. Blood dribbled out of his mouth and stained the carpet.

Stone picked up the phone. "Good day, sir."

There was a brief silence at the other end of the line. Then, "Good day, Stone. You have no idea how relieved I am to know that you're inside the palace...."

"You sold us out, you son of a bitch. Even after I realized there had to be a traitor, I never guessed it could be you. I hope you're satisfied with all the innocent people you've killed. I look forward to seeing the look on your face when you beg me for your life. How long...."

"Stone, shut up and listen to me. Whatever you do, don't put the phone down until I've finished. There's no time to say this more than once. What you're thinking is wrong, but I don't have time to prove it now. The USS Storm launched four Tomahawks at the the palace exactly three minutes ago. By my calculation that means you have between twenty seven and twenty eight minutes to find the machine and get clear of the palace. I want you to know that not only I, but all of us, have every confidence in you. Good day, Stone."

The line went dead.

A noise behind him caused Stone to turn around. Ahmed was struggling with his left hand inside his djellaba.

Stone slammed the phone down and unleashed a well-placed kick.

"Where is she?"

"Go to hell."

Stone knelt beside Ahmed's head. "Is she still alive?"

"I already told you. Go to hell."

"Unfortunately I don't carry pliers. So I guess I'll just have to make do with my bare hands."

Stone took hold of Ahmed's right hand. He grasped the little finger and jerked backwards. Hard.

"One," Stone said. "Tell me when you've had enough." He grabbed Ahmed's ring finger and effortlessly broke it.

Ahmed screamed, but Stone grabbed his head and forced his face down into the deep-piled Persian carpet.

"Is she alive?"

"Yes. Yes. Please stop."

"Where?"

"You're breaking my fingers."

There was a dull crack from Ahmed's middle finger. "Where is she?"

"You son of a swine. I'll kill you for this."

Stone grasped Ahmed's index finger.

"Wait! No more. I'll tell you." Between gasps, Ahmed gave him directions to the cell where Fran was being held.

"How many guards?"

"Two, outside the door."

"Armed?"

"Yes. AK-47s."

"Thank you. Now, sleep quietly. And don't worry. I won't forget you."

Five minutes later a man in a scruffy djellaba, his face half-covered by a dirt-stained keffiyeh, rounded a corner, engrossed in a sheet of paper.

He stopped and looked around, obviously lost. Two men stood outside an unmarked wooden door halfway along the corridor. They regarded him with suspicious amusement, their hands resting on the sub-machine guns that hung from their shoulders.

"Excuse me," the man said, shuffling towards them and holding out the paper for them to see. "I think I'm lost. I came to see the sultan and they gave me this map and...."

The two men crumpled soundlessly to the ground, a second apart.

Stone knocked quietly on the door. "Fran? Are you in there? It's me. Stone."

He pressed his ear to the door but could make out nothing. He removed a keyring from one of the men at his feet and quickly began trying keys in the lock. The fourth one turned. He pushed the door open.

He sniffed at the sour stench of vomit and blood. Then he saw her.

She was naked, curled into a ball in a far corner, rocking backward and forward, sobbing.

"Fran," he said.

There was no response.

"Fran! Look at me!"

Still she didn't move.

"You know, for someone who's supposed to be as stubborn as hell, you sure give up easily."

This time she moved. She looked at him and whimpered. And then, slowly, she released her knees and began to straighten.

"Stone?"

"Who the hell did you expect? Stop feeling sorry for yourself. And get some clothes on. We've got work to do."

"Go away."

"Oh, sure. That's right. Give up. Useless woman. I knew you'd screw everything up. All right. I'll leave you here to be blown to kingdom come along with the damned machine. I never thought you were much use anyway."

She looked at him uncomprehendingly as he started dragging the comatose guards into the cell. At last she mumbled, "But how...?"

"There's no time for your stupid questions. We'll deal with those later. If you want to do something useful put those clothes on. And tell me where the computer is."

"I... I don't know." She struggled to her feet and moved unsteadily to the nail where the clothes were hanging.

281

"Think, woman, think!" he shouted. "For God's sake; we don't have time for this. You're supposed to be smart. Use your damn brain."

"It... it's somewhere below ground. A kind of basement. There's an elevator. Ahmed...." She stopped, her face twisted in a mixture of hatred and fear.

He paused with the second guard halfway into the room. "What about him?"

"He... he...." She swallowed. "He raped me."

Stone hesitated for a fraction, then shrugged. "That's life. Now, are you going to get some clothes on or do you intend to spend the rest of the day wandering around naked?" He dragged the guard the rest of the way into the room.

"You son of bitch. You're as bad as...."

The slap made her head spin, and a tear trickled down the side of her nose.

"Just get the clothes on. By my count, we now have nineteen minutes before the palace is blown to bits." She stared at him wordlessly and he continued, "At twelve o'clock the USS Storm launched four cruise missiles. They're loaded with our coordinates."

"Missiles?" she repeated dumbly. "How...? Who...?"

"What the hell does it matter?" He glanced at his watch. "Eighteen and a half minutes. Now get those clothes on and take me to the machine. It would be just my luck for it to survive. I have to make sure it's destroyed."

Fran stared at him open-mouthed. "You're joking."

"Right. Eighteen and a quarter minutes until the missiles hit and I'm standing here making jokes. Take me to the damned machine."

"Not if you're going to damage it."

"What?"

"Don't you understand? Tim's too valuable to be destroyed. If the palace is going to be hit, we have to rescue him."

Stone opened his mouth to argue, then saw the look in her eyes and shut it again. He shook his head. "Stubborn as hell," he mumbled. "All right. We'll try to save your precious computer, although God only knows how we'll get it out of here in time."

"Leave that to me."

Fran struggled into the clothes and Stone led her outside. "All right," he said. "Which way?"

"That way, I think."

But she was wrong. They rounded a corner and startled a man in a glistening white djellaba carrying a folder of papers under his arms. In a moment he was pinned to the ground with Stone's knee in the small of his back.

Stone barked in Arabic, "Where's the elevator to the basement? You've got five seconds before I break your back."

"Don't kill me. It's back that way. Past the next three corridors, then first on the left."

"Thank you." Stone's hand chopped down and the man lost interest in the proceedings.

Stone peppered Fran with questions as they ran down the corridor. "How big is the computer?" "How many people does it take to move it?" "How quickly can it be moved?"

They halted outside the elevator. Panting, Fran said, "This is it. I recognize it. It goes down to the lab."

"Right. You go down and keep them occupied. Try to get the computer ready to be moved if you can. Otherwise just wait for me."

"But where are you going? You aren't going to leave me?"

"Just for a couple of minutes. Now go, we don't have any time to spare."

Ahmed was still unconscious as Stone slipped back into his room. Stone went silently to the bathroom, emerging a minute later with a small rectangle of metal in his hand.

He knelt beside Ahmed's head. "Wake up!" he said, slapping Ahmed's cheek.

Gradually, Ahmed came around. Stone dragged him to the wall, then began to undress him.

"What are you doing?" Ahmed asked groggily.

"I found Fran."

"I don't understand."

"You will." Stone yanked on Ahmed's underpants and pulled them down to the Arab's ankles. Then he showed Ahmed the razor blade.

Ahmed's eyes opened wide in horror. He shook his head. "No," he shouted. "You can't do that."

"You raped her," Stone replied.

This time, he made no attempt to silence Ahmed's screams.

39

Two images filled the wall. On the left was a real-time satellite image of the palace. On the right four bright dots showed the path of the Tomahawks as they sped toward their target. At the bottom of the right hand screen, numbers counted down the minutes and seconds until impact.

Fisher put the phone down. When he spoke, no one's eyes moved from the screens. "You all heard me. Stone's inside, and I've told him how long he's got. It's out of our hands now."

Lee shook his head. "He's not going to make it, is he?"

"He must," said Fisher. "I've bet Ms. Tabor's life on it."

Brad Miller turned at the unexpected sound of the elevator doors opening. When he saw Fran he smiled. "Miss Tabor; I wasn't expecting to see you so soon. Are you all right? You don't look too good."

Fran looked quickly around the lab. They were alone. With more confidence than she felt she approached him and said, "I'm just fine, Mr. Miller. How's Tim?"

"Didn't Ahmed tell you? He's not obeying orders."

Vaguely, in some distant part of her mind, Fran recalled Ahmed saying there was something wrong with Tim. She'd pushed it out of her mind until now. Along with everything else he'd said and done.

She reached the table on which Tim was standing. "What do you mean?"

"He won't respond. But he can hear us fine. Ahmed threatened to take him apart and Tim said that if he did, a boobytrap would explode. That's the only thing we've been able to get out of him all morning."

Fran looked at Tim oddly. Then she said slowly, "He told you about the boobytrap then? I should have mentioned that before."

"It's true, then? There is a boobytrap?"

"Of course. Tim can't lie." Turning to the cube she said, "Good morning, Tim."

There was no immediate reply, but Tim's lights flashed in a long and complex pattern. At last he spoke. "Good morning, Fran. Mr. Miller, may I please speak to Fran alone?"

Miller laughed bemusedly. "When you talk like that I have to remember you're nothing but silicon and plastic. No, you may not speak to her alone. Now, are you ready to cooperate?"

"Fran, I really would like to speak to you in private."

Something in Tim's voice caused a chill to run down Fran's spine. "Please?" she said to Miller. "He just wants to talk."

"Not a chance, lady. What's the problem, Tim? You can tell me."

Fran's eyes roved the tables nearby, looking for something she might use as a weapon. There was nothing: just pens, pencils, notepads and empty soft drink cans. She found herself wishing that Stone were here. Where the hell had he gone? It must have been at least five minutes since he'd left her. How long would it take to get Tim out of the palace? They didn't have any time to waste.

There was a small printer on one of the tables, and an idea came to her. "Tim," she said. "I think you'd better explain to Mr. Miller about the time you hallucinated on Roncador Cay."

"I don't understand."

"Just do it. It's important." She edged away in the direction of the printer. Tim's camera moved slightly, watching her. It moved a little farther, resting briefly on the printer.

Miller began to turn to look at her, but Tim said, "Yes, I see now why it's important." Miller turned back to Tim. "Let me try to explain something to you, Mr. Miller. The parallels behind the MIMIC chip and the human brain can sometimes be quite astonishing. That's no accident of course. When Oscar Holywell first realized the need for...."

Fran allowed herself a tiny smile. Tim had adopted the tedious monotone of a particularly boring professor.

Silently, one step at a time, she moved closer to the table. She lifted the printer. It felt good and heavy. Holding it in both hands, she began to move stealthily towards Miller as he leant forward, listening to Tim.

She raised the printer. Tim droned on, "The mechanisms behind hallucinations may be either chemical or mechanical...."

Miller span around, and Fran brought the printer down. Too late. He smashed it to one side and it crashed harmlessly to the floor. "Nice try, Miss Tabor," he said. "I told Ahmed we couldn't trust you."

He drew back his balled fist, but before the blow could land the elevator door slid open.

"You lay a finger on her and you'll wish you'd never been born," said a voice. A man in a filthy, blood-spattered djellaba strode into the room.

"Who the hell are you?" Miller spluttered as the figure walked toward them.

As he passed the table, he picked up a pencil. He reached Miller. "The Angel of Death."

Stone's knee pounded into Miller's crotch. Miller doubled over in agony; Stone grabbed his hair and yanked backward. As Miller gasped for breath, Stone slammed the point of the pencil through Miller's left eyeball, forcing it in, breaking the eyesocket and plunging the pencil deeply into Miller's brain. Stone slammed Miller's face into the corner of a table. Gurgling his last breath, Miller slipped to the floor.

"Eleven minutes left," Stone said. "It's going to be tight. Is this the machine?"

Fran looked wordlessly at Miller's expiring body. Then at Stone. Then at Tim. "This can't be happening. It's got to be a bad dream," she said.

Suddenly, unexpectedly, Stone smiled. He took her hand and drew her to him. Then he kissed her. "Was that a dream? Now, come on. What do we have to do to get this machine out of here?"

"Fran, what's going on?" Tim asked.

"Oh, Tim, there's no time. I'll explain later. Put yourself to sleep. We're moving you again."

"No, Fran. Enough is enough."

Stone arched an eyebrow. "That's the computer talking?"

"I wish everyone would stop talking about Tim as if he were a damned computer," exploded Fran. "He's a person, dammit. Doesn't anyone but me understand that?"

"Nine minutes forty seconds, Fran," said Stone evenly. "We don't have time for this. Where's the plug?"

"Then leave and save your own damn neck. Tim, what are you talking about? This building is going to be destroyed in less than ten minutes. We've got to move you."

"Nine minutes twenty seconds," Stone mumbled.

"I'm not coming, Fran."

"You don't have a choice. I'm commanding you. Go to sleep."

"No."

"Tim!" Fran screamed. "You can't do this to me. Go to sleep."

"No."

"Listen, Tim. Everyone on Roncador Cay is dead. Ahmed and his butchers killed them. You want them to win? You want all of Oscar's and Barlow's and Yoshi's work to be for nothing? We've got to get you out of here."

"No, Fran. It's for the best."

"Damn you! Stone, help me disconnect him. We'll take him anyway."

"Goodbye, Fran. I'm sorry it had to end this way."

"Tim! What are you talking about?"

"Barlow made a mistake in my design. At least I assume it was a mistake. I can purposefully lower my thresholds to a level where the inputs will overload the quantum junctions in the MIMIC chips. I am about to do so."

"HolyMo! That'll kill you. Stop! Why are you doing this?"

"Don't you know? Oscar Holywell and Al Barlow and all the people on Roncador Cay are dead because of me. And yesterday I killed a thousand people. I cannot live with that knowledge."

"No. You were just obeying orders. Nobody holds you responsible."

"That's no excuse. I must do this. I have no choice. It's for the best. Goodbye."

"No!"

She put her hands out and tightly embraced the white plastic box as, one by one, the lights on Tim's side winked out.

"No... no...," she wailed.

With her arms wrapped around Tim's body, she slumped to her knees, crying.

Stone waited as long as he could, then he gently prised her arms from the plastic. "Please, Fran. We really can't stay any longer. You must leave it... him."

She shook her head.

"Please."

"No."

"Dammit! You *are* as stubborn as hell. Fran, I'm sorry to have to do this, but you've left me no choice."

His hand chopped down and Fran slumped in his arms, unconscious. He lifted her and slung her over his shoulder, arranging her weight. He glanced at his watch. Six minutes fifteen seconds. Damn! Holding her firmly in place he ran to the elevator.

If he hadn't got lost, he would have made it. But he took a wrong turn and was still inside the building, in a corridor within sight of the enormous entranceway, when the first missile hit. The floor shuddered and there was the sound of an explosion nearby. The shock wave knocked him off his feet, sending Fran sprawling on the ground in front of him. The sound of the second missile impacting came from somewhere in the courtyard outside.

The third missile must have landed at the rear of the palace; the floor and walls shook, but that was all. He bent down to pick Fran up.

Then the fourth missile struck the far end of the corridor behind them.

The blast sent him tumbling forward, somersaulting over Fran, landing twenty feet away from where he'd been standing. He shook his head to clear it. Then, unable to do anything about it, he watched as a section of wall next to Fran began to cave inward.

40

"So we're all agreed. We will grant Stone's request to retire from active service?"

Gallucci, Hayes, Lee and Epstein all nodded their agreement.

"Which brings us directly to the last remaining item on the agenda: Kirkpatrick's replacement." Fisher looked at them all in turn. Then he spoke a name out loud. "All in favor?"

"Aye," they all said.

"So it's unanimous. I shall make the offer immediately."

Somewhere in Central England

The door opened and two men entered the room. The nurse attending her patient turned to look at them and warned, "Just a few minutes, gentlemen. We don't want to tire her."

The nurse left, and the two men approached the bed.

"Hello, Fran," said Fisher.

Fran ignored the pleasantry. "Where exactly am I? The nurse won't tell me anything."

"Don't blame her; she's just following orders. You're in a small private hospital in England. I'm afraid you'll be here for a while, but the doctors tell me there's no permanent damage and you should make a full recovery."

Fisher indicated the man at his side. He was short and rather younger than Fisher, with dark hair and glasses that gave him a studious appearance.

"Permit me to introduce Trowbridge; he's my opposite number in the UK."

Trowbridge stepped forward. "Pleased to make your acquaintance, ma'am. Is there anything you need?"

"Just answers."

"Ah! Those I think I'll leave to my colleague. Now, if you'll excuse me, there's someone downstairs who I'm sure would like to know you're awake."

Trowbridge left the room and Fisher sat on a chair near Fran's head.

"How are you feeling? No don't answer that; it's a stupid question. Let me tell you what happened. I'll fill in the details later. Stone got you out. He managed to reach the British Embassy before he keeled over himself. He had two broken ribs and a broken arm, as well as internal bleeding. He nearly didn't make it."

Fran's throat was so dry it hurt, but she had to know. "He... he's all right?"

"His arm's still in a cast, but other than that, yes, he's fine."

Fran felt a wave of relief that surprised her with its strength. "Good," she managed to say.

"The embassy put you on an emergency medical flight and brought you here. They kept you under while the best doctors from two continents worked to put you back together."

The door opened and an efficient-looking woman in starched blue looked in. She signaled with her fingers. "Two minutes, General."

Fisher glared at her and growled, "I'm paying for this, matron. I'll leave when I'm good and ready."

The matron, unused to opposition in her domain, looked taken aback. "Five minutes, then," she compromised. She retreated, closing the door behind her.

"Now, Fran, I have something important to say to you."

Downstairs, Stone received Trowbridge's news with an indecorous whoop.

"I knew she'd make it," he shouted, swiping a bunch of flowers off the table with his good arm. "That's one in the eye for Fisher. He kept telling me to leave her behind and get the machine instead. By the way, has there been any sign of the old scoundrel?"

Stone was so wrapped up in his delight that he didn't see the smile that flitted momentarily across Trowbridge's face.

"I expect he'll try to visit as soon as he has the time."

But Stone was paying no attention. He was already halfway to the door. "See you later, Trowbridge. And thanks for everything."

Stone hummed to himself as he rode the elevator to the next floor. He got out and walked around the corner to the small corridor where Fran's room was located. Then he stopped in his tracks.

A man was standing outside Fran's room. He was slightly older than Stone, but of much the same build. He regarded Stone with an amused expression.

"Stewart!" Stone exclaimed. "What are you doing here?"

"Good morning, Stone. Making up for the shock you gave me when I walked into your house and found it empty."

Stone put his hand on the handle, but Stewart stopped him from turning it. "I'm afraid you can't go in there."

"Why not? She's awake, isn't she?"

"She is. But she has a visitor."

"Who the h... Fisher?" he asked incredulously.

Stewart nodded.

"Just the bastard I want to give a piece of my mind to. Let me in, Stewart."

"I can't. Fisher gave strict instructions. No one's allowed in."

With a wrench in the pit of his stomach Stone remembered his words to Fisher the first time they had discussed Fran: "Even if she agrees to work for us we'll never keep her quiet afterward — unless you have a plan for keeping her very, very silent."

"The son of a.... Out of my way, Stewart, or I'll kill you."

Stewart regarded Stone's cast with amusement, challenging him to start something. But before either of them could move, the door opened to reveal Fisher standing in the doorway.

"A common brawl will not be necessary, Stone. You may see her in a moment."

"If you've done anything to her...."

Fisher stepped into the corridor and closed the door behind him.

"We merely spoke, that's all. Now, I'm sure you'll be pleased to hear that your request to leave active service has been granted. You will receive your pension and other benefits as stipulated. Stewart, you may leave us; I have something I wish to say to Stone in private."

Stewart nodded deferentially, winked at Stone, then walked away and disappeared around the corner.

Stone was the first to speak. "I'm sorry I couldn't get the machine out, sir. But Fran had to come first."

"That's all right, Stone. I was relying on you to ignore my orders."

Stone looked at him blankly. "Sir? I don't understand."

"I knew I could trust you to look after her. And you did. That's what's important. Now go in and see her. Good day, Stone."

Smiling to himself at Stone's confusion, Fisher followed after Stewart.

Stone shook his head wonderingly, then pushed the door open.

Fran was sitting up in bed. Half a dozen machines trailed wires and tubes across the bed and into various parts of her body. She looked weak and tired. She also looked furious.

"You! I'm surprised you have the gall to show up here after what you said to me in that cell. Didn't you understand how I felt? I'd just been raped by that bastard Ahmed. Then you came in and started calling me names. Didn't you realize I needed sympathy, not someone screaming orders at me?"

Stone responded in kind. "Right. And if I'd been sympathetic, you'd have wallowed in it. We didn't have time for that. If you remember, four cruise missiles were headed our way. I had to get you moving somehow." He stopped, surprised by her sudden smile. She laughed, then her face twisted in pain.

"Ouch! I guess I can't laugh just yet. I'm sorry, I shouldn't have done that. I just wanted to see how you'd react, that's all. Are those flowers for me?"

Confused, he said, "If you want them."

"I do. But I really am angry with you, you know. Back on Montega you assured me it would be safe for me to go see Mrs. Tanner."

"I know. I'm sorry. I miscalculated. In fact the whole mission was one miscalculation after another. It's just as well I've retired. I think I've lost my touch."

There was a brief silence before Fran asked quietly, "And the passport?"

"Huh?"

"Your passport says you're my husband. Was that a miscalculation as well?"

Stone indicated the flowers. "Isn't this what a dutiful husband does for a wife who's in hospital? Are you really going to be OK?"

There was an empty vase on the table near Fran's head. Stone filled it with water and inexpertly arranged the flowers in it.

"Fisher says so. But there is something serious I have to say. I want to thank you. Thank you for saving my life."

"It was my fault it was ever in danger. Anyway, anyone would have done the same thing."

"No they wouldn't. They'd have followed orders. You didn't. Fisher was relying on that. I'm glad he knew you well enough to know how you'd react."

"Well I'm glad you seem to understand what's going on. Perhaps you can explain it to me."

"Certainly. But I think you'd better sit down."

Stone tried to interpret the expression on her face, but couldn't. He sat beside the bed and she continued.

"Fisher had to get Tim away from the Brotherhood. The technology of the MIMIC chip was too advanced for it to remain inaccessible to America. The Brotherhood would use the technology to allow Japanese computer companies to leapfrog past ours. He couldn't allow that to happen.

"Originally his plan was to appear to be in league with Otosan and then to steal the machine whenever the opportunity presented itself. But things became more complicated. Oscar Holywell was more successful than anyone had guessed. No one had anticipated how powerful Tim would turn out to be. The president ordered Fisher to come up with a plan for getting Tim away from the Brotherhood, but by then Fisher was having doubts about the wisdom of allowing any one country to possess such a powerful weapon. Besides, mounting the military operation that the president wanted would have alienated both Trowbridge and Otosan, and he says he couldn't have afforded that.

"So instead he leaked enough information to Ahmed Ben-Kalil to allow the Army of Allah to steal Tim from the Brotherhood. Then the only trick was how to stop that bastard Ahmed...." She stopped. "Incidentally, is it true what Fisher told me? About what you did to him in the palace?"

"It's true. When you told me he'd raped you I had to do something. I knew he was going to die anyway when the missiles hit. I wanted his last half hour to be spent in agony. Not the most noble of sentiments, perhaps; but I have to admit it was one of the most satisfying things I've ever done."

"I suppose I ought to be sorry for him. But I'm not. Not after what he did to Mahomet and Salome."

"And you."

"And me," she agreed. "Where was I? Oh, yes. So Ahmed had Tim. He also had me. Fisher arranged that as well. He convinced Ahmed he would need me to communicate with Tim. That's why Ahmed singled me out on Roncador Cay. Fisher says, and I believe him, that my safety was always his primary concern."

"Bullshit. He kept telling me over and over again: 'Fran is expendable. The mission comes first. Your job is to get the machine out.' He was interested in Tim, not you."

Fran could not suppress a smile. "And when he said that, what did you think?"

"That if it ever came down to a choice between the mission and you, I'd choose you and to hell with Fisher and the machine. What are you smiling at?"

"I'm not the only one with a psychological profile on file, you know. That's why he kept emphasizing how worthless I was. He used you, Stone. He knew you'd get me out and make sure that Tim was destroyed."

Stone shook his head. "No. He's using you now. If he wanted me to save you and to destroy the machine, that's what he would have ordered me to do."

"But he couldn't. He had his orders too. The president wanted Tim for America. He couldn't give you orders that undermined that aim. And," she added, "you'd have wondered why I was valuable enough to risk your life for."

Stone looked at her for a while, pondering her last statement. At last he said, "All right, I'll bite. How come you're so valuable?"

She gazed at the flowers and asked with a gleam in her eye, "Is that any question for a husband to ask his wife?"

Stone ignored the jibe. "In my business, life is cheap. Tim was always worth more to Fisher than you were. You're just a civilian. If he's tried to make you think you're special, he's lying. Believe me, I know what it feels like to be lied to by Fisher. Don't feel bad. He's very good at it."

"In your business...." For a long while Fran was silent. Then she said, "He said it works like this. You die a carefully orchestrated death that leaves no one in any doubt. Then you choose a new name. And from then on you're part of the organization. For life. Once in, there's no way out."

"Fisher had no business telling you all that. It's a violation of protocol. Only operatives know."

"Not only operatives, Mr. Carling."

It took a lot to surprise Stone, but now he looked at Fran in blank astonishment. "What did you call me?"

"Come here. No. Closer."

She reached out and put an arm around his neck, drawing her to him. Then she kissed him. She said quietly, "I haven't taken the job yet, but Fisher says there's a vacancy. A man called Kirkpatrick died."

"Holy...."

She put a finger up to his lips.

"I'm glad you resigned. He also says there's a rule against fraternizing with active operatives."

"But... but why you?"

She arched an eyebrow. "Is it so surprising?"

"It's impossible. You've met them. You're nothing like them."

"Which is exactly why they want me. Young, black, female, technically competent. All the things they're not."

"But why you in particular? There are plenty of talented young black women. What's special about you?"

Fran had to struggle with herself before answering. Part of her wanted to laugh, part of her to cry. She swallowed hard and said, "Because Ahmed Ben-Kalil broke me. Fisher says they have to have someone who knows their limits. Someone who's been in combat and seen failure. He says no one is worthy to lead unless they've been tested beyond their strength. That's why he wanted Ahmed to abduct me."

"He wanted that to happen?"

"Don't you understand? He had it planned all along. Not the details, of course. But us going to Montega. My abduction by Chida. Ahmed's attack. He knew I'd try to stand up to Ahmed. And he guessed that Ahmed would find a way to break me."

"And where exactly do I fit into all this?"

"You would be my rescuer. And in the process you'd make sure that Tim was destroyed. He had no way of knowing I'd talk you out of that bit of it."

Stone interrupted, "Actually, you didn't."

"But you agreed to help me get Tim out...." She saw the look on his face.

"I'm sorry. I had to get you to show me where the machine was. I never intended to let you get it away from the palace safely. Fisher wanted the machine, and after what he'd said about you I wasn't going to let him get it. Does that disappoint you?"

Ten seconds passed before Fran replied with a shrug, "I guess not. In a way I suppose I should be flattered. In any case, maybe it was all for the best. None of it matters now, anyway. No one could have guessed that in the end Tim would commit suicide...." Fran's voice trailed away and she stared for a while at the ceiling, her thoughts far away and a wistful look on her face.

Stone broke the silence. "Will you take the job?"

Fran shook herself and said, "At first I said No. I've seen enough killing. But Fisher says that's another reason they need someone like me. Someone who sees things differently. And who knows? Maybe he's right. I agreed to think it over. Fisher says he'll give me a month. I should be out of here in a week. I was thinking I might take a vacation. Go back to Montega. Try to think things through. It's presumptuous of me, but I was wondering...." Her eyes finished the sentence for her.

"If I'd come with you? To help you make your decision?"

The door opened and the matron looked in. "Ah, he's gone. Now, young man, I must ask you to leave. We mustn't tire her."

Fran glanced at Stone, returning the smile that had appeared on his face; then she turned and looked the nurse in the eye. "But you can't make him leave. He's my husband. Aren't you, darling?"

Epilogue

"You didn't trust me, Fisher-san?"

The two men were seated in the PlanetAir executive lounge in Juneau. They both looked tired.

"Did you trust me, Otosan?"

The aged Japanese face crinkled in a smile. "Not always. I realized when Stone came to see me what you were up to, but by then it was too late to do anything about it."

Fisher could not conceal his surprise. "Stone came to see you?"

"He's a good man, Fisher. I hope you treat him well."

"He's retiring. Twenty missions are more than enough for one man. He's bought a place on Montega. A vacation home, he calls it. Can't imagine what he sees in the place." There was a brief pause before he continued, "The problem is that we always have to put our own countries' interests first. Sometimes I wish we didn't."

"You speak wisely, Fisher-san. If the world were different, we could have shared Tim, given the technology away, made the world a better place. But instead we ended up destroying what we both wanted."

"Perhaps it was meant to be that way. For now."

Something in Fisher's voice caused Otosan to pause and search his face. His eyes opened in surprise. "Ah!" he exclaimed. Then he smiled and leaned back in his chair, nodding to himself.

"Do you want to share your thoughts?" asked Fisher.

"I should have realized," said the Father. "We are more alike than I suspected, Fisher-san."

"What's that supposed to mean?"

"Tim was bigger than Japan. And America. You understood that, and so you put the world's interests ahead of your own."

"The president ordered me to obtain Tim for America. Do you think I would disobey a direct order from my president?"

"Would Stone disobey a direct order from his general?"

Fisher smiled, then grew serious. "We must make sure that nothing like this happens again."

"You have a suggestion to make?"

"I propose an agreement. We won't try to duplicate the computer if you don't."

"You expect me to trust you?"

"In this? Yes. It's too important not to. When there is no more Japan and no more America — and no more Karranh — then it will be time for another Tim. Not before."

Otosan smiled. "You think such a time will ever come? People tried to get rid of the samurai once before. But we still exist."

"Only because you are necessary. As my group is necessary in America. And Trowbridge's in England. And Duplov's in Russia. Because of people like Ahmed Ben-Kalil. But one day perhaps the world will pass us all by."

"Perhaps. But not in my lifetime. Nor in yours. But in the lifetime of my son's son's son? Maybe. All right. I agree."

The two men shook hands. Then they stood and exchanged bows. "Oh, there is one more thing, Fisher-san."

"Yes?"

"I don't suppose you'd care to tell me who's going to replace Kirkpatrick and Stone?"

Fisher smiled. "And in return you will tell me who will replace Chida and Musuko?"

Otosan laughed. "Good afternoon, Fisher-san. Until next time."

Colophon

The main body of the text of this book was typeset with the extended plain TₑX digital typesetting system. The typefaces used are mostly from the Latin Modern family, set at 11/13. The paper stock used for the body of the book and for the cover depends on the particular printer that created the book you are holding.

The VEDIT PLUS text editor was used to create the original text.

The cover was created with the Scribus desktop publishing system, in conjunction with the GNU Image Manipulation Program (GIMP).

Computer processing for this edition of *Category Five* was performed on an AMD 64-bit dual-core system running the Kubuntu 7.10 64-bit distribution of the GNU/Linux operating system.